Praise for *Rules of Engagement*

"A fast and furious tale of cyberwarfare . . . Bruns and Olson kick off their new series with a thundering bang."
—*The Real Book Spy*

"Fans of the cyberwarfare genre will enjoy this novel's snappy pace, broad cast of characters, and timeliness."
—*Kirkus Reviews*

"With their background in the U.S. Navy, both Bruns and Olson have the right stuff to create a realistic military tale."
—*Booklist*

"Compelling characters and high octane narrative drive define *Rules of Engagement*. In a global tour de force, Bruns and Olson deliver a crafty villain, patriotic protagonists, and a truly frightening and unique World War III scenario. A must read for all fans of thrillers of every variety!" —Anthony J. Tata, Brigadier General, US Army (Ret), national bestselling author of *Dark Winter*

"In this terrifying age of hacking that threatens not only our elections, but every infrastructure from our power grid to our economic system, the ultimate threat would be a cyber war tha' *les of Engagement* lay rio in one of those fant n. Hell of a fine read!' rk
bestselling author

RULES

OF

ENGAGEMENT

DAVID BRUNS

AND

J. R. OLSON

St. Martin's Paperbacks

This is a work of fiction. All of the characters, organizations, and events portrayed in this novel are either products of the authors' imaginations or are used fictitiously.

Published in the United States by St. Martin's Paperbacks, an imprint of St. Martin's Publishing Group.

RULES OF ENGAGEMENT

For information, address St. Martin's Publishing Group, 120 Broadway, New York, NY 10271.

www.stmartins.com

Library of Congress Catalog Card Number: 2019001793

ISBN: 978-1-250-25322-4

Our books may be purchased in bulk for promotional, educational, or business use. Please contact your local bookseller or the Macmillan Corporate and Premium Sales Department at 1-800-221-7945, ext. 5442, or by email at MacmillanSpecialMarkets@macmillan.com.

Printed in the United States of America

St. Martin's Press hardcover edition / June 2019
St. Martin's Paperbacks edition / April 2020

10 9 8 7 6 5 4 3 2 1

TO MELISSA AND CHRISTINE

THE AMERICANS

UNITED STATES NAVAL ACADEMY

Don Riley, Deputy J2, US Cyber Command; guest lecturer, Cyber Security Studies Program

Janet Everett, Midshipman First Class

Andrea "Dre" Ramirez, Midshipman Second Class

Michael Goodwin, Midshipman Fourth Class

Watson, Captain, USN; Commandant of Midshipmen

US INTELLIGENCE COMMUNITY

Elizabeth "Liz" Soroush, Assistant Director, FBI Counterterrorism Division; married to Brendan McHugh

Brendan McHugh, Captain, USN; head of the CIA Trident program

Rick Baxter, Deputy Director of National Intelligence

Judith Hellman, Director of National Intelligence

Sarah Jackson, Lieutenant, USN; US Cyber Command watch officer and midshipman liaison

Trafton, Admiral, USN; head of US Cyber Command

Martha Raddabat, CIA Senior Intelligence Service Officer; Brendan's boss

Jenkins, Trident program watch supervisor
Tom Price, Brigadier General, USAF; J2 and Don's boss
Roger Trask, Director, Central Intelligence Agency

US NAVY SEVENTH FLEET
Martin Cook, Vice Admiral; Commander
Bernard "Sauce" Benson, Captain; Chief of Staff to
    Commander

USS *GERALD R. FORD*, AIRCRAFT CARRIER
Manuel "Han" Manolo, Rear Admiral; Strike Group
    Commander
Diane "Ralph" Henderson, Captain; Air Wing Com-
    mander
Jim Gutterman, Captain; Commanding Officer

USS *BLUE RIDGE*, SEVENTH FLEET COMMAND SHIP
Weston Merville, Lieutenant Commander; IT Depart-
    ment Head and Systems Administrator
Jason Karrick, Commander; Executive Officer
Jurgens, Petty Officer First Class; IT Division

USS *KEY WEST*, LOS ANGELES-CLASS FAST ATTACK SUBMARINE
Langford, Commander; Commanding Officer
Gordon Cremer, Lieutenant Commander; Executive
    Officer
Dawkins, Lieutenant (j.g.); Junior Officer
Williams, Petty Officer Second Class; Radioman

SEAL TEAM
John "Winky" Winkler, Lieutenant Commander; Team
    Leader
Sidney, Winkler's Belgian Malinois working dog

OTHER CHARACTERS

THE NORTH KOREANS

Pak Myung-rok, special projects officer to the Supreme Leader

Rafiq Roshed, a.k.a. Jung Chul, Covert Actions Division agent and international terrorist

Yun So-won, cyberwarfare specialist

Kim Jong-un, Supreme Leader of the Democratic People's Republic of Korea

Kim Daiwoo, defector; former DPRK ambassador to the United Kingdom

Kong Sung-il, second deputy to the North Korean ambassador, based in Hong Kong

THE RUSSIANS

Borodin Gerasimov, Russian arms dealer

Alexi Aminev, head of the Far East Russian Bratva

THE CHINESE

Lieutenant Liu Wen, Chinese fighter pilot

Captain Sun, Commanding Officer, Chinese submarine *Changzheng 5*

Captain Li Sandai, Commanding Officer, Chinese frigate *Yangcheng*

Lieutenant Wei, officer of the deck, *Yangcheng*

Lieutenant Han Bingwen, 820th Brigade, Second Artillery Corps

THE JAPANESE

Captain Akihiko Amori, Commanding Officer, Japanese frigate *Sawagiri*

Admiral Hideki Tanaka, Commander, Japanese Maritime Self-Defense Force

MINOR CHARACTERS

Lieutenant Commander Jake "Tracker" Hanson, P-8 Poseidon pilot

Lieutenant Max "Taxi" Weber, P-8 Poseidon copilot

Richard "Dickie" Davis, private security contractor

Nigel Okumbe, private security contractor

Marco Gonzalez, CIA Chief of Station, Buenos Aires, Argentina

Admiral Tom Williams, Commander, US Pacific Fleet

Captain Bill "Handsome" Ransom, Air Wing Commander, USS *Reagan*

PROLOGUE

Allegheny Power and Light Operations Center
Jamestown, Pennsylvania

The email arrived in his inbox just as Randy Waters was thinking about shutting down his computer for the day. He knew that most of the others in his office left their computers and monitors running all night, but for God's sake, they worked for a power company. At least make an effort at conservation.

The email was from his mom. *For your father's birthday?* the subject line read.

His heart went out to her. His father was in the hospital again. Pancreatic cancer, stage three. Dad wouldn't be coming home, the doctors said.

His mother couldn't drive on her own anymore. In fact, Randy was just about to pick her up to make their twice-daily visit to the hospital to see his father. During the day, while Randy worked, she surfed the internet, killing time. Based on the subject line of the email, it seemed the obsession of the day was what to get his eighty-four-year-old, terminally ill father for his birthday next week. All the poor man probably wanted was a shot at another birthday to spend with his wife of fifty-seven years.

Randy opened the email. There was a single line of text, *I think he would like this,* followed by a link. None of her usual "Dear Randall" or "Love, Mom." His mother had never really mastered the informality of email. Normally her messages read like letters, complete with a salutation, an opening paragraph about the weather, then whatever she wanted to say, followed by a nice "Sincerely" to tie everything off with a neat bow.

Randy frowned. Maybe Mom needed to see someone, a therapist or something.

He clicked on the link without bothering to study it. His screen flashed to an Amazon page with a nice message saying they couldn't find the article he was searching for.

Randy shook his head. Poor Mom. It seemed even a simple cut-and-paste task was beyond her now.

He shut down his computer and grabbed his jacket off the back of the door. By the time he reached the elevators, he'd forgotten all about Mom's email.

Within a few milliseconds, the malware unleashed by Randy's indiscriminate link-clicking had found its target, an open security flaw in the recently updated driver for the color printer in the copy room. Before Randy's computer had shut down, the virus had infected every running computer networked to that color printer.

By the time Randy pushed the elevator call button, the malware was waiting on the desktop of the plant operations manager, Herman Moison.

At 6:45 P.M., just as he did every evening before going home, Moison logged in to the supervisory system for the power plant that loomed outside his office window. He studied the SCADA screen showing him the status and operating parameters of all twenty-six generators that fed electricity to the greater Midwest node of the national power grid.

Herman nodded with satisfaction. He didn't really understand all the numbers, but the red and green color-coding was very helpful. Green was good; red was bad. The electrons were going the right way, as his engineers liked to say. He noted that generator 24 was still down for maintenance.

Herman's screen flickered. He cocked his head. Something seemed different on the display, but he couldn't make out what it was. The red-green color-coding hadn't changed, so he figured all was okay. It had been a long day. The engineers would call him if anything went wrong overnight.

Herman shut off his office lights as he left, leaving the room bathed in the glow of his computer screen.

The malware that entered the power plant Supervisory Control and Data Acquisition system executed the first part of its payload: It shifted the generator-numbering system by one digit. Any commands being sent to generator 1 would be executed on generator 2, and so on.

Dustin Taft, the incoming shift supervisor, settled into his chair with a fresh cup of coffee. The plant staff was on four twelve-hour days now, a concession made by the union in the last negotiation. It took a little getting used to, but he found he liked it. That regular three-day weekend was pretty sweet.

"Shift Supe," one of his two operators called out. "Maintenance team requests permission to clear tags on gen twenty-four."

Taft nodded. "Permission granted. We'll test it after the dinnertime bump is over." Power usage peaked by as much as twenty percent between the hours of five and ten in the evening. That was a lot of TVs being switched on. It was even worse in the summer, with all the air conditioners running.

Their customer, Midwest Power Distributors, had installed a complete smart-grid system last year, allowing real-time access to power-demand data across the entire system. The upgrade helped them shift loads faster, but the dinnertime bump was just the nature of the beast. When people demanded more power, Taft made more electrons. Simple supply and demand.

"Tags cleared, Supe," the operator called. "Ready for testing whenever you are."

"Acknowledged." Taft watched his screen. "We're going to need more juice here soon. Let's bring gen twenty-three online."

The operator, a local kid, ex-navy, repeated the order and punched a series of commands into his keyboard. "Bringing twenty-three online now."

Taft sensed a dull thud under his feet, and the windows rattled. His monitor flashed red.

"What the hell happened?" Taft whirled in his seat. "What did you do?"

The operator's face was bathed in the pulsing, bloodred glow of his own screen. "I—I don't know . . . it just—"

Taft shifted his gaze to the security camera feed from the floor of the generator building. It took him a full second to realize that he was looking at the picture sideways. The camera must have been knocked off its mount.

Explosion. His mind rejected the idea. That was impossible in a modern power plant. . . .

Smoke or dust filled the screen with a mysterious swirling motion as if teasing him for the big reveal. He moved his face closer to the monitor, his nose almost touching, muttering to himself a steady mantra of *no, no, no, no.* . . .

A rip formed in the veil of dust, and Taft experienced a moment of light-headedness. The area that had once housed generator 24 was a smoking wreck of twisted metal and cracked foundation. Taft could see bodies on the floor, and one of the panels was on fire.

"You idiot, you tried to put gen twenty-four online!" Even as he shouted at the operator, Taft knew this didn't make any sense. There were software interlocks to prevent this kind of accident. Was it possible they'd all failed at the same time?

"Don't just sit there, dammit!" Taft bellowed, trying to keep the panic out of his voice. "Call an ambulance. We've got men hurt down there." Dead, probably. A fifty-thousand-pound steel turbine shredding itself into deadly shrapnel . . . His brain balked at the thought of what that could do to the men—his friends—on the plant floor. His mind raced back to the pre-shift briefing—who was down there? He couldn't even remember their names.

His training kicked in, finally. Taft snatched the phone from its cradle on his desk. With the whole plant down hard, Midwest Power needed to know they wouldn't be back online anytime soon. His eyes found the clock on the wall. Four minutes had elapsed already. It was strange they hadn't called him yet.

He started talking as soon as someone answered the phone. "This is Taft over at Allegheny. We're down hard. Major accident, the whole plant will be offline for . . . I don't know how long. I'll let you know—"

"Look, Taft, we got bigger problems over here. The whole friggin' East Coast is offline. When you're operational, call us back."

The line went dead.

CHAPTER 1

Grace Hopper Cyber Security Studies Center
United States Naval Academy, Annapolis, Maryland
One year later

"Thirty-six million people—including this institution—without power for nearly twelve hours. Forty-six traffic fatalities, twelve people dead in hospitals with inadequate backup power systems, and three men dead in an explosion at ground zero of the hack: Allegheny Power and Light."

Don Riley paused, allowing his gaze to roam over the dozen uniformed midshipmen in his seminar class. He always included this incident in the syllabus, since they'd all lived through it or at least knew someone who had.

Nearly all the midshipmen were seniors—first-classmen, in Naval Academy parlance—except for two. Midshipman Second Class Andrea Ramirez's dark eyes followed him like a hawk as he spoke. She seemed to be committing to memory not just his words but every move he made. Next to her sat a fourth-class midshipman—a freshman, or plebe as the upperclassmen called them.

To have a plebe in an advanced seminar broke every rule of Naval Academy etiquette, but Don had insisted.

Midshipman Fourth Class Michael Goodwin was no ordinary plebe. He was Don's special project.

The Academy, like every other institution of higher learning in America, had a well-established recruiting program for athletics. No one thought twice about spending money and resources to track down and lure the best possible athletic candidates to the academy. Don just applied the same recruiting logic to the Cyber Security Studies program. After all, that was why US Cyber Command lent him to the Academy as a guest lecturer: to get first crack at the new talent like Goodwin.

By any measure of intellect, Michael Goodwin was a prodigy. By any measure of societal norms, the fact that he was sitting in this classroom was a miracle.

Goodwin's face was still as he watched Don, his dark skin smooth, his jaw relaxed, his eyes vacant as if he were daydreaming. Don had seen this look before on Goodwin. He wasn't daydreaming, he was seeking inputs.

Don cleared his throat and continued. "The attack originated via an email to a midlevel employee in the admin department of Allegheny Power. The user clicked on a link which downloaded malware onto his computer. The malware used a security flaw in a print driver to infect any computer that was connected to that printer."

There was a snort of disbelief from the back row. "Problem, Midshipman Powers?" Don asked a tall, whip-thin brunette sporting the rank of a company commander on her collar.

"It's just amazing how stupid people can be, sir. I mean, who clicks on random links?"

Don pursed his lips. "Would it change your mind if I told you that this email was supposedly from the individual's mother? Also, the subject line indicated that it was about his father, who happened to be in the hospital receiving treatment for advanced pancreatic cancer. Would that change your attitude, Ms. Powers?"

The midshipman dropped her gaze to her desk.

"Given this new information, what can we surmise about this attack, people?"

"That the employee was targeted," said a voice.

"Exactly!" Don's gaze sought the person who'd answered. A stocky young woman with dirty-blond hair. "Midshipman Everett, please elaborate."

"Well, the fact that it was from his mother and regarding his father indicates the attacker knew his subject. He probably hacked the mother's email account to avoid the spam filters and wrote a subject line that would increase his chances of getting a click."

"That's exactly correct," Don said. "This was not some random internet virus you pick up when you visit porn sites—which I know midshipmen never do." He got a few laughs out of that line. "This was a very sophisticated spear-phishing operation, a targeted attack on a single individual. This person was surveilled, and his weaknesses exploited.

"But there's another reason we study this cyberattack. The actual code itself was a masterpiece. A virus within a virus within a virus. The first layer exploited the security flaw in the printer driver to gain access to as many workstations as possible. Then it waited for someone to access the power plant SCADA system." He paused. "By way of review, what does SCADA stand for, Mr. Nelson?" He called on a first-class midshipman in the second row who was nodding off. The young man's head snapped up.

"Supervisory control and data acquisition system, sir," the midshipman said in a near shout.

"Thank you for your enthusiasm, Mr. Nelson," Don replied, smiling along with the laughter of the class. "If you're feeling sleepy, perhaps you'd care to stand?"

The midshipman hoisted himself out of his seat, and Don continued. "The third layer of the virus was again targeted and clever. Instead of trying to crash the system, it changed just one parameter: the numbering system for the generators. When a technician tried to change an operating parameter on a generator using the SCADA system, he was actually sending the command to a different machine. When the control room thought they were bringing a spinning generator online, they were actually connecting a nonoperational unit to the power grid. What happens when you try to make a rotor go from zero to thirty-six hundred RPMs in a split second, Mr. Nelson?"

"Boom, sir?"

"Boom." Don stopped pacing and faced the room. "In addition to killing three men, the resulting explosion destroyed most of the Allegheny P&L generating capability. But our little piece of malware had one final mission.

"The term *national power grid* is often tossed around as if it's one monolithic entity. It's not. It's a patchwork of fiefdoms and legacy operating systems from the last hundred years. There's a reason the hackers chose to attack Allegheny P&L. Their plant is colocated with Midwest Power's distribution operation. This site is the link between the East Coast and the Midwest transmission networks. These are two separate companies, operating two separate software systems with two separate levels of cybersecurity.

"The malware jumped the fence from Allegheny to Midwest and proceeded to take down every distribution node on that network. The only way they were able to contain it was to take their entire operation offline for eight hours and bring the system back online one network at a time."

Don let the information sink in.

"All that damage, all those lives lost, all from one email. It does no good to complain about the guy who clicked on a link in an email from his mom. People are people; they will do things you don't want them to do. We're not here to try to change human nature, we're here to find the bad guys and shut them down.

"Make no mistake about it, people. What is going on out there is a war, right under our noses. We are under attack every day from all sorts of people with all sorts of reasons to want to hurt us. Non-state actors, the Russian 'patriotic hackers,' the North Koreans, China's cyber corps, even Israel's Unit 8200—yes, even the countries we give billions of dollars to—love to hack us. And don't get me started on the private sector."

"Sir?" It was Everett again. "Who did it? The Allegheny hack, I mean."

Don gave her a grim smile. "The thorny issue of attribution, Ms. Everett. Hackers don't just leave a calling card. We need to pick apart their code, look at the context of the hack, backtrack on where the emails came from, and so on. Then, and only then, can we make some educated guesses about who did the deed."

"So who did it?"

Don shrugged. "In this case, it was simple. The hack was claimed by a group affiliated with ISIS—Daesh, as the rest of the world knows them. According to our current rules of engagement, we retaliated with increased bombing and drone strikes. All of the suspected perpetrators were killed."

"And is that what happened?" It seemed Everett was not going to let it go.

"Why do you ask, Ms. Everett?"

"Well, sir, you just described a scenario that was part intelligence operation and part hack. ISIS has not shown that level of capability before or since."

Don considered her. He needed to pick someone from this class, and she seemed to be the most engaged so far. "The topic of attribution and public acknowledgment is for another class, Midshipman. Class dismissed."

Everett hung back as the room emptied out. "That's not really what happened, is it, sir?"

"Ms. Everett, I'm the deputy J2 at Cyber Command. You know what that means, right?"

"Yes, sir. You help run the military's cyberwarfare operations. You complement what the NSA's already doing."

"Right. My stint here as a visiting lecturer is contingent upon following some strict security protocols. If I tell you that's what happened, then you have to accept that answer at face value." Her bright blue eyes met his without reservation.

In Don's experience, there were two types of midshipmen: those who were naturally gifted and those who worked their asses off every day to stay above water. Janet Everett was the latter, a striver, the kind of midshipman who put in the hours needed to get the job done. "Even if there's another answer that I can't talk about," he finished softly.

She gave him a curt nod. "I understand, sir."

"Midshipman Everett, what do you think about the underclassmen in the seminar?"

Her brow wrinkled. "I know Ramirez, we've had other classes together. She's solid. The plebe? Goodwin? Seems strange to have a plebe in an advanced course like this. I heard he's a real brain."

"You could say that." Don resisted a laugh. "Brain"

didn't begin to cover Michael's pattern-recognition skills. "Do you expect there to be any tension with the other upperclassmen?"

Everett's broad shoulders shrugged. "Could be. He has to learn to deal with it. It's the system."

"We'll be breaking into teams after the next class. I want you, Ramirez, and Goodwin on the same team. Understood?"

Don knew his request—she would interpret it as an order—was unfair. She was a young officer, not a baby-sitter. He had no business saddling her with a couple of underclassmen, but his gut told him she was the right person for the job.

Everett had every right to ask him why or what was in it for her. Instead, she nodded without hesitation.

"Understood, sir."

CHAPTER 2

Secret Intelligence Service (MI6)
Headquarters, London

In the movies, defector debriefings were tense affairs filled with sharp questions designed to catch the witness off guard. The answers always revealed some brilliant new plot twist.

Real debriefings were much less exciting. Every minute of face time with a defector required at least ten minutes of preparation. You only got one chance to ask a fresh question and see his initial expression, to judge if the defector was real or some kind of double agent. Of course, the British had had this guy in custody for weeks. The chances of two US agents being able to find an unanswered question was nil.

FBI Special Agent Elizabeth Soroush studied the small monitor showing an image of the interrogation room. Kim Daiwoo was a slight, wiry man, but carried a shadow of past malnutrition in the lines of his face. Was it possible that even a third cousin of the Supreme Leader might have known hunger in his past?

"Ready?" said the man at her elbow. Reggie Bowerman, a Canadian by birth, was a strapping man with a perpetual five-o'clock shadow who probably weighed twice what the North Korean did. As a representative of the US Treasury Department's Terrorist Financing and Financial Crimes Division, he was assisting Liz on the money-laundering aspects of the counterterrorism case.

She flashed him a smile. "Let's do this. I'll take point, you jump in with technical details, just like we agreed, okay?"

Reggie popped up his thumb in answer.

Kim looked up as Liz entered the room with Reggie hulking behind her. He got to his feet in a controlled manner and offered a short bow, then seated himself after Liz had taken her seat.

She opened her folio on the table and drew a pen from the pocket of her jacket. The entire interview was being recorded, but she liked to take notes anyway. It helped her think.

"Good morning, Mr. Kim. My name is FBI Special Agent Elizabeth Soroush, and this is my colleague Agent Reginald Bowerman of the US Treasury Department. I run the United States Joint Terrorism Task Force—do you know what that is, sir?"

The diplomat spoke in a cultured accent, reflecting his British education. "I presume you investigate acts of terrorism against the United States. But this is England; why are you here?"

"When an investigation of terrorism takes us outside the borders of the United States, Mr. Kim, we follow." She placed a photo in front of him. His eyes widened for a split second, and a shadow flickered across his features.

"You know this man, Mr. Kim?"

The diplomat's calm exterior slipped back into place. "Yes, I know him. Pak Myung-rok, the Supreme Leader's man . . . I believe the American term is 'fixer'?"

Liz and Reggie exchanged looks. "What does that term mean to you, Mr. Kim?" Reggie asked.

"When Kim Jong-un needs something done outside the normal channels of business or diplomacy, he calls this man." Kim tapped the photo.

"I see," Liz said. "We have reason to believe that Pak is involved in money laundering, both in the US and in Europe. Do you have any knowledge of this?"

Kim relaxed in his chair. "Oh, yes, I'm certain he is involved in money laundering. What do you want to know?"

Reggie leaned over the table and began to pepper Kim with questions. The North Korean defector answered everything immediately and truthfully as far as Liz could tell, but her mind was stuck on his initial reaction to the charge of money laundering.

He had relaxed, as if he was expecting her to ask about something else. Something much worse.

Reggie was writing furiously. Times, dates, bank visits, diamonds smuggled in diplomatic pouches, illicit weapons deals, oil smuggling. It looked as if Kim was a gold mine for Treasury.

Finally, Reggie leaned over toward Liz. "I'm good," he said.

Liz focused her gaze on Kim, saying nothing. The diplomat's smile faded as the silence lengthened. Reggie shifted in his seat and she willed him to be quiet. Kim dropped his gaze to the table.

"What did you think I was going to ask about, Mr. Kim?"

He attempted another smile. "I don't know what you mean, Agent Soroush. I've just provided you with plenty of information about Pak's illegal money-laundering efforts. My answers were truthful. There is nothing else."

"Tell me, Mr. Kim."

The North Korean squirmed, his eyes pleading with her.

"Reggie," Liz said. "You can go."

"But the briefing plan. We got what we wanted, right?"

"Mr. Kim and I have another topic to discuss. I'll see you back at the hotel."

After her partner had departed, Liz let the silence drag on. "I'm not leaving until you tell me," she said.

"Have you seen my family? Are they safe?" Kim asked. His unflappable diplomatic shell had evaporated, replaced by a hunted expression.

"They're safe—provided you cooperate completely."

Kim sighed. "Pak is a playboy. He leads a charmed life. Favored by the Supreme Leader, he goes on expensive European business trips and does deals for the regime. Everyone knows he skims money off for himself, but he's always willing to share with his friends. Everybody loved Pak."

"Loved?" Liz asked. "That's changed now?"

"Four years ago, Pak brought a foreigner to Pyongyang. He convinced the Supreme Leader to give the man asylum. Before long, Pak was doing more than money laundering. He used this man to carry out secret assignments for the Supreme Leader. That reporter in Germany who was investigating food shipments to North Korea?"

Liz vaguely recalled a car accident and conspiracy theories. She nodded.

"That was him," Kim said.

"How do you know this? Did you see him do it?"

Kim shook his head. "No, not that one." He was sweating freely, and his eyes roamed around the room.

"Then it's just a rumor."

"No, I know because I smuggled him into the United Kingdom."

"And he did something while he was here."

Kim nodded. "It was easy," he said. "He's nearly six feet tall, has European features, and speaks English with a Spanish accent."

Liz felt a chill run up her spine. "What did you say?"

Kim mopped his brow with a silk handkerchief. "Which part?"

"His accent," Liz whispered.

"Spanish, but not Continental, more like—"

"South American," Liz finished for him.

"Exactly."

Liz stood so quickly that Kim drew back in his chair. She stabbed out her hand. "Thank you for your time, Mr. Kim. I wish you the best. You will have my recommendation for asylum."

She made her way out of the room and found the nearest office. "I need a secure line to the CIA. Quickly, please."

Her hand shook as she dialed her husband's assistant in Washington, DC. The minutes dragged by as they tracked Brendan down. She tightened her grip on the receiver. Could it really be him? After all this time?

"Liz? What's up, honey? Is something—"

"I found him, Brendan. I know where he is."

"Who?"

"Roshed. I found Rafiq Roshed."

CHAPTER 3

Undisclosed location in the Russian Far East

The hood came off Pak Myung-rok's head with a snap of cloth. He squinted in the bright lights of the airplane cabin.

"Welcome to Russia," said one of his escorts in broken English, followed by a harsh laugh. His companion joined in.

"Enough!" A new voice, a voice Pak knew. Borodin Gerasimov had to stoop in the confines of the Gulfstream cabin. Relief flooded through Pak at the sight of his well-tailored friend cursing out the guards in Russian.

He turned back to Pak, extending his hand. "Come, my friend," he said in English, their only common language. "They're waiting for us."

Pak took the immaculately manicured hand and stood. He smoothed the front of his Armani suit. Wrinkled—not the way he wanted to meet members of the Bratva, the Russian Brotherhood, for what might be the most important meeting of his career.

The chill night air was refreshing after the stuffiness of the Gulfstream cabin. The guards had smoked and played cards the entire four-hour flight without so much as offering him a glass of water.

"How is the Supreme Leader?" Gerasimov said, his cultured English accent betraying his Western education. He'd once joked that British boarding school was the best possible education for an international arms dealer.

"The Supreme Leader is in good health," Pak replied. "He looks forward to a fruitful business relationship with our Russian friends."

Gerasimov's smile glinted in the darkness. "Trust me, Pak. If you play your cards right on this deal, we all get rich. You, me, and the Supreme Leader." He paused before a low-slung building and dropped his voice, his breath smoking in the air. "There's only one man you need to care about tonight. Alexi Aminev runs the Far East Bratva; this is his home. Be careful—the man is an animal."

Pak nodded. "Is there someplace I can freshen up? Maybe get my suit jacket pressed before the meeting?"

Gerasimov's laugh rang loud and lusty in the night air. "My friend, you won't need a suit for this meeting." He placed a hand on Pak's back and ushered him through the door. The interior was warm and humid, with a faint chlorine smell in the air. Gerasimov shucked his suit coat. "We'll be taking this meeting *au naturel,* as the French say." He handed his jacket to a woman in a bikini.

Pak stood rooted to the spot. They were having a business meeting naked?

Gerasimov snapped his fingers. "They're waiting, Pak. Get a move on."

A hand tugged at the lapel of his jacket and he looked up to find another scantily clad woman trying to undress him. He did not resist and soon he was standing in his underwear. The woman held up a snowy white bathrobe.

Gerasimov paced. "Pak, we need to do this deal before they get too drunk. Hurry!"

Pak turned away and slid his boxers to the floor. The woman draped the bathrobe over his thin shoulders. The material was soft and fluffy to the touch, expensive.

Gerasimov seized his elbow and steered him to the door.

For a moment, Pak wondered if they'd somehow walked into a high-end European spa. Italian tiles in tasteful earth tones covered the vast room. Pools of various sizes and shapes spotted the space with broad tile walkways between them. All were lit from underwater, lending an unearthly glow to the room. At least a dozen nude young women lounged in and around the pools, some carrying trays of drinks, others plastered to the sides of hairy Russian men. Europop played in the background.

Pak drew in a deep breath. This was the business meeting? As Kim Jong-un's major representative for alternative business relationships, he'd seen and enjoyed many, many scenes, but this was unique. He was supposed to negotiate an international arms deal in front of two dozen people?

"Borodin!" came a booming voice from the other side of the room.

Gerasimov went into full salesman mode. With a huge smile painted on his face, he threw his arms wide and strode down the tile walkway, still herding Pak forward. "Alexi!" he bellowed back.

The man in the pool stood in the waist-high water, shaking off the girls on either arm. Gerasimov shucked his bathrobe, and waded into the pool, leaving

Pak behind. He embraced Alexi Aminev, the pair exchanging a volley of Russian that Pak had no hope of following.

Aminev was half a head shorter than Gerasimov, with powerful shoulders, and a thick mat of graying hair covering his chest. With a square jaw and a generous mouth, the man looked friendly, like someone's grandfather.

But the man's eyes told Pak the real story. Flat, dark brown, like stone, they captured Pak's gaze and held him.

"So this is your North Korean friend, Borodin," Aminev said in a gravelly tone. His English was passable.

"Allow me to introduce Pak Myung-rok, the personal representative of Kim Jong-un."

Pak held Aminev's gaze, willing himself not to be the first to look away. Finally, the Russian nodded and slapped the water. "Join us, Mr. Pak."

He allowed one of the ubiquitous young women to slip the robe off his shoulders, acutely aware of how scrawny and hairless he appeared next to these brawny, bearlike men. He stepped into the water. It was hot, searing, but he kept his face blank.

Aminev offered a thin smile as Pak seated himself, the water reaching his chin. He breathed through the discomfort. Gerasimov settled himself on the opposite wall, his arms spread across the tile rim of the pool.

"Borodin has told you about our needs?" Aminev asked finally.

Another test. "Borodin has told me you have a business proposition for the Democratic People's Republic of Korea, that's all."

Aminev held out his hand and one of the girls passed him a glass of vodka. He drank it off, then pointed at Pak. The girl swam across the pool with a fresh glass. Pak downed it and handed it back to her.

It was chilled, and the clear liquid burned straight down to his gut. He smiled at Aminev. "Good."

It was good, and it took the edge off the pain from the hot water. Pak swiped the sweat from his brow but kept his eyes on the Russian. He was willing to wait as long as necessary for the other man to speak.

"Borodin says you have computer weapons on the internet." He looked at Gerasimov for the right word.

"Cyber," Gerasimov replied.

"Yes, cyberweapons. Computer viruses."

Ah, thought Pak, *now we're getting somewhere.*

"The Supreme Leader has made great investments in the realm of cyberwarfare. We rank among the most powerful nations on earth."

Aminev narrowed his gaze to slits. "Why cyberweapons? I thought all Kim cared about was his nuclear program."

Pak blinked the sweat out of his eyes. "Our nuclear weapons are for self-defense. Cyberwarfare gives us the ability to attack the United States in more . . . subtle ways."

Aminev tossed off another vodka and indicated for the girl to give another to Pak. "We have a job for you."

Pak tilted the shot of vodka down his throat. "I'm listening."

"Our weapons sales in the region have dropped off. Things are too peaceful. We want you to . . ." He twirled his finger in the air and looked at Gerasimov.

"Stir up trouble," Gerasimov supplied. "Alexi wants to goose his sales by ratcheting up tension in the region. No real conflicts, understand. Just bad feelings between neighbors."

"What did you have in mind?" Pak asked.

Gerasimov shrugged. "Hack into Chinese military databases, leak some of their military plans to the Vietnamese, the Philippines, the Malaysians—that sort of thing. We want everyone to feel off balance, a little on edge. Nervous nations buy weapons."

He leaned forward. "You must understand, Pak, this operation requires finesse. We don't actually want to start a war, just stir things up enough for everyone to open their pocketbooks. Maybe even start a bidding war on a few of the more hard-to-get items."

"Russian military surplus?"

Gerasimov threw back his head, letting his laugh echo through the room. He quickly translated for Aminev, who joined him in the joke. Pak knew the arms dealer had a network that allowed him to skim seemingly unlimited quantities of weapons from the Russian military. He often wondered what would happen if Russia actually needed to mobilize a fighting force.

Pak pulled a thoughtful face as he accepted another vodka. The water was just the right temperature now. This was his favorite part of a negotiation: the part where he got paid. "Cyberwarfare is expensive," he said.

Gerasimov and Aminev exchanged glances. "We were thinking twenty million US dollars, processed discreetly, of course."

"Hmm, that's funny, Borodin," Pak replied. "I was thinking forty million—with a three percent surcharge for handling." Pak drank off the vodka. One point two million dollars in his private account!

It took another hour and three more shots before they agreed on 32 million dollars with an additional 1.2 million on the side for Pak.

His legs wobbled as he climbed out of the pool. Gerasimov caught his arm, steering him toward the locker room.

"Pak!" Aminev called after him.

With Gerasimov's help, he turned back to face the head of the Bratva. "Just computers, got it? Cyber only. No shooting. Bad for business." The Russian was standing in the pool, his matted chest hair sluicing water. He'd drunk at least eight shots of vodka with Pak, but it seemed not to affect him at all.

Using Gerasimov as a stabilizer, Pak made a mock bow. "Just computers, Alexi. You have my personal guarantee."

CHAPTER 4

CIA Headquarters, Langley, Virginia

Captain Brendan McHugh blew out a long breath and leaned back in his office chair until he could see the ceiling tiles. He'd just completed his fourth meeting of the day on his least favorite topic: budgets. Thank God he wasn't the one doing budget briefings to Congress. They'd never get any funding.

"Tom, how long till my next meeting?" he called through the open door.

"Fifteen minutes, sir. In the ops center," his admin called back. "I left a printed copy of your schedule in your inbox."

Brendan dug through the stack of paper until he found the sheet. So much for the paperless office. "Thanks, Tom."

He sipped at his now-cold coffee, enjoying a moment of calm before his next bureaucratic skirmish. His gaze strayed to the family picture on the corner of his desk. Liz, her raven hair grown out longer than at any time since he'd known her, and their two children. Beth, their oldest, had inherited her mother's Iranian features—dark hair, olive skin, and firm jaw. Ahmad, despite being named after Liz's father, tended toward Brendan's Irish heritage with fine, strawberry-blond hair and a sprinkle of freckles across his nose.

Beth had a T-ball game tonight, he reminded himself, and he made a note on the paper schedule. It was his turn to make the game. Juggling Liz's FBI career and his own assignment with the CIA made for a hectic home life.

"Sir?" Tom appeared at the door. "You're meeting in the ops center in five."

Brendan hoisted himself out of his chair. His knee popped, and he grimaced at the expected pain. The ancient injury from a young North Korean sailor that had ended his career as a Navy SEAL was the gift that kept on giving. He forced himself to put weight on the knee as he walked down the hall. According to the doctors, the only way to keep the joint healthy was to keep using it—no matter the discomfort.

Stepping onto the Trident watch floor was like shedding his skin. On one side of the door was all the paperwork and budgets and infrastructure; on this side he could at least maintain a tenuous connection to his time in the field with the Feisty Minnow program, the precursor to Trident.

It was hard to believe that all this had started with one lonely cast-off sailboat from the US Naval Academy sailing fleet. At the beginning, Feisty Minnow was one step above a harebrained idea: take a civilian sailboat, outfit it with the latest in signals intelligence monitoring, and sail it around the globe. He'd skippered the *Arrogant,* a fifty-four-footer, posing as a rich software executive with more money than common sense. With his small crew of five, they'd broken some of the best SIGINT of their time.

Partly as a result of his success, the fleet expanded to

six sailboats stationed all over the world. Feisty Minnow, the program with the ridiculous name, became so successful it was taken over by the CIA and Brendan was pulled out of the field to run it. That was nearly six years ago.

Brendan swept his gaze across the massive wall screens that dominated the room and the two dozen watch officers on duty at computer workstations. This was the headquarters for Trident, the most expensive and ambitious signals intelligence monitoring program in the history of the world. Trident connected an unimaginable variety of floating platforms into a network of what his analysts called v-SIGINT, short for "viral signals intelligence." And they were just beginning to scratch the surface of what they could do with this capability.

As he always did, he searched the wall screens for *Arrogant,* his old command.

"She's off the coast of Turkey, sir," called one of the techs.

Brendan spotted the dot on the map and blushed. "Thanks, Jenkins." Some days he felt like an old high school quarterback reliving his glory days.

He strode to the center desk, where the watch supervisor was waiting for him. "What's our status, Supe?"

"The network's in good shape this morning, sir. We've got full coverage in the Med and the IO, pushing ninety percent around Japan and Taiwan, but we're not even at sixty in the rest of West Pac."

Brendan studied the vast stretch of ocean from Taiwan to Malaysia as the man spoke. "That's a lot of blue water to cover. How're the installs going on the merchant ships?"

The supervisor nodded with enthusiasm. "Really

well. We'll be ready to flip the switch this week. The analysts estimate we'll have greater than ninety percent coverage across the whole region within a month or so."

Brendan chewed his lip. Tying military ships into a consolidated surveillance network was one thing, but using civilian ships worried him. The CIA had developed a "black box" the size of a phone booth that could be installed on any vessel. Cooperative shipping lines were paid a handsome fee to supply a 220-volt line and ask no questions. The unit automatically gathered and uploaded signals intel wherever the ship went. For shipping lines that were unwilling to participate, the CIA had developed a version with a fuel-cell power source. The unit was simply bolted into a shipping container and shipped as regular cargo from one CIA front operation to another.

The supe cleared his throat. "What's the approval status of Piggyback, sir?" His voice had a hopeful tone.

Brendan tried not to frown. The watch supervisor was in his midtwenties, one of the new breed of CIA officers who believed with all their being that every problem could be solved through the application of technology. If you just had the right app, you could sit behind a desk and all the questions of our complex world would be served up in a spreadsheet.

I'm getting old, he thought. A feeling that seemed to be looming in his consciousness more often lately.

"They're briefing the Hill today," he said finally. "I expect it'll get approved."

The watch supervisor pumped his fist. "That's awesome, sir."

"Yep, awesome." Brendan returned his attention to the wall screens.

In the last decade, threat assessments had highlighted the vulnerability of the United States' space assets. From global positioning system satellites to comms birds that connected the fleet, the expected first move in any global conflict was for the opposing side—the Russians or the Chinese were the perennial favorites—to destroy the US military satellite network. Of course, the US would do the same to them, so after the first few hours, the world would have two blind war machines squaring off.

Trident changed all that. The program that had begun as a passive signals intelligence collection platform had graduated to a distributed analysis network with independent computer processing capacity on every platform. Now, with Piggyback, it was ready to take the next step: viral communications. When the CIA platform achieved the right amount of coverage in the right places, the plan was to use Trident as an independent command and control network. In the event of loss of satellite coverage, the US would have a viral network of ships and planes blanketing the world.

He'd seen the cool graphics of an entirely interconnected fleet with bright yellow lines bouncing from ship to ship to ship, without ever needing a satellite. It made for a really slick presentation for congressmen.

But all that connectedness worried him. What if this all-encompassing network got hacked? Had these people never seen *Battlestar Galactica*? The Cylons decimated the über-networked human fleet with a single computer virus. He'd actually brought that analogy up in a staff meeting once, and the room of twentysomethings looked at him like he'd farted in church.

Maybe I've been doing this too long, he thought.

"Will that be all, sir?" the watch supervisor asked.

"Yeah," he replied with a sigh. "That's all for now." His eyes searched for the little blip on the map that represented *Arrogant.*

CHAPTER 5

*Covert Actions Division, Ministry of the People's
Armed Forces Pyongyang, North Korea*

The desk between them was a cheap affair of metal and
plastic laminate, built for a much smaller frame than his
own. When Rafiq Roshed bothered to visit his office,
which was infrequently, he managed to bang the tops
of his knees against the drawer every time.

He allowed the slight man in the well-cut, Western-
style business suit to speak first.

"How are you getting on these days?" said Pak.

Rafiq shrugged and lit one of the vile sticks that
passed for cigarettes in the DPRK.

"Ah!" Pak said. He slid his hand into his breast pocket
and pulled out a red and white package. Marlboros. "Try
one of these."

Rafiq immediately crushed out his own butt and
seized the unopened pack. As he tore the foil, the scent
of real tobacco filled the tiny office. He tapped out a cigarette and lit it, drawing deeply.

"Your brother's brand, remember?" Pak said with a
smile.

Rafiq considered the burning end. He hadn't thought
about Hashem in months. His only link to this greedy

little man who'd given him shelter in the rogue state of North Korea. A gift of sorts, with strings attached.

"Half brother," he replied. He stowed the pack of Marlboros in his breast pocket. Pak pretended not to see his petty theft even though real cigarettes were like gold on the thriving DPRK black market.

Rafiq flexed his shoulders. The dark green uniform he was forced to wear in this formal office setting pinched in all the worst places. He told himself it was because the tailors of this godforsaken country only knew how to sew for two sizes: concentration-camp-thin or as fat as the Supreme Leader, who smiled down at them from his picture on the wall.

"Half brother, then," Pak said, watching him closely. "A good man all the same."

Rafiq grunted. His feet were like ice in the thin uniform shoes—also too small for him. They never turned the heat on in these damn buildings. . . .

"I have a job for you, Rafiq," Pak said.

Rafiq. He'd called him Rafiq, not Chul, his new name in North Korea. Was this Pak's subtle way of telling him this was a special task?

"What kind of job?"

Pak produced a second pack of Marlboros from his leather valise and lit one. He left the open pack sitting on the desk between them. He continued in English, a fact that caused Rafiq to sit up in his chair.

"A job that requires finesse." Pak pinched the cigarette between his thumb and forefinger and aimed it at Rafiq like a dart. "A skill that is sorely lacking in many of our operatives."

Rafiq nodded. The problem with a cult of personality like North Korea was that it killed independent thought, let alone initiative. The people of this damned country were a hammer and every problem was a nail. Threaten to attack, shoot a missile, test a nuclear weapon. Then what?

"I had an interesting trip to Russia. The Bratva is seeking our help. They want to—how do the Americans say it?—create a seller's market, I think."

Rafiq reached for the open pack of Marlboros and took one, leaving the pack on his side of the desk. "Explain."

"Cyberwarfare. They're looking for a third party to hack the Chinese and spread disinformation throughout the region. Release war plans, diplomatic cables, that sort of thing."

"So the Russians can sell more hardware?"

Pak nodded.

Rafiq drew on his cigarette, holding his breath, finally expelling a long stream of smoke at the ceiling. "Too risky," he said, pointing to the picture on the wall. "He'll never agree to it."

"The Supreme Leader already has agreed to it."

Rafiq hid a smile behind another drag of his cigarette. "The Russians have legions of hackers. Why not do their own dirty work?"

"Because they want the best—"

"We're not the best, not even close."

Pak's lips tightened.

"They want plausible deniability, Pak. If this goes wrong, it could start a shooting war. The Russian Brotherhood doesn't want to be left holding the bag and they certainly don't want any suspicion to fall on the Russian government. That's why they want you to do it."

Pak stayed silent.

Rafiq smoked his cigarette to the butt, then tapped another out of the pack. "It's a tricky job. 'Finesse' is a good word to describe what's needed."

"So you'll do it then?"

"How much are you getting under the table?"

Pak reddened. "That's insulting. How can you suggest I—"

Rafiq leaned across the desk. "You know what's insulting, Pak? I've built the Supreme Leader's covert-action capabilities into a world-class operation and I'm still freezing my balls off in this office. Your suit costs more than I made in the last six months. Every meal I eat is some sort of rice mixed with mystery meat—if it has meat at all." He took a deep breath. "Answer me: How much are you skimming?"

"A million," Pak whispered.

"Which means it's actually one point five. I want half—and a way out of here when the time is right."

Pak nodded.

"Good." Rafiq sat back in his chair. "I need full authority—no interference from the chain of command. I report to you and you alone."

"That can be arranged."

"I already have a core group of cyber people. I'll need a squad of commandos for overseas work. Handpicked by me. I don't want any informants in the group."

"You already have a plan," Pak said.

Rafiq shrugged, his shoulders straining at the confines of his uniform. "I've got something that has been waiting for an opportunity."

"Tell me."

Rafiq smiled but stayed silent. Pak snorted as a reply. This was a familiar dance between them. Rafiq Roshed delivered results, and Pak had learned not to interfere.

"Anything else, Rafiq?"

"A location. Someplace remote, secure, but with facilities for a top-notch cyber war room."

Pak brightened. "I know just the place."

CHAPTER 6

South China Sea

Lieutenant Commander Jake "Tracker" Hanson slipped his headphones off and hung them on the hook next to his pilot's chair. The P-8 Poseidon aircraft rode high in a sun-drenched, cloudless sky over the sapphire blue of the South China Sea.

He flipped his sunglasses up on his forehead and pinched the bridge of his nose. The steady drone of the jet engines was putting him to sleep. These freedom-of-navigation operations, or FONOPs, were his least favorite part of his job. Sure, they were great for racking up flight hours, but he preferred at least some activity. This run was a straight shot from Okinawa to Singapore—with a short dogleg to make sure they crossed within ten miles of a Chinese-made "island" in the Spratlys.

"You've got it," he said to his copilot, Lieutenant Max "Taxi" Weber. "Going for coffee."

"I got it," Taxi acknowledged. "We're coming up on our turn in ten minutes. I expect the Chinese will have something to say about our flight plan."

Tracker laughed and called over his shoulder, "Stand by to get talked to death in bad English."

He made his way down into the heart of the aircraft, passing the banks of electronics used for their main mission: hunting submarines. Two of the crew had a panel racked out and were running a diagnostic.

"How's the coffee?" Tracker said to the chief petty officer.

"Black and bitter, like my attitude, sir," she replied with a wry grin.

Tracker chuckled as he poured his coffee. As he added powdered creamer, he felt the aircraft start a gentle turn. Within a few minutes, they'd get the typical verbal warning about how they were approaching Chinese territorial waters and to reverse course. He wondered idly if they had that message prerecorded or if they had someone read it each time.

He could remember flying over Fiery Cross Reef years ago as a newly minted ensign on a training mission. The place had been nothing but a bump in the ocean. But the Chinese had carted in rock and soil and sand and made an island, complete with a harbor, a short airstrip, and buildings. The Chinese had some brass ones to pull that off, but what really amazed him was how the rest of the world just let them do it. He had to hand it to them, the Chinese knew how to play the long game. They'd taken decades to attain full control over the Spratlys, and there was no way they were leaving.

Now pilots like him were stuck playing this silly game of "violating" a fictional twelve-mile boundary on a fictional island instead of hunting submarines like he was trained to do. It was a waste of time and resources in his opinion, but who else was going to challenge the Chinese besides the good old US Navy?

He licked a drip of coffee from the stir stick and dropped it in the trash.

Tracker was just sliding back into his seat when his copilot called out. "Crossing the twelve-mile boundary on Fiery Cross Reef, sir."

He fitted his headphones over his ears. "Very well. Stand by to be jawboned."

As if on cue, the radio sounded in his ears: "Unidentified aircraft, you are operating in the sovereign waters of the People's Republic of China. Please reverse course and leave this area immediately."

Tracker winked at Taxi. "I'll take this call." He cleared his throat and keyed his mic. "We are a US Navy aircraft operating in international airspace en route to Singapore. We intend to maintain course and speed."

The Chinese broadcast continued: "Unidentified aircraft, you are operating in—"

"Incoming bogeys, Captain!" the crew chief broke in, her voice tight with tension.

Seconds later, two Chinese J-11 fighters streaked by the windscreen with a thunderous roar. The Poseidon wobbled in their wake, alarms flashing on the control panel.

"Off autopilot!" Tracker yelled, seizing the aircraft controls. "Repeat the warning, Max."

Weber keyed his mic. "We are a US Navy aircraft operating in international airspace en route to—"

"They're coming back for another pass," the crew chief said over the open channel.

"Acknowledged, Chief. Maintaining course and speed. Max, keep broadcasting."

Tracker gripped the steering yoke, his eyes searching the blue sky for the two Chinese fighters.

There! A dot on the horizon separated and grew larger at an alarming rate.

"Closing speed Mach two," the chief called.

Tracker gritted his teeth as he acknowledged the

chief. There was nothing to do but stay on his present course. He had a fleeting glimpse of the lean fighters flashing by the cockpit. He felt the sound of their passage in the muscles of his belly, and he forced himself not to duck in response to their supersonic passage.

"They're carrying PL-12 air-to-air missiles, sir," the crew chief said.

"Any sign we're being targeted, Chief?"

"Negative, sir. I'm reading only nav radars."

Tracker took a deep breath but kept a firm grip on the yoke to still his shaking hands. "How long till we're past twelve miles, Max?"

"Two minutes."

"They're coming back again," the chief called out.

Tracker steeled himself. "Acknowledged."

"They're slowing, sir . . . matching speed . . ."

A shape loomed in Tracker's peripheral vision. He stared over at the Chinese fighter fifty yards off his wingtip. The craft's angular design and swept wings looked lethal next to the lumbering Poseidon.

"Coming up on twelve miles."

Just before the fighter peeled off, Tracker raised his right hand and flipped the Chinese pilot the bird.

CHAPTER 7

Rick Baxter came to attention as the president entered with his entourage.

The seats around the table filled rapidly with a who's who of political and military power, and the overflow spilled into chairs against the wall. In addition to the directors of the FBI, CIA, and national intelligence—Baxter's boss—there were the secretaries of state and defense, the vice president, the chairman of the Joint Chiefs, and the national security adviser.

Far too many people, in Baxter's opinion, but his boss did enjoy making a splash with her announcements.

After the normal pleasantries, the DNI took charge of the meeting. Judith Hellman was a tall, angular woman with shoulder-length red hair and a noncommittal smile derived from years of political maneuvering. "Good morning, Mr. President. The briefing today is seeking your approval for an operation to take out the terrorist Rafiq Roshed."

"Public enemy number one is still out there after all, huh?" the president said. "I was hoping maybe the Iranians had taken care of him by now."

"Unfortunately, sir," Baxter said, taking his cue from the DNI's lead-in, "it looks like it's up to us. We have new intel about Roshed's whereabouts, as you can see in this debriefing video." He punched his keyboard to start the video clip. The screen showed a thin man with Asian features sitting across from Rick Baxter.

"Meet Kim Daiwoo, third cousin once removed to the Supreme Leader himself. Mr. Kim was a North Korean diplomat assigned to the UK. Three weeks ago, he defected, along with his wife and son. From the perspective of gathering intel on the DPRK's nuclear program, he was a bust. However, he had a very interesting tale to tell on another topic."

The Korean defector spoke in excellent English. "There is a man, a foreigner, in the Covert Actions Division. He has dark skin and dark hair and speaks English with a Spanish accent. He knows Arabic, too. We needed him to translate for us once."

"When did he come to North Korea?" Baxter asked.

The defector considered the question. "Maybe five years ago. Difficult to say. He lives on a special compound outside of Pyongyang—and he goes on secret assignments for the Supreme Leader. Overseas assignments. I was told to bring him into the UK on a diplomatic mission two years ago." He hesitated.

"Go on," Baxter urged.

"There is a rumor in my homeland—my former homeland—about this man."

Baxter said nothing. The diplomat shifted in his seat.

"It's only a rumor, you understand. I am not vouching for this as fact."

"I'm waiting."

"The attack on the American power grid last year. It was done by this man."

Baxter exchanged a glance with the DNI as a collective gasp sounded in the room. *Mission accomplished.*

He stopped the video. "It is our assessment that Roshed is hiding out in North Korea and the defector's rumor is at least plausible. Furthermore, we have a plan to take him out."

The vice president frowned. "Please tell me you're not going to recommend we run a covert operation inside of the DPRK."

"No, sir," Baxter replied, ignoring the sharp look from DNI Hellman that said, *Get on with it!* "We've been able to correlate a number of unrelated incidents that directly benefited the Kim regime with times when this individual was outside of the DPRK."

"So when he's out of his hiding place doing the Supreme Leader's dirty work," the president said, "you're going to nail him."

"Exactly, sir."

The JCS chairman, Admiral Henley Reeder, leaned into the table. "If you can ID him outside of North Korea, we have lots of options to take him down. JSOC, a drone strike, even a small CIA direct action team."

The DNI coughed gently. "Those are all very viable options, Admiral, but we recommend using outside assets."

"Explain that," said the national security adviser in a sharp tone.

The DNI nodded at Baxter to continue. "We want him eliminated—with firm proof, of course. Verify the kill and destroy the remains, bin Laden–style. But when we went after bin Laden we found his hideout and planned a direct action mission over many months, including numerous rehearsals by SEAL Team Six." He flipped to a map of North Korea.

"With Roshed it's a different game. We need to nail

him up on the run. His hideout has thousands of miles of coastline and borders Russia and China, so our ability to nab him leaving or reentering North Korea is almost zilch." Baxter let that last statement sink in.

"And that leaves us where?" the chairman said.

"We need to pre-position strike teams where we think he *will* be." He flipped to a world map. "We're proposing three teams. One in Argentina, near his children; one in Africa, his last known location; and one in Lebanon, to cover the eastern Med. We think these three locations hold the highest probability of his next appearance."

"Tell me about his family situation again, Rick," the president said.

Baxter punched a key on his laptop, and side-by-side images of two dark-haired children popped onto the screen. "The mother was killed by the Iranians when they came hunting Roshed. The two children survived. They still live on the family ranch in Argentina with an aunt."

"And the story about the flowers?" the president persisted. "That's true?"

"It is, sir. White roses on his wife's grave on the anniversary of her death, every year like clockwork. Other than that, there's no indication Roshed's in contact with his children."

The CIA director, Roger Trask, cleared his throat. "If I could bring the discussion back to the operation, Mr. President. Three US teams undercover in foreign countries for an unknown period. It's a logistical nightmare—what if they get discovered? The political fallout would be a disaster." Trask was a man predisposed to more caution than courage. Baxter could see that Trask's comments had not landed well with the president.

"That's why we're not proposing to use US teams," the DNI replied, her cryptic smile in place.

"You're going to contract it out," the president said.

"Exactly, sir," Baxter jumped in. "We hire three hit teams through the CIA's Special Activities Division— all through shell companies, completely deniable. We assign them a geography and they get paid only if they bring us DNA-based proof of Roshed's demise."

"And what happens when one of these teams gets discovered?" said the vice president.

"It's on them," Baxter said. "These guys know what they're getting into when they sign on with a private security firm. If they get caught, it's their problem to sort out."

"But we'll use our own assets if we have the opportunity, right?" The chairman's face was red, and Baxter could see his jawline working. The admiral knew he'd been outflanked by the DNI and was not happy about it. His boss could handle that mess.

"Absolutely, sir," Baxter said. "This is just a low-risk way to have assets in place if we need to act on immediate intel."

"Can't we just run a drone over North Korea and drop a Hellfire on this guy?" asked the vice president.

The room went quiet. The national security adviser spoke finally. "Sir, we'd be risking the DPRK lobbing a nuke into South Korea—or maybe even Japan. That's not a risk we can take, even for an animal like Roshed."

The president looked at the CIA director. "What about human assets inside the DPRK? Can we take him out that way?"

Roger Trask shook his head. "No, sir. Our assets on the ground in North Korea are sparse to say the least. Getting close to Roshed with the assets we have would take months, maybe years, and even then, there's no guarantee of success. The analysis says we could burn a lot of assets and a lot of time with little to show for it. In the meantime, we have no idea what Roshed is cooking up next. This plan is a calculated risk, but it's the right one. I guess I support it."

The president took his pen out of his breast pocket. He fixed Baxter with a fierce glare. "Then let's make sure we get him this time, Mr. Baxter."

"Aye, aye, sir."

CHAPTER 8

White House, Washington, DC

As he hustled up to the staff entrance at the White House, Don Riley put his hand in his bag for his ID, but the pocket where he normally kept the badge was empty. Don cursed to himself, then placed the bag on the dewy pavement to perform a more methodical search.

He checked his watch and let out a hiss of frustration. If he'd left his credentials at home, there was no way he could retrieve them in time to make the meeting. And one did not show up to a meeting with the director of national intelligence wearing a temporary badge. His fingers touched a thin plastic card between his laptop and his iPad.

"Don?"

Brendan McHugh stood over him, a half smile on his face. "Lose something?"

Don held up his ID triumphantly. "Not anymore." He scrambled to his feet and hugged his friend. "What are you doing here?"

"Briefing. You?"

"Same." Their eyes met, and Don knew his friend

was thinking the same thing he was. Ever since Liz had picked up the trail of Rafiq Roshed, Don had been dreaming about getting some payback on that bastard. Maybe this was it. "Liz going to be here?"

Brendan shook his head and passed through the metal detector. "Not that I know of."

Maybe he was wrong after all. It was hard for Don to believe that Liz would be excluded from a Roshed manhunt. She had as much history as either of them. He passed through the metal detector and picked up his bag off the belt. "How're the kids? Got a recent picture?"

Brendan thumbed his phone on and swiped through the camera roll. He held the phone out to Don. Liz's face had thinned with motherhood, but she had the same stocky, muscular physique he'd always known. Her dark hair was longer now and held by a silver clasp at her nape. She was swinging a raven-haired girl up in the air.

Don handed the phone back. "Your wife is more beautiful than ever. You, on the other hand . . ." He laughed as he spoke, but it was true. His friend's dark hair was shot with gray and permanent lines had settled into his face. Shadows filled the hollows under his eyes.

Brendan gave Don a tired smile. "Yeah, I know, you don't have to say it: I look good, too."

He was interrupted by an approaching staffer, who said, "The director is ready for you. If you'll follow me, please."

Director of National Intelligence Judith Hellman was seated alone at the table in the secure conference room. She rose and shook their hands, adding a perfunctory nod at two folders on the table. "Before we begin this morning, we'll need each of you to sign a special NDA."

Don flipped open the cover to find a multipage

nondisclosure agreement with the label Operation Parable Cleaver. He chuckled to himself at the computer-generated name. The program was designed to ensure that no trace of the actual mission was inadvertently signaled in the name of the operation, but it often resulted in some ludicrous word combinations. He scanned the document, noting the extreme penalties for disclosure, and signed his name at the bottom.

The door opened and a tall black man in civilian clothes walked in. He nodded at the DNI. "Sorry I'm late, ma'am. Accident on the Beltway."

The DNI gave him a frosty nod and turned to Don and Brendan. "I believe you both know Rick? He's running point on Parable Cleaver. Now that you've signed, I'll get right to business. We're confident that Rafiq Roshed is in North Korea. We want him captured or killed. Either way is fine with the administration."

Baxter took over and played a video clip of his interview with a North Korean defector. Brendan and Don exchanged looks when the man claimed Roshed was responsible for the attack on the US power grid. That accounted for the new focus.

"We did some checking on old video footage suggested by the defector," Baxter said. "We came up with this." He pushed an 8×10 black-and-white picture across the table.

It was a shot of a man from the waist up, taken from a distance and through a wrought-iron fence. He was the right height and build for Roshed, but the jawline and profile seemed off.

"Cosmetic surgery?" Don asked.

Baxter nodded. "That's likely. It's also interesting to note that at the same time as this photograph was taken, one of the principal negotiators for the multiparty talks on the North Korean nuclear deal died in a car accident while on holiday. He was having an affair and had a known drinking problem, so the death was ruled accidental." His lips tightened. "We're working with the assumption that Roshed was brought in to silence a very vocal critic of the Supreme Leader."

The DNI broke in as if impatient for Baxter to get to the point. "Based on the defector's testimony, we believe Roshed comes and goes from North Korea at the bidding of Kim Jong-un—for special assignments. Parable Cleaver authorizes us to nail him if he pokes his nose outside of the DPRK. You both have a unique understanding of Roshed, and Rick feels it is in our best interest to read you into this special access program. It's very possible that our first hint of Roshed will come from a lateral source, something that you might come across during the course of your normal duties."

Brendan cleared his throat. "If I may, ma'am. The connection between Roshed and the North Korean regime was initially uncovered by an FBI agent. I'm wondering why the FBI is not being read into this SAP?"

Don tensed. Hellman's desire to keep the entire operation under her purview without FBI involvement was understandable, but it smacked of politics and Brendan knew it.

The DNI's red lips tightened. Baxter tried to intervene, but she waved him off. "And you know this how, Mr. McHugh?"

"The FBI agent was my wife. She uses her maiden name professionally. Soroush."

"I see."

"She has a personal stake in getting this guy, ma'am. He almost killed her. Twice."

Don flinched. A flush of color rose up the DNI's throat. "May I remind you, Mr. McHugh—"

"Captain."

"Pardon?" The interruption seemed to break her train of thought.

"I'm a captain in the navy. An O-6."

"Very well, *Captain* McHugh. This is not a personal decision. There are very good reasons, operational reasons, for not involving the FBI. And since you've already signed on to the SAP, you will abide by my decision."

Brendan sat back in his chair. "Yes, ma'am." His jaw was set in a rigid line.

The DNI rose. "I'll let Mr. Baxter finish the briefing. I have another meeting." She did not offer to shake hands on the way out of the room.

An hour later, Brendan and Don stood on the sidewalk outside the White House.

"Well," Brendan said, "now we know why Liz wasn't invited this morning." He sighed. "I can't believe Hellman. Liz found Roshed again for God's sake. If it wasn't for her, we'd still be chasing our tails."

Don squinted up at the watery sunshine. He couldn't imagine the relationship dynamic between Liz and Brendan now that Brendan was assigned to the SAP and was forbidden to even mention it to his spouse. He knew his friend would follow orders. "Yeah. Now we know."

"Do you think it's really him?"

"It's him," Don said. "It all fits: North Korea, special assignments. He's a psychopath with a need to destroy those who took his family away from him. He's willing to let the world burn and North Korea is the only place crazy enough to take him."

Brendan nodded. "Too many people—good people— have died by this man's hand. It's time we stop him once and for all."

Don watched a blood vessel throb in Brendan's temple, the only outward sign of his friend's rage at this monster. Twice before, Roshed had eluded them. In his wake, he'd left a trail of bodies and destruction that had sown grief into the lives of Don, Liz, and Brendan. Rafiq Roshed needed to end and they were the people to do it.

Brendan shook Don's hand and then strode away, his broad back blending into the pedestrian traffic on Pennsylvania Avenue.

The rational part of Don's brain knew that what the DNI said was correct: The hunt for Rafiq Roshed was not personal.

Except it was.

CHAPTER 9

Covert Actions Division site
Pyongyang, North Korea

The headlights on Pak's limousine illuminated the heavy steel door set in a wall of concrete. So this was where Rafiq had set up shop for his new assignment. No wonder he hadn't returned any of Pak's messages. This place probably didn't even have a working phone.

He considered the muddy ground and his Italian leather shoes. Maybe he'd wait until tomorrow and send another message demanding Rafiq come to his office.

Pak sighed and signaled for his chauffeur to open his door. The news he had was too good not to share now. He stepped out. Thankfully, the mud was mostly frozen.

He approached the guard shack. "I'm here to see Jung Chul," he said to the stone-faced soldier, using Rafiq's Korean name.

"No one enters," the guard replied.

A stray gust of wind whipped the back of Pak's coat. "Do you know who I am?"

"My orders are no one enters," the guard replied.

"Call him," Pak said.

The guard eyed the expensive car. Finally, he backed

up and rapped on the steel door. A peephole slid open, and he spoke rapidly into the opening. The plate slid shut.

"Wait here," the guard said to Pak.

"I'll wait inside where it's warm."

The guard shook his head. "Wait here."

After a few minutes, Pak returned to his vehicle, alternately fuming and glaring at the guard. After a wait of nearly thirty minutes, the door opened, and another guard appeared. Pak put down his window to hear the sentry.

"He will escort you to Jung Chul," the soldier said.

Pak waited until his chauffeur reopened his door to step back into the cold and stalked through the now-open door into the bunker.

Although there was no wind, the cold of the bunker seeped through the thin soles of his dress shoes. He passed two more manned guard stations before finally arriving at a brightly lit room, filled with rolling whiteboards. A bank of glowing electric heaters took the edge off the chill. Against the far wall were a cot covered with rumpled bedclothes and a small table with a laptop. Rafiq paced in front of two whiteboards covered with pictures of young men and women.

Pak wrinkled his nose. "You live here?"

Rafiq glanced his way, then turned back to the boards. His face was thick with salt-and-pepper stubble, and his eyes were red. "What do you want?"

"I have news."

"You found a place to base my operation?" Rafiq said without turning around.

"We got paid."

Rafiq grunted, not bothering to turn around.

Pak frowned. He had gone to a lot of trouble to make sure he'd set up Rafiq's funds in a secure way. It benefited them both. If the Supreme Leader found out Pak was skimming money . . .

"I have your Swiss bank account information here." He handed Rafiq a slip of paper. The man stared at it for a few seconds, then handed it back.

"You can keep it," Pak said.

"No need." Rafiq was staring at the pictures again.

"I recommend you move these funds as soon as possible to a new account. I use the Caymans. I can recommend a good banker. Very discreet."

The other man nodded absently.

"Dammit, Rafiq. What are you looking at?"

"My team," he replied, waving at a grouping of twenty or so pictures. "These are the coders. I've worked with most of them before. Just filling in a few gaps."

Pak plucked a picture of a young woman off the board. Her thin cheeks were pocked with acne and she was glaring at the camera. "I recognize her."

Rafiq snatched the picture back. "Her name is Yun So-won. My star pupil." He pointed to the adjoining board. "These are the assault teams. Still working on them." He yanked one of the photos from the board, pursing his lips as he read the back. Then he ripped it in half and let it drop to the floor, joining a pile of dozens of other torn photos.

"Assault teams?" Pak said. "I thought this was a cyberoperation. What do you need assault teams for?"

"Security," Rafiq mumbled.

"What does that even mean? Security for what?"

Rafiq started pacing again. Pak tried a new tack.

"I found you an operational site," he said.

Rafiq wheeled around, his eyes alight. "Show me." He drew Pak to a table where he had a stack of maps. Pak watched him flip aside a street map of Beijing to reveal a map of North Korea. He pointed. "Where?"

Pak traced his finger along the east coast of the DPRK until he found the city of Hwadae. He tapped a small island just off the coast. "Yang-do Island," he said. "This used to be a missile launch facility. We stopped using it a few years ago after we commissioned the new base to the north. Power and telecom are supplied via submarine cables from the mainland. Very secure."

Rafiq scratched at his beard, nodding. "Perfect. When can we move?"

"Depends, Rafiq. When will the code be ready?"

Rafiq looked at him with surprise. "The code's done. It's been ready for nearly a year. All that was lacking was the right opportunity. Once I have my assault teams, we can start. Maybe a month of training."

Pak remembered the map of Beijing. "Tell me again why you need assault teams."

Rafiq smiled. Not a nice smile. "Security. Some of the code has to be handled using new methods."

"I don't understand."

"You don't need to, Pak." He considered Pak's Italian loafers with a look of disdain. "We each have our part to play. You concentrate on getting paid. I'll do the rest when I'm ready."

"And when the Supreme Leader gives his permission, right?"

But Rafiq had turned back to his whiteboard of young North Korean faces. "Of course, Pak. Whatever the Supreme Leader wants."

CHAPTER 10

Best. Thanksgiving. Ever.

If the statement wouldn't have hurt her parents' feelings so much, that's what Dre Ramirez would have said to her mother in her daily call home. She slipped her phone back into her hip pocket and hurried across the parking lot to catch up with Goodwin and Everett.

Although none of them had slept more than a few hours last night, they were all raring for a full day at US Cyber Command. The Hopper Center at the Naval Academy was a state-of-the-art facility, but this was so much better. This was the real deal, where real people were on the front lines of the cyberbattle that was happening every day.

And she was about to be part of it.

Even better, Goodwin and Everett were willing to give up their Thanksgiving break to stay in Maryland and work at CYBERCOM for the long weekend.

"You guys ready?" Dre said, catching up to Janet and Michael.

Janet winked at her. "We're going to the show, Dre. On the watch floor. Time to stop some cyber bad guys."

Dre let the laugh that was inside her bubble out. "What about you, Mike? Not every plebe gets to do this."

Goodwin gave her a faint smile, as if he knew that a smile was something he was supposed to do in this kind of social situation. Dre punched him on the arm. He was a good kid, sort of like a little brother in a way. A strange duck to be sure, but the more they worked together, the more she felt like they were bonding.

Janet approached the security desk in the lobby. "Midshipmen Everett, Ramirez, and Goodwin here to see Lieutenant Jackson." The sergeant on duty examined their IDs, then punched a button on his keyboard.

"She'll be down in a minute." He eyed their service dress blue uniforms. "Are you guys officers or what?"

"We're midshipmen from the Naval Academy in Annapolis," Janet replied. "I'm a first-class—a senior. Ramirez is a second-classman, a junior, and Goodwin is a plebe, a first-year. Think of us as baby officers. And yes, you do salute us."

"Helluva way to spend your Thanksgiving, that's all I'm saying," he replied. "Ma'am," he added.

Lieutenant Sarah Jackson appeared behind the security desk. She held her badge over the scanner until it turned green. "Send them through, Sergeant. I've got them."

She set off down the hallway at a clip that made them hurry to keep up. "How we doing this morning, Midshipmen?" she asked.

"Fine, ma'am," Everett answered for them.

"You're done with indoc, so today we go onto the watch floor. It's a lot to take in, so just try to keep up, okay?"

"Yes, ma'am," they replied in unison.

Jackson halted outside the door to the watch floor. "All right, we'll be 'ma'am'ing and 'sir'ing each other to death here, so let's agree on first names. I'm Sarah, and you are?"

The three midshipmen each offered their first names.

"Okay, now that we've got that out of the way. Here's the basics: CYBERCOM JIOC is the joint intel operations center. The 'joint' part means you'll see officers and enlisted from all the services here, as well as plenty of civilians. We don't often get midshipmen, so I'm sure you'll get a few odd looks. It's part of the drill."

She paused outside a set of double doors. "Behind here is the watch floor, where the action happens. I've got you all set up with your own workstations. If one of the watch standers wants to talk, that's fine, but otherwise leave them be. You never know what they're working on. Got it?"

Dre nodded along with her colleagues. Jackson pushed the doors open.

The room was set up amphitheater-style, with the overhead lights dimmed. Four rows of computer workstations faced massive wall screens, the center one containing a world map. Arcs of color bounced across the map at a startling rate.

"The moving lines represent attacks—incoming and outgoing. Color-coded based on severity. Yellows are nuisance, red are the ones we really care about. This is mostly used for an overall view of the traffic level out in cyberland." She stopped, watching the expressions on their faces.

"Pretty scary, huh? At any minute, there are hundreds if not thousands of attacks going on against the US government and our infrastructure facilities. That doesn't even begin to consider private servers or passive attacks, like phishing emails."

Dre watched the screen, trying not to let her mouth hang open. They'd seen simulations like this, of course, but this was real. These attacks were actually happening right this second.

Jackson moved them farther along the last row. "When we find a DDoS event going on—distributed denial of service—we take steps to isolate the problem, but mostly we're looking for an ancillary attack. Lots of times the bad guys use an assault on the front door as a way to mask something subtler going on, a sneak attack, sort of." She stopped in front of a workstation manned by a young Hispanic man in an air force uniform. "Vasquez here is writing a script to search for instances of malware in"—she peered at the header on the screen that was waterfalling lines of code—"what looks like a water plant in California."

"There," Michael said, pointing at the screen.

Vasquez halted the screen flow. "Where?"

"Right there." Michael reached across the enlisted man's shoulder to point at a line. "This has been repeated three times since we've been standing here."

"Vasquez?" Jackson asked.

"Holy shit, ma'am, I think he's right." He adjusted the script and his screen lit up with highlighted text. "Wow, you just saw that by standing there for ten seconds?"

"Midshipman Goodwin specializes in pattern rec," Everett said. "It's kind of his thing."

Vasquez shook his head. "Well, Midshipman Goodwin can come sit next to me on watch anytime he wants to. He just saved me about a shift's worth of work staring at a screen."

Jackson led them to the far side of the room to three empty workstations. "Okay, now I see why Mr. Riley wanted you guys here. That was pretty impressive, Michael." She turned to the two women. "If he's the pattern-rec savant, what do you two do?"

"Dre's our coder," Everett said. "She's able to take

what Michael needs and turn it into code. She's good, she's fast, and she knows Michael." Dre blushed.

Jackson nodded. "And you?"

Everett shrugged. "I guess I'm the project manager. I keep us on the right track. It's weird, but we just work better as a team. Mr. Riley saw that and wanted us here together."

Jackson's gaze roamed over the trio. "Well, if Don thinks it's the right thing to do, then I'm sticking with him." She looked over Everett's shoulder. "Speak of the devil, here's Mr. Riley now."

Dre turned to find Don Riley crossing the watch floor with a four-star navy admiral in tow. She whirled to where Everett and Michael were inspecting their work-stations. "Guys, get up! There's an admiral coming."

The other two scrambled to attention as Don arrived. He grinned at them. "Good morning, Midshipmen."

"Good morning, sir."

"Admiral, may I present Midshipmen Janet Everett, Andrea Ramirez, and Michael Goodwin. Mid-shipmen, this is Admiral Trafton, head of US Cyber Command."

The admiral was a tall, rangy woman with mouse-brown hair drawn back in a severe bun. Her eyebrows ticked up when she saw Michael's bare uniform sleeves, indicating he was a fourth-class midshipman. "A plebe, Don? You're starting them young, aren't you?" To Dre's ears, she didn't sound happy about it.

Riley's laugh was strained. "No worries, Admiral. Mr. Goodwin has already validated all of his plebe-year courses and most of his second-year as well. He's part of a pilot program to recruit the best cyber talent in the country."

The admiral studied Michael. "Where are you from, Mr. Goodwin?"

"Lennox, California, ma'am," he said.

"Whereabouts is Lennox, California?"

"Have you ever flown into LAX, ma'am?"

Trafton nodded. Her eyes never left Michael's, as if she was challenging him.

His gaze stayed steady. "Just before you touch down on the runway, if you look down, you'll see Lennox."

"I see. Not the best neighborhood, I take it."

Michael said nothing.

The admiral frowned for a second, then said, "Enjoy your time here, Midshipmen. I hope it's informative."

As she stepped away from the group, Dre heard her say, "Okay, Don, you've got them here, but I'm holding you responsible if there are any issues."

CHAPTER 11

Yang-do Island, off the eastern coast of North Korea

The island location provided by Pak was perfect. Only a few miles off the coast of North Korea, the oval-shaped blob of land in the Korean East Sea was close enough to the mainland to receive supplies, but far enough away to discourage unwanted visitors. Originally a missile launch site, the island came complete with barracks for a full company of men and a blast-proof underground bunker with a missile command and control center and an independent satellite communications array. In the end, the island's size and lack of mainland access proved to be its undoing. When the Supreme Leader wanted to expand his missile inventory, the entire operation moved to the brand-new Musudan-ri missile launch site, a brightly lit complex visible on the horizon.

The facilities were perfect. The personnel he'd recruited, not so much.

In the past, when in the throes of planning a major operation, Rafiq experienced calm, a satisfaction drawn from being deeply knowledgeable of every detail, completely in control of his emotions. His results spoke for themselves: All on his own, he'd come within a whisker of detonating a nuclear device on US soil and had masterminded a series of worldwide terrorist attacks—and lived to tell the tale.

Pak's cyber mission should be easy by comparison. He had the backing of an entire nation. He should be supremely confident about this operation.

Except he wasn't.

Even worse, he didn't know why.

The snow-covered ground sparkled in the light of his headlamp. They were on another night march, with Rafiq setting a grueling pace. Not that his team of North Korean commandos needed additional exercise—they were in peak physical condition—but because he wanted to provoke them.

The idea for the forced march had formed earlier in the day, when he was watching the men eat. They were all here because they were assigned to him. There was no unifying cause, no factor to motivate them, no sense of mission. Add to that, Rafiq was an outsider. These soldiers had been raised in a closed society. From birth, they were fed the lie that everyone who didn't look like them was an untrustworthy outsider—and Rafiq definitely did not look like them.

They reached the high point on the island, a windswept patch of rock half the size of a soccer pitch. To the west, he saw the city of Hwadae, where their power and internet connections came from, and to the north, the distant halogen lights of the Musudan-ri missile complex.

"Take a break," he called in Korean.

He heard someone deep in the ranks make fun of his accent.

Rafiq slowly turned. The wind turned the sweat on his cheek to ice, and his breath smoked in the air.

"Who said that?"

No one spoke. Their combined exhalations fogged the air within their ranks, then were whipped away by the breeze.

"No one wants to speak?" He pointed at a random man. "You. Stand up."

The man stood, his eyes searching back toward his comrades.

Rafiq stepped forward and punched the man in the throat. He went down gagging. A ripple of discontent ran through the squad.

"I'll ask again: Who said that?"

No response. Rafiq pointed at another random soldier. "You—"

"I said it." The man who stood was half a head taller than the rest, and well muscled. One of the few who had received proper nutrition as a youngster. Probably a politician's kid.

Rafiq motioned him forward. "What is it you wanted to say?"

The soldier smiled and shot a look back toward his comrades. "We are professionals. We don't need some fucking foreigner telling us how to prepare for an operation."

"You doubt my orders?"

The man shook his head. "I doubt the judgment of a foreigner."

Rafiq slid his knife out of its sheath. He pointed the tip at the soldier. "You want to teach me a lesson? How about right now?"

The man's face hardened, and he whipped out his own blade. The blade reflected the combined light from the squad's headlamps.

"Ryoko, not a good idea," one of his comrades called.

"I'm going to teach this fucking foreign pig a lesson

about the Supreme Leader's finest troops." He moved forward in a fluid motion, his knife slashing silver against the night sky.

He was fast, Rafiq could see that, and he knew how to handle a knife. But he was also young and cocky about his ability to take on an older man, and a foreigner. He stepped into the soldier's attack, allowing the blade to cut into his heavy jacket. He felt the edge bite into his flank, but Rafiq was close enough now to trap the soldier's knife hand. With his free arm, he smashed an elbow into the younger man's face, breaking his nose. He released the soldier's arm and let him stagger back.

The soldier dropped his knife, putting both hands up to his face.

"I give," he said in a thick voice.

"Yes, you do," Rafiq said. He let his anger take over, let his rage at the years of exile drive him forward. In one sweeping motion, he stepped forward and drove his knife up through the man's jaw and into his brain. He let go of the hilt and the soldier fell back into the snow. The warm blood flowed dark, steaming in the cold white light of the headlamps.

"Anyone else want to teach this foreigner a lesson?" he barked at the squad.

The only answer was the wind. Even the smoke of their breaths seemed to have stopped.

"Good." Rafiq said. "We leave for Beijing in the morning. Leave the body for the rats."

Rafiq could feel the cut in his side bleeding freely. It would need stitches. He turned on his heel, careful not to let the men see any sign of his injury, and breathed deeply. A smile of satisfaction warmed his face.

Now they had a unifying cause: their fear of him.

CHAPTER 12

USS Blue Ridge *(LCC-19)*
South China Sea

Vice Admiral Martin Cook, Commander, US Seventh Fleet, put two fingers to his lips and let out a shrill whistle in the confined space of the Joint Operations Center, or JOC, the admiral's command and control center buried deep in the superstructure of the massive USS *Blue Ridge*. The hubbub of multiple conversations ceased.

"Let's work the problem, ladies and gentlemen. Chief of Staff, status report."

Captain Bernard "Sauce" Benson spoke up in a crisp voice. "Admiral, we appear to have two separate incidents of Chinese aggression within the fleet operating area." He nodded at the operator to project the information onto the 3-D BattleSpace table display and whipped out his laser pointer.

"The Chinese have two destroyers harassing a Japanese patrol craft in the waters off the Senkakus, south of the Japanese mainland."

"Define 'harassing,'" the admiral replied.

"The two destroyers are riding herd on either side of

the smaller Japanese boat, broadcasting their usual line about the Japanese invading their territorial waters."

"Any contact? Is our Japanese friend just crying wolf?"

"No, sir, no contact. Threatening actions—but they seem to be operating a lot closer than normal—and the usual BS about territorial waters."

Cook nodded, relaxing the tiniest bit. The Chinese were contesting every rock in the waters around their mainland as theirs by historical decree. The Japanese Senkaku Islands—or the Diaoyus, as the Chinese called them—were a string of rocks stretching from the Japanese archipelago south to Taiwan. Same argument, different day. He sorely wished someone had shown the balls to stand up to the Chi-Comms thirty years ago when all this bullshit started. Now the United States was just pissing in the wind. Hell, the Chinese probably claimed the wind as theirs, too.

"All right, let's get some eyes on the situation. What's next?"

Benson directed the operator to change the Battle-Space display, zooming out, then back down to a map of the Paracel Islands, off the coast of Vietnam. Cook gritted his teeth as he studied the familiar terrain. Following their stunning success in building working naval bases out of the Spratly Islands, south of the Philippines, the Chinese promptly set to work trying to further advance their claim on the Paracels.

Any idiot with half a brain could see what they were doing. If the Chinese controlled both groups of islands, they effectively created a choke point for shipping in the South China Sea. If the main mission of the United States Navy was to keep the shipping lanes open across the globe, then in his book, this constituted a big problem.

"What've we got, Sauce?" he said to the chief of staff.

"Same thing, sir. Two Chinese ships ganging up on a small contingent from the Philippine Navy. The language is the same, but they're a lot more aggressive than usual. The Filipinos are asking for assistance, sir, as are the Japanese."

"Assistance, huh? What are our options under current rules?" The Rules of Engagement was the guiding document for everything they did in-theater, and it stated in plain language that they were not to escalate a situation with the Chinese. Cook knew the answer to his question, but having his chief of staff ponder it gave him a chance to think. Besides, maybe Benson would come up with a creative option he hadn't thought of.

Cook certainly hoped so, because in this particular scenario, the rules didn't sit right with him.

He raised his eyebrows at Benson. "Well, Sauce, what are our options?"

"Not a lot of good ones, sir. The *Ford* is on station near the Paracels. I recommend we reposition her closer to the scene of the incident. Show the flag."

Cook stroked his chin. First the P-8 Poseidon getting nearly sideswiped by a pair of Chinese fighters on a routine flight from Okinawa to Singapore, now two Chinese maritime challenges in two different parts of the South China Sea at the same time.

Something was rotten here. Very rotten.

Cook straightened up. It was time for some definitive action. "All right, here's what we're going to do. See if we can get some fighters from Okinawa to overfly the Japanese ship in the Senkakus. I want those fighters to buzz the Chinese destroyers as close as allowable under the ROE, but no closer. Supersonic flyby is authorized. Let's make some noise over these assholes. Second, direct the *Ford* to initiate immediate flight operations. Let's fill the sky over our Chinese aggressors with some good old US of A flying metal. Any questions?"

Benson nodded. "Aye, aye, sir." He whirled around and began issuing orders to the watch standers. When the JOC had resumed its typical high-energy hum of operations, Cook motioned for Benson to join him. They passed through a series of hatches, emerging on the Flag Bridge. A stiff wind greeted them.

Cook turned his back on the long blue line of horizon and crossed his arms. "That was a clusterfuck in there, Sauce," he said.

Benson flushed. "I'm sorry, sir, I—"

"Not your fault, Sauce. I should've seen this coming. When was the last time the Chi-Commies ran two naval interference ops at the same time? Answer: Never. What if one of those Chinese ships had run into a Japanese boat? Is that an act of war? Do we engage?"

Cook leveled his gaze at his chief of staff. "The Chinese are stepping up their game, and our pants are down around our ankles. I want some goddamn clear guidance from Pac Fleet or higher. If this happens again, I want a plan in place to make sure these bastards go home with a bloody nose or at least some wounded pride. Get on the horn and get me some answers."

Benson set his chin. "Right away, boss."

CHAPTER 13

Midshipman First Class Janet Everett focused on her single computer screen. She was acutely aware that Goodwin and Ramirez were running the same exercise as she was, but on multiple screens. Ramirez had two monitors engaged and had probably hacked together a nice piece of code to do all the work automatically. Goodwin was running three screens, his finger on the down-arrow key, eyes shifting from screen to screen looking for anomalies.

She was near the top in her graduating class at the academy and these two made her feel slow. She focused harder on the screen. Slow and steady wins the race, she told herself.

The three of them were running a random security audit on a DOE agency—she didn't even know which one—decrypting their SSL streams for suspicious activity. Not exactly glamorous work, but Mr. Riley assured her that some of the greatest hacker discoveries had come from good old detective work.

And so Janet and her two midshipmen friends were spending their second holiday camped out at Fort

Meade. According to Riley, Christmas break was an especially good time to survey government organizations for suspicious activity, since network usage tended to be low.

She saw an outgoing ping on the network. She followed the signal to a URL, nucleartreaty.org. Odd to have an outgoing packet from a secure government site relayed to a .org site. She used her network admin access to check the system. There were only twenty or so users logged on, and none of them had sent the file.

Janet shot a sideways glance at Ramirez and Goodwin but hesitated to say anything. She wasn't even sure if they were looking at the SSL stream from the same agency. No, she would make sure this was an actual hack before she called it.

She ran back through the logs, looking for another ping to the same outside URL. It took her another half hour of backtracking to find it. Janet stared at the screen, a growing sense of excitement bubbling up in her chest. It had been five hours between pings. She scrolled back through the historical record, seeking the time stamp from five hours prior.

There it was. The same .org site receiving another outgoing packet.

"Hey, guys, I think I've got something here," she said to Goodwin and Ramirez. "Come check this out."

She quickly recapped the random pings and external website. Ramirez scrambled back to her station and typed in a quick search. "Website is registered to a Richard Grayson."

"You need to let Lieutenant Jackson know about this," Goodwin said. "This is really good work, ma'am."

Janet felt a glow of pride from the praise. Sure, he was only a plebe, but he was easily the best hacker she'd ever met. "I told you to call me Janet when we're out of the Yard. When we're away from the academy, we're equals, Michael."

"Okay, Janet," he replied with his slight, lopsided grin. "It's still good work."

Janet raised her hand. "Lieutenant Jackson, I think we've found something."

Jackson, who was doubling as the watch supervisor that day, made her way to Everett's workstation. Her eyes grew wide as Janet laid out her case. She touched the microphone at her throat. "Listen up, all watch standers, we've got a possible hack in progress." She nodded for Janet to put her monitor on the big wall screen. "Our midshipmen trainees may have uncovered something big here. They've identified an outgoing ping of a zipped file leaving the Department of Energy at regular intervals going to a dot-org website registered to a Richard Grayson."

"Dick Grayson. The site is registered to the superhero Nightwing. Classic hacker move," one of the watch standers called out.

Jackson nodded. "Agreed. Let's find out where this hack is coming from and how it got there." She turned back to the midshipmen. "Good job, all of you."

"It was Janet, ma'am," Goodwin said. "She's the one who found it."

Janet found herself blushing. "How can we help?" she said to cover her embarrassment.

"We need to determine the five w's on this case: who, what, when, where, and why. You've already given us a good starting place, but now the real work begins. We need to find out as much as we can without tipping off the hacker. From the looks of it, these guys have been there for a while, which means they're dug in and probably have backup systems in place if we try to shut them down. There'll be an executable file on the network somewhere that's running the show—probably embedded. We need to find that file."

"We're on it, ma'am," Janet said.

Jackson smiled. "I'm sure you are."

Janet turned to her friends. "Let's do this, guys. How do we track down this executable?"

Ramirez posted her chin on her fist. "Well, there's got to be some kind of pattern to the usage, right? I mean, the hackers are using this program to capture data, zip it into a packet, and send it off-site. They need to feed the outgoing stream, which is on a schedule." She sat up and pulled her rolling chair toward the monitor. "It stands to reason the executable is on a schedule, too. Maybe I can write a script for Michael that feeds him all the programs with a regular start-stop cycle and he can look for a pattern."

Janet shook her head. "That's got to be thousands of programs, cycling all the time. We're talking millions of lines of code."

Ramirez was already hammering at her keyboard. "It's the best we've got for now."

Within the hour, she'd hacked together a monitoring program to allow Goodwin to see the inner workings of the Department of Energy network. The young midshipman had set up his three monitors in a band shell–style arrangement so he could watch all three without moving his head. Ramirez routed the feed to his screens, and they waited.

Michael sat perfectly still, his eyes scanning across the code as it rolled down his screens. Minutes turned into hours, but the midshipman sat still as a stone.

"What's he doing?" said a voice from behind Janet.

It was Don Riley. "Sorry, didn't mean to startle you,"

he said. "Jackson called me. Said you guys had uncovered a hack in progress. He's looking for something on the DOE network?"

"Dre wrote a program that lets us look for a suspicious start-stop cycle on the network. He's looking for a pattern in the data, hoping it will lead us to the hidden executable."

"By himself? Can he really watch three screens at once?"

Janet shrugged. "If anyone can do it, it's Michael. He's been at it for nearly three hours without a break."

"I got it," Michael said. "At least, I think I do. Stop the feed, Dre." His normally calm voice held a trace of excitement. Using his cursor, Michael highlighted one line of code on each screen. "These all point back to a DLL file."

Ramirez already had the file open and was scrolling down the screen. "Holy shit, you did it, Michael! This has got to be it."

Jackson crowded close, peering over Ramirez's shoulder. Janet watched the lieutenant's eyebrows arch up, and then she looked back at Don Riley, nodding.

Riley's gaze went from Goodwin to Ramirez and finally rested on Janet. A warm feeling of pride filled Janet. Her team did this. *Her* team.

Riley rubbed his jaw and smiled. "Well done, Midshipmen, dinner's on me tonight."

CHAPTER 14

Beijing, People's Republic of China

Rafiq peered through the smudged warehouse window into the grimy Beijing night. The air outside was a choking blend of smog and airborne dust blown in from the Gobi Desert. Car headlights from the never-ending traffic on the S30 Jingjin Expressway crawled along a mere stone's throw from the window. Beyond the highway, the details of the twenty-foot-high double fences topped by razor wire were completely obscured by the thick atmosphere.

China's infamous Unit 61398 was housed there. A shadowy branch of the Chinese military, this elite unit was responsible for some of the most notable hacks in recent history, including *The New York Times,* the European Central Bank, and the US government's Office of Personnel Management. This was the group everyone loved to hate, the group everyone in the world would be happy to blame for causing a cybercatastrophe. More importantly, Unit 61398 was in charge of cybersecurity for the entire Chinese military command and control network, a gateway to the crown jewels of the People's Liberation Army forces.

But how to get inside their impenetrable network? Rafiq had pondered this problem during his years as a guest of the Supreme Leader. For what he had in mind, he needed to upload gigabytes of code. Even assuming he managed to break in via a cyberattack, getting that much data on their servers undetected would be impossible.

Unless he was already inside.

The idea had come to him in a clash of two random events. During his indoctrination into North Korean culture, Rafiq had been shown the tunnels North Korean soldiers had dug under the DMZ into South Korea in the 1970s. The tunnels were two meters high, and wide enough for two soldiers to march side by side. The idea was to break through to the surface far beyond the well-guarded DMZ, putting hundreds of DPRK soldiers behind South Korean lines in advance of a military attack. The idea ultimately failed, but the concept stuck with Rafiq.

Then, one afternoon not long before Pak brought him the Russian assignment, Rafiq passed a group of maintenance workers digging up the street in front of the Pyongyang Covert Actions Division headquarters. They had just opened a junction box with a Chinese label on the cover. The interior was filled with fiber-optic connections.

Rafiq told his driver to stop, and he got out. The foreman of the work crew, a wizened man with only a few wisps of silvery hair, nodded to Rafiq as he approached, curious what this foreigner dressed like a North Korean wanted.

"Where do these fiber-optic lines go?" Rafiq asked in his accented Korean.

The man pointed to the Covert Actions building.

"You can access any line going into that building?"

The man shrugged.

"Show me," Rafiq said.

For the next half hour, Rafiq watched as the IT worker in the crew attached an adapter to each line and measured the signal.

"If I wanted to, I could read this traffic?" Rafiq asked.

The IT worker seemed glad to be the center of attention. "If it's unencrypted, you could read it."

"What about upload? Could I send a file on this line?"

The IT worker shook his head. "Not on this line, but you could use one of the spare lines as long as it was connected on the other end."

"Show me."

The man pointed to the box. "We always draw extra cable and hook them up. That way when we do an expansion, we have the capacity ready to go without having to lay new cable."

By the time Rafiq got back to his car, he knew how he was going to hack the Chinese.

The shrill *beep-beep-beep* of the Caterpillar loader backing up interrupted his reverie. The loader parked, and the operator shut down the engine. In the sudden stillness, Rafiq could hear the steady drone of traffic noises.

He smiled to himself. Hundreds of thousands of Chinese citizens had passed by this warehouse over the past three days and not a one of them could imagine what kind of crimes were being perpetrated behind these walls.

But first they had to dig.

He made his way to the table in the center of the warehouse floor, next to a six-foot square hole cut into the concrete. A ladder disappeared into the depths.

He nodded to the man on duty, an impassive North Korean soldier dressed in the clothes of a common laborer. A dirt-smudged drawing was spread over a piece of plywood suspended on a pair of sawhorses. "Where are we?" Rafiq said.

The man stabbed his finger on a city map of the area with underground utilities in dotted lines. A red pencil line was drawn across the highway outside. "Another hour more, maybe two," he said.

"Good. Wake up the tech team. Tell them to be ready to go."

The man nodded and stalked away. A second soldier, bare to the waist, climbed out of the hole carrying a load of dirt on his back. He dumped it in the bucket of the waiting Caterpillar. Rafiq wrinkled his nose as the man passed him. Last night, the digging team had mistaken a sewer pipe for their destination and raw sewage had partially flooded the tunnel.

It took his team three hours to put a patch on the pipe. The amount of human waste, dead animals, fish carcasses, and all manner of other filth that entered the tunnel during that time was overwhelming, but they kept digging after the hole was patched. Twelve hours later, the heavy stench remained.

Rafiq swung down the ladder and squatted to inspect the narrow conveyor belt his team had set up to move dirt out of the tunnel. He breathed through his mouth to avoid gagging on the smell.

The tunnel itself was about four feet square. A tight fit for his frame, but a breeze for the shorter-statured North Koreans.

Getting his team into China had been the riskiest part of the operation so far. These were soldiers, raised in a totalitarian culture, with no concept of how "normal" people acted. Still, with the number of people he needed to dig a tunnel and hack the fiber-optic network, it was too big a risk to use native Chinese. Someone would talk.

So, while he'd come into China under a false passport as a Canadian businessman, his team had crossed the China–North Korea border disguised as laborers and driven north to Beijing in the back of a truck.

He picked up the radio hanging on a ladder rung and called for the conveyor belt to stop. Clearing a space off the belt, Rafiq stretched out on his belly. The belt reversed direction, drawing him into the tunnel.

A single light illuminated the two men at the end of the downward-sloping tunnel. One dug, the other loaded the loose dirt onto the belt. Smiles formed white slashes in their dirty faces. Rafiq willed himself not to gag, but these two men seemed unaffected by the smell.

"Almost there," one said.

Rafiq nodded. He'd paid a small fortune for this warehouse and a copy of the underground schematics. If they were off by as little as a few feet, they would miss the concrete pipe housing the fiber-optic lines. The incident with the sewer pipe worried him. He'd allowed his enthusiasm to cloud his judgment. It would not happen again.

"Continue," Rafiq said. He squeezed to the front and picked up a spare shovel, hacking at the thick clay. He lost track of time as he sweated and breathed in the dank air, rich with the smell of human waste.

His shovel struck something solid. Rafiq exchanged a glance with his digging companion and they both redoubled their efforts. Soon they had the side of a concrete pipe exposed. It was smooth and professionally finished. This had to be it.

"Bring down the concrete saw," Rafiq said to the man moving dirt onto the conveyor.

Three hours later, they'd cut a two-foot-square plug out of the concrete pipe, careful to angle the edges so the piece could be replaced and sealed. The ground around the pipe was soupy from the water they'd supplied to the concrete saw, which only added to the sewage aroma. Rafiq's ears rang from the scream of the machine, but he didn't care.

Yun So-won arrived on the conveyor belt, holding a small plastic suitcase. She slipped into the narrow hole, shimmying out of sight. "I can see the junction box," she said, her voice muffled.

Rafiq stuck his head in the hole. She was ten feet forward. All he could see was the bottom of her shoes and the halo of her headlamp.

He wanted to be there, wanted to watch her probe each connection, but there was no space for him. The success of the entire operation rested on the shoulders of a twenty-four-year-old North Korean girl who until last week had never left Pyongyang.

He heard her crack open the case. "I'm going to start," she said.

"Okay." Rafiq's voice stuck in his throat, so the response came out like a croak.

If he angled his head just so, he could almost see her clamp a device on a fiber-optic line. "Active," she said. She repeated the process until finally she said, "Dark."

Rafiq held his breath as she connected her suitcase to the junction box. Another interminable minute passed before she said, "I'm in."

Rafiq let out a sigh.

"Come," he said, pulling a thumb drive from a lanyard around his neck. She wriggled backwards until their hands touched.

He heard her slip the drive into the USB slot and tap the keys of her panel. "Uploading," she called.

Rafiq held his breath. If they were going to be discovered, this was the moment. Two minutes passed . . . four minutes . . . eight minutes. He lost track of time.

"It's done," she said.

Rafiq emerged from the hole in the warehouse floor and turned to offer So-won his hand as she stepped off the ladder. Mud plastered his body from the waist down, and he smelled like a public toilet. The entire team gathered around the hole, watching him.

He held up her hand like he was announcing a winner at a boxing match and let out a shout of approval. The group stared at him. They'd never seen Rafiq show any positive emotion before.

Then they raised their hands and screamed along with him.

When they stopped, the only sound was the roar of the Beijing traffic outside the warehouse window.

"Fill in this hole," Rafiq said. "It's time to go home."

CHAPTER 15

CIA Headquarters, Langley, Virginia

Brendan slid into his seat next to Baxter in the secure conference room and accepted a stack of three dossiers from his former boss.

"Here's the guys you're going to meet," Baxter said. "Good operators, but private companies sometimes have lower standards on behavior, so calibrate your expectations."

"Well, I guess once you're no longer an officer, you don't need to do the gentleman part either," Brendan replied.

Baxter gave a short laugh and shot an inquiring look at the videoteleconference technician.

"Still waiting on the team from Brazil, sir."

"All right, just put up the other two teams for now," Baxter said. "If the third team shows up, you can patch them in."

The screen lit up with two faces. Brendan shuffled the dossiers so the order of the files matched the lineup on the screen.

"Good afternoon, sir," said a square-jawed black

man. Nigel Okumbe, his file read. Former Delta Force operator.

"Greetings, gentlemen," Baxter said. "We're waiting on one more to join us, if you can stand by for a few minutes."

The second man nodded but said nothing. Brendan checked his file. Soohan Kim, former SEAL.

"I assume you're waiting for Dickie Davis, sir?" said Nigel. "I heard he was your man in South America. If I know Dickie—and I do—he's knee deep in some—"

The third screen lit up and a red-haired man with white, freckled skin appeared. "Aw, fuck you, Nigel. I thought I was going to work with some quality contractors this time."

Brendan started to smile, but a look at Baxter told him his boss did not find Davis's banter amusing. He scanned the file on Richard Davis. Washed out of Air Force Combat Controller training, left the service after four years to join the former Blackwater group. Investigated for excessive use of force in Iraq, but no charges filed. A note at the bottom of his file listed BASE jumping and free-diving as his hobbies. An adrenaline junkie.

Baxter cleared his throat. "Gentlemen, let's start again. Now that your teams are in position, we'll have a weekly meeting to update you with any new intel on Roshed. To my right is your briefer today, Captain Brendan McHugh. Brendan has had personal experience with Roshed. If we get immediate actionable intelligence, he will get it to you via secure comms."

Brendan picked up the briefing. "Roshed's last known location was Africa and we believe he still maintains a strong network there. He also has ties with Hezbollah, so we've placed another team in Lebanon. Our analysis shows Roshed has been hiding out in North Korea, acting as a special projects man for the Kim Jong-un regime. In this capacity, he travels outside the DPRK. That's where you come in."

"So why am I fucking off down here in South America then?" Davis said.

Brendan frowned. "In the mission briefing material provided to your company, it says that Roshed has family in northern Argentina. Two kids."

"No wife?"

Nigel rolled his eyes, and Brendan gritted his teeth. "Wife was killed when the Iranians tried to roll him up a few years back."

"Oh," Davis said.

"We've got continuous surveillance on all modes of transit exiting North Korea. If we pick him up on the outside, we will task one of your teams to go after him."

Baxter broke in, clearly annoyed by Davis's lack of preparation. "I want to make one thing clear. This is a kill mission, but we require positive proof of Roshed's death before payment is made. You have biometric kits. We require pictures, DNA, fingerprints, the whole shebang. It's all in the kit, so no mistakes."

All three nodded.

Davis spoke up. "So that's it? We're just going to sit and hope he comes out of his hidey-hole?"

Brendan could feel Baxter bristling again.

"This is not Pakistan and Osama bin Laden," Brendan said, working to keep the irritation out of his tone. "There's no way we could do a clean op in North Korea. They're nuclear-capable now and the Supreme Leader is bold enough to threaten to pop one off if he thinks he's being attacked."

Davis shook his head. "That's not what I'm talking about, Brian."

"Brendan."

"Whatever. Listen, we hold the keys to the kingdom. Let's make him come to us."

Brendan and Baxter exchanged glances. Baxter's dark skin was flushed with anger.

Davis held up his palms to the camera. "Hear me out here, Baxter. We have his kids, right?"

"We're not using his children as bait," Baxter replied.

"Not what I'm talking about," Davis said. "What if we picked up some random North Korean *diplomat*"—he waggled his fingers as air quotes—"and rough him up a little. Then we tell him to deliver a message to the Supreme Leader's pet that we're coming for his kids."

"Too risky," Baxter said. "We would be letting the regime know that we've located Roshed."

"We don't even know if he cares about his kids anymore," Brendan said.

Nigel broke in. "Wait a minute, Brendan. Your intel package says he sends flowers to his wife's grave every year on the anniversary of her death, right? That doesn't sound like a man who's given up his family. Isn't it at least worth a shot? It might flush him out in a way that we can use to our advantage."

"I'm not authorizing you to use a man's children as bait!" Baxter said.

Davis gave an exaggerated wink at the camera. "Got it, boss. We are directed to sit like good little boys and wait for an international terrorist to come to our town."

Nigel and Kim stayed silent.

"Dammit, Davis, you listen to me—"

"Easy, Baxter, I'm just messing with you." Davis's tone was not convincing.

As they ended the call, Brendan noticed that Baxter was gripping the edge of the table.

CHAPTER 16

Chinese frigate Yangcheng
10 miles off the Senkaku Island cluster

Captain Li Sandai pushed through the door onto the bridge of his ship. *His* ship.

Finally, after twelve years of groveling and fighting for scraps, he had his first command at sea. First in his graduating class at Dalian Naval Academy to get a command pin. Not bad for a boy from Wuhan who'd never seen the ocean until he joined the PLA Navy.

"Report, Mr. Wei," he snapped. The key to command was to be unpredictable, make his crew think he was watching them as individuals. Keep them on their toes. Then they would respect him.

"No surface contacts within ten thousand meters, Captain," the officer of the deck replied from the red-lit bridge. The sun had gone down only a few minutes ago, and Li noted with satisfaction that his OOD had already rigged for night running.

"Very well," he said as he strode onto the bridge wing.

This command wasn't much as far as ships went—only a frigate, after all—but he'd turn this into a platform to really launch his career. After two years of command, he'd secure a shore tour in Beijing at the People's

Liberation Army Navy headquarters. From those contacts, he could get command of a cruiser. Maybe even an aircraft carrier someday.

The line of the horizon was clear against the darkening sky. The stars were just starting to gain real brightness.

"Mr. Wei," he called into the bridge. "Set a course to take us within five miles of the Diaoyus."

"Aye, aye, sir," came the prompt reply.

The ship heeled to starboard and the engines thrummed under Captain Li's feet. A white wave curled out from the bow as the *Yangcheng*—his ship—cut through the water. He smiled into the freshening wind.

"All ahead full, Mr. Wei," he shouted. "Let's show these thieving Japanese fishermen the power of the Chinese navy."

"Aye, aye, sir," came the faint reply. The bow wave grew wider. He gripped the railing.

Wei appeared at his side. He leaned in and shouted in his captain's ear. "New radar contact, Captain. Classified as a fishing vessel."

Li stepped back into the shelter of the bridge, his ears ringing in the stillness. The radar operator stepped to the side so the captain could view the screen. "Only six thousand meters off the coast, Captain. Well within our territorial waters," Wei said.

Li nodded, pinching his lower lip. Perfect. A golden opportunity to set an example with these Japanese fishermen, let them know there was a new Chinese captain patrolling these waters and he was not about to let anyone violate the sovereignty of the People's Republic of China.

"Set an intercept course, Mr. Wei."

The ship came into sight. The *Yangcheng* reduced speed, and the OOD brought a pair of binoculars to his captain on the bridge wing. As they suspected, a Japanese trawler, barely making way, but no nets out. Lit up like a Spring Festival parade.

"Rig ship for shouldering operations, Mr. Wei."

"Captain?"

Shouldering operations, where a ship would bump another to alter its course, were normally done in daylight, although there was no regulation against doing them at night.

Be bold, Li thought. *You are in command.*

"Did I not make myself clear, Mr. Wei?" he said in a voice loud enough for the whole bridge to hear. "Rig ship for shouldering ops."

The general-quarters alarm rang, and the *Yangcheng* filled with the sounds of running feet, his men taking their stations.

Li took the radio himself. "Japanese trawler, this is the People's Liberation Army Navy warship *Yangcheng.* You are violating the sovereign waters of the People's Republic of China. You will turn back to sea. Immediately." He nodded in satisfaction at his bold tone.

A long blast of Japanese, interspersed with blasts of static, came back.

"Where's our translator?" Li demanded.

"Petty Officer Wu is on leave, sir. The only Japanese speaker on board is Seaman Hai."

"Well, get him up here!" Li fumed. He would have words with the senior enlisted man who set the watch stations. Translators should be part of the watch rotation.

Seaman Hai was a skinny, acne-pocked kid still in his teens. His eyes were wide with apprehension as he stepped onto the bridge. "Reporting as ordered, sir," he said to the OOD. Wei pointed at the captain, who was pacing between the radio and the radar station.

"You speak Japanese?" Li demanded.

Hai nodded. "Yes, sir," he whispered.

Li thrust the radio handset at him. "Talk to them. Tell them to move out to sea."

A long exchange ensued between Seaman Hai and the Japanese trawler. "They say they are making best speed, but their ship is slow," Hai said. He shifted from one foot to the other. "Their accent is very strong, and they are talking very fast. My translation is limited, sir."

Li nodded. "Tell them to turn to seaward. We will escort them."

Another long exchange as the trawler made minimal progress away from land.

The OOD approached Li. "Captain, they may have engine trouble. Maybe we should wait until morning—"

Li raised his binoculars. "They have men on the fantail. They're putting out nets! They're just ignoring us." He dropped the binoculars. "All ahead two-thirds, Mr. Wei. Let's give them a push in the right direction."

The radio erupted in another volley of Japanese and static. Seaman Hai looked frozen to the deck.

"Captain, I recommend we—" the OOD began.

"Mr. Wei, I have the conn." On the ship-wide system: "All hands stand by for shouldering operations."

As the announcement rang through the ship, Wei tried one more time. "Sir, we're moving quite fast—"

"You stand relieved, Mr. Wei."

Captain Li stepped up to the bridge window to better judge his speed and angle of attack. The bright lights of the trawler made for an easy target and he could see the Japanese men watching him from the fantail.

He'd done this simulation a hundred times. Match their course, take an oblique angle, and bump them as his ship went past. Normally, the drill called for the shouldering ship to match speed, but the trawler was barely moving. He'd give them a glancing blow, a tap and nothing more.

"All ahead one-third," Li said.

"One-third, aye, sir."

The speed didn't die off as fast as in the simulator and Li considered putting on a backing bell to drop his speed. Not needed, he decided. He'd just clip them on the way past.

The water at the stern of the trawler boiled as they tried to get away. Li's lips curled back in a smile.

Finally, you start your engines, you lying Japanese bastards.

"Captain, I think maybe one of their engines is out! Recommend we break contact!" Wei had binoculars to his eyes and his voice cracked with concern.

Li raised his own binoculars. Wei was right: the boiling of water was only on the starboard side of the fantail. He watched the fishermen scramble away as the Chinese frigate bore down on them.

Then, under the force of one engine at full power, the Japanese trawler began to turn—right into the frigate's path.

"All back emergency!" Wei screamed. "Hard right rudder!"

The helmsman hesitated, looking from his captain to Lieutenant Wei.

Those precious few seconds were all it took. The lights of the trawler flashed by the bridge of the *Yangcheng* and Li heard the sickening crunch of metal on metal. The *Yangcheng* slowed for an instant, then plowed forward.

Li raced to the bridge wing. The bow of the trawler was gone—sliced off by the sharp keel of the frigate. The fishing vessel, her front a gaping hole, plowed into the next wave and sank out of sight.

CHAPTER 17

Tokyo, Japan

The subway tunnel was damp and warm. Rafiq stripped off the bright yellow jacket of the Tokyo-based Nikkei-Addams engineering firm and dropped it to the ground. He left the white hard hat on and grinned at So-won.

"We're in," he said into his radio.

The young woman pulled the mask away from her nose and mouth. "Can I take this off now?"

Rafiq struck off down the tunnel without answering her. He'd come to Japan prepared to dig another tunnel. In fact, he'd gone to great lengths to select North Koreans with Japanese ancestry—a relic of the "comfort women" from World War II—for his team. So-won was obviously of North Korean descent, and her mannerisms did not allow her to blend in with the Japanese population. Nevertheless, Rafiq trusted her and only her to do the connection and upload, so he solved the issue by making her wear a face mask in public, a common enough practice in Japan.

It turned out all his advance planning wasn't needed. In the few months since he had selected the dig site, the Tokyo Ministry of Transportation had started work on a new subway extension less than a kilometer from the gates of the Yokosuka naval base. The telecom junction box he needed had already been uncovered.

A mixed blessing, he soon found.

"Their network admins will certainly be on alert for any suspicious activity," So-won told him. "Beijing was easy. They never suspected anyone could access that junction box, much less tap into it. This one could be tougher."

Rafiq considered the problem for a full day before deciding to move forward. To increase their chances of success, he planned an additional level of subterfuge. While they were accessing the Japanese network, he would have a team launch a dedicated denial-of-service attack as a distraction.

So-won entered the chain-link fence surrounding the telecom junction box and opened the relay center. The interior of the junction box was a wall of blinking fiber-optic connections, easily ten times the size of the dedicated box in Beijing. Rafiq fretted. This might take longer than he'd planned.

The young woman set up her suitcase and started connecting alligator clips to the lines. She quickly determined which block to probe, but she needed to find the lines dedicated to the naval base. Thirty minutes ticked by before she said, "I'm in. Tell them to go ahead."

Rafiq tapped out a secure text and received a one-word reply.

So-won stared at her screen, monitoring traffic levels. Another twenty minutes crawled by, leaving Rafiq wondering if their attempt to ghost-net thousands of Chinese computers into spambots directed at the Yokosuka naval base was going to get him the reaction he wanted.

"It's working, Chul," the tech whispered in Korean. "They're reconfiguring their servers now."

Rafiq had been briefed that this was standard practice. If the network detected an attack, the first defensive measure was to wall off its most critical servers from the outside world—except Rafiq and his technician were already inside. While the Japanese network admins worked feverishly to protect themselves from the exterior denial-of-service threat, Rafiq would be uploading the program to their servers.

"Do it," Rafiq said, glancing at his watch. "Hurry." Nearly two hours gone.

"Nani o shiteru no?" What are you doing?

Rafiq whirled to find an older Japanese man in the tunnel. His heavy workman's coveralls were unzipped to his waist, and a dented metal lunchbox dangled from his hand. His broad smile faded at the sight of a foreigner in the secure work area.

Rafiq scooped up the bright yellow jacket with the fake ID tag. "Nikkei-Addams," he said, in deliberate syllables, in English. "En-gi-neer-ing." He motioned at the roof structure.

"Ah," said the old man brightly. "Engineering," he repeated. His gaze shifted to the tech in the cage. "Telecomm," he said.

Rafiq smiled and stepped between the man and the fence containing the junction box. "That's right, telecom."

But the worker kept moving forward. Inside the cage, So-won looked up. Her eyes met the worker's. Too late, Rafiq saw she'd forgotten to put on her mask. As if to accentuate the issue, So-won let out a curse in Korean. There was no mistaking her North Korean accent.

The worker stopped short, a puzzled expression on his face. "Korean?"

Rafiq lashed out with a right hook that sent the man to the ground. The man's eyes grew wide as the big foreigner knelt on his chest and wrapped his hands around his neck. His cries reduced to choking gurgles, then nothing. Rafiq waited until the man's legs stopped moving; then he stood.

"Are you finished yet?" he snarled at So-won.

She shook her head. "Ten more minutes, at least."

Rafiq's blood was up now. Taking a life excited him in a way he didn't understand but enjoyed all the same. He jogged to the end of the tunnel, the way the worker had come in. Was it possible the man was just early for his shift? Or were there more workers in the area?

When he strode back to the telecom cage, So-won was packing up the suitcase with shaking hands. She handed him the thumb drive containing the source code.

"You uploaded the program? You're sure?" Rafiq grabbed her arm in a tight grip.

She nodded, her eyes cutting to the dead body a few feet away.

He released her. "Put your mask on." Rafiq slipped on his yellow jacket and grabbed the worker by the collar, dragging him back the way they'd come.

As they exited the tunnel into the wide expanse of what would someday be a new subway station, Rafiq spied a backhoe. He loped toward it, the body bouncing along behind him. He dropped the corpse, swung into the operator's chair, and started the machine. The deep rumbling made a fearful noise in the space.

He raised the bucket. "Put his head under the bucket," he called to So-won.

She was trembling all over and the dead man's body was heavy, but she did as Rafiq directed. He leaned over to make sure the alignment was right, then released a lever. The heavy metal bucket, its edges shiny from wear, crushed the unfortunate worker's upper torso and skull.

Good luck figuring out he was strangled, Rafiq thought.

He shut off the backhoe, and silence settled over the area. Rafiq swung down, dropping lightly to the ground next to the partially crushed corpse. So-won's eyes were wide over her white face mask.

Rafiq grinned at her. "That'll teach him to show up to work early, right?"

His laugh echoed in the pit.

CHAPTER 18

US Cyber Command, Fort Meade, Maryland

Midshipman Fourth Class Michael Goodwin leaned back in his chair, watching his screen. It was hard to believe he was seeing an actual hack take place on an actual bank. To make it even more surreal, his job was just to watch it happen.

"If it's not in our national interest," Lieutenant Jackson said over his shoulder, "we don't touch it. We just observe and learn."

"Yes, ma'am."

"Nice job on the entry, Goodwin. The Dubai Islamic Bank is no pushover on network security."

"Thank you, ma'am."

He was far ahead in his classes at the academy. Far enough, in fact, that he was released to Cyber Command for a three-day weekend once a month, along with Ramirez and Everett. Working as part of a team was a new experience for Goodwin. To his surprise, he found he kind of enjoyed it. His teammates balanced him, made him better. Dre Ramirez could visualize and write code faster than anyone he'd ever met, and Janet

Everett saw the big picture, helped them focus their energy on the right areas.

Lieutenant Jackson and Mr. Riley had taken to calling them the Triad. Michael smiled to himself. For the first time in his life, he was part of a gang. Ironic, considering he'd spent most of elementary school trying to stay out of gangs.

Back in his old neighborhood in Lennox, gang life was the only life. When he closed his eyes at night, Michael could still hear the big jets coming in for a landing at LAX, their screaming engines shaking the walls of his tiny bedroom. Funny, after a while, even a noise that loud became background. You just stopped hearing the jets.

Same with the gunshots.

His mother was killed in a drive-by shooting when he was ten. A stray bullet, the cops said. The gang-bangers hadn't even been targeting his house. His mother was just collateral damage.

If he concentrated he could remember the contours of her face, the way her skin crinkled when she laughed, the rumble of her voice when she sang him to sleep between the cries of the screaming jets.

And then she was gone. Erased from his life.

Although he didn't know it at the time, Michael was "on the spectrum," as the current lingo went. He didn't experience emotions like other people, that's what the doctors told his mother. Maybe not, but he felt a hole in his heart when his mother disappeared, no matter what they said he had going on in his head.

Miss Eustace came into his life at that point and everything changed for Michael. What had been his disability magically became a skill set people found amazing. Private boarding schools, early acceptance to MIT, and then a visit from Mr. Riley and off to the US

Naval Academy. Michael's life was not his own, but right now he was okay with that.

"Earth to Michael." Dre waved her hand in front of his face. "Come in, Michael."

"Sorry. What'd you say?"

Everett laughed. "Lieutenant Jackson wants us to follow this hack and file a full report. Are you up for that or do you need a break?"

Michael straightened in his chair. "No, I'm good. Just spaced out there for a second. I'll figure out how the hacker got in if you guys want to backtrack and figure out who he is."

Janet nodded. "Let's do it."

Michael submerged himself in the code. It was odd. He wasn't good at writing code, but he had a knack for reading it. The trick was not to absorb every line but to try to see through the body of the program . . . like trying to see a 3-D picture. If you stared at the dots, you'd never see the picture. But if you let your mind relax, the picture popped into view.

Using the Cyber Command toolbox, he set to work following the hacker's digital trail within the bank network. This guy was professional, almost surgical with his movements. After a solid hour, Goodwin isolated his entry point to a vendor's network.

"We tracked it back to the Russians," Janet said. "The Golden Bear." Pseudomilitary groups like this one were covertly funded by Putin's government to collect information that could be used to disrupt government operations all over the world.

Jackson circled back to them for an update. She swore under her breath. "We're finding these guys all over the place. See if there's any chatter about that zero-day flaw being sold on the vulnerability markets in the last few weeks. They probably bought their way in."

Dre pulled up a new screen. "I'll do it." New weaknesses in software were being discovered all the time. Some enterprising criminals had figured out a way to set up an auction site to sell these vulnerabilities to the highest bidder.

"Stay on it, you three," Jackson said. "Janet, you're in charge of writing up the report."

"Yes, ma'am. As soon as our plebe figures out how they got in in the first place, I'll have it ready for your review."

Michael looked up, his feelings hurt. Then he saw smiles all around. *They're teasing me,* he thought. He curved his lips into a grin.

"You're not losing your edge, are you, Goodwin?" Lieutenant Jackson said.

"No, ma'am," Michael said. "As long as I've got my teammates with me, I'm good."

Janet and Dre exchanged glances.

Michael frowned. "Did I say something wrong?"

Dre punched him on the arm. "Nope, you're good, plebe. Now get back to work."

CHAPTER 19

Hong Kong, China

Despite the late hour, Kong Sung-il left the North Korean Consulate General building with a spring in his step. The door on his limousine closed behind him with a satisfying thump.

"Apliu Street," he said to his driver, a longtime Hong Kong resident. The man's eyes flicked up to the rearview mirror.

"A little relaxation this evening, sir?"

Kong smiled and looked out the window at the bright lights of the vertical skyline. So different from home. The skyline in Pyongyang was beautiful, but not exotic like this. Hong Kong was beyond anything he could have imagined growing up in the DPRK.

Unlike many of his diplomatic colleagues, Kong did not have a Western education. His family circumstances had been, well, less connected. His job here, as second deputy to the ambassador, was the sole result of his wife's family connections.

Fortunately, she had returned to North Korea for an extended visit with her mother, leaving him with free time to sample the darker delights of Hong Kong.

He settled back in the soft leather seats. The first Western woman he'd seen naked had been a redhead. Kong had grown up in a land of skinny, flat-chested, dour women with straight black hair. The image of the prostitute's fiery red hair, pillowy breasts, and ample bottom still excited him to this day.

Others came after that. Blondes, brunettes, Chinese, Russian, curly-haired, tattooed . . . he sampled as much variety as his wife's travel schedule allowed.

He was careful, of course. It wasn't sexually transmitted diseases that worried him, it was the Chinese intelligence services. If he was compromised, he'd be sent back to Pyongyang—or worse.

So, he made his selections carefully, never using the same girl twice, never on a regular schedule. Like tonight, he only sought out pleasure when his schedule permitted.

The car swung into the seedier section of New Kowloon, past the all-night flea market. Multistory shops and rent-by-the-hour hotels lined the street to his right.

"Stop here," he called, and waited for his driver to open his door.

He stepped into the night air. To him, it smelled fresh. He didn't see or smell the rotting garbage a few meters away. He rubbed his crotch. His quarry was close, and his blood was hot with desire. He was a hunter on the prowl.

"Don't wait. I'll take a cab back to the embassy." He took off on foot down the narrow street. Although he hadn't visited this exact street before, they were all the same. Shops, hotels, food vendors all blending into the sounds and smells of nighttime in Hong Kong. But if you looked on the corners, or in the shadowy alleys or lounging in doorways, you would find girls. Lots of girls.

An almond-eyed Chinese girl with short dark hair and the glazed look of an addict strutted across his path. She met his gaze, but he passed her by without a second glance. Too ordinary. A rail-thin blonde, her bleached hair limp in the dampness, called to him from a doorway. Kong sized her up. A possibility, but he'd walk the block before making his choice.

At a street-side bar, a redhead lit a cigarette and locked eyes with him. She crossed her milky white thighs, giving her barely-there miniskirt a suggestive tug, and blew out a long stream of smoke in his direction.

Kong felt his mouth water, his heart rate tick up. This was the one. She tapped her cigarette and a fleck of ash fell to the street. He adjusted his suit jacket to hide his growing erection and stepped toward her.

"How much?" he said.

She pursed her ruby lips and drew on her cigarette again. Hard. "More than you have," she said in a cloud of smoke.

Kong licked his lips. Feisty.

He pulled a wad of cash from his pocket and peeled off a few hundred RMB notes, dropping them on the table. The red-haired woman looked away and Kong's eye followed the curve of her neck. She was magnificent.

He doubled the amount of money on the table and she scooped up the bills with a broad smile. "Follow me," she said in Mandarin, crossing the street. Kong stayed close until she stepped into an alley.

"C'mon," she called, holding out her hand. "The entrance is back here. The room's on me, by the way."

Kong smiled. He would get a discount after all. Taking her hand, he stepped into the darkness. Afterimages from the bright streetlights clouded his vision.

He felt a sharp prick on his neck, then strong arms held him. He struggled to breathe.

A sharp, searing scent snapped Kong awake. He cursed in Korean.

"Morning, sunshine," said a male voice. Mandarin, passable but with a Western accent. American?

His arms and legs were strapped to a chair and he was naked. The room was stifling, damp, with an undertone of rot. A basement. He closed his eyes against the harsh light shining in his face.

"I am a diplomat of the Democratic People's—"

The hand came out of nowhere, whipping his head to the side with a slap. His ears rang.

"Shut the fuck up, asshole. We don't care who you are. It's not you we want."

A glimmer of hope. "Who is it you want?"

Another slap. Kong's eyes watered, turning the light into a glimmering blob in his vision.

"We ask the questions. You speak when spoken to. Understand?"

Another slap.

"I understand," Kong sobbed.

"Good. Now take a nap." A hand holding a needle stabbed him in the shoulder.

Darkness.

The searing scent snapped him awake; the light blinded him. His tongue felt like it was glued to the roof of his mouth and he desperately wanted a drink of water. How long had he been asleep? Hours? Days? Surely his driver would have reported him missing now. Then he remembered he'd sent the driver away.

The slap came out of the darkness. The side of his face throbbed with every heartbeat.

A new voice. Male, but his Mandarin was better. "Rafiq Roshed. Where is he?"

Kong looked up into the light. His hearing seemed muffled on his right side. Had they burst his eardrum?

"I don't know who that is," he said, trying to keep the hysteria he felt out of his voice.

"You're lying." The needle appeared again. A sharp stab in his shoulder. Darkness.

The acrid smell blasted him awake for the third time—or was it the fourth? His naked thighs were sticky with his own urine.

It had to be days later now. His people would be looking for him, his wife worried. A new fear crept into his thoughts. What would they do when they found him? Would they consider him a traitor?

"Poor baby." Her voice was gentle, her Mandarin excellent. The light angled down at the floor and the redhead stood before him. She had on jeans, a silk shirt, and a short leather jacket.

"You!" Kong tried to spit at her, but his mouth was too dry.

"Shh!" She held her finger to her lips. "Do you want them to kill you? I just about have them convinced to let you go. Don't make trouble." She produced a cool washcloth and knelt in front of him. The dampness felt wonderful on his skin. "You need to do something for them."

Kong drew back. "I will not betray the Supreme Leader—"

"Relax." She laid one long hand with elegantly painted fingernails on his thigh. Her perfume washed over him, drowning out the dank smell of the room. "No one would ask you to betray your leader. You're too strong for that. They're after someone else. A foreigner."

Kong recalled them shouting a name at him. Rafiq Roshed. He had no idea who that person was. "What do I have to do?" he said.

Her voice was like honey in his ear. "All you have to do is deliver a message."

Kong's voice cracked. "I—I don't know—"

"Shhh." The girl put her index finger on his cracked lips. The red nail caressed the underside of his nose. She held up a picture. "Do you know this man?"

Kong looked at the image. He nodded. It was Pak Myung-rok, close confidant to the Supreme Leader himself.

"This man brought a foreigner to North Korea maybe four or five years ago. Rafiq Roshed. He now works in the Covert Actions Division. Find Pak and deliver a message to him—and only to him. Can you do that?"

Kong nodded.

"If you fail to do this within two days, they will have no choice but to tell your country you've been compromised. You know what happens to those who betray the Supreme Leader?"

"Death," Kong croaked. He'd seen the public executions on state TV many times. "But how will they know?"

The prostitute smiled. "They'll know."

"What is the message?"

She leaned so close her soft cheek rubbed against his. Her breath was warm in his ear. "Listen carefully."

Kong woke up on a park bench a block from the North Korean embassy. He struggled to his feet. He was fully dressed in his own clothes, his face washed. Apart from the headache and the pain in his jaw, he felt fine. He touched his shoulder, wincing at the tenderness where his skin had been punctured multiple times.

No, it wasn't a dream.

His wristwatch said it was 6:00 A.M., and the pre-dawn streets around him were mostly empty. He walked stiffly to the embassy entrance, where the guard on duty saluted.

"What day is it?" Kong demanded.

"Friday, sir."

Kong turned away to hide his shock. He had been gone for six hours.

"Are you feeling all right, sir?" the guard asked.

"Of course!" Kong snapped back, marching through the gate. He avoided the living quarters, heading to the office area. Not even the secretaries were in this early. He climbed the steps two at a time, his pulse hammering in his ears. He bypassed his own desk and made his way to the ambassador's office. He would need a secure line to call home.

His keys jangled in his hand as he sorted through them to find the one that opened the ambassador's office. The door opened easily, and he stepped onto plush carpet. Morning sun touched the rich red of the DPRK flag posted behind the ambassador's desk.

Kong perched on the edge of the ambassador's high-back leather chair as he slid open the drawer. He breathed a sigh of relief at the sight of the official directory. He flipped through the pages, wanting this all to be over, until he found the number for the residence of Pak Myung-rok.

It took Kong three tries to dial the number. He pressed the receiver to his ear as it rang with the digital warble of a secure line. Once, twice, four times . . . six times. Kong felt hot tears of frustration prick the corners of the eyes.

A voice, groggy with sleep, answered the phone.

"Listen to me," Kong said, almost shouting in relief, "I have a message for Rafiq Roshed."

Kong could feel the tension on the other end of the line. When the man spoke again, there was no trace of sleep in his voice. "I'm listening."

Kong thought of the redheaded woman with her gentle hands and her voice like honey, and he repeated the message word for word.

CHAPTER 20

USS Gerald R. Ford *(CVN-78)*
150 miles south of Taiwan

Heavy rain lashed the carrier's superstructure as Rear Admiral Manuel "Han" Manolo, strike group commander, entered Flag Watch.

"Admiral in Flag Watch!" the petty officer at the door called out as he stepped into the room.

He joined the air wing commander, Captain Diane "Ralph" Henderson, at the BattleSpace display. "How's the recovery going, Ralph?" he said, using the pilot's call sign.

"We've got twelve birds out, sir. This little squall will slow us down, but we're on track for a clean recovery. Easy day."

BattleSpace, a square tabletop display twenty feet on a side, gave him a holographic 3-D representation of the area surrounding the carrier. It was currently set at a range of thirty miles and was operated by a lieutenant wearing VR goggles over his eyes and a manipulator glove on his right hand.

Manolo nodded as he studied BattleSpace. The US Navy could land a plane in almost any weather short of a typhoon. A little rain and sketchy visibility was useful to keep the pilots on their toes. One of the tiny planes in the display changed from green to yellow as it lined up behind the carrier for a landing approach.

A watch stander behind them called out, "Flight Ops reports Zip Lip recovery in progress. First aircraft is two miles out, on glide slope." For training, the carrier routinely recovered aircraft in a "Zip Lip" condition: without the use of any active radar or radio transmissions.

"Very well," Henderson replied.

Manolo thought about donning rain gear and heading out to Vulture's Row, the adjoining bridge overlooking the flight deck. The incoming F/A-18 would appear any second now, slamming onto the deck of the carrier at a relative speed of one hundred miles per hour, preferably snagging the third of four steel cables to slow itself. He'd seen it—and done it—thousands of times and he never tired of experiencing carrier landings. Tonight, he decided to stay dry.

"Ma'am," a petty officer called with a hitch of anxiety in his voice, "we've got four fast-movers on an intercept course. Probable Chinese J-11 fighters."

Henderson cursed and stalked to the edge of the BattleSpace display. "Track them, Lieutenant. Let's see what these guys are up to." The operator expanded the display range to show four incoming jets marching across the distance between the Chinese coast and the *Ford*. In a few minutes, they'd cross paths with the scattering of US jets circling the carrier.

Outside, Manolo heard the supersonic boom as the incoming Chinese jets passed the carrier.

Henderson snatched up a handset and spoke to her air boss in charge of recovery operations. "Agreed," she said. "Put them in a holding pattern until these Chinese assholes clear out. I'll tell the captain."

Captain James Gutterman, commanding officer of

the *Ford,* entered Flag Watch with his typical brusque style. "I was just about to call you, Captain," Henderson said. "I've suspended recovery ops until we're sure the pattern is clear."

Gutterman, a short, swarthy man with a jutting jaw, addressed Manolo. "This is bullshit, sir. We're in international waters and they damn well know we're recovering aircraft."

"Calm down, Jim," Manolo said. "They had their fun, let them clear out." His words were meant to placate his team, but Manolo was worried. He was convinced that this increased Chinese activity was part of a larger, more aggressive pattern. The briefing he'd received just a few hours ago confirmed his suspicions that Sino-American relations were sinking, and fast.

The Chinese fighters settled into a wide loop around the massive ship, crossing the flight path of the incoming planes, ensuring that the carrier could not recover her aircraft.

Gutterman fumed, gripping the railing around the BattleSpace table with his beefy hands as if he could choke the problem to death.

"Any response to your warnings?" Henderson asked, breaking the tension.

"Not a peep from those fuckers," Gutterman replied through clenched teeth.

"Join me on the Row," Manolo said to the two other officers. He stepped out of Flag Watch onto Vulture's Row. The rain had stopped, but the wind, chilled and heavy with moisture, still blew in gusts. He turned. "Options," he said.

"Let me light them up with a fire-control radar," Gutterman said. "That'll send them heading for the hills."

Manolo hid a smile. "As much as I'd like to do that, Jim, you know it's against the rules of engagement. If

World War Three starts tonight, it's not going to start here. Not on my watch."

Henderson spoke. "The closest bingo airfield is Kaohsiung in Taiwan. We've got another ten minutes before we have to divert our birds."

Ten minutes. Manolo glared down at the idle flight deck, tamping down a deep burning anger at these irresponsible Chinese pilots who were putting his people at risk. He eyed his two commanders in his peripheral vision. Henderson was concerned but seemed in control. Gutterman, on the other hand, felt on the edge. The last thing he wanted to do was inflame the carrier CO into doing something stupid. Even though he would dearly love to give the order to blast those Chinese planes out of the sky, he needed to keep cool, stay level.

This is how wars get started, he reminded himself. *When people take things personally.*

"Start the clock," Manolo said. "I'm going to call Admiral Cook at Seventh Fleet."

He stepped back into Flag Watch and ordered a watch stander to get him a secure linkup with Commander Seventh Fleet.

"Cook here." His boss's voice warbled slightly from the scrambled digital signal.

"Admiral, we've got a situation brewing. Four Chinese fighters are disrupting recovery ops for a dozen aircraft. No response to hails. In another ten minutes, we're going to have to divert to Taiwan for refueling, sir." He hesitated. "That briefing we received this afternoon about increased Chinese aggression. It's happening."

Cook swore.

"Look, Manny, I know this is going to hurt, but do not provoke the Chinese. If you have to divert, then that's what we'll have to do. For now. This thing has gone to the White House already and they are terrified of starting a hot war from this penny-ante bullshit."

"Aye, aye, sir."

"If it's any consolation, I'll take it to Pac Fleet right away and they'll take another run at Washington. For now, our orders are to play nice. Understand?"

As Manolo hung up the phone, Henderson approached. "We're three minutes from bingo on fuel, sir." She raised her eyebrows at him.

Manolo watched the team gathered around the brightly lit BattleSpace display and gritted his teeth.

"Order the divert. I want those birds right back here as soon as they've refueled."

Pyongyang, North Korea

Pak Myung-rok paced the hardwood floor of his study, fuming. What was taking so long? Rafiq and his god-damned security protocols. He needed to speak with him *now*.

His mobile phone beeped, indicating an incoming message. He thumbed to the screen to find the number for Rafiq's daily burner phone. Pak's breath hissed through his teeth as he dialed the number. Even with these elaborate precautions, their call could still be intercepted by the Americans.

He resumed his pacing as the phone rang.

Rafiq's voice was low and cool. "I'm working. This better be important."

"I need you back now."

"I told you, I'm working."

"We've been compromised. Get back here now."

The line was silent.

"Hello?" Pak said letting his impatience show in his tone. "Did you hear me? We've been compromised."

"Explain." Rafiq's voice was softer now, less demanding.

"I received a call from the Hong Kong embassy this morning. A low-level staffer was kidnapped and sent back with a message for you. They knew to call me to get to you and they asked for you by name. Not your Korean name. Your real name."

"What was the message?"

Pak blew out a blast of frustration. "That's not important. These people had skills. They knew who to target and how to get to you. Your cover is blown, my friend. Get back here now."

"The message, Pak."

Pak hesitated. Until the call an hour ago, he'd never given a thought to Rafiq's family. He knew his wife was dead and he seemed to recall Rafiq had children, but they had never spoken of them.

"Pak. The message." Rafiq's tone was like steel.

"They said they're coming for your children."

"Who?"

The skin on the back of Pak's neck prickled. "I don't know."

The line was silent, waiting.

"He said he thought they might be American," Pak said finally. "We need to get you back now, Rafiq. The whole operation rests on you. The Supreme Leader is depending on you to fulfill the Russian contract . . . Where are you?"

"Australia. For now."

Pak held the dead phone to his ear for another moment. Australia. What the hell was Rafiq doing in Australia?

CHAPTER 21

Admiral Henley Reeder, Chairman of the Joint Chiefs of Staff, was normally a calm man. Some of his subordinates had even described his leadership style as placid. He radiated quiet confidence in everything he did.

But today, the long face beneath his graying fringe was fiery red and far from calm. "Mr. President, with all due respect, sir, we are looking like a bunch of lily-livered wusses out there!"

The secretary of defense tried to signal the admiral to dial back his rhetoric, but the man wasn't finished yet.

"We have evidence that the Chinese are behind the latest hack into the Defense Department database. They got service records, DNA profiles, even security background checks."

"Allegedly," the national security adviser said. "That investigation is not complete yet, Mr. Chairman."

"Allegedly, my left foot!" the admiral shot back. "This is on top of their harassing a P-8 on simple freedom-of-navigation operations. But this latest act is the final straw. They disrupted recovery ops on the *Ford* operating in international waters and forced a dozen US Navy aircraft to divert to Taiwan. This is not—"

"Admiral," the president said. "You've made your point."

Reeder took a deep breath. "Yes, sir." The chairman leaned back in his chair.

The president pinned State and Defense with his gaze. "Options, gentlemen."

Defense cleared his throat. He was thin to the point of gauntness, with an Adam's apple that bobbed as he spoke. "Sir, I agree with the chairman. We need to give our frontline commanders more tools to combat Chinese aggression."

"Specifics, please," the president replied.

"Well, sir, for close-aboard situations, I recommend we authorize shouldering procedures for our surface fleet if the situation warrants."

The president stroked his chin. "Actually make contact? Push the Chinese vessel off course?"

Defense and the chairman nodded in unison.

"What about aircraft? That seems to be where a lot of these incidents are happening."

"Light 'em up, sir," the chairman said. The secretary of state started to object, but the chairman pressed on. "These Chinese aircraft have buzzed our flight path and disrupted recovery operations for an aircraft carrier of the United States Navy. In another time, that would have been enough for a declaration of war, sir. They have disrespected us long enough. If a Chinese pilot has to put on clean underwear after hearing a fire-control radar lock on his ass, then next time he won't be so eager to play in our airspace."

The president nodded. "That's it? Shouldering and targeting? Seems like we should have more than those two options in our bag of tricks."

Defense's Adam's apple was doing the herky-jerky up and down his neck. "One more, sir. We recommend you give the theater commanders the option to fire a warning shot, if warranted by the situation."

The room went still. The national security adviser and State tried to speak at the same time, but the president cut them off. "No," he said. "I know what you're going to say, and the answer is no. The Chinese have brought this on themselves. Our military needs clear guidance and responses that are in line with what we're seeing out there. If our operational commanders on the front lines believe the best play is a shot across the bow, then I'm giving them that option. If you don't like it, then give our diplomats in China a boot in the ass."

NSA and State glared at the military side of the table.

"Mr. Chairman," the president continued, "bring me the revised Rules of Engagement and I'll sign them. Also, instruct the Seventh Fleet commander that I want him to double freedom-of-navigation operations in the region. Paracels, Spratlys, Senkakus—I want the Stars and Stripes in evidence for our allies and the rest of the world to see."

"Yes, *sir*," said the chairman. "You'll have them on your desk by this afternoon."

State tried again. "Sir, I have to say—"

"Adrian, the time for talk has passed, I'm afraid. I need you to communicate our intentions to the Chinese ambassador. Make it clear to him that increased Chinese aggression in the western Pacific will not be tolerated. He must acknowledge that any further activities like the one that forced our aircraft to divert will be considered a hostile act. Understood?"

"Understood, sir, but we haven't addressed the hacking. I agree with the chairman. Although the investigation is not one hundred percent complete, it is pretty clear the Chinese were behind it. Do we wrap additional actions into this communiqué?"

The president pursed his lips in thought. "No," he said finally. "Let's complete the investigation, make absolutely sure it was them before we go accusing the Chinese of another dirty trick. This latest fiasco with the *Ford* is all over the news. Let's play this one out before we open up another can of worms."

CHAPTER 22

Darwin, Australia

Weston Merville tossed down another tequila and slammed the shot glass back on the wooden bar.

"Hey, mate!" the bartender shouted at him over the din of the dance music. "I asked you not to do that. It puts dents in my bar."

The bartender was a wiry guy with shaggy blond hair. Weston could take him if he had to. "Shut up and pour me another."

"You gonna mess up my bar?"

Someone bumped into him from behind before he could answer. Weston whirled around to find himself nose-to-nose with a pair of deep blue eyes attached to a luscious body. His eyes slid down her very deep cleavage, catching more than a peek of black lace. He licked his lips. "'Scuse me."

She gave him elevator eyes, pausing for a moment on the bulge in his trousers—or was that his imagination?—before locking eyes with him again. "No problem, sailor." Her Australian accent made her seem even sexier.

A man tugged on her arm. Tall, well-built, but older than the woman by at least ten years.

"Sabrina, come on," the man said. Sabrina winked at him before she allowed herself to be pulled away.

Weston watched her follow the man to a table on the far side of the dance floor. Every few minutes, she sneaked a glance his way.

He turned back to the bar, not believing his luck. First night of liberty and he was hot on the trail of some grade-A Australian pussy. He thought about the officers in the wardroom back on the *Blue Ridge* and checked his phone to see if any of them had shown up on social media. If he could get a picture with *her* . . . He sneaked another glance across the dance floor. Sabrina was looking at him.

"Still want that drink?" the bartender asked.

"Yeah, rum and Coke." He found that a few of his shipmates had tweeted about being at the Blue Dog Bar. He looked it up on his phone. It was only a few blocks away.

He sipped the fresh drink. As the IT department head and systems administrator on the USS *Blue Ridge,* Lieutenant Commander Weston Merville was in charge of command and control systems for the entire Seventh Fleet, from Singapore to the South Pole to Hawaii and everything in between. Those assholes in the wardroom were either junior officers who worked for him or ship drivers who thought he was just a glorified computer nerd.

They had no idea how hard his job was. The Seventh Fleet covered vast distances, including hundreds of ships, thousands of computers, and dozens of different communications networks. That shit didn't just happen, he *made* it happen. Every day.

What a bunch of ungrateful assholes.

Even his superiors didn't see his real worth. They wrote crap on his fitness reports about how his work was technically perfect, but he needed to "work on his leadership skills" to take the next step in his career. That line especially made him want to barf on the captain's desk and grab his crotch with both hands. *I got your leadership skills right here, Captain, you prick.*

He finished the drink and signaled for another.

Which led him to tonight. A port call in Darwin after a solid fourteen days at sea, and he was free as a bird, because the engineers wanted to take down the power to most of his equipment. He peeked over his shoulder for another look at Sabrina. Her beautiful brow was creased with anger and she seemed to be arguing with her date. As Weston watched, she stood and threw a drink in the man's face. Sabrina cut through the dance floor, making a beeline for Weston.

Her face was flushed, and she stood close enough to him that he could smell the perfume wafting up from her open blouse. "Take me out of here. Please."

Weston threw a wad of bills on the bar and followed her onto the street.

Sabrina clutched his arm. "You're a lifesaver. That was the mother of all bad blind dates. I'm Sabrina, by the way."

"Weston," he said. "That was a blind date?"

"Don't remind me." She looked at her watch. "It's only a little after one. Let me buy you a drink to say thank you, Weston. What's your pleasure?"

"Do you know where the Blue Dog Bar is?"

Sabrina slid her arm into his. "Sure. Let's go."

Weston made sure Sabrina's hefty breast was crushed against his biceps when they walked through the door of the Blue Dog Bar. His gaze found the group of junior officers from the *Blue Ridge,* and he stared at them until one of them noticed him. Then he looked away.

He and Sabrina stood together at a high-top in the bar area, his back to his crewmates.

"I think some of the guys over there are watching us," Sabrina said.

"What guys?" Weston pretended to look around. He spied the table and waved. "Just some officers from the ship. Probably jealous, you know."

"Really?" Sabrina sidled up next to him. "Well, why don't we give them something to be jealous about, my knight in shining armor?" She ran her knee inside his thigh as she nuzzled his neck. "Do you have someplace we can go, Weston? Someplace private?"

The night air cooled his face as they walked back to his room at the SkyCity hotel. He was glad now that he hadn't agreed to share a room with another officer from the wardroom. She pulled him into an alley a block away and ground her hips against him. "I want you, Weston."

His head swam. Her heat, her scent; it consumed him. He weaved his way through the lobby with Sabrina glued to his side, a raging hard-on straining at his trousers. At his door, she licked his ear as he fumbled for the room key. Inside, she pinned him against the wall, crushing her body against his, another rush of perfume sending his senses into overdrive. He gripped the back of her neck and drew her mouth to his.

Sabrina broke off the kiss, her chest heaving. "I'm going to visit the little girls' room before we get busy." She fished a silver flask out of her purse. "Have a shot of this, big fella, and get undressed." She watched as he drank deeply. Sweet, like crème de menthe or Irish cream. "I'll take that." She plucked the flask away from him and pushed him toward the bed. "Now go get yourself ready."

Weston staggered into the bedroom and sat down. He fumbled to untie his shoes, wishing now he'd had a little less to drink. Sex with this magnificent woman was an experience he wanted to savor. He thought about his phone. Maybe she would let him record it.

"Almost ready?" she called.

Weston stood, his head woozy. He struggled out of his shirt, then stepped out of his pants. Sabrina struck a pose in the bathroom door, her voluptuous body silhouetted in the light. The black lace brassiere was the perfect complement to the creamy white skin of her full breasts. She plucked the strap of a matching black lace thong on her hip. "You like it?" she whispered.

"Yes," Weston rasped out. His vision was swimming, but his body was willing. She stepped closer, taking his hand and placing it on her chest. Her soft flesh quivered at his touch. His groin responded.

Sabrina unsnapped the bra, letting her heavy breasts swing free, releasing another cloud of intoxicating perfume. She cupped a breast and offered it up to Weston.

He leaned closer, but his balance was off. He focused on the deep pink flesh of her nipple, pursing his lips to kiss it, but Sabrina stepped back.

Weston lost his balance, and the rough blue carpet of the hotel room rushed up to slam him in the face.

Bright lights burned Weston's retinas.

"Wake up, sir!"

His head pounded; his stomach was on the edge of purging its sour contents.

"Wake up." Someone slapped him on the face. Hard.

Weston struggled to sit up, suppressing the urge to blow chunks all over himself. Where was he? Fragments of memories floated in his mind, just out of reach.

Australia . . . shore leave . . . drinking . . . girl . . . sex! His eyes sprang open. He was about to have sex with the Australian girl . . .

"Sabrina," he croaked.

"Is that the woman's name, sir?" the deep voice said. "Sabrina?"

What was a man doing in his hotel room? Weston struggled upright. "Who are you? What are you doing in my room?"

The man stepped past Weston and turned on the light next to the bed. He was wearing a policeman's uniform. "We had a call for disturbing the peace, sir." He consulted his notebook. "Are you Lieutenant Commander Weston Merville of the USS *Blue Ridge*?"

Weston rubbed his face. His mind was still so foggy. "Yes, why are you in my room?"

The policeman pointed past Weston, forcing him to turn around. Sabrina was splayed across the far side of the king bed. Her black lace thong was caught on one ankle, her breasts flopped to one side—and there were bright blue bruises on her neck.

Weston's knees gave out and he was kneeling on the floor, his eyes on a level with Sabrina's body. "I—I," he whimpered. Tears streamed down his cheeks.

"Did you get a little rough last night, Weston?"

"No, no, I . . . don't remember." His breath was coming in great gulps, but he seemed unable to get any oxygen into his system.

"I wager to say she doesn't remember anything either." The policeman had an odd accent, almost Spanish, but not quite. "How did you meet Sabrina Douglas, sir?"

"You know her?" Weston looked up at the cop.

"Oh, sure," the cop said. "Well-known prostitute in these parts. Liked it rough, too. The choking was probably her idea, you know. We figured it was just a matter of time before she ended up like this."

"She told me she was on a blind date and I rescued her."

The cop laughed. "She got you good—and now this. You're screwed, Weston. When the navy finds out about this, your security clearance is toast. And Australian prisons . . . well, they'll use you like a pincushion."

"Oh my God, oh my God, oh my God," Weston repeated.

"That said," the cop continued, "Miss Douglas was far from a model citizen and I'd hate to derail the career of a navy man. For a price, I can make this all go away, Weston."

Weston stared up at the cop, not believing what he was hearing. "You—you can make this disappear?" He gestured at the body.

"Like it never happened."

Weston got off his knees and sat on the edge of the bed. "How much?"

The cop sat on the edge of the bed. He gripped Weston's chin and forced him to meet his gaze. "I don't want your money, Weston. The men I work for, they want favors from powerful people. People with access, if you get my meaning."

His security clearance. They wanted him to spy for them. The whole thing was a trap. He ripped his chin away from the man's grasp and looked back at Sabrina's body. He gagged.

A girl—another human being—had been killed so they could set him up. His mind raced through the evening. The bar where all of his crewmates had seen him with Sabrina, the hotel lobby with her all over him— that had to be on security cameras. His DNA was surely all over her corpse.

He was fucked.

"I'll do it," he said, not looking at the police officer.

"Good choice, Weston. Get dressed, go back to your ship, and pretend nothing happened. My people will be in touch."

Weston nodded. "One last thing," he said.

The cop raised his eyebrows.

"I want to touch the body."

The other man stood. "Knock yourself out, sailor. I'll be back in ten minutes."

CHAPTER 23

Pyongyang, North Korea

Pak paused outside the doors of Kim Jong-un's office. He drew a deep, calming breath. Face-to-face meetings with the Supreme Leader were always touch-and-go affairs, completely at the whim of the great man. What sort of mood would he be in today?

The heavy gold-inlaid double doors swung open and Pak was announced. Smiling, he strode into the room, trying to exude more confidence than he felt.

Kim Jong-un's office was styled in lots of gold, mirrors, the obligatory enormous self-portrait, and a desk piled with stacks of important-looking—and never read—papers.

The Supreme Leader rose and waited for Pak to approach. Pak halted a few feet away and bowed formally.

"You are back from Russia, yes?" the great man said, striding around the massive desk. He seated himself in a gaudy golden chair with golden pillows, waving Pak to a similar seat opposite. This was the Supreme Leader's informal "talking circle"—a welcome sign that his mood was positive today.

"I've just returned, Excellency, my third trip," Pak said. "The Russians wish you well in the new year."

The other man's substantial jowls shook as he laughed. "I doubt that, Pak. Tell me: Did you get paid?"

Pak answered in a cautious tone. It was unlike the Supreme Leader to ask about money so soon in the conversation. For one moment of blinding terror, he wondered if his boss knew how much Pak was skimming off the transaction. It was more than usual, since he had to account for Rafiq's cut as well, but he had taken extra precautions.

"Yes, Excellency, the Russians paid promptly. Thirty million US dollars." He coughed into his fist. "I've already routed it through the normal process. The treasury will have access to the funds in another twenty-four hours."

Kim pouted.

"Is there a problem, Excellency?"

"We should have charged them more. We're taking all the risk so they can make billions in profits."

Pak smiled, back on firm ground. "This is just the beginning. Once we've established ourselves with the Bratva, we can charge more."

Kim plucked a grape from the lavish golden bowl on the coffee table between them and popped it into his mouth. "Try a red one. They're from California."

Pak detached a grape. The flesh of the fruit was firm between his fingers and glistened with moisture. He knew that each individual grape had been inspected for flaws and hand-washed before it ended up on the Supreme Leader's plate. He placed it on his tongue and bit down. Sweetness exploded in his mouth.

"It's magnificent," he said.

Kim chuckled. "Yes, they are. Tell me about Jung Chul, my secret weapon."

That was how the Supreme Leader referred to Rafiq—his secret weapon. Indeed, he was not far off the mark. In the years since Pak had brought Rafiq to the DPRK, the man had performed some valuable services for the regime. The assassination of an unfriendly European bureaucrat, blackmailing of a nuclear inspector, no fewer than four arms deals with various Middle East factions, hacking the US power grid, and Pak's personal favorite: the elimination of his half brother, Kim Jong-nam.

It turned out hacking the US power grid had been a step too far. It had taken all of Pak's influence to convince the Supreme Leader not to take credit for the attack. While Kim was delighted with his cyber prowess and wanted to show off his abilities to the world, Pak assured him the Americans would consider the hack an act of war—a prophecy that was borne out by their response when Rafiq convinced ISIS to claim responsibility.

"Roshed continues to carry on his good work for your regime, Excellency. His methods are unorthodox and bold, but he gets results. He is almost ready to begin this endeavor supporting the Russians. Do we have your permission to begin?"

Kim clapped his hands together. "Well done. I want to move forward immediately. I want you to give the order today."

Pak cleared his throat.

Kim narrowed his eyes. "What is it, Pak?"

"Rafiq has taken some time off."

"I don't understand."

"He was in Australia two days ago and now he's disappeared."

Kim's brow wrinkled, and a shadow of fear flickered across his features. "Is he compromised? Have the Americans found out about our plan?"

He leaped to his feet, pacing the room. For all the regime's media bluster about attacking America, the Supreme Leader feared the Americans more than any other country, including the Chinese. The omnipresent threat of US forces only a few miles beyond the DMZ was a constant reminder of his tenuous grasp on power.

Pak rose immediately, following his leader. "No, Excellency, I don't believe so. I spoke to Rafiq before he disappeared. He said he had to take care of a family matter."

Kim stopped pacing. "What does that mean?"

"I'm not sure, sir. His wife is dead, that's all I know."

"And you're sure he'll be back?" The Supreme Leader's dark eyes pinned Pak in place.

Pak swallowed. "Absolutely, Excellency. I'd stake my life on it."

CHAPTER 24

Brendan studied the giant wall screen on the Trident watch floor. "Well, Supe, are we there yet?"

"Ninety-one percent and holding steady, sir."

"How's the coverage in the Java Sea?" he said.

"Ever since we added the break-bulk freighters to the mix, we're consistently meeting our coverage targets."

Brendan nodded. Adding the phone booth–sized black boxes to foreign-flagged vessels was not his idea, but it had worked well. In that part of Indonesia, much of the freighter traffic was done by so-called break-bulk ships, operated by independent carriers who made their living hauling anything not in a standard shipping container from port to small port.

Besides, the large container ships had refused the CIA's efforts to permanently install the comms nodes on their vessels, forcing the spy agency to resort to a complicated plan of placing the black boxes in shipping containers without the company's knowledge. Brendan had added a full-time staffer just to coordinate the shipping schedules needed to ensure continuous coverage.

But it was done. And it worked. They now had full viral network coverage of all the hot spots on the globe.

"That's a long way from a couple of guys in a sailboat, hey, McHugh?" Baxter's voice was a welcome relief to Brendan's overworked brain. He shook his former boss's hand warmly.

"You here to see the show?" Brendan asked.

"Show?" Baxter turned in a slow circle, surveying the rows of computer workstations. "I don't follow. You planning on showing a movie on the big screen?"

The watch supervisor made a face, and Brendan led Baxter away from the supe's desk. "We've been holding at ninety percent coverage now for the better part of a week, so I've been authorized to turn on Piggyback."

Baxter gave a low whistle. "Whoa, that's big. You're running months ahead of schedule, right?"

"Yeah, I'm getting pushed and I'm not liking it." Brendan looked around. "Let's go into my office."

With fresh cups of coffee, the two men settled into chairs in Brendan's office.

Baxter spoke first. "Okay, McHugh, spill it. You're running one of the most successful intel programs in CIA history, you're months ahead of schedule, and you're about to release an entirely new comms capability. Yet you're still down in the mouth. Talk to me."

Brendan stared at his coffee cup. "I feel like we're going too far, too fast. We are building the largest-ever network of communications and supercomputing assets, but I don't feel like we're giving enough attention to the downside."

"The downside?"

"Trident goes beyond anything anyone's even conceived of before. We're setting up a viral network that includes the CIA, NSA, CYBERCOM, and the fleet—all interconnected." He pointed at his office door. "The average age on the watch floor is twenty-seven. These are kids who believe if we *can* build it, we *should* build it."

"So you're worried about security?"

"Damn right! If someone did manage to get inside, there's no limit to what they could access. It could make the hack on the power grid look like a tea party."

"And you've expressed these concerns?"

Brendan snorted. "The average age of the people at the next level is thirty-two. I'm a fossil, Rick! Hell, Riley has midshipmen on the CYBERCOM watch floor. I'm too old for this, man." He sipped his coffee. "I'm sorry, I'm talking your ear off. What did you come down here for anyway?"

"Update on Parable Cleaver."

Brendan brightened. "Roshed. Have they found him yet?"

Baxter shook his head. "Our friend hasn't poked his nose out of North Korea yet."

"That we know about, you mean."

"That we know about. I'm hoping Trident will give us a few more assets to use in the hunt. In fact, I'm headed over to see Riley at CYBERCOM to see if he's got any ideas on how to find Roshed." He glanced at his watch. "Speaking of which, I'm late."

"Tell Don to stay on his toes. Anytime I question network security they tell me not to worry, that's CYBERCOM's responsibility. I long for the old days when we had signs everywhere: If you see something, say something."

"You're showing your age, Brendan." Baxter's face took on a serious cast. "Don't stop voicing your concerns just because they're not listening. They need to hear from us fossils."

There was a knock at the door and Brendan's aide poked his head in. "They're ready for you, sir."

Brendan stood. "Well, this dinosaur is about to make spy history, Rick. Sure you can't stay?"

Baxter stuck out his hand. "Nope, I'm already running late."

Brendan made his way back onto the dim watch floor where his team was assembled. The wall screen was covered with hundreds of active Trident sites. And he was about to link them all together.

"We're at ninety-two percent and holding, Captain McHugh," said the watch supervisor. His eyes were dancing with anticipation. Brendan looked around. The entire watch section was tense and happy. He cleared his throat.

"You all have worked really hard on Piggyback," he said. "This system upgrade was completed months ahead of schedule and that was entirely due to your hard work and dedication. For that I am both proud and grateful. You all deserve a big round of applause." He clapped and they all responded in kind.

"All right," he said, "are we ready to do this?"

He got a few "yeahs" from the crowd.

"Okay." Brendan stepped behind the operator at the watch desk. "Make it so, Number One."

The operator swiveled in his chair to look at Brendan. "Come again, sir?"

Brendan looked around. "No *Star Trek* fans in here?"

Blank looks.

Brendan sighed. "You can turn on Piggyback." Everyone watched the wall screen as the dots—each representing one node in the network—blinked, then turned green. It took a few minutes for all the contacts to convert. The group whooped and high-fived each other.

Brendan leaned down to the watch stander. "What if I had said 'Engage'? Would that have worked?"

The man leaned back in his chair and cocked an eyebrow at Brendan.

"Nope."

CHAPTER 25

Estancia Refugio Seguro, Argentina

Dickie Davis held on to his Heckler & Koch G36 as the four-wheel-drive vehicle careered through another pothole. Its headlights carved a cone of white in the inky darkness of the winding jungle road.

"Can't you drive any faster?" he said.

"Not unless you want me to leave an axle on the road, Dickie," the driver replied through clenched teeth. "Keep your pants on. The team's in place and we have the target under surveillance."

Davis gripped the armrest even tighter. "Just drive faster."

Hiring a few freelancers to pick up a North Korean diplomat in Hong Kong was about to pay off handsomely. It was the perfect crime. Baxter hadn't thought to put any coverage in Hong Kong, and that place was crawling with North Koreans. One phone call to a few ex–air force buddies was all it took to rattle Rafiq Roshed's cage.

He chuckled to himself. And Mr. Stick-up-his-ass Baxter would be none the wiser.

The fact that he'd only had to pay his Hong Kong

team twenty thousand dollars and he was about to get a ten-million-dollar payday made it all the sweeter.

All they had to do was kill Roshed and get the DNA evidence. Then Dickie Davis was on permanent vacation.

Davis had been on his way to a weekend in Buenos Aires when the tip arrived from one of their informants. Someone claiming to be Rafiq had contacted the local Hezbollah cell. When he'd first arrived, Davis had been surprised to find how active the Iranian-backed terrorist group was in the tri-border area of Brazil, Argentina, and Uruguay. There were dozens of cells and thousands of Hezbollah fighters and supporters in the region.

Davis wasn't above using terrorists as informants. Everyone—even the terrorists—spoke the language of dollars, and he let it be known he'd pay well for any information about Rafiq Roshed. At the same time, his men set up a listening post near Estancia Refugio Seguro, where Rafiq's children still lived.

Consuela and Javier. Children of the most wanted man in the world, living free on their old man's money. And now their old man was coming home.

The truck skidded to a halt at the end of the dirt road. Davis energized his headlamp, swung to the ground, and jogged into the dense foliage. Their listening post was a few hundred yards into the jungle.

Four men looked up as he burst into the tent. "What've we got?" he demanded.

They were hunched over a map on the table. His crew chief, Finn, stabbed his finger at a thin line about five miles away. "The suspect took a bus to here and is heading this way on foot." He tossed a phone to Davis. "We got pictures. Doesn't look like Roshed, boss."

Davis studied the screen, blowing up the image to study it more closely. A dark-haired man, with vaguely

Middle Eastern features, and a salt-and-pepper scruff. He was the right age range, and the right build for their target. It had to be him.

"Probably had cosmetic surgery," Davis said, tossing the phone back.

"Maybe, but we can't be sure," Finn said. "Should we pick him up?"

Davis studied the map. "You said he got off the bus and he's headed this way?"

Finn nodded.

"Show me the live feed from the Puma."

Finn spun the ruggedized laptop around and hit a few buttons. The IR video feed from the unmanned aerial vehicle came in clearly, showing a man walking on the familiar dirt road. He zoomed in on the IR image, looking for a cool spot at the small of the man's back indicating a handgun.

"Bingo," Finn said.

"Welcome home, Rafiq," Davis said. "Set the Puma on autonomous flight and have it orbit over . . . here." He tapped on the detailed topographical map at a sharp bend in the road that led to the ranch house.

"Tell the boys to set up for a chat with our visitor."

Rafiq listened to the sounds of the jungle around him. He breathed in the earthy scent of rotting vegetation and dampness. He missed this place, these smells, this life.

Estancia Refugio Seguro—"*refugio seguro*" literally meant "safe haven"—was the one place on earth where he'd been truly happy. It had been a sanctuary for him, a place far from the endless fighting and the petty factions of his native Middle East. In that part of the world, who you were was decided before you were even born.

In Argentina, he'd found a new world, a place where a man was defined by the sweat of his brow and the people around him. He'd married Nadine, had two beautiful children with her, inherited a vast *estancia* . . . and he had believed—if only for a short time—that his life was changed.

It wasn't.

His Iranian half brother Hashem had called him back into action. Rafiq and the small nuclear device he had shepherded across the ocean and secreted in the wine cellar of the *estancia* were called back to the fight. He was the fail-safe. When his brother's attack failed, Rafiq was assigned to attack the United States.

Hashem died in the sands of Iran. Rafiq could have disobeyed the call to action . . . but he didn't. He left his wife and young family to undertake one last mission for a cause that no longer seemed to be his.

Even now, the moment when he'd said goodbye— his last goodbye—to Nadine still made his eyes sting. What if he had refused the order from Hashem? His beautiful Dean would still be alive, his children would know their father, this dirt he was burrowed into would still be his. . . . What if?

A cracking branch shattered the stillness, snapping Rafiq back to reality. Twenty meters away, the shadows shifted, and he caught a glimpse of a man's silhouette. He smiled to himself. The time for *what if* was over. He might be an absent father, but no one would threaten his family and get away with it.

Rafiq turned on his night-vision goggles, and the forest took on a ghostly green clarity. He studied the terrain. This bend in the road, affording a clear line of fire from both directions and ample cover, was the natural spot for an ambush.

The man to his left was one. A second figure crept

forward from Rafiq's right. Two. A movement in the brush where the road turned. Three.

Rafiq angled his wrist to see his watch. Any minute now the man he'd hired would come walking down the dirt road from the main highway toward the ranch house. The man's only crime was that he was the same height and build as Rafiq. He never even asked the man his name.

Two men appeared on the road coming from the direction of the ranch house. They hugged the edge of the woods, their weapons at the ready. Four and five.

A figure, walking in the center of the dirt road, appeared from the direction of the highway. The bait was in place, but Rafiq needed to find one more player in the game. He squinted at the foliage behind the unsuspecting victim. The last man would be there to make sure their quarry didn't slip away and wasn't being followed.

A branch moved in the distance. Six.

Rafiq bit his lip with anticipation. The table was set. Now for the main course.

The target walked with quick steps, like a man with someplace to be. Rafiq had hired him to pick up a package at the ranch house and bring it back to Buenos Aires. He might have hinted that the package was full of money. He'd even given the man a handgun for protection.

The man reached the bend in the road, where the two mercenaries intercepted him.

"*Hola,*" one of the armed men said.

The fighters on either side of Rafiq crept forward until they were a few meters from the edge of the road. The man in trail stepped onto the road. Their target was surrounded.

Except for the man hidden in the brush on the far side of the road, Rafiq had a clear shot of all the players.

"Where are you going, my friend?" the lead man called, stepping closer. The muzzle of his weapon hung midway between the ground and the man. "It's late—or early, depending on your point of view."

"I'm here to pick up a package," the bait said. His hand inched toward the pistol at the small of his back.

"A package? At this hour, you must know the family very well to just show up, yes?"

The bait went for his weapon.

"Gun!" the man in trail shouted. His weapon snapped up and he ripped off a three-round burst. The target went down.

"Stop!" the lead man called. He ran forward and rolled the body over. "Goddammit, Lem. There's six of us and one of him. Couldn't you have just wounded him?"

"Sorry, Dickie. Is it Roshed?"

Rafiq smiled from his hiding place. *No.*

The lead man spoke into a throat mic. "All stations, report status."

The two men in Rafiq's sight reported the area was clear. They made their way to the road.

The brightness of a flashlight cut through the dark.

"Is it him? Is it Roshed?"

The man called Dickie, the leader, grunted. "Can't tell." He touched his throat mic again. "Nestor, bring up the biokit. On the double."

The brush on the opposite side of the road moved, and another mercenary stepped out into the open, lugging a bulky suitcase.

Rafiq let out a sigh of relief and hefted his sniper rifle. *Six.*

CHAPTER 26

CIA Headquarters, Langley, Virginia

Brendan's admin poked his head inside his office door. "Sir, I've got Marco Gonzalez, Buenos Aires station chief, on secure VTC. He says it's urgent."

Brendan dropped the report he was reading and swung his chair toward his computer screen. "Put him through, Tom."

He'd met Marco a few times and had always been struck by the man's sense of style. Always dapper, impeccably groomed, and outfitted in the latest in men's fashion, Gonzalez could have graced the cover of *GQ*. But the man who appeared on the screen was dressed in jeans and a dirty polo shirt, and his black curls were raked back from his face. Dark circles shadowed his eyes.

"Bad night, Marco?"

The man's face twisted into a snarl. "Not funny, McHugh. I knew you had some op going on down here, but your boys stepped in some deep shit last night."

Brendan leaned toward the screen. "Estancia Refugio? Roshed?"

Marco nodded wearily, grinding his hands across

his stubbled chin. "Yeah, it's a fucking bloodbath. Six men in paramilitary kit killed on the dirt road leading up to the ranch house. No ID, no serial numbers on the weapons, nothing, but it's all top-of-the-line shit. Mercenaries? Really? I know how bad people want Roshed's head on a plate, but I should have been told if you had a team in my backyard."

Brendan stayed silent. There was nothing he was allowed to say, and Marco knew it. Better to let the man vent.

Marco looked like he wanted to spit at the screen. "Look, I don't know who's calling the shots up there in DC, but I've got seven bodies and the ambassador is crawling up my ass. I hope you guys know what you're doing."

The screen reverted to the CIA logo, signaling the end of the call.

Brendan gripped the armrests on his chair. Dickie Fucking Davis had gone off the reservation, that had to be it. Baxter was going to blow a gasket over this. They had been crystal clear with Davis that he was not to use Roshed's kids as bait. Now, because of one rogue operator, they had the makings of an international incident on their hands.

"Tom!" he roared out. "Get me Rick Baxter on the phone. Secure line."

It had to be Roshed, he reasoned. Six operatives dead, and not just ordinary hired guns. These were highly trained ex-military, many with special ops background. It would have taken a cunning mind to outwit a group with those kinds of skills. A mind like Rafiq Roshed's.

Brendan sat back in his chair, struck with a sudden thought. If it was Roshed, then they knew where he'd been. If they had a starting point . . .

"Tom! Cancel Baxter. Get me Don Riley on VTC."

A minute later, Don's round, freckled face filled the screen. "Brendan, to what do I—"

"No time for chitchat, Don. We've got a lead on Roshed."

Don's face went serious. "Really? Where?"

"Our covert team in South America was wiped out last night. All of them."

Don's face slackened in surprise. "All of them? And we know it was Rafiq?"

"Not exactly," Brendan replied. "Details are still coming in and the local station chief has his hands full, but who else could have pulled off that kind of stunt?"

"What about the kids, Brendan?"

"Don, wake up! We know where Roshed is"—he looked at his watch—"or where he was, at least, less than twelve hours ago. You've been trying to track him down, right? Well, here's your chance."

Don sat up, his face alert. "I'm an idiot. Of course, you're right. If I have a starting point, I can find him, and I've got just the team for the job. My three midshipmen," he said with a note of pride in his voice.

"Midshipmen? Don, this is serious. You're tracking the most wanted terrorist in the world and your crack team is three midshipmen?"

"You wouldn't believe these kids, Brendan. They're perfect for this job."

"Whatever you say, Don. Just find him."

"Will do." Don hesitated. "You didn't answer my question. What about Rafiq's kids? Are they okay?"

"I don't know. I'll find out and get back to you." Brendan ended the call.

He stared at the blank screen, collecting his thoughts. He realized he hadn't asked Marco about Roshed's children. He hadn't even really cared about the covert team, either. None of it mattered; his only interest was Roshed.

He reached for the file on Roshed, the one that never left his desk, and flipped it open to the old picture of Rafiq, before he'd had cosmetic surgery.

The most wanted terrorist in the world had the fine, clean-cut features and ice-blue eyes you might see on one of those ridiculous overpriced-perfume commercials that aired around the holidays. He could have been anything in this world, and he'd chosen to be a killer.

He flipped the page to the pictures of Roshed's children. They were teenagers now, a few years older than his and Liz's kids. How could a man with so much evil in his heart produce children so beautiful? The girl—her name was Consuela—had her father's chiseled good looks, right down to the cleft chin and the striking blue eyes. The boy, Javier, was the spitting image of his mother, with a mass of loose, ebony curls and flashing dark eyes.

He slapped the file shut. It was his job to make sure they both grew up fatherless.

Tom's face appeared in the window of his closed office door. *Baxter,* he mouthed, miming a phone with his hand. Brendan waved him in.

"Put him through, and then call back Marco Gonzalez in Buenos Aires and ask him if the children are safe."

"That's it? Are the children safe? He'll know what I'm asking about?"

Brendan nodded. "Just that: Are the children safe?"

CHAPTER 27

US Cyber Command, Fort Meade, Maryland

The man sitting next to Don Riley in the conference room had a visitor's badge clipped to the lapel of his dark blue business suit. Janet saw that Ramirez and Goodwin had left the seat between them empty. She shut the door behind her and slid into the waiting chair.

They were back at CYBERCOM, this time giving up their spring break. She knew she should feel like she was missing out—her roommates were headed to Utah for spring skiing—but this was really where she wanted to be.

Don Riley cleared his throat. "Midshipmen, this is Joe Quigley from the CIA. He's here to read you into what's known as a special access program. Do you all know what that means?"

Ramirez raised her hand. "I'll ask the dumb question, Mr. Riley. What's a special access program?"

Quigley spoke in a low, intense voice. "The United States government has a number of activities that are not public knowledge."

"Like a covert action program, sir?" Goodwin asked.

Quigley nodded. "An SAP offers an added level of

security. The information is compartmentalized such that very few people know the entire scope of the operation. That way, if someone in the field is compromised, they can only give away a piece of the puzzle." He opened a file and distributed a sheet of paper to each midshipman. "You have been selected to be read into an SAP so that Mr. Riley can utilize your skills. What you have here is a nondisclosure agreement. I urge you to read it very carefully before signing."

The tone of his instruction made Janet slow down and absorb the contents of the page. Her eyebrows went up as she read further. As excited as she was to be doing real work for CYBERCOM, the NDA gave her pause. This was serious stuff.

Janet was aware that the younger mids were watching her. She took a pen from her breast pocket and signed the document. As she handed it back to Quigley, she said, "Thank you, sir. You can count on us."

Quigley met her gaze. He had hard brown eyes that matched the intensity in his voice. "Yes, Midshipman Everett, I believe I can." He collected the signed sheets from the other two mids and stood. "They're all yours, Don. Good luck."

Riley waited until Quigley had closed the door behind him. "Do you remember the terrorist attack at the Mall of America?"

Janet nodded. She'd been entering high school when that happened.

"That was planned by a man named Rafiq Roshed, the most dangerous man no one's ever heard of. The Mall of America attack occurred at the same time as attacks in Helsinki and London. Dozens of civilians died. A trusted friend of mine was killed trying to bring Roshed down in Africa." Riley paused.

"He escaped, unfortunately, and disappeared. Recently,

we believed him to be hiding in North Korea, but we had no way of taking him down until he left the country. The game has changed." Riley opened his laptop and spun it around to face the mids. It showed a map of South America.

"Less than twelve hours ago, Roshed killed six people near a ranch in Argentina." He tapped a key that zoomed in and dropped a pin on a remote countryside location. "We know where he was, and we know he will eventually head back to North Korea. I want you three to pick up his digital trail and track him down. Passport records, flight manifests, border crossings, private jets—if you can think of it, I want you to check it out. To travel internationally, Roshed has to be on the grid somewhere. I want you to find him for me."

Janet stared at Riley. This was real spy stuff. "Why us?" she asked.

Riley grinned. "I've seen you three work together. You've been here enough times to know the systems and what we can do. I've seen Ramirez write some kick-ass code and feed Goodwin three streams of data at once. I've seen you, Everett, keep this team on task for days at a time. You three are a unit. Three brains, one output." He slapped the laptop lid shut.

"Look, I've been hunting Roshed for years. I've seen good people die. I know that we're not going to catch him by following the same old playbook. He's too smart for that. You guys are different. I'm hoping that's the edge I need to win."

Janet set her chin. "We won't let you down, sir." Ramirez and Goodwin nodded.

"There's one more thing you should all know. Remember in class at the academy when we did the case study of the power grid hack?"

The three mids nodded.

"Everett asked me if I really thought ISIS was responsible. I gave her the party line about claiming responsibility and appropriate retaliation. Well, I lied." He gave them a rueful smile. "Occupational hazard. The truth is that ISIS only claimed the credit, but the hack was done by North Korea. I firmly believe Roshed was behind that attack. I'm telling you this because he's planning something new, something big. I can feel it."

Riley leaned across the table. "Roshed will stop at nothing to bring us down. Track him down and figure out what he's up to. Whatever he's got planned, you can bet it will hurt a lot of people."

Riley sat back in his chair. "Now, get to work, Midshipmen."

CHAPTER 28

Yokosuka Naval Base, Japan

Lieutenant Commander Weston Merville's mobile phone rang just as he was crossing the bow of the USS *Blue Ridge* on his way home. Certain it was the duty officer with some stupid question about the maintenance work for the night shift, he answered without looking at the caller ID.

"Hello," he barked into the receiver. It was best to be gruff with his department, so they thought twice about calling him after-hours.

"Do you recognize my voice, Weston?"

Merville felt a chill run up his spine. *Him.* He'd waited in agony for weeks, wondering what the man from the SkyCity hotel would want him to do. And the woman, Sabrina, with the bruises around her neck and the chill of her skin . . .

It took him a few days to figure out how he'd been set up. The woman's special flask, with the sweet liqueur, had been drugged. He'd been roofied. And then they—whoever *they* were—had killed the girl and put her in his bed.

They were willing to kill someone to force him to

cooperate, so he knew they were serious, but who was behind it all? The man pretending to be a cop, with his dark hair and olive complexion, looked Middle Eastern, but his English had a Hispanic accent. Then again, maybe these clues were all designed to throw him off and the Russians were behind the whole thing.

In the weeks after the *Blue Ridge* left Australia, Merville wrestled with whether to turn himself in. He'd been compromised, that much was clear, but he hadn't actually done anything yet. A dozen times he'd approached the XO, but he always chickened out at the last minute.

His crewmates had seen him with the girl, and the fake cop had pictures of him with the girl's body. In any scenario, there would be an investigation, a scandal; his career would be over. And when he was really honest with himself in the dead of the night, his career was all he had. He had no wife, no friends, no strong family ties to speak of. If he couldn't get up every day and put on his uniform, he truly had nothing.

And besides, if he turned himself in, the guys in the Blue Dog Bar would know the truth about Sabrina, the girl he had flaunted in front of them that night. When he got back to the ship the next morning, still shaking from his encounter with the cop, they had looked at him with newfound respect. And despite the sick feeling in his stomach, he'd played along, making sly double entendres about sex during dinner in the wardroom that same night. The woman was dead! What was wrong with him?

"Weston? Are you still there?"

He'd stopped walking. People were flowing around him like he was a rock in a stream. They were all going home to their families, to people who cared about them.

"I'm still here," he whispered.

"You have a reservation at the Hitorizawa driving range in an hour. Don't be late."

The phone went dead.

Merville threw his car keys on the table and went straight to the liquor cabinet. He poured himself a healthy measure of whatever was closest at hand and drank it off in one go. The burn of the alcohol revived his brain.

He poured another shot and carried the glass to the counter. He slipped out his phone and thumbed to the XO's personal number. This was it. He was officially compromised. It was time to turn himself in.

Drink in hand, Merville poised his thumb over the call button. He waited so long the screen dimmed and went dark. Finally, he swallowed his drink and went to find his golf clubs.

Normally, the drive to the golf club was relaxing, but this afternoon Merville hunched behind the wheel of the car, barely seeing the road. He arrived early and parked, intending to stay in the car until the very last minute, but nervous energy drove him to movement.

He stalked through the aisles of the pro shop, buying a glove he didn't want and a box of tees he didn't need. As he was paying, a teenaged boy came up to him and bowed. "Lieutenant Commander Merville?"

Merville froze. Good God, were they going to make contact with him right in front of everyone?

The boy handed Merville a slip of paper. "Your reservation is for box twenty-eight. I can carry your golf clubs, sir."

"Thank you," Merville managed to reply after his heart stopped hammering.

The boy admired his custom KZG clubs as they made

their way down the row of tee boxes facing the driving range. "Very nice golf clubs, sir. Very expensive."

Merville smiled at him. "I appreciate the finer things in life," he said. The set had cost him over four thousand dollars and he didn't even like golf all that much. But every time he took those clubs to the range, someone noticed.

The boy set up his bag at the last tee box, brought him a bucket of balls, and left. Merville was sad to see him go. He was alone now, just him and his bad choices.

Might as well make this look good, he thought. He dumped out the balls and placed one on a tee. A heavy slice curved the ball far away from his intended path. Merville cursed and placed another ball, correcting his body and swing as the horrendously expensive golf pro had taught him last year. The next swing was a little better, but not much. He'd gone through a dozen shots when he heard someone clear their throat behind him.

The man was short and solidly built, his face like a blank slate. He was of Japanese descent but mixed with some other heritage that made his features seem heavier. Chinese, maybe? Is that who he was dealing with?

The man handed Merville a mobile phone.

"Hello?" he said.

"Weston, good of you to show up, but I'm a little disappointed in your game. For a guy who's using KZG clubs I expected a better performance."

Merville looked around. Four tees away was another golfer, but he was concentrating on his game. The sun was setting, darkening the edge of the course. Was he hiding in there?

"Don't bother looking around, Weston. You won't see me."

The short man in his tee box tapped him on the shoulder and handed him a USB drive the size of his thumbnail.

"My associate is giving you a thumb drive. I want you to insert this into the systems administrator server on the USS *Blue Ridge*. When the light turns green, remove the drive and throw it into the ocean."

"I can't do that!" Weston said. "There's too many people around. That server is off-limits."

"Weston, why do think I chose you? I have complete faith in your ability to get the job done."

"I won't do it!"

"Put the phone on speaker, Weston."

He touched the appropriate button. The man barked out an order in a foreign language. Not Japanese. Chinese? Russian?

The man drew a pistol from under his jacket and held it at his side.

"I just ordered my associate to shoot you if you don't put the drive in your pocket and nod to him. Ten seconds, Weston. By the way, I'll still release the pictures of dear dead Sabrina after you're gone so your ex-wife can have the satisfaction of knowing she was right about you all along."

Merville's eyes flicked to the golfer four tees away, but he was still absorbed in his game. He slid the drive into his pocket and nodded at the man with the gun.

"Wise choice, Weston. You have forty-eight hours. I'll be watching."

CHAPTER 29

*Japanese Maritime Self-Defense Force
Headquarters Ichigaya, Japan*

US Pacific Fleet Commander Tom Williams popped a quick salute as he left his car. "Be back in forty-five minutes, Petty Officer Binder," he said to his driver. He hurried up the stone steps of the JMSDF headquarters building without waiting for a reply. Admiral Hideki Tanaka valued punctuality above all else.

"Tom, how good to see you," Tanaka said as Williams was ushered through the door. "I was about to send out a search party."

"I'm two minutes late, Hideki," Williams protested.

"I thought the first rule of the Naval Academy was that on time means five minutes early, or am I mistaken?" Hideki's weather-beaten face broke into a wide smile. "But since we're old friends, I'll let you slide this time. Tea?"

"Of course." Williams followed him to the far side of the office, where a small sitting area overlooked a tiny garden. He accepted a cup of tea and gestured at the window. "It's beautiful, Hideki."

"I use that tiny bit of nature to calm myself, especially these days."

Williams sipped his drink. He'd grown to like Japanese tea. It had a heavier taste than teas from the US, but he found it satisfying. He set his cup on the lacquered table between them. "What's the latest with the Chinese?"

Tanaka shook his head. "More aggressive than we've seen them in years, and more determined than ever to push their claim on the Senkakus. Now, there's a move afoot in the National Diet to charge the Chinese with war crimes over the sinking of the Japanese fishing boat. The boat's engine was out! And they ran it down. Politicians are calling me three times a day demanding I do something, but no one seems to agree on what that should be."

Williams nodded, letting his friend vent. He'd known Hideki Tanaka since they attended the US Naval War College together as senior officers over a dozen years ago. Their families had lived on the same street near downtown Newport, Rhode Island, and many a happy evening had been shared between the Williamses and the Tanakas. That relationship had only deepened when Williams was tapped to command Seventh Fleet from their headquarters in Japan five years ago. After a two-year stint as vice chief of naval operations in DC, Williams was glad to be back in the region, this time as Commander, US Pacific Fleet, based in Pearl Harbor.

But the action right now was in the South China Sea, hence his visit to his old friend in Japan.

"I can't tell you how relieved I am that you're in charge of Pac Fleet, Tom," Hideki said. "I've got a bad feeling about this. The Chinese don't seem to be sending a message this time; I feel like they're doubling down. This could be the Big One."

The Big One—the scenario they talked about endlessly at the War College. How some minor incident triggered an out-of-control global cataclysm. Lord knew politicians around the world were talking tough about China, but no one had acted yet. Some days, Williams felt it was just a matter of time before the right mixture of oxygen and jet fuel met the spark of an international incident.

And right now, the Chinese seemed overly anxious to create as many sparks as possible.

"So, let's talk specifics, Hideki. What are they doing now that's different than six months ago?"

Hideki frowned as he sipped his tea. "The PLA Navy has always been visible in the waters off the Senkakus, but as you saw with the fishing boat, they've taken to more aggressive moves, like shouldering, to harass the fleet. The number of Chinese fishing vessels in the territorial waters around the Senkakus has doubled and they've even taken to sending over Chinese coast guard ships!"

Williams frowned. The last was a real insult to Japanese pride.

"Well, Hideki, we feel like we've gone out of our way to be patient with the Chinese and it's gotten us nowhere, so effective tomorrow, there's a new sheriff in town." He slid a manila folder from his briefcase.

"I've ordered the *Reagan* and the *Teddy Roosevelt* into the region. Three carriers send a pretty strong message that we mean business. Furthermore, the president has signed new rules of engagement that give in-theater commanders a lot more options for dealing with China's aggressive posture."

Hideki's face grew still as he listened to his old friend outline the new engagement protocol for the US fleet. He nodded when Williams finished. "That's very comforting to hear—and long overdue, I might add. Still, I'm worried about the root cause. Have your diplomats been able to glean any insight into why the Chinese have changed their tactics?"

Williams sighed and sat back in his chair. "No, we get the same old doublespeak about territorial waters and so on. That's what concerns me most. We're addressing a symptom, not the cause, and if the underlying issue isn't put to rest, we could be creating a lot of sparks."

Hideki offered a tight smile. "All the same, I'm glad to hear the US is taking these threats seriously. That will go a long way to soothe the angst of the politicians that are calling me every day."

Williams held out his cup for a refill. "We aim to please, sir. What are friends for?"

CHAPTER 30

USS Blue Ridge *(LCC-19)*
Yokosuka Naval Base, Japan

The sky was still pitch-black when Lieutenant Commander Weston Merville crossed the quarterdeck of the USS *Blue Ridge* and made his way belowdecks. He hadn't slept a wink in the previous twenty-four hours, and his nerves felt raw, exposed. He jumped as a young petty officer rounded the corner in front of him.

"Watch where you're going, goddammit!" he yelled.

"Yes, sir." The young man's eyes were red from lack of sleep; he was probably just coming off watch. "Sorry, sir."

Merville calmed his racing heart. "It's okay, just slow down, all right?"

He stepped into the wardroom and was surprised to find the XO sitting at the long table with a bowl of oatmeal. "Morning, Weston." Jason Karrick was a heavy man, with placid features and a walrus mustache. "Coffee's fresh."

"Thanks, sir." Merville's hand shook as he poured himself a mug. The tiny thumb drive felt like an anvil in the breast pocket of his khaki uniform. Surely, the

XO's presence was a sign from above that he was supposed to turn himself in. Right here, right now.

"Join me, please," the XO said. Merville pulled out a
chair and sat. He gripped his thigh to stop his foot from
jiggling.

"I come in early to avoid the temptation," the XO
said.

"Pardon, sir?"

He pointed at the bowl of oatmeal. "Cholesterol's
high and my wife says I need to lose ten pounds before I come home to San Diego. If I come in for regular breakfast, everybody'll be having bacon and eggs
and sausage and toast . . ." He sighed. "So I eat early to
avoid the temptation."

Merville nodded and sipped his coffee.

"What about you?"

Merville started. "Me?"

"Yeah, you're in awful early."

I'm going to betray my country! "I, uh, needed to talk
to the night shift," he lied. "Didn't want them to have
to stay late, being in port and all. So I came in early."

The XO spooned another glop of oatmeal into his
mouth and made a face.

"Sir, can I talk to you about something?"

The XO dropped his spoon into the bowl. "Sure,
what's up?"

Just then, the wardroom door opened, and Lieutenant Goren strode in, the duty officer keys hanging from
his neck. "Good morning, XO," he said. "And Lieutenant Commander Stud Muffin." He winked at Merville.
"Get any postcards from Down Under, sir? She was to-
tally into you."

"Lieutenant," the XO said in a sharp tone, "we were
having a conversation."

Goren flushed. "Sorry, sir, I'll grab a coffee in the

crew's mess." Silence settled over the room as the door shut behind the junior officer.

The XO considered the bowl of oatmeal, then pushed it away with a look of disgust. "You were about to say, Weston?" His eyes searched Merville's face. Surely the man could see how guilty he was, Merville thought.

Merville stood. "I need to get moving if I'm going to catch the off-going watch, sir."

The XO shrugged and turned back to his oatmeal.

Merville strode through the hard steel passageways into the heart of the USS *Blue Ridge,* the command and control center. He accessed the cipher lock that gave him entry into the server room. The room was a chilly sixty degrees, making Merville shiver in his short-sleeved uniform. The first-class petty officer on duty jerked his feet off the desk when he saw Merville.

"Good morning, sir!" He stood, shifting from foot to foot. "Chief Reynolds doesn't get in till six, sir."

"That's okay, Jurgens. Sit down. Just came in early to do a walk-through."

"Yes, sir." The petty officer stayed on his feet.

"Maintenance logs, please," Merville said. Jurgens handed him a clipboard, which Merville pretended to study. He looked around and snapped his fingers. "Petty Officer Jurgens, I left my coffee cup in my office. Can you fetch it for me? Command cup with my name on it."

"Sure, sir, but I'm still on watch."

Merville shrugged. "No problem. I'll stay here till you get back."

"Yes, sir. I'll just be a minute."

Merville waited until the door closed behind the petty officer, then moved swiftly to the server at the back of the room. His hand was steady as he unbuttoned his shirt pocket and drew out the tiny USB drive. He snapped it into the slot and folded down the keyboard. Merville drew a sharp breath as the drive registered on the screen. Twenty-five gigabytes. He hoped whatever install program was on that drive was smart enough to disguise the upload of a file that large.

Ninety seconds later, it was done. Merville unplugged the drive and slipped it back into his pocket just as he heard the cipher lock on the door click. Jurgens stood in the doorway, holding a white coffee cup with the ship's logo on the side.

"Found it, sir," he said. His gaze slid to the lowered keyboard on the system admin server.

"Thanks, Jurgens." Merville slammed the maintenance log clipboard down on the desk. "By the way, the keyboards on these servers are filthy! I want every single one of them cleaned before you go off watch."

The petty officer's face fell. "Yes, sir."

Merville was gripped by a sudden urgency to put all this behind him. He'd saved himself, that was the important thing. What was done was done. Now he could move on.

The sun was rising out of the ocean as he stepped onto the deck of the USS *Blue Ridge*. The superstructure of the ship rose behind him like a gray cliff glistening with dew in the light of the dawn. A weary petty officer wearing a white watch belt and a sidearm saluted him as he walked by. Merville returned the salute and approached the railing.

Sunlight bronzed the ripples in the water as Merville palmed the thumb drive from his pocket. With a quick flick of his wrist, the tiny device arced over the water, catching the sun for a brief moment before making a tiny splash.

CHAPTER 31

Yang-do Island, North Korea

Rafiq sipped his tea, keeping his face the very picture of calmness. The four large wall screens at the front of the stadium-style room were blank, waiting for inputs. The dozen operators sat behind their computer workstations, idle.

He'd shaved and donned his olive-green North Korean officer's uniform. The rest of the operators were similarly dressed in their best, their dark hair combed, caps resting in their laps.

"Chul, it's time," said So-won. Her thin face had a glow of excitement.

Rafiq nodded but said nothing. This was their moment of truth, the moment when they found out if their audacious plan was going to work. He was confident about their ability to control Beijing and Japan, but the Americans worried him. The US physical security was too great: too many layers, too many opportunities for failure. But every network, no matter how secure, was only as strong as its weakest link.

Rafiq believed he'd found his weak link, someone who could circumvent all that security and take Rafiq's code right to the heart of the network. But finding and compromising an inside operative was a tricky business. Some people, no matter how good they looked on paper, when faced with a moral choice found a core of confidence even they didn't know they possessed. Others, unable to live with the potential consequences, tried to hurt themselves. There were relatively few who could handle the pressure of being compromised and still perform.

Money was rarely the difference. Often the telltale pressure points were minor in the grand scheme of life, but they mattered a great deal to the individual. Things like pride. And shame.

Rafiq had a nose for weakness. He knew how to ferret out individuals with a fatal character flaw and exploit that softness to maximum effect.

Lieutenant Commander Weston Merville had been his choice. Now Rafiq would find out if he had chosen wisely.

He set his teacup down with care and leaned over the keyboard, entering the command to ping the program sleeping on the servers of the USS *Blue Ridge*.

If it was even there.

He sat back and folded his hands in his lap, waiting.

The cursor blinked as steady as a metronome beat.

"It may take some time, Chul," So-won whispered.

They were in uncharted waters. No one had any idea how long it would take for the command ping to establish contact with the program residing on the USS *Blue Ridge*.

If the program was even there. If Merville had done his job.

The cursor blinked.

This could take minutes, maybe even hours. He passed his teacup to a soldier, amazed that his grip showed not even a tremble to reveal the quaking mass of anxiety roiling in his gut.

"More tea, please," he said.

The soldier nodded and hurried off.

The cursor blinked.

What would he do if the access to the US network failed? Pak would still be pleased. The access to the Chinese and Japanese networks alone was more than enough to fulfill the assignment from the Russian Bratva. Hell, if he believed the intelligence reports from the DPRK Special Branch, the Chinese were already causing havoc in the region—and Rafiq had yet to do anything!

Pak would take credit for it, of course, but that was Pak's reason for being. Just as Rafiq could size up an individual and see immediately how the person could be exploited, Pak could size up any situation and assess his personal gain from it just as quickly. He had a nose for profit. He was just born into the wrong society.

The tea arrived and Rafiq accepted the cup without so much as a ripple in the surface of the liquid. Meanwhile, So-won shifted in her chair and fretted next to him. She reached for the keyboard and he stayed her hand.

"Wait" was all he said.

She nodded and leaned back. Rafiq sipped his tea. The operators in the room all watched them, watched *him*. What would they do if the command ping failed? Surely there was at least one spy in the group. He had chosen his people carefully, but in North Korea, spying was assumed as a fact of daily life. Children spied on parents, neighbors spied on each other, people spied on strangers on the bus. In a way, it was the genius of the DPRK: a self-policing state with a completely flat hierarchy of power. There was the Supreme Leader, then everyone else. But everyone else believed that if they could just amass a certain amount of notice, they would be elevated above the crowd. They would find themselves on a new level of power beneath the Supreme Leader.

It was a fallacy. Rafiq had seen the Supreme Leader execute peasants and his most trusted generals on the same day for the same offense: lack of loyalty. Even the great man's uncle and half brother had fallen prey to his need for unquestioned faithfulness.

Rafiq tore his eyes away from the screen and scanned the room. *At least one of you is a spy. Show yourself.*

"Look," So-won said, pointing to the screen.

The cursor had stopped blinking.

Rafiq sat up in his chair. Was the program hung up? Should he send another ping? He reached for the keyboard, but So-won stopped him.

"Wait," she said.

The cursor seemed to flicker; then a torrent of code spilled down the screen, faster than Rafiq could absorb it.

So-won, still sitting next to him, wept.

The screen resolved into a map of the western Pacific. The label at the top of the screen said US SEVENTH FLEET. As more data flowed in, new contacts began to show up on the map.

Rafiq tapped in a sequence of commands, and the wall screens at the front of the room displayed the picture. The operator's mouths opened in wonder. Spontaneously, they began cheering and clapping.

Rafiq stood and waved.

His gamble on Merville had paid off. Let the chaos begin.

CHAPTER 32

CIA Headquarters, Langley, Virginia

Martha Raddabat was a squat woman with the shoulders of a linebacker, the eyes of a fox, and the temperament of a bear. The angry, no-nonsense kind of bear, not the Gentle Ben type. She was also the CIA senior intelligence service officer, the equivalent of a two-star admiral, and Brendan's boss.

"What's going on with my brand-new, multibillion-dollar intelligence network, Captain McHugh?" Raddabat said.

"We're not sure, ma'am. It started after we turned on Piggyback, but my techs say that has nothing to do with it."

"And you believe them?" Her gaze raked across his face. She had a reputation throughout the agency as a tough boss and her temper, when engaged, was legendary, but Brendan had always found her to be fair.

"I do. We have no indication the two issues are linked. I'd rather change as few variables as possible and keep troubleshooting."

Raddabat grunted and stole a look at her wristwatch. "What's the possibility this is something more serious?"

She didn't say the word "compromised," but her message was clear to Brendan.

"We've run diagnostics and there's no evidence of any firewalls being breached anywhere," Brendan said. "I'm told there's zero chance we've been compromised. They're saying there's just a latency issue in the system."

The woman snorted. "Zero, my ass. Sounds like geekspeak for 'We don't know.'" She waved her hand. "Keep troubleshooting. Keep me posted. Don't be afraid to ask for help if you need it."

When Brendan returned to the ops center, the watch floor was abuzz with activity. Most of the techs were pulling double shifts until they fixed this latency problem.

"What's our status?" he asked the watch supervisor.

"No change, sir. We see a brief outage on a single platform, but by the time we get it back online there's no evidence of an issue. We've checked and double-checked everything." By "platform," the supervisor meant a node in the Trident viral network.

Brendan rubbed his jaw. "And it never shows up on the same platform twice?"

"We haven't seen that behavior—at least not yet."

"And we're not doing any sort of software update that would cause this type of behavior? You know, like when I update Windows I have to reboot . . ." His voice trailed off when he saw the pitying look from his supervisor.

"Sir, this is not *that* kind of system."

Brendan squinted at the wall screen, searching the eastern Med for his old ship, the *Arrogant*. "I think we need more horsepower on the problem," he said. "I'm calling CYBERCOM in for a tech assist."

The young man flushed. "Sir, I don't think that's necessary. We've got everyone here focused. It would take CYBERCOM days to get up to speed."

Brendan kept his eyes on the screen. The sour feeling in his stomach would not go away. "Your objections are noted, but I'm making the call."

Don's haggard face on the VTC screen made Brendan flinch. His friend's eyes were red-rimmed and shadowed by dark circles.

"Jesus, Don, you look like hell."

Riley replied with a tired laugh. "Whoever said age is just a number is full of shit. I'm trying to keep up with my midshipmen and it's not going well."

"Have you tracked down Roshed yet?"

"We've found a few crumbs, but the big prize still eludes us." Don scrubbed his face with both hands. "But you didn't call to talk about my problems. What's up?"

"Trident. We're getting a ton of network noise and outages ever since we turned on Piggyback. My techs say it's a latency issue, but I'm worried. I'd like a second opinion."

"Latency, huh? That's what we geeks say when we don't know what the real answer is. Tell me what's going on."

Brendan pulled out his notebook. "The whole system is based on a viral network comprised of hundreds of platforms from navy ships to merchants carrying our black boxes—"

Don held up his hand to the camera. "Brendan, you do know this is what I do for a living, right? You don't have to explain how Trident works."

"Just bear with me, Don. We're seeing intermittent outages on these platforms. A trawler drops off the grid for thirty minutes or so, then pops back on. Nothing out of the ordinary shows up on diagnostics, no firewall breach—that we can find."

"But ships come on and off the viral network all the time, right? The network is always changing. Maybe it's system capacity limits."

"True, the network elements come and go, but this seems . . . 'scheduled' is the only word I have to describe it."

Don posted his chin on his fist. "Well, to be honest, it does sound like a latency issue. Maybe. It would take some investigation to really figure that out."

Brendan saw his assistant motioning him from the window. The young man tapped his watch, a signal that Brendan was screwing up Tom's carefully crafted schedule.

"I'll check with Ops to see if someone's running a Red Team infiltration drill on you guys," Don said. "If that comes up empty, I'll see if I can put my midshipman team on your problem."

"Midshipmen? Really? That's what you got for me?"

Don grinned at the camera. "Only the best for my oldest friends, Brendan. Only the best."

CHAPTER 33

Pyongyang, North Korea

Pak looked up in surprise as Rafiq walked through his office door. Pak's new—and very attractive—secretary followed him with a flustered expression on her face.

"I'm sorry, sir," she said. "He just—"

"It's all right," Pak replied. "Jung Chul is just anxious to be early for our appointment." He waved at her to shut the door behind her.

Rafiq took a seat without invitation and slouched low in the chair. The last time Pak had seen Rafiq, he'd seemed like a caged animal. Now, his chiseled features showed a flush of energy and his eyes danced as if he was anxious to share a secret joke with Pak.

"You're looking well, my friend," Pak said.

"And you've traded in your secretary for a younger model," Rafiq shot back. "Well done, old man."

Pak bristled. "From your attitude, can I assume you are bringing me good news about the project?"

"Beware the Ides of March, Pak Myung-rok," Rafiq replied.

"What does that mean?"

Rafiq pointed at the calendar on Pak's desk. "Today.

It's the Ides of March." He waited for Pak to respond. "C'mon, Pak. Shakespeare? Julius Caesar's assassination? The first step in the Roman civil war?" Pak shrugged, and Rafiq threw up his hands in mock dismay. "Your expensive Western education was a waste of money, Pak."

The North Korean absorbed his friend's unusual high spirits with a growing sense of unease. "The project, Rafiq. What is the status of the project?"

Rafiq grinned at him for a few seconds before replying. "We are ready. I've confirmed the code is active and ready to deploy. Just say the word."

"And it will do all that you claim? You will be able to access the Chinese and Japanese networks?"

Rafiq's grin grew wider. "Oh, yes, and much more."

Pak had had about enough of this insolence. "Your orders are explicit. We want to raise tensions between China and her neighbors, not cause an international incident."

"There's an American saying about omelets and eggs. It might apply to this situation."

"Will you please be serious for a moment, Rafiq?"

The other man sat up in his chair and delivered a mocking half bow. "I apologize, Pak. My good humor has gotten the best of me, I'm afraid. Please continue; I'll do my best to contain my exuberance."

Pak placed his elbows on his desk and leaned forward. "That would be much appreciated. Now, is the project ready to launch?"

"Yes, all three sites are active and ready to deploy as soon as we have the Supreme Leader's approval."

"Three sites? I authorized two sites: Beijing and the Japanese naval base. What is the third?"

"We took advantage of proximity to develop a third option."

"Speak plainly, Rafiq. What is the third site?"

The corners of the man's lips turned up. "The American Seventh Fleet."

Pak fell back in his chair, aghast. "The Americans? How? Who gave you . . ." He thought of the Russian's warning about keeping the cyberwarfare in the virtual world. The Americans?

"No," Pak said, leaping to his feet. "Absolutely not. We are not authorized to take action against the United States. The Supreme Leader did not authorize that at all."

"Relax, Pak. It's an option at our disposal, nothing more. Why not mention it to the Supreme Leader and see what his reaction is? A trial balloon?"

Pak stared at him, acid churning in his stomach. This was his project. He was responsible. Anything that went wrong would fall completely on his shoulders.

"That is a ridiculous idea. One does not float trial balloons with the Supreme Leader, Rafiq." A misplaced trial balloon was a quick trip to a firing squad.

Rafiq shrugged. "Then we can keep it between us. Makes no difference to me."

"And?" Pak said.

"And what?"

"What do you want in return?"

To Pak's surprise, Rafiq rose to his feet and placed both hands on Pak's narrow shoulders. "My friend, you were there for me when the world was against me. I owe you everything and ask for nothing in return. Consider my debt to you paid in full."

In the blink of an eye, Rafiq's mood had turned solemn—another mood change. Pak tamped down the lingering twinge of unease. "Friendship is a treasure, Rafiq, but I prefer cash." He retrieved a slip of paper from his desk. "We've received the final payment from the Russians. Here's your cut."

Rafiq pressed the paper back into Pak's hand. "I want you to have it."

Pak's fingers closed around the slip. It was nearly four hundred thousand dollars. "I don't understand."

"Money's of no matter to me. Take it. I want you to have it."

Pak slipped the paper into his pocket, feeling suddenly guilty at having shortchanged Rafiq on his cut. "If you insist . . ."

"I do." The secret smile returned to Rafiq's lips. "And now I must take my leave, good sir." He made an elaborate bow to Pak. "I return to my island to await your call."

Pak stared at him. Had the man lost his mind with all the stress? He'd been on the run for the better part of a decade, without his family, always one step ahead of the authorities. No matter how this operation turned out, Rafiq's erratic presence could be a liability in the future—a liability he did not want the Supreme Leader blaming on him.

Pak's next trip out of North Korea would be his last. It was time to run. He'd saved enough money to live a secret life of luxury abroad, far from the clutches of the Supreme Leader.

On impulse, he hugged Rafiq. "Goodbye, my friend."

Rafiq hugged him back. Further proof that his friend was losing his mind.

"Goodbye, Pak. Take care of yourself."

Pak smiled. Taking care of himself. That was something he'd never found difficult.

CHAPTER 34

USS Key West *(SSN-722)*
International waters outside Yulin Naval Base,
Hainan, People's Republic of China

Lieutenant Commander Gordon Cremer spun the periscope barrel and dialed the handle to increase magnification.

"New contact, designated Sierra five-nine, a surfaced Chinese Shang-class submarine on this bearing. Mark." The quartermaster called out the bearing.

"Conn, Sonar, confirm contact," came the reply from the sonar shack, a few steps away.

Cremer cleared his throat. "Attention in Control, my intention is to trail our Chinese friend and see what they're up to. Diving Officer, make your depth one-five-zero feet. Set the tracking party."

The periscope optics submerged, and he activated the hydraulics to lower the scope back into the submarine. The smooth greased periscope barrel glistened as it slid into the well underneath the control room.

He turned his attention to the sonar "waterfall" display, a measure of the overall noise in the ocean around them. So named because of the snowy picture that scrolled down the monitor, the device provided a visual representation of broadband noise. Short spurts of noise, such as a whale sounding, might appear as a bright blip that traveled down the screen. Loud continuous noises, like the surfaced submarine they were seeking, showed up as a bright trace, and signals with movement relative to the *Key West* showed up as diagonal lines across the screen. It was a crude but effective way to gain a passive assessment of the world outside the submarine pressure hull.

Right now, the surfaced Chinese submarine showed up as a thick, bright trace that cut across the screen at a shallow angle.

"Conn, Sonar, Sierra five-nine is slowing. She's submerging, sir."

"Very well, Sonar. Let's establish her narrowband signature quickly so we have something to track out here."

When the Chinese submarine submerged, all the broadband prop noise on the waterfall display would disappear. The *Key West* would look for "tonals," narrow frequencies of sound from individual elements on board the sub, such as a pump whose casing was touching the hull, radiating noise into the ocean.

"Conn, Sonar, we're seeing additional ships getting under way from Yulin Naval Base."

Cremer studied the waterfall display as the new contacts registered on the screen. At this distance from the multiple contacts, all he could make out was a froth of noise that showed up as a thick white band. He stepped into the sonar shack, a cramped room filled with floor-to-ceiling displays and young sailors wearing headphones. "How many, Supe?" he asked the first-class petty officer supervising his team. He also wore headphones and routinely switched between different audio feeds as he monitored his operators.

The young man handed him a spare set of headphones. "More than two, sir. Might be as many as six."

Cremer slipped on the headphones and closed his eyes. The noise created by massive propellers thrashing seawater into foam sounded like a fleet of distant washing machines. He could make out at least two distinct platforms.

"All right," he said, handing back the headphones. "I'm calling the captain to recommend we break trail and head up top for a look-see."

Cremer strode into control and snatched a telephone handset from the rack. A few moments later, the captain entered the control room.

Captain Langford was a tall man whose features looked as if they might have been carved out of ebony. The CO's eyes flitted around control, taking in details. Cremer tried to keep up with his gaze and failed.

"Report, XO."

"Captain, we were establishing trail on a Shang-class submarine when we picked up indications of as many as six ships departing Yulin."

Langford's eyebrows ticked up a few millimeters, the equivalent of a shout for this reserved man. "Six? That would be unusual."

"I agree, sir. I recommend we break trail and investigate."

Langford rubbed his jaw. The *Key West*'s mission was to track Chinese submarines, and the best time to establish trail on a modern submarine was when it left port. Finding the ultraquiet Shang-class sub again in the open ocean would be like looking for a needle in a field of haystacks. The captain called for headphones and jacked into the sonar feed. He closed his eyes and slowed his breathing while Cremer fretted. He should have said two, not six. If he said six and they went to periscope depth and found two ships, he'd look like an idiot. If he said two and they found six, he'd be vindicated.

Langford opened his eyes. "Take us up, XO."

The scope optics broke the surface and Cremer spun in a quick circle to ensure there were no ships about to hit them. "No close contacts!"

He turned in the direction of the port and dialed up the magnification on the scope. "I have one, two, three . . . *seven* contacts in view. Two Kilo-class submarines, two destroyers, and three Yuhai-class landing ships."

He took his eyes off the scope. The captain was studying the TV monitor that mirrored the image on the periscope. "Did we receive any notice of Chinese naval exercises, XO?" Langford asked without taking his eyes off the monitor.

"No, sir."

Langford nodded. "I don't like the look of this. Let's get a flash message off to Pac Fleet while we're still at PD. Then, find that Shang-class sub again."

"Aye, aye, sir."

CHAPTER 35

US Cyber Command, Fort Meade, Maryland

Midshipman Everett knocked on Don Riley's office door. "Sir?"

Don took a second to focus on her. He'd spent the last hour concentrating on his computer screen as he went through data logs from Trident platforms that had gone offline without warning. So far, all he'd gotten for his efforts was a headache.

"What can I do for you, Janet?" He stretched his arms over his head to relieve the stress in his neck and shoulders.

"I think we found him."

"Him?" Don blinked, unsure what she was talking about. Then he sat forward in his chair. "You mean Roshed?"

She nodded.

"Show me."

The corner of the CYBERCOM watch floor had been dubbed "Midshipmen's Row" by some of the staff. Don liked to believe it was a testament to how much of their own time the three midshipmen had put in at the site, but he was sensitive to the fact that some of the permanent watch standers might not have meant the designation in a positive way. No matter. His job was to find the best people, and so far the mids had been performing.

Ramirez and Goodwin were waiting for them. Both had taken off their service dress blue jackets and rolled up the sleeves of their white uniform shirts. All three looked as exhausted as he felt, Don realized.

Everett led the briefing. "We assumed our target would be coming from somewhere in Southeast Asia between the dates you provided, so we started there. After narrowing down the pool using gender, age, and height as factors, we created a pool of candidates that had entered any airport within a day's drive of the ranch."

Don scratched his chin. "That's got to be thousands of candidates."

"Three thousand six hundred and seventy-two, sir," Goodwin said. "That's just the ones who came into South America via airports without fingerprint scanners."

Don nodded. That was one part of his disguise that Roshed would not be able to alter easily—his fingerprints. He could use overlays, but that increased his level of risk.

Everett continued, "Dre—I mean Midshipman Ramirez—figured out a way to feed video footage from the area of the murder into our facial recognition program to see if we could find a match. It took five days for us to come up with this."

Ramirez tapped her keyboard, and a grainy image of a man pumping gasoline showed on the screen. A passport photo appeared on the adjoining screen. The man's face was thicker than Don remembered, but the eyes were the same. He caught his breath. He was looking at Rafiq Roshed.

"This man entered South America via Santiago,

Chile, three days before the murders, under a Mexican passport in the name of Ricardo Matalan. To confirm, we traced the license plate number on the vehicle he was fueling. It was registered to a shell company in Uruguay, which led us to a law firm in Panama, which has ties to Guardian Security, in Sterling, Virginia. We did some digging and that's—"

"A private security firm," Don finished. "The fucker killed them all, then took their car."

The midshipmen stayed silent until Don told Everett to continue.

"Twenty-four hours after the murders, Mr. Matalan flew from Asunción, Paraguay, to Bogotá, Colombia. From there he traveled to French Polynesia. His choice of airports supports our theory that he is avoiding checkpoints that require fingerprint scans. Mr. Matalan's records say he was there on a tourist visa and intended to stay for two weeks."

Don felt a surge of hope. "So he's still there?"

Everett shook her head. "That's what we assumed at first, but he had taken so much care to hide his tracks, it seemed unlikely he would just hang out on the beach. I mean, he knows we're after him, right? He even took the mercenaries' vehicle as a way to taunt us."

Don looked at the midshipmen sharply. He hadn't told them the murdered men were mercenaries. "I'm listening."

"Less than twenty-four hours after landing in French Polynesia, this man flew from Papeete to Manila, using a Spanish passport and the name Miguel Sandoval."

Ramirez put the passport photos for both men on the screen. Sandoval had bleached-blond hair, an earring, and brown eyes, but those were just distractions. Don studied the facial structure. "What's the facial-recognition level of certainty?" he asked.

"Eighty-nine percent," said Everett.

Don pinched his lip. It seemed too easy, but Rafiq's trip to South America felt personal, not related to his mission with the North Koreans. It was possible he'd gone rogue, which meant he'd be using his aliases and fake papers as judiciously as possible.

"Where did Mr. Sandoval travel to?" he asked.

"Back to Manila, then immediately on to Osaka, Japan."

"When did he get to Japan?"

"Five days ago."

"And he's still there?"

Everett shrugged. "Impossible to tell. If he's left Japan, he didn't use any official ports."

Don nodded, more to fill the time than to offer a response. A small boat could make the trip from the Japanese west coast to North Korea in a day, and the Sea of Japan was filled with boats of all shapes and sizes.

"This is excellent work, all three of you," Don said. "I'm setting up a briefing with the J2 and CYBERCOM commanding officer for this afternoon. I want you three to give the briefing. Just like you did for me. Lay out the facts and let them absorb it, okay?"

The three were all nervous glances and smiles. "We'll be ready, sir," Everett said.

"I have no doubt," Don said, turning on his heel and hurrying away. Behind him he could hear the mids trading high-fives. Hell, they'd earned it. Because of three midshipmen, they were only a few days behind the most wanted terrorist in the world.

CHAPTER 36

Yang-do Island, North Korea

The huge wall screens showed a panoramic view of the western Pacific Ocean from the Strait of Malacca to Japan. Once he gave the signal, the seas and landmasses on the maps would fill up with hundreds of live military installations. The Chinese PLA, the Japanese JMSDF, the United States Seventh Fleet. All assets under his control.

Rafiq felt a lightness in his chest. This was what real power felt like. *His* power.

He shot a sidelong glance at the young woman seated next to him. When he first arrived in North Korea, So-won had been a lowly computer coder. He'd been sent to Covert Actions for indoctrination on Pak's word alone. He soon found that the word of Pak Myung-rok carried little weight with the military.

Without a direct endorsement from the Supreme Leader, the general in charge of the Covert Actions Division saw no need to spend any of his precious time on a foreigner. As Rafiq barely spoke any Korean yet, the assignment to teach him about the workings of North Korean covert operations fell through the bureaucratic ranks like the proverbial stone until it landed on So-won's desk. Her only distinctions were that she had no underlings to slough off the assignment to and she spoke English. Excellent English, to Rafiq's surprise.

The introverted young woman was more than happy to sit in her cubicle all day, fiddling with code and speaking to no one. But Rafiq saw the possibility in the young woman. In her, he saw native intelligence and creativity so often quashed in the DPRK youth.

She was also obsessed with the concept of machine learning, a basic form of artificial intelligence. On her own, the young woman had obtained a bootleg copy of the code for IBM's Watson computer and was experimenting with ways of modifying it for use by the department. Rafiq learned more about cyberwarfare in a few months with this girl than he had in his lifetime. Most of all, he saw a way for a small country like North Korea to have a major impact on the global stage.

His experience with changing world events was deep. The attempt to detonate a nuclear device in Minneapolis had been foiled by an alert FBI agent who had followed her instincts. In hindsight, the Minneapolis strategy had been shortsighted. To risk all his resources—and his life—on a single event was pointless, too easy to stop.

He decided he needed a bigger stage, a wider platform, to strike terror in the hearts of more people. His next attempt was to dupe impressionable Muslim youth into protests that he hoped to turn into bloodbaths that would escalate into worldwide anger. Planning those events had taken nearly two years.

Rafiq had achieved partial success. He'd managed to get a global response and excellent news coverage, but it died quickly. He needed to go even bigger, unleash even more destruction.

Cyberwarfare was the wave of the future, he was sure of it, and as time went on, his opinion was validated. The Chinese managed to hack the US Office of Personnel Management, netting millions of personnel records from US government employees. The Russians, using a combination of covert and overt attacks, successfully manipulated the US election in favor of Donald Trump. The follow-on hand-wringing of its intelligence community only served to show the weakness of the US government.

Rafiq was eventually pulled away from his new computer friend, given a new identity, and directed to perform a number of sensitive tasks for the Supreme Leader—under Pak's direction, of course.

But when he'd laid in enough political capital, Rafiq asked to create a small team of cyberwarriors with Yun So-won as their leader. He chose their first target carefully. Rafiq knew it needed to be something patriotic that would catch the Supreme Leader's fancy, so he chose a massive entertainment multinational that had just released a ridiculous movie spoofing the Supreme Leader.

Rafiq was amazed how easy it was to gain access to the private company. If these were the kind of cyberdefenses he could expect from a supposedly cutting-edge corporation, anything was possible.

Their next target was the US power grid. It was a raging success, throwing the US government into churning chaos. Then Pak got cold feet. Instead of taking credit for the hack, he convinced the Supreme Leader to allow ISIS to take credit. Rafiq was denied the sweet taste of victory yet again.

So-won came to Rafiq's office a few weeks later. "I have an idea," she said. She was still a shy young woman, but Rafiq had encouraged her to develop her new cyberoffense. "I call it Snakehead," she said, after explaining how the code worked.

Rafiq raised an eyebrow in question.

"The snakehead is a fish, an ugly beast, but it's a survivor. If the body of water it lives in is drained or becomes contaminated, the fish will crawl across land to find a new home." So-won smiled at her analogy.

"Snakehead," Rafiq said, savoring the name. "Tell me more."

The phone at Rafiq's elbow buzzed. Everyone in the room tensed. This was the call he'd been waiting for.

"Chul?" Pak's voice, and he sounded drunk.

"Yes." Rafiq kept his tone neutral. After this call, Pak's assistance would no longer be necessary.

"I've just met with the Supreme Leader. Your project has been approved. Remember, as we agreed, just the Chinese and Japanese. Is that clear? Leave the Americans out of it. We don't want this to get out of control."

"I understand." Rafiq hung up the phone.

He turned to So-won. "Bring up the Chinese network." The young woman nodded and bent over her keyboard.

The phone buzzed again. Rafiq ignored it.

The screen began to populate with Chinese ships, aircraft, and missile batteries. Rafiq had received the intelligence briefing about the Chinese sortieing their fleet in response to the Americans sending two additional aircraft carriers into the South China Sea. The area around the three Chinese claims—the Spratlys, the Paracels, and the Senkakus—was teeming with Chinese vessels. He watched as each contact appeared on the screen, then shifted from yellow to green.

"We have established control of the Chinese fleet," So-won said, her voice hoarse.

Rafiq nodded. "Bring up the Japanese network."

Slowly, the Japanese Maritime Self-Defense Force assets dotted the map. The Japanese had increased their presence in the Sea of Japan and the East China Sea. By the time all the Japanese and Chinese contacts showed green on the screen, nearly three hours had passed.

"Control over the Japanese network is in place," said So-won. She was beaming. Rafiq reached across and gently gripped her shoulder.

"Now the Americans," he said.

So-won licked her lips. For a brief moment, Rafiq wondered if the young woman might refuse. Taking on the United States was a big step. Would she question Rafiq's order?

So-won hammered at her keyboard. The US Seventh Fleet began to populate the screen, but much slower than during the prior two connections.

"What's wrong?" Rafiq asked.

So-won shook her head. "I don't understand. There seem to be many more contacts in the US fleet than there should be. The system is maxing out our bandwidth as it tries to process all the data."

"Will they be able to detect us?"

"Not a chance; the program has been running in the background for weeks, cataloging the fleet and establishing back doors. It's like tapping into a database now. All the hard work has been done." So-won shook her head. "Still, there's something wrong. I'm seeing thousands of contacts, far more than I expected."

"Should we drop the connection?" Rafiq asked.

She hesitated. "Let it run," she said finally.

So-won called a few of her programmers over, and a long discussion ensued, of which Rafiq comprehended only a fraction. Finally, the young woman turned back to Rafiq, a look of worry on her angular features.

"We've tapped into something big. The Americans

have built a massive distributed computing and communications platform. It's acting like a viral network."

"Explain."

The young woman tore off a sheet of paper. She peppered the sheet with dots. "Imagine each dot is a ship. If you want to talk to another ship and it's within line of sight, you beam your communications signal directly to them. But if you're calling a ship hundreds of miles away, you send a signal to a satellite and it beams the signal back to the other ship." She began to draw lines to connect all the dots together. "The Americans have built a network filled with line-of-sight communication nodes, so they never have to use a satellite if they don't want to or—"

"Or if the satellite isn't there," Rafiq finished.

"That's not all," So-won continued. "Each node has spare computing power, meaning that if one ship is damaged, as long as it has a communications link, it still has the ability to fight. They've built a worldwide viral network."

Rafiq studied her face. "But you're worried."

So-won nodded. "Our system can't process that many contacts. We need to install more servers." She drew a deep breath. "I recommend we disconnect from the US network—for now."

"Do it. We'll get started with the Chinese first." Rafiq pulled a bottle of rice wine from his desk drawer. He poured a measure into So-won's teacup and then into his own. He raised his cup. "Your toast, my friend."

"To Snakehead!" So-won shouted.

"To chaos," Rafiq replied. The rice wine had an aftertaste like gasoline, but to Rafiq it tasted like victory.

CHAPTER 37

Brendan stared at the giant wall screens in the Trident ops center. He sipped his coffee. "Tell me again what I'm supposed to be looking for."

"There," the watch supervisor said, pointing at the center screen. "The *Ford*. The system status hesitated for a split second before it updated."

Brendan had come to the morning briefing expecting to be happy that the intermittent system outages had passed, but his watch supervisor had told him about this new issue.

"I saw the hesitation," he said, "but isn't that just the system updating? I've been around military hardware all my working life and that kind of update lag is nothing. Besides, these ships are on the other side of the world, for God's sake."

The watch supervisor shook his head. "No, sir, that's not how these systems are designed. There should be zero lag. This is the same system they use to fly combat drones."

Brendan rubbed his chin. That made more sense.

It always amazed him how the military could operate a UAV on the other side of the world from a trailer in Creech Air Force Base in Nevada.

"What are you saying, Jenkins? We've got a hardware problem, a software glitch, we've been hacked, what? Give me something to work with here."

Jenkins threw up his hands. "Whoa, sir, no one said anything about a hack! This is system-wide; there's no way someone could break into Trident and own it like that. It's just not possible. I'd say we're looking at a relay error somewhere in the comms hardware."

Brendan tried to read the man. He was clearly bothered by the issue, but he seemed to be trying to minimize it at the same time. That kind of behavior worried Brendan. He tried a new approach.

"Let's go worst-case here, Jenkins. Say we were hacked—"

"Captain McHugh, we were not hacked. There's no way."

Brendan sat down and waved at Jenkins to do the same. He rolled his chair to close the space between them and lowered his voice. "All right, Jenkins, just you and me talking here. No attribution, we're just spitballing, okay?"

Jenkins nodded nervously.

"Good. Now, say the absolute worst case is a hack. Does that explain all these symptoms?"

"It could."

"Okay, so assume the worst for a moment. How could this happen?"

"It couldn't, sir. The firewalls are—"

Brendan resisted the urge to throttle the man. If he heard one more Ph.D. tell him how good their firewalls were, he was going to use him as a punching bag. "Enough with the firewalls, Jenkins. They're impenetrable, I get it. Is there a way into the system that doesn't involve breaching the firewalls?"

Jenkins cocked his head as he considered the question. "An inside job," he said finally.

"Meaning?"

"Someone with system administrator access could upload a program directly into Trident."

Brendan looked around the room and dropped his voice even further. "You mean someone in this room would have had to upload it?"

Jenkins shook his head. "No, sir. It could come from any Trident network node—as long as the person had system admin access, of course. The system is a viral network. Once you're inside Trident, everything is connected to everything else, that's the whole point— complete interconnectedness."

Brendan licked his lips. "But you'd see someone upload a file, right?"

Jenkins grimaced. "Probably . . . maybe. We're moving gigs of data every millisecond, sir. A few gigs here or there wouldn't be noticed, especially on the major hubs." He hesitated. "Sir, this idea's really out there. We have internal defenses designed to sniff out malware, there's no way it could get past them." He rolled back his chair. "Look, sir, I'm still on duty here. I've got to get back to work."

Brendan spun his chair to face the wall screens. Around the world, there were thousands of Trident nodes, and how many people with system admin access? Hundreds? The idea that one of them could have compromised the entire network gnawed at him. He wanted to dismiss the idea. Every single one of them had passed a security background check and annual reassessments. These were some of the most trusted people in any branch of government.

And also some of the smartest. Was it conceivable there was another Snowden out there?

Brendan didn't like to think about it, but if there was even the slightest chance that they'd been hacked, he needed to tell someone.

Martha Raddabat's executive assistant was an older man with a droopy mustache and a blue and gold bow tie. "Is she in?" He knew he was taking a risk coming to her office without an appointment.

The EA cocked a skeptical eyebrow at Brendan. "She's got five minutes before her next appointment. I assume it's important?"

Brendan nodded. The man rose from his desk and poked his head in Raddabat's office.

She stayed seated when Brendan came in the door and waved him to a chair. He perched on the edge of the cushion, feeling like a plebe on report. This was a stupid, half-cocked idea, he thought.

"I'd offer you coffee, but I don't think you'll be here that long. What's on your mind?" Her voice was raspy, and Brendan noticed a pile of cough drops on her desk. Bad timing for bad news.

"Ma'am, I'm concerned about Trident."

"You said that in our last meeting. What's the issue this time?"

"There's some latency issues—" He knew as soon as he said the word "latency" that he'd made a mistake. "Delays in data processing, I mean."

Raddabat's face was clouded. "What about the intermittent outages?"

"They're gone, ma'am."

"Well, that's good news, right? These delays—are they affecting system performance?"

"Not that we can tell, but they shouldn't be there."

"I've got a bunion on my right foot that shouldn't be there either, Captain, but I keep walking."

Brendan took a deep breath. "But what if we were hacked?"

Raddabat stared at him for a full three seconds before she said, "I suppose you have some data to back up that idea?"

"It's one possibility we're considering, ma'am," Brendan said.

"You're starting with the worst case and working backwards? I appreciate your logic, but I've got an operation to run here." She unwrapped a cough drop and popped it into her mouth. "The US taxpayers have spent billions of dollars building the most capable network in the history of the world—and it works. Some days I pinch myself. Do you know how many times we've dropped a billion or so and the project failed? I've been around awhile. It's happened. More than you think."

She softened her tone. "Look, Brendan: The director is happy, the president is happy, the Joint Chiefs are happy, even frigging Congress is off my ass at the moment. And now you come in here and tell me our network might have been hacked? Where's the data? How did it happen? Who did it? You've got to give me something besides your gut."

Brendan felt his face growing warm. "I understand, ma'am."

"Look, I know you're just doing your job, but you need to get out of my office now. Bring me something I can hang my hat on and we'll revisit this."

Minutes later, his face still red from frustration and the fast walk back to his office, Brendan was on a secure VTC link with Don Riley at CYBERCOM.

"Whoa, you look like somebody pissed in your Wheaties, man," Don said. "What happened?"

"I did a stupid thing in front of my boss. Look, you were having your team look into the Trident comms outages—what did you find?"

Don looked sheepish. "Sorry, Brendan, I put the resources on tracking Roshed. The good news is they found something."

"Really? You know where he is?"

"I know where he *was*. As of last week, our man was in Japan. The midshipmen team I told you about? They were the ones who tracked him down. I'm telling you, these guys are good."

"How good?"

Don looked at him. "Why?"

Brendan filled him in on his theory—unproven theory—that Trident had been hacked.

When he'd finished, Don looked doubtful. "Do you know how crazy you sound right now, Bren?" he said, shaking his head. "You jumped right from a few microseconds of latency to the biggest hack in the history of United States intel community? In front of your boss, no less. Really?"

Brendan gritted his teeth. He knew what it sounded like, but this whole thing smelled wrong to him. He managed a smile.

"Look, man, can you help me out here? I know you can't put real assets on it, but are your mids good enough to assess the system and tell me if there's a problem? Please?"

Don sighed and rolled his eyes. "They're here on the weekend. I'll put them on it."

After the call ended, Brendan sipped cold coffee from the mug he'd abandoned hours ago. He swished the bitter brew around his mouth as he thought.

Maybe he was looking at this backwards. Combing through every Trident node for a possible event would take weeks, if not longer. But what if he could narrow down the field?

Don's intel put Roshed in Japan in the last week. The US Seventh Fleet was headquartered in Japan. . . .

Brendan picked up the phone and called the ops center. Jenkins answered.

"Get me a list of every person with system admin access to Trident who was in Japan in the last two weeks."

CHAPTER 38

Yang-do Island, North Korea

Rafiq hadn't slept since So-won's Snakehead system had come to life. He watched the wall screens obsessively, studying how the ships from the various fleets intermingled.

The timing for his intervention could not have been better. In fact, he worried that his meddling might not even be needed to set off a spark in the region. The Chinese, always quick to defend their perceived territorial rights, were occupying forward positions in contested waters and challenging the Japanese fleet at every turn.

The Americans were repositioning aircraft carriers in the region, to include the Senkakus, no doubt intending to use the enormous ships and superior airpower as a massive show of force.

Rafiq had a window of time to act before they arrived.

He sent for So-won. She arrived in the control room within minutes, her eyes puffy with sleep.

"It's time to make our first move," Rafiq said.

So-won moved behind a pair of workstations, manned by two technicians. Rafiq changed the view on the center wall screen to zoom in on the East China

Sea between Taiwan and Okinawa. A lone Japanese destroyer, the *Sawagiri,* occupied the ocean, a forward picket for the force surrounding the Senkakus.

A combat air patrol had just taken off from Yiwi Air Base on the Chinese mainland. Four Shenyang J-16 jets, the Chinese answer to the American F-15E Strike Eagle. According to the Snakehead program, they were armed with upgraded YJ-8 antiship cruise missiles.

A perfect choice for his opening move.

"Take control of the Chinese communications network," he said to So-won. "Let's see how well the Chinese pilots follow orders. And how good the Japanese air defenses are."

Rafiq leaned back in his chair to watch the scenario unfold. The lack of sleep left him hyperaware, floating in an altered state of wakefulness. More alert, he thought, better able to perceive his next moves.

His thoughts drifted to Pak. His old friend would be blamed for this. The Supreme Leader would have dear old Pak's skull for a mantelpiece ornament. Rafiq felt a flicker of guilt, but it passed like a moth in the wind. Pak had served his purpose and Rafiq was free to discard that relationship like he had discarded all the others in his life.

Save one. Only one relationship in Rafiq's life had ever mattered. *Nadine.* If he closed his eyes, he could feel her thick curls brushing past his cheek, snagging gently in the scruff of his beard, the rich, earthy smell of her flesh, the way her body pressed down on his . . .

"Chul?" So-won's voice intruded on his thoughts.

He opened his eyes and Nadine was gone. A wave of loss passed through him. She was gone.

So-won's face held a questioning look. She glanced back at the console. "We wait for your order," she said.

Rafiq let the loss morph into anger. Rage simmered

in his belly, filling him with heat, energy, power. He stood.

"Very well," he said in a clear voice. "Order the Chinese fighters to attack the Japanese destroyer."

CHAPTER 39

Japanese destroyer Sawagiri (DDG-157)

Captain Akihiko Amori stalked onto the darkened bridge, ignoring the quartermaster's warning to all the watch standers of "Captain on the bridge."

The officer of the deck appeared at his side. "Good morning, Captain."

The CO responded with a thin smile. "Good morning, Kiko. Don't mind me, I'm just an old man who's forgotten how to get a full night's sleep."

The OOD saluted and moved away.

The captain stepped onto the bridge wing, letting the moist sea air soothe his mind. The low-hanging cloud cover left him with a hemmed-in feeling, as if the sky itself were falling. A pregnant night, he decided.

The business of running a modern warship flitted through his mind as he stared at the horizon. Two weeks they'd been on patrol near the Senkakus and already it felt much longer. It was difficult to maintain crew morale when you spent your days carving a racetrack into the ocean.

Although the Chinese were very active north of their position, his crew had seen no contact with the PLA

Navy fleet. It might be good if they did see some action, he thought. A way to break them out of their complacency. He'd studied the Chinese navy a long time, and he was convinced its behavior this time was different. The Spratlys, the Paracels, and now the Senkakus. The Chinese were solidifying their grip on this region of the world, and few would stand in their way.

There was a buzz of activity on the bridge, and the OOD appeared in the doorway. "Captain, CIC reports two incoming PLA fast-movers from Yiwi Air Base on the mainland." Another burst of dialogue behind him, and the OOD leaned backwards for a second, listening. "Make that four, sir."

"Very well." The captain followed his OOD back onto the bridge. A routine combat air patrol, no doubt.

"CIC reports the contacts are on an intercept course with our position, sir."

The captain shook his head. Aviators, always showing off. They'd probably perform some low-level flyby to show their incredible speed, then head back home. For a brief moment, Captain Amori considered setting general quarters and lighting up the Chinese flyboys with the *Sawagiri*'s OPS-24 fire-control array. He smiled to himself, then dismissed the thought. Their orders were not to provoke their PLA foes.

"Time to intercept?" he asked.

"Three minutes, Captain."

The captain borrowed the OOD's binoculars and stepped out onto the bridge wing again. At least he could enjoy the show.

Even though they had their navigation lights on, they came in so fast he almost missed them in the darkness. He managed to catch a glimpse of one jet. It was one of the new Shenyangs, and it was carrying missiles. His ears rang from the thunderous roar of their engines.

A few seconds later, the OOD appeared in the doorway. "The jets broke to the north, sir. It looks like they're setting up for another pass."

Captain Amori had had enough. He strode onto the bridge and picked up a handset to connect him with the CIC watch officer. "CIC, this is the captain, anything showing on ESM?"

"No, sir. The scope is clear . . . wait." The man's voice seized with concern. "Incoming contacts. Four, six, eight contacts, moving at Mach two. Bearing two-six-three. They're missiles, sir!"

Captain Amori dropped the handset and rapped out orders automatically. "Left full rudder, steady new course two-six-three. All ahead flank. Sound general quarters!"

The alarm pulsed through the ship like a living thing. The captain believed he could feel the drum of footsteps on steel deck plates.

"CIC," he barked. "Range to incoming contacts."

"Fifteen miles and closing, sir."

"Fire chaff at six miles."

"Fire chaff at six miles, aye, sir."

Seconds later, the captain heard the chaff canisters on the ship's deck launch with a *pop,* and an explosion of tiny metal fibers filled the air around them. The cloud would create an enormous target for the radars on the incoming missiles, much larger than the *Sawagiri.* At the same time, the wind would carry the chaff cloud away from the actual ship's location. Hopefully.

"Captain!" The OOD was pointing out the front windows of the bridge, his binoculars clamped to his eyes.

Captain Amori could see the points of light on the horizon, closing fast. They leaped across the open sea and slammed one after another into the hull of the *Sawagiri.*

One . . . the deck buckled under his feet.

Two . . . the bridge windows shattered inward.

Three . . . the blast swept the captain off his feet and smashed him back against the cold steel bulkhead.

Captain Amori snapped awake into a tilted world. He raised his head. The front of the bridge was gone. He struggled to his knees and found the tilted sensation was not his addled imagination. The ship was listing to starboard, the angle increasing with every passing second.

He pawed at a khaki-clad body next to his. The OOD. He blinked. Kiko's head was missing.

He crawled forward and gripped the 1MC handset. "Damage report," he said. His voice echoed around him. The captain looked again at the where the bow of his ship should be, dark water swirling over the remains of the deck.

Hopeless.

"All hands, abandon ship," he said into the handset. Again, his voice echoed through what was left of the *Sawagiri.*

"Captain?" said a petty officer, crawling in from the bridge wing. "We have to go, sir."

Amori nodded and let the young man help him to his feet. His left leg would not respond, so he slung his arm over the petty officer's shoulder for support. Together, they hobbled onto the twisted metal stub that had been the bridge wing.

Bright yellow rafts had deployed automatically. They bobbed merrily on the black sea, lights blinking. A few heads poked out of the water, far fewer than the *Sawagiri*'s crew of two hundred.

The ship groaned and lurched to starboard. Any second now, she would roll.

"We need to jump, sir." The water was only a few meters away.

Amori leaned forward, letting gravity tear him away from the dying *Sawagiri*.

CHAPTER 40

He'd gotten away with it. That was Lieutenant Commander Weston Merville's conclusion. In retrospect, he wasn't really sure what he expected to happen. Red flashing lights? Armed men breaking down the door of the server room?

Instead, nothing had happened. He'd monitored system performance across the Seventh Fleet, and while the ships at sea were whining about latency issues and random comms outages, what network didn't have those issues?

Not only had he gotten away with it, he'd outsmarted them all. His gamble had paid off. As usual.

Not that he hadn't had some sleepless nights. Merville had installed security cameras around his house and packed a "go bag" in case he needed to leave town quickly. But none of that had been needed—all because he was smarter than the average bear.

It was as simple as that. Now if these dolts he worked for would just recognize him for the genius he was, his life would be complete.

The phone on his desk buzzed, signifying an internal call.

"Merville," he answered.

"Weston, it's the XO. I need to see you in my stateroom ASAP."

A finger of doubt probed Merville's gut. "Right away, sir. What's it about?"

"Just get up here."

It was nothing, he told himself on the way up to see the XO. He knocked on the door, opening it when he received a gruff "Come!"

The XO was not alone. A pair of civilians, a man and a woman, occupied the sofa wedged against the wall, visitor's badges clipped to their lapels. They stood when Merville entered. He tried not to stare at the woman's sidearm.

"You wanted to see me, XO?"

Commander Jason Karrick heaved himself out of his chair, motioning to the visitors. "Agents Mincer and Zach. NCIS."

"Like the TV show?" Merville said with a smile.

The woman seemed to be in charge. She flexed the corners of her lips at his comment.

"They're here on serious business, Weston. NCIS believes a breach in the Trident network originated from this ship."

It took an act of will for Merville to maintain his smile. "Here? Part of my team? That's not possible."

"It's possible, sir," the woman said. She had a throaty growl in her tone that might have been appealing if she actually smiled. "The fleet was infected with a computer virus that started from this ship."

"You're sure?" Merville said.

The woman did not answer him. He flicked his gaze

to the XO. Karrick's round face was flushed red, and his walrus mustache quivered.

"I'm sorry, Weston, but it was Petty Officer Jurgens."

Merville's vision went out of focus for a second as relief swept through his body.

"Jurgens, sir? A spy? You're sure?"

The man spoke finally. He held out a photocopied paper with three dates circled in red. "It happened on one of these three days, sir. Probably during a maintenance period on the night shift. Jurgens was the only watch stander on the night shift all three days with system admin access." He paused. "Unless you know differently."

Merville studied the paper with steady hands. "No, that's correct. Petty Officer Jurgens always takes that shift when we're in port. He's going to school, uses the time to study." He handed it back. "You know he's off today, right?"

Agent Mincer nodded. "We have him under surveillance, hoping he does something we can use as leverage. Before we picked him up, we wanted to let the command know what was happening. See if there's anything you can add."

Merville shook his head, his face a mask of concern. "Jurgens is a good sailor. I'm having a hard time believing he did something like this. How good is your case against him?"

"Circumstantial," Mincer said. "We've had to backtrack through logs and reconstruct events. The original virus disappeared after being uploaded, which is why we've had such trouble pinpointing the origin site. We may need your expertise after we question Jurgens, sir."

"You've got it, Agents. Whatever I can do to help."

When the NCIS agents were gone, the XO collapsed in his chair. "I can't believe it, Weston. Jurgens? A traitor?"

A sudden thought struck Merville. He'd taken care of the video logs and the record of the cipher lock on the computer space being opened, but what about Jurgens himself? He would tell them Merville had been alone in the server room. Would he remember the keyboard on the system admin computer being down?

Merville stayed just under the speed limit all the way home. Pre-rush-hour traffic was light, and he checked his rearview mirror frequently to see if anyone was following him.

He needed to think, maybe even run. At least he needed to be in a position to take action. The plan was to pick up his go bag and spend the night in a cash-only hotel under an assumed name from a fake passport. If things went south, he needed options.

In the morning, assuming all was clear, he'd just show back up to work as if nothing had happened.

He pulled in to his garage and immediately lowered the door. The house was silent and stuffy, since the timer on the air-conditioning hadn't kicked in yet. He dropped his keys on the table and bounded up the steps to the spare bedroom.

In spite of the danger, he felt a thrill of excitement. Sometime over the last week or so, his fearful thoughts had shifted to dreams where he was the hero, a Bond-like character who had every detail planned out, staying one step ahead of his less-capable pursuers.

In the bedroom closet, he pulled up the carpet and pried up the square of plywood he'd cut out of the floor to create a space to hide his go bag. In there, he had it all: cash in multiple currencies, a forged passport, clothes, even a wig and glasses in case he needed a disguise.

Merville drew in a sharp breath. The space was empty.

He reached his hand into the opening, grasping at air, still not comprehending the situation.

Merville scrambled to his feet and ran into the hall. He needed to get away. Now. He descended the stairs two at a time into his kitchen.

NCIS agent Mincer stood behind his kitchen table, the contents of his go bag emptied onto the wooden surface. Behind him, the air-conditioning kicked on. Mincer's lips flexed, and she spoke in her husky voice.

"Lieutenant Commander Merville, you are under arrest for treason."

CHAPTER 41

North of Fiery Cross Reef
Spratly Islands, South China Sea

There was nothing better than seeing the sunrise from the cockpit of a fighter plane, thought Lieutenant Liu Wen. He nudged the stick, and the aircraft banked in a long, sweeping curve to starboard.

He and his wingman had just been ordered to monitor another US Navy aircraft that had violated China's sovereign airspace off the Spratly Islands to the west of the Philippines. Wen didn't really follow politics, and the Spratlys seemed an awful long way from the Chinese mainland, but whatever gave him an excuse to fly was fine with him.

The warning from the land-based crew on Fiery Cross Reef came across his radio: "United States Navy aircraft, you are in violation of the territorial waters of the People's Republic of China. Reverse course immediately."

The American response came back immediately. "This is US Navy aircraft. Be advised we are operating in international airspace. We intend to maintain course and speed."

A message from the Ground Control intercept station on Fiery Cross Reef flashed on Wen's heads-up display. *Flyby on US aircraft is authorized.*

Wen acknowledged the order. Ground Control had left the mission parameters up to him, so in his mind, supersonic was a viable option. At least, they hadn't said it wasn't allowed. Besides, what were the Americans going to do about it? Complain to his wing commander?

He glanced out the window at his wingman and keyed his radio. "You take port, I'll take starboard side. Match my speed."

He steered toward the blip on his radar and hit the afterburners, grinning as the g-forces crushed him back into his seat. Out of the corner of his left eye, he saw Dang, his wingman. He had his sun visor snapped down against the glare of the new morning. His oxygen mask hid the matching grin Wen knew was there.

He spotted the American aircraft on the horizon, a P-8 Poseidon, really just a glorified 737 commercial jet. Nothing like the sleek, powerful weapon of the sky that he commanded.

He and Dang rocketed by the Poseidon at a closing speed well over Mach 1. He imagined he glimpsed the shocked faces of the US Navy pilots as his plane broke the sound barrier right next to their cockpit. Over the radio, he heard Dang laughing.

The US Navy pilot came back on the radio, his tone angry, almost shouting his message. "We are a US Navy aircraft operating in international airspace. Please refrain from supersonic flybys. Such moves are dangerous and could cause the loss of both of our aircraft."

Ground Control started in with their standard script.

Wen put his aircraft into a wide turn. "We've got the fuel. How about we go again, Dang?"

His copilot agreed. Wen laid in a course and was just about to punch the throttle when his heads-up display pinged him with another message.

Weapons release authorized. Destroy enemy maritime patrol aircraft.

Wen blinked and reread the message. What the hell? Those bastards in Beijing must have lost their minds. This was peacetime. In most cases, even doing a supersonic flyby was enough to get you called up in front of the wing commander. He'd only risked it because things seemed to have gotten a little looser of late.

He keyed his radio. "You got this engagement message?" he asked Dang.

"Yeah." Right now, Dang was probably glad he wasn't the mission commander.

Wen punched in a response. *No hostile intent with US aircraft. Request you confirm engagement orders.*

The confirmation came back within seconds. Far faster than he would have expected military bureaucracy to move.

Destroy enemy maritime patrol aircraft.

Wen keyed his radio. "Attack order confirmed. On me." He punched the arming sequence on the PL-21 air-to-air missiles slung under his wings. His pulse thundered in his ears as the full import of the order hit home. He was about to shoot down another aircraft. For real. *Be calm,* he told himself. *You've done this exercise hundreds of times in simulators.*

The Poseidon, twenty miles ahead of him, had not deviated from its prior course and speed. Wen eased his aircraft into a trail position and energized the EOTS-86 fire-control radar. He could imagine the panic in the

American crew when they heard the warbling of the deadly radar.

The fire-control system issued a flat tone, indicating a lock. Wen toggled the first missile. The jet gave a slight lurch as the long projectile dropped from the wing; then the missile's booster kicked in, and it shot forward in a trail of fire. "Missile one away."

He repeated the sequence. "Missile two away."

He felt . . . nothing. He'd completed those actions so many times he could have done them with his eyes closed. "Time to impact: thirty-eight seconds." Wen kept one eye on the radar, the other on the horizon. The system registered two hits. A gray smudge appeared on the clean line that defined the border between the sea and the sky.

Wen keyed his radio. "Let's go in for a look." He eased the throttle forward, feeling the jet respond to his command.

The Poseidon's port engine was gone, and she had a gaping hole in her starboard side. The plane was depressurized and the control surfaces on the port wing were hardly functional, but somehow the pilot had managed to keep the plane in the air. Wen was impressed.

His radio squawked. "Mayday, Mayday, Mayday, this is US Navy patrol aircraft—"

"Dang, finish them off," Wen ordered.

"Yes, sir." Dang never called him "sir."

Wen watched as first one, then a second PL-21 missile streaked off the rails of Dang's jet. They crossed the distance between their position and the foundering Poseidon in seconds. The first missile passed directly through the fuselage, exploding in a spectacular ball of flame. The second missile only added to the carnage.

Chunks of fire rained down on a slate-blue sea.

Smoke formed a dark cloud in an otherwise pristine morning. It was already starting to dissipate.

There were no parachutes.

Lieutenant Liu Wen messaged back to Ground Control.

Target destroyed.

CHAPTER 42

USS Gerald R. Ford *(CVN-78)*
100 miles south of Taiwan

Admiral Manolo reread the flash message. The Japanese destroyer *Sawagiri* had fallen off the comms network a few hours ago and was now designated as lost at sea. The Japanese had already started a search for the missing ship and were asking for American air assets to join in. Most troubling of all, they were blaming the Chinese.

He handed the message to the lieutenant running the BattleSpace display. "Show me these coordinates." The man snapped down his VR goggles and manipulated his right hand in space. The 3-D display loomed out, then collapsed in on the new coordinates.

"What range, Admiral?" the operator said.

Manolo chewed his lip. "Hundred-mile radius on the last known position."

There were three Japanese UH-60J search-and-rescue helos crisscrossing the display, and two JMSDF warships. A red pin pulsed at the last known position of the *Sawagiri.*

"Show me all historical activity in the area for the last eight hours, Lieutenant."

BattleSpace took a long time to update. "The only

activity in the database is a Chinese flyby about five hours ago, sir. Looks like four Chinese Shenyangs out of Yiwi. The quality of the information is pretty spotty because the system was offline for part of it. I'll play out what we have."

The four red tracks entered the BattleSpace display on an intercept track for the *Sawagiri,* then stopped about twenty-five miles short. "That's all we have, sir," the operator said with a note of apology in his voice.

When BattleSpace first entered the fleet, it had been nicknamed the BS system for the quality of the information it provided. As command and control networks advanced, so too did BattleSpace, until it was the primary decision-making tool for fleet commanders. This kind of poor coverage was like a throwback to the old days. Manolo fretted that his staff might not know what to do without their holographic view of the world.

He studied the high-tech display. Would the Chinese be stupid enough to start a shooting war over a few rocks in the middle of an ocean? Up until the last week his answer would have been an emphatic *no.* But now . . . his gut told him otherwise.

The air wing commander, Captain Diane Henderson, loomed out of the dimness of Flag Watch. "Sir?"

"Yeah?" Manolo managed to tear his eyes from the BattleSpace display. Henderson's look told him that more bad news was coming.

"Sir, we've lost contact with a P-8 we had en route from Okinawa to Singapore. FONOPs mission through the Spratlys." She motioned to the operator to reconfigure the 3-D display.

The table zoomed out, then dropped in on a block of water near the Spratly Islands, southwest of the Philippines. Another red pulsing pin showed on the display. "What do you mean lost contact?" Manolo said.

Henderson fidgeted. "We're still having major comms issues, so it could be nothing. Still, they should have checked in an hour ago." She hesitated. "There's more, sir. We were tracking a Chinese CAP, two J-20s, in the area before we lost contact with the P-8. There's no evidence the two incidents are related, but I've got a bad feeling about this."

Manolo felt his jaw tighten. First the *Sawagiri* mysteriously disappeared, then a Poseidon didn't check in, and the common denominators were communication issues and Chinese fighter aircraft. "Get Gutterman in here," Manolo said.

Captain Jim Gutterman, CO of the *Ford,* was standing in front of his boss within five minutes.

"Jim, I'm hearing a lot of chatter about comms issues. What's going on?"

Gutterman's prominent jaw was rough with salt-and-pepper stubble. "I wish I had a good answer for you, sir. I've got every man jack working on it, but frankly it's kicking our ass. As soon as we think we've got the problem solved, it seems to jump to a new system. Even my best people have never seen anything like it. We've had to resort to cold-starting every hour."

Henderson showed up again, lines of worry carved on her face. "Sir, sorry to interrupt, but we've got unconfirmed reports of a navy Poseidon sending out a Mayday off the Spratlys." Her face went tight. "It came in off the internet, so I'm not calling it real—yet. But it's too much of a coincidence that we're missing a P-8 and rumors start showing up . . ."

Manolo let a blast of anger show. "I will not run the goddamn navy from fucking Twitter. Get me some facts. Now."

Henderson nodded. "Aye, aye, sir."

Manolo turned to Gutterman. "I don't like this

situation one goddamn bit, Jim. I'm putting the strike force at general quarters." Manolo barked at his Flag Watch team. "Get me Seventh Fleet on the horn ASAP."

Manolo experienced the communications issues first-hand over the next fifteen minutes. After three tries using the secure military EHF, he was forced to speak to his boss using an Iridium commercial satellite phone.

He stepped onto Vulture's Row and looked down on the flight deck of the *Ford* as he briefed the Seventh Fleet commander on the situation.

"First the Japanese destroyer missing and now a Poseidon possibly lost—it's just too much of a coincidence for me, sir. I've put my carrier strike force at GQ. But I wanted to make sure we're on the same page in terms of response. This could get ugly real fast."

"I agree, Manny," his boss replied. "The new rules of engagement give us much more leeway. From here on out, you will interpret any Chinese provocations as hostile, understood? If the destroyer and the P-8 really were attacked, then this has already turned into a shooting war and we just don't know it yet. Use your fire-control radars. If they shoot, you blow them out of the water, is that clear?"

"Yes, sir."

"And get your comms outages fixed. We've got a navy to run."

CHAPTER 43

Lieutenant Commander Cremer yawned, stretched, and gulped his third cup of coffee in the last hour. At this rate of caffeine consumption, they'd be peeling him out of the overhead by the end of the watch. He stared at the waterfall sonar display. The wide white line running down the side of the display was the USS *Ford* carrier strike group, still nearly fifty miles away.

Cremer made a circuit of the control room watch standers: diving officer, fire-control technician, quartermaster, and the three-man tracking party. The officer of the deck was one of their more promising junior officers but only recently qualified, hence Cremer's presence as a senior adviser while the submarine was in trail of a Chinese sub.

Trailing another submerged contact was like playing a game of 3-D chess blindfolded—a delicate dance of staying hidden in the other submarine's baffles, the acoustic blind spot behind their screw, but still remaining close enough to hear their target. Since they relied entirely on passive information, it often took precious minutes to gain a clear picture of the tactical situation.

That lag had drawbacks: if the submarine you were trailing had just reversed course, you might not know it until he was right on top of you, the so-called Crazy Ivan maneuver from the Cold War. Understanding a complex tactical situation was a lot of responsibility to put on the shoulders of a newly qualified, twenty-four-year-old lieutenant junior grade.

"Conn, Sonar, contact aspect ratio is changing . . . he's turning, sir. Possibly clearing baffles."

Cremer bit back his automatic response, allowing Lieutenant (j.g.) Dawkins to respond with "Sonar, Conn, aye."

"What's your next move, OOD?" Cremer asked.

As Dawkins studied the sonar display, Cremer prompted him. "Let's think about the big picture here." He led the junior officer to the tracking chart. "This guy is obviously in transit. He's not running drills, he clears baffles on a set schedule every hour, he's just driving straight. When was the last time he went to PD?"

The young officer gave Cremer a blank look and earned a disappointed headshaking in response. "You should have gotten that from your watch turnover," Cremer said. "Quartermaster, when did our Chinese friend last make a trip to periscope depth?"

"Six hours ago, sir," came the crisp reply. The tracking team was enjoying seeing the young OOD squirm. Cremer pulled him back to the sonar display, away from the tracking party. "If we have to clear traffic every eight hours, you can bet they're on some kind of similar schedule, right?"

Dawkins nodded.

"Conn, Sonar, contact is slowing and we're detecting hull popping noises. He's headed to PD, sir."

"Sonar, Conn, aye," Dawkins said. Even in the dimness of the control room, Cremer could see the young man blushing. Good, that meant he wouldn't forget this lesson.

"Let's break trail and make a trip topside to get our own radio traffic, OOD," Cremer said.

"Aye, aye, sir." Dawkins's tone told him the kid had recovered from his embarrassment. He slid into the familiar routine of taking the ship shallow and clearing their own acoustic baffles before they ventured to periscope depth.

"Request permission to raise the mast and query the satellite," said the radio operator when they were at PD. Cremer watched the monitor while Dawkins manned the periscope. It looked like a beautiful morning in the South China Sea.

"Permission granted, Radio," the OOD called out, never taking his eyes away from the scope.

A sharp burst of static sounded, indicating that the radio operator had sent a signal to the satellite.

"Conn, Radio, we got no response from the satellite. Request permission to retransmit."

Cremer put a hand on Dawkins's shoulder before the young officer could reply. "Radio, this is the XO. Recheck your lineup and retransmit." Every bit of electromagnetic signal they released was another opportunity for them to be detected. He let irritation bleed into his voice. That was just sloppy work. Here they were, sitting on China's doorstep and having to retransmit!

"Aye, sir. Lineup rechecked. Retransmitting."

Cremer waited.

"Conn, Radio, no response from the satellite."

Cremer said to the OOD, "I'll be in Radio."

The radioman on watch held the locked door open so the XO didn't have to input the cipher. "It's not on our end, sir. I checked and rechecked. The satellite's not responding."

Cremer studied the young petty officer second class. He had a reputation for being a smart kid and detail-oriented. Maybe there was something wrong with the satellite. "Is there an alternate bird we can query?"

The radioman nodded. "We've got another coming into range in three minutes."

Cremer chewed his lip. "All right, check everything again and query the new bird as soon as it's available." He pulled a handset off the rack and dialed the captain's cabin.

"XO, sir. We weren't able to clear traffic." He shot a look at the sweating radioman. "We believe it's a satellite problem, so my intention is to stay at PD and catch another bird in about two minutes." He waited for the CO's assent, then ended the call.

By the time he was back in the control room, Captain Langford was there. The XO spoke to his captain in a low tone. "Sir, Williams is on watch in radio. If he made a mistake on the first query, I seriously doubt he'd make the same mistake again." Cremer couldn't remember the last time they'd experienced an unannounced satellite outage.

"Conn, Radio, querying the satellite." A short burst of static followed. "No response from the satellite, sir."

Cremer raised his voice. "Chief of the Watch, have the radioman chief lay to the radio room ASAP."

Captain Langford pinched his lip. "Radio, this is the captain. Raise the BRD-7 mast. See what you can find on commercial traffic. XO, go listen in while the chief works the problem."

Cremer entered the tiny radio space and slipped on a pair of headphones. "What do you want to hear, sir?" Petty Officer Williams asked.

"Gimme CNN, I guess," he said.

He caught the tail end of a commercial; then the

top-of-the-hour news summary began. "Our top story this hour is the reported loss of a US Navy maritime patrol aircraft near the Spratly Islands, southwest of the Philippines. A commercial fishing vessel reported a Mayday call from the US Navy aircraft early this morning. The island chain has been a source of friction between the United States and China, which claims the islands as part of its territorial waters. Sources tell CNN the US Navy P-8 Poseidon aircraft was shot down while on a routine freedom of navigation flight near the contested Fiery Cross Reef in the Spratly Islands. There has been no official confirmation from either the Chinese or the United States."

Cremer snatched the mic from the hook over the operator's head. "Captain to Radio, sir."

Langford appeared a few seconds later, concern etched on his face, and Cremer stepped aside so his CO could edge past him to the headphones. Langford's stern face went still as he listened to the CNN broadcast.

He ripped off the headphones and said to Cremer, "Take us deep, XO. And find that Chinese submarine."

CHAPTER 44

Chinese submarine Changzheng 5

Alone in his tiny cabin, Captain Sun reread the flash message from South Sea Fleet headquarters.

Intercept US carrier. Launch attack. The latest co-ordinates, speed, and direction of the American carrier strike group ended the message.

The message was classified as eyes-only for the captain.

This was insanity, he thought. A US carrier had lay-ers of protection—destroyers, antisubmarine aircraft, other submarines. To attack such a ship was madness. Unless . . .

He put down the message and picked up his tea. The surface of the amber liquid quivered.

Unless this was a preemptive strike against the Amer-icans, a move to even the odds before the real battle be-gan. In a way, it made sense; the US had three aircraft carriers in the waters around the Chinese homeland. The Chinese had one, and she was untested in combat of any kind. Nearly all Chinese air power had to launch from land-based sites, a distinct disadvantage against the highly mobile American navy.

But a preemptive attack, a submarine attack, on one or more carriers could tilt the scales a bit in China's favor. And the Americans would be caught unawares. They would be at a peacetime posture, ready, dangerous, but unsuspecting. If he could get close enough, his missiles just might be able to penetrate the layers of defense that surrounded the aircraft carrier.

Captain Sun strode into the control room, nodding curtly at the officer of the deck. He made his way to the quartermaster's plot, where he read off the coordinates from the message. The young quartermaster found the spot and marked it with a pencil. The captain read off the last known course and speed, and the petty officer turned the dot into a vector. Nearly fifty miles distant, running perpendicular to their own track.

"OOD," the captain called. He tapped the track of the US carrier group. "Make best possible speed to intercept this track."

The deck of the *Changzheng 5* tilted forward as the ship went deep. The pressure hull popped and creaked, and the powerful engines made the deck plates quiver under his feet.

USS Key West (SSN-722)

Cremer paced back and forth between the diving officer's chair and the sonar shack. While the *Key West* had wasted precious minutes at periscope depth waiting for satellite availability, the Chinese sub had disappeared.

"Anything, Sonar?" he called out. That was his third request in ten minutes, and the sonar supervisor made no attempt to hide his frustration in his response.

"Conn, Sonar, we're not seeing him, sir. Recommend you come to new course one-eight-seven to give another angle on the array and change depth to three-five-zero fifty feet."

Cremer gave the orders for the recommended depth and course, then resumed his pacing.

Reacquiring a submerged contact after breaking trail was a tricky business. You could make assumptions about his course and speed, but they were only guesses. If the Chinese sub had received new tasking during his trip to periscope depth, he could be headed in any direction at any speed. Or he could have rigged for ultraquiet and reduced his speed to fool his American trackers.

Cremer stopped. If the Chinese boat had received new orders . . . what if his new tasking was to intercept the *Ford* strike group?

"Sonar, assume our contact is attempting to intercept the carrier strike group. Focus your search on that bearing."

"Aye, aye, sir. This new depth is much clearer. Stand by."

The minutes ticked by and Cremer paced. He accepted a fresh cup of coffee from a steward and sipped as he walked. Five steps across the control room, turn, five steps back.

"Conn, Sonar, we've got him. Hull pops indicate he's changing depth. It looks like he's going deep and increasing speed."

"Give me your best guess on course and speed, Sonar. I intend to stay with him."

Cremer had the quartermaster lay out the Chinese sub's vector as well as the last information they had about the *Ford* carrier group. He called the captain.

Captain Langford loomed over the chart, listening to Cremer's theory. He nodded gravely. "You recommend we try to trail him at speed, XO?"

"Normally, sir, I'd say we go to PD and phone home, but if we can't rely on the satellites that would just be a waste of time. I say we stick with this guy and see what he's up to."

Langford tapped the chart a few inches ahead of the carrier strike group's track. "There's another option. We try to get there first and wait for him."

Cremer hesitated. Their passive sensors were useless at high speed. If his guess about the Chinese boat's final destination was wrong, they'd never find him again. "What if he doesn't show?"

"Then my faith in the sanity of man will have been restored, XO." He looked at the quartermaster. "Plot a course to this point."

When the USS *Key West* slowed more than two hours later, Cremer waited impatiently in the entrance to the sonar shack. They'd gone deep and run as fast as possible without causing cavitation of the massive screw that drove the submarine.

He glared at the four sonar operators, trying to will them to find the Chinese submarine.

"Sir, it's going to take a few minutes," said their supervisor. "We need to recalibrate the towed array and do a full sweep before we can tell you anything."

Cremer stepped back into the control room, resuming his pacing. The captain stood between the scope wells, his feet planted, arms crossed.

"Conn, Sonar, we've got a possible contact bearing two-seven-three. The signal's weak, but the tonals match. I think it's our guy, sir."

Cremer breathed a sigh of relief. "Good job, Sonar—"

"Conn, Sonar, we're getting transients! He's flooding tubes and opening outer doors!"

A burst of sonic energy from the transient noise showed up as a bright spot on the waterfall display.

"Conn, he's launching, sir!"

Captain Langford's voice rapped out, "Snapshot, tube one, bearing two-seven-three."

At the sound of the emergency launch order, the fire-control technician sprang into action, punching buttons to flood the torpedo tube, open outer doors, and launch a weapon. Seconds later, Cremer's ears popped as the pressure changed in the ship due to the torpedo launch.

The general-quarters alarm pulsed in the background. "Sonar, report!"

"Contact launched two weapons, sir. Looks like cruise missiles. He's on the move, sir."

"What about our torpedo?"

"Torpedo is acquiring, sir. Shifting to high speed." Sonar put the audio feed over the intercom. The high-pitched drone of the torpedo's engine was interspersed with sharp pings from its active sonar. The pings shifted to a steady beat that increased in intensity as the seconds crawled by.

"Torpedo has acquired, sir."

The explosion of the Chinese submarine exceeded the range of speakers. The USS *Key West* rocked gently in the depths of the China Sea.

CHAPTER 45

USS Gerald R. Ford *(CVN-78)*

Rear Admiral Han Manolo could almost hear his wife's voice echoing in his head: *They're professionals. They know what they're doing and you screaming at them is not going to make them work any faster.*

He folded his arms, gripped his biceps until it hurt, and kept his mouth shut as the barely controlled chaos roiled around him in the Flag Watch of the *Ford*.

The strike group was still at general quarters—and would stay there until they had reliable communications restored—so he had a petty officer on sound-powered phones following him everywhere he went in Flag Watch, feeding him updates from around the ship.

"Bridge reports they have restored ship-to-ship secure comms, sir," said the petty officer.

Manolo nodded in response.

A lone voice cut through the hubbub of Flag Watch. "We've got incoming! Two missiles, port side. Probably submarine-launched . . . time to impact . . . *one minute.*"

Manolo rushed to Vulture's Row, shading his eyes to squint at the horizon. One of the destroyers was accelerating, trying to get between the missile and the carrier. It was a bold move, but Manolo could tell at a glance it wasn't going to work.

His mind raced. The missiles had to be sub launched. How else could they have gotten so close?

He could see the missiles now. Two fiery streaks headed right at them, barely skimming the wave tops. Their speed was breathtaking. A slew of SeaRAM missiles launched, and he heard the steady *bzzzt* of the Phalanx close-in weapons systems spewing forty-five hundred rounds per minute of depleted-uranium bullets at the bogeys. He recalled a Command School instructor's famous line: *If you have to rely on a CIWS, you're fucked.*

One of the incoming missiles wobbled, then spun out of control. Pieces hurtled toward the *Ford,* causing Manolo and the petty officer shadowing him to duck.

The second missile escaped the stream of bullets and slammed into the hull of the carrier a mere twenty feet above the waterline. The massive ship lurched, and a rumble came from deep within the superstructure as if some enormous giant had belched. Smoke began to pour out of the port-side hangar deck.

Antisubmarine warfare helos lifted off from the destroyer and the carrier.

Manolo knew they could handle one hit and live, but how many more Chinese submarines were out there?

"Sir," the petty officer said. "Alpha Xray reports the attacking Chinese sub was killed by the USS *Key West,* approximately twelve miles off our port beam." AX was the undersea warfare commander in the *Ford*'s combat center. Manolo swore. The entire strike force structure was designed to protect the carrier and they'd failed—badly.

"Damage report," he said.

"Missile struck amidships," the petty officer said. "Hangar deck and engineering sustained damage. Crew quarters, too. Fires are not yet under control. Estimate at least twenty dead, another twenty injured. Port-side hangar elevator is out of commission and we have damaged aircraft. Damage-control teams are on scene."

The smoke from the burning ship—*his* flagship—stung Manolo's eyes. He blinked. A ship of the United States Navy had been attacked by a foreign power. American sailors killed. His mind grappled with the concept for a split second, then snapped into focus. He threw open the door to the chaos of Flag Watch.

"Listen up, everyone." A hush fell. "We have been attacked by the People's Republic of China. We are weapons free on all platforms. You shoot first and ask questions later. Any questions?"

There were none.

CHAPTER 46

US Cyber Command, Fort Meade, Maryland

Don was logging off his computer for the day when Lieutenant Jackson called his office. "Sir, I think you'd better come out to the watch floor. It looks like all hell is breaking loose in West Pac."

The mood on the watch floor was tense, edgy, and ominously quiet. The normal chitchat between watch stations was absent, he realized. He found Jackson at the supervisor's station. "What's up?" Don realized he was whispering.

"We're getting news media reports of a P-8 Poseidon shot down near the Spratlys, and a Japanese destroyer patrolling the Senkakus has disappeared. Both point to Chinese involvement. I think we should get authorization to use Happy Panda, sir."

Don frowned. What most people never fully understood about the cyber world was that hacking was a long game, played out over days, weeks, even months or years. Big splashy events, like denial-of-service attacks to shut down a website, got all the press, but the most successful hacks were the ones you never heard of—because they were never discovered.

Happy Panda was the longest of games. Over six months ago, the NSA had discovered a flaw in the Chinese elite military cyber corps known as Unit 61398. Using Cyber Command resources, the NSA had exploited the flaw, turning it into an entry point, a back door to China's deepest military secrets. After some initial probing, a joint decision was made to let the back door go dormant to reduce their chances of discovery. The top minds gambled that a day would come when they needed an ace in the hole with the Chinese and Happy Panda would fit the bill.

The problem with knowing about a hidden ace is that everyone wants to use it for their pet issue. Don knew requests for Happy Panda access were sent to his boss at least once a week and they all got shot down.

"Where are we with the communications issues on the Trident network?" he asked in an attempt to change the subject.

Jackson shook her head. "Not much progress. It's definitely a systems problem and it's worse now that we're having spotty outages on the satellites."

A petty officer rushed into the room with a clipboard, which he handed to Don. "Flash message, sir. You need to see this now."

Don read the words, shook his head, and reread them.

"What is it?" Jackson asked.

He handed her the sitrep from the USS *Ford*.

. . . HIT BY CHINESE ANTISHIP CRUISE MISSILES. TWENTY DEAD, FIFTY PLUS CASUALTIES. ATTACKING PLAN SUBMARINE DESTROYED BY USS KEY WEST . . .

"It's happening," he whispered.

Jackson handed the clipboard back to the messenger without a word. Don's phone beeped with a tone indicating a secure text.

POTUS AUTHORIZED DEFCON 3.

He showed the text to Jackson. "Get everyone in here. If they're on leave, recall them. We go to twelve-hour shifts, full staffing, effective immediately. I need answers to those comms outages and I need them now."

"Aye, aye, sir." Jackson slipped on her headset and started to address her watch team. She stopped and turned back to Don. "What about the midshipmen, sir? Do you want them called in, too?"

"Absolutely, Lieutenant."

She flashed him a quick smile. "I think that's a call you're going to have to make, sir. They're not in my chain of command."

"Try anyway. I'm going for approval on Happy Panda. Let me know if you have any issues with the academy."

The events whirled in Don's brain as he strode back to his office. These kinds of attacks by the Chinese made no sense. The Chinese were consummate strategists; they always played the long game. Shooting a random P-8 patrol craft out of the sky and sinking a Japanese destroyer were nuisances at best to a force as powerful as the United States Navy. Even attacking an aircraft carrier with a single submarine was ridiculous. Why attack a carrier without putting in place the force necessary to kill it?

Taken as a whole, these all seemed like random actions designed to provoke the Americans, not hurt them. It went against everything he knew about the Chinese battle plans, which made this scattershot approach especially unnerving. What if every response, every battle contingency the US had in place to fight the Chinese was wrong? Did this signify a change in military strategy or even a military coup?

Whatever the reason, they needed answers and Happy Panda was one way to get them. Once inside his office, he placed a secure call to Admiral Trafton. Her admin put him through immediately.

"Trafton."

"Ma'am, it's Riley. I wanted to talk to you about—"

"Happy Panda," the admiral interrupted.

"Yes, ma'am. I think we need to consider—"

"Do it." Her words were sharp and clipped.

"Ma'am?"

"Look, Riley, if there was ever a rainy day, this is it, right? I've already cleared it with NSA. I can't believe the friggin' Chi-Comms would be so stupid as to attack a US Navy carrier. It's like they *want* to start World War Three. We need answers—and fast."

"I'll get Panda activated ASAP. We'll start digging."

"Be careful, Riley. This thing stinks to high heaven. In retrospect, considering all the stupid things we've seen China do in the last few hours, I'm wondering if Panda is even real."

"You mean they want us in their system?"

"I mean it's pretty convenient we have a back door into our enemy's network right when they start operating off the reservation. It could be part of a trap."

Don hadn't considered that. "I think it's still worth using Panda, ma'am."

"I agree, just keep in mind the lesson of the WMDs." Prior to the invasion of Iraq, the entire US intelligence establishment had put together the case for Saddam Hussein's possession of weapons of mass destruction. In hindsight, it had become an exercise in groupthink, where the people in power cherry-picked the pieces of intel that supported their conclusion and sidelined intel that didn't. The result was the greatest failure in the history of modern intelligence—and a Middle East destabilization that remained a source of US foreign policy woes.

"I understand, ma'am."

He'd no sooner ended the call than another one came in, this time from Jackson. "No dice on the midshipmen, sir. The dean won't approve the request."

Don fought back the urge to say something snarky. He kept close tabs on the grades of his midshipmen and he knew there was no academic reason to refuse his request. "I'll handle it," he said. "Jackson, we've got approval to open up Happy Panda. Get the SCIF set up. I'll be on the floor in ten minutes."

He thumbed through his mobile phone until he found the personal number for the commandant of midshipmen. She answered on the third ring.

"Mr. Riley, what a surprise. I just got a message from the dean saying you might be calling. What can I do for you?"

"Good evening, Captain Watson. I'm afraid the size of my request has increased since Lieutenant Jackson's call to the dean. I'm calling to ask that Midshipmen Everett, Ramirez, and Goodwin be transferred to CYBERCOM until further notice."

"Mr. Riley, I'm afraid that's—"

"Ma'am, I don't want to be rude or dramatic, but have you seen the news or read your message traffic in the last hour?"

"No . . ."

"Here's a recap: The Chinese have shot down a Poseidon P-8 on FONOPs, sunk a Japanese destroyer, and launched an attack on the USS *Ford* that killed twenty sailors. The president has just authorized DEFCON Three. Those three midshipmen could make a difference over here."

The captain's voice tightened. "I understand, Mr. Riley. I'll get them to Fort Meade myself."

Nimitz Library, US Naval Academy
Annapolis, Maryland

Miss Eustace Jenkins came into Michael Goodwin's life after his mother was killed in their living room in Lennox, California. He'd barely heard the distant gunshots over the roar of a jet passing overhead as it made a landing at LAX. One minute his mother was dozing in front of the TV, the next a bullet hole in her neck was fountaining blood down her chest.

So much blood.

The police called it "drive-by collateral," their term for the stray bullet that took the life of the only person who had ever loved Michael.

He sat alone in the police station on a plastic chair scarred by the many people who had sat in this chair before him. Michael twisted in his seat so he could study the graffiti on the chair back, his mind automatically seeking a pattern to the random scrawls of criminals and orphans.

"Can I get you a soda, son?" The police officer was a white man, with short black hair already going gray. He had a growly voice but a smile on his face. "We called CPS, but sometimes it takes them a long time to get here."

CPS. Child Protective Services. He was an orphan. His mother was dead. He had no other family.

He was alone.

Michael's mind turned this new set of facts over and over, examining it for patterns.

"Are you okay?" the cop said. "How about that soda?"

"No, thank you, sir," Michael replied, still pondering. He heard the cop say "I think the kid's in shock" to one of his colleagues, but Michael knew he wasn't in shock. He was special. His mother told him that every day.

Michael Goodwin, you are special. Your mind works in mysterious and wonderful ways. And she would always kiss him on the forehead when she said it.

It occurred to Michael that there would be no more forehead kisses and no more daily affirmations. He wasn't sure how he felt about that new fact.

"Michael." A new voice. Soft, but deep, with a hint of a timbre that told him this was a woman who liked to sing. She had a voice for the Lord, his mother would have said. A voice for gospel.

A pair of shoes entered his downcast field of view. Black, sensible heels, but expensive; a dark blue pantsuit sheltered a set of sturdy legs.

"Michael, look at me." The voice was not to be trifled with. He raised his gaze.

The woman was his height, built like a person who had known hard labor in her life, but her hands were soft, uncalloused. She wore a suit that looked expensive to his untrained eye and a blouse that he guessed was silk. She wore no jewelry except for pearl studs in her ears that shone against her dark skin. When she smiled at him, her whole face moved.

"My name is Eustace, Michael. I'm a friend of your mother. She told me how special you are and asked me to be your legal guardian if anything happened to her. Is that okay with you, Michael?"

Michael stood and held out his hand. It was what his mother would have wanted. He watched as Eustace showed a sheaf of papers to the policeman and signed forms.

Life with Eustace Jenkins was very different. She taught him about computers and how his need for order was a skill, not something to be ashamed of. Also, she was rich, and sent him to private school. It was at St. Anthony's that Michael learned about libraries. The library there was more than a collection of books, it was a place of solitude for Michael. Tall stacks with their books in ordered rows sheltered him from the outside world, allowed his mind to find a precious moment of calm.

When he arrived at the Naval Academy eight years later, Michael sought out Nimitz Library as soon as he could, and what he found was even better than St. Anthony's. The stacks at Nimitz were endless, and sprinkled among the tall stacks of books were study desks with high sides where he could be completely alone.

He thought he heard a voice calling his name, but he ignored it, still lost in thought.

"Hey, plebe. Are you Goodwin? Michael Goodwin?" He felt a hand on his shoulder and spun in his seat, startled. Another midshipman, a third-class by the stripes on his service dress blue uniform, stepped back at the suddenness of his response. "Whoa, didn't mean to scare you, man, but I saw your name tag when you sat down. Are you Michael Goodwin?"

"Yes, sir."

The mid pointed at the ceiling. "They've been calling your name for like the last ten minutes."

"Midshipman Fourth Class Michael Goodwin, please report to the circulation desk," came over the PA system.

Michael quickly gathered his books and hurried to the steps. Dre Ramirez was waiting for him at the front desk. She started waving her hands at him as soon as he came into sight. She raced up to him and grabbed his arm, dragging him toward the door. "Where have you been? Your phone was off, and no one could find you." She punched at the heavy steel and glass door with her hip, not letting go of Michael's arm.

"What's going on, Dre?"

When they were outside on the broad stone expanse

of Rickover Terrace, she let go of his arm but set off at a quick pace. Past the edge of the plaza, the lights on the athletic fields blazed in the dark night. "The 'Dant wants to see us," she called over her shoulder. "C'mon, Michael. Don't keep the woman waiting."

He broke into a trot. "The commandant? Why? Her office is that way, Dre." He pointed to the right.

Dre paused at the edge of the broad stone steps that overlooked the athletic fields next to the liquid blackness of the Severn River. An SH-60 Seahawk helicopter sat in the center of the soccer field, its whirling blades a disc of silver in the cold lights. Well back from the helo stood two figures, their uniform caps tucked under their arms to avoid any possibility of them getting sucked into the helo's twin engines.

Michael recognized Janet's familiar shape and blond hair. The other woman had four broad stripes on the sleeve of her uniform. Captain Watson, the Commandant of Midshipmen.

Dre's smile was electric white in the reflected light of the fields. "Janet's gonna kill you, plebe. She's been making small talk with the 'Dant for twenty minutes."

Then she raced down the steps two at a time.

CHAPTER 47

Yang-do Island, North Korea

Rafiq stood up from his command chair and stretched. His nervous energy was fading. Fatigue cloaked his body like a blanket. Sleep. He needed sleep.

"I'm going to rest," he said to So-won.

She nodded, her eyes still on the screen.

"Monitoring only. No more offensive actions for now."

She nodded again without looking up at him.

Rafiq wondered about her at times like this. Lost in the code, marveling at her creation, but seemingly unaware of the effect her actions were having in the real world. He hadn't even needed to deceive her. From the moment he conceived of the idea for a self-learning computer virus, she was in—just to see if it could be done. As his plans grew in scale, her excitement matched it, heedless of the potential global devastation they could cause.

"Do you understand, So-won?"

She looked at him, finally. Her eyes were red from staring at the screen but alive with energy. "Yes, Chul, I understand. Get some sleep." She patted the side of the workstation. "Our pet doesn't need sleep and neither do I."

Their pet. When they'd first started the program, Rafiq had called the cyberweapon an artificial intelligence, or AI. So-won corrected him time and again, insisting that he was misusing the term. What they were really building was a virtual pet, a machine they could train to follow their commands.

But they needed to make sure it had the *right* training, and in Rafiq's view that was a slow but steady buildup of small skirmishes designed to confuse everyone. Rafiq wanted maximum confusion, best achieved by a series of seemingly random, small-scale events. Shooting down a patrol plane and blocking the outgoing Mayday call. Sinking an isolated destroyer under the cover of heavy clouds to shield their actions from the prying eyes of American satellites. Launching a pair of cruise missiles at a carrier and watching the Chinese sub get destroyed.

And that was just his warm-up act for the Chinese command and control network. It astonished him how simple it was to order these small attacks. All these ships and planes from the opposing forces were armed to the teeth and operating in close proximity to one another. Meanwhile, politicians from both sides spouted angry rhetoric across the twenty-four-hour news cycle. When Rafiq intervened in this already tense situation, all he had to do was give a single command and watch the weapons fly.

And with each event, his pet learned a new lesson in cause and effect.

The Chinese were the easiest to manipulate; that was why he'd started there first. Between the Americans, the Japanese, and the Chinese, the Chinese military machine was the most centrally commanded force of the three.

Beijing liked to hold all the cards, delivering orders directly to individual units rather than delegate power.

The Japanese had modeled themselves after the United States, giving their theater commanders more latitude to operate but restricting them from any sort of first strike. Rafiq smiled to himself. The strikes he'd launched via the Chinese military, especially against the US Navy aircraft carrier, would soon loosen those bureaucratic shackles.

He splashed water on his face in his private bathroom, then inspected himself in the mirror. If his Nadine were still alive, would she recognize him? Would she care that his jawline was heavier, that his cheekbones were softer? The cosmetic surgeons had done a respectable job, but even after all this time, he still felt like he was seeing a stranger every time he saw his own reflection.

He lay down on his narrow bed, trying to will himself to sleep. Despite the ache of tiredness in his muscles, his mind raced.

They would begin teaching the Japanese network next. The virus they had uploaded had distributed itself across the network, hiding itself as code fragments amid actual programs, spreading its tentacles into every program and platform across the extensive network. A hacker's version of hiding in plain sight.

But the American system . . . this was a puzzle. He'd expected a similar architecture to the other two countries, but they had found a vast number of communications nodes in their command and control network, reaching far beyond the western Pacific.

What were the Americans doing with this unknown capacity? The processing of so many sites had all but overwhelmed Rafiq's computer resources, but the prize was too tempting to ignore. Controlling the Japanese and Chinese networks gave him access to Asia, but the American network promised so much more.

Enough, he thought. *Get some sleep.*

He pictured his old home in Estancia Refugio Seguro, imagined walking up to the front door, seeing each flagstone and tree in intricate, loving detail. From the direction of the stables, he could hear little Javi shouting and smell the heavy odor of horses in the afternoon heat. The front door opened, and Nadine was there, her dark hair spilling over her shoulders, her dark eyes flashing with the passion he knew so well—

His satellite phone rang. Rafiq's eyes flew open.

"*Anyoung haseyo?*" he said.

"What have you done, Rafiq?" Pak's voice had a hysterical edge, and his Korean spilled out so fast Rafiq struggled to process the words. "Too much!"

"How so, old friend?"

"Don't 'old friend' me, you bastard! You were supposed to create tensions, not start a war."

"I don't know what you mean."

"The Chinese launched an attack against an American aircraft carrier! You were behind it, I know it."

"You give me far too much credit, Pak."

Pak gained some semblance of control. "You're sure you had nothing to do with this?"

"Nothing."

"No matter. Kim has decided to end your operation. He wants to see you in Pyongyang immediately."

"I can't do that, Pak," Rafiq said. "I'm needed here."

"Didn't you hear what I said? The Supreme Leader himself wants to see you. The operation is over. Shut it down. Now."

"No."

Pak's voice tightened again. "No? What do you mean, no?" The line went silent. "It was you, wasn't it?"

"It's all part of the plan, Pak. You've been very helpful, by the way."

"Whose plan? Rafiq, I beg of you, don't do this. Stop now, come back to Pyongyang, we can smooth this over with the Supreme Leader."

"Goodbye, Pak. If you have an escape plan, I suggest you use it now."

"Wait, I—"

Rafiq ended the call. He stooped to pull on his shoes. When Pak reported his disobedience to the Supreme Leader, their first course of action would be to cut off his communications with the mainland.

When he entered the watch floor, So-won looked up in surprise. "Couldn't sleep?"

Rafiq smiled. "No rest for the wicked. Switch from landline to satellite uplinks."

"So soon?" she said.

Rafiq ignored her. "Then bring the Japanese network online."

CHAPTER 48

USS Gerald R. Ford *(CVN-78)*
65 miles south of Taiwan

Admiral Manolo pursed his lips as he surveyed the BattleSpace display dominating the center of Flag Watch. The holographic representation showed an eighty-mile radius around the *Ford* strike force. The lieutenant operator, flexing the manipulator on his right hand, waited for his orders.

Manolo looked through the hologram at Captain Henderson. "What's the status of our AWACS support from the air force in Okinawa?" The damage from the Chinese cruise-missile strike had put a serious dent in their air coverage. They'd lost nearly a third of their air wing, including two of the four E-2D Hawkeyes the strike group depended on for organic early-warning air support.

"Kadena's got them in the air, sir. They'll be on station within the hour."

The admiral growled. He rubbed his face, feeling the coarse stubble grind against his palms like sandpaper. The day had been consumed with damage-control reports, getting the remaining air wing flying again and establishing a functional screen around the carrier.

And always hindering their progress were the random comms outages that had continued all day.

The loss of the Hawkeyes partly deprived him of long-range early warning and a solid overall view of his environment. The BattleSpace table worked best with lots of data to process, and the Hawkeyes generated a lot of data.

"Lieutenant, have the *Zumwalt* move to five miles off our starboard beam." He watched as the operator reached into the hologram to touch the tiny representation of the navy's state-of-the-art destroyer. The ship's information flashed onto the wall screen, along with a command to reposition to their new station. The ship's acknowledgment flashed on the same screen.

Manolo cursed to himself. They needed better top-down coverage. He needed to see where the goddamn Chinese were! He strode across the room and pushed open the door to Supplementary Plot—or SUPPLOT, as it was called—the tiny top-secret space dedicated to keeping the strike group connected to national intelligence agencies.

"Commander," he barked at the intel officer on duty, "where's our satellite coverage? We're fighting blind out here."

The intel officer, or N2, had a ruddy complexion and a spare tire that sagged over his belt line. "We've got satellites repositioned, sir, but we're still seeing connectivity problems."

"Very well," Manolo replied, even though it was anything but. He returned to his post at the railing overlooking the BattleSpace display. As he watched, the scale of the space expanded.

"Admiral," said the BattleSpace operator with a note of relief in his tone. "We're receiving a data link from the AWACS. Processing now." The operator's gloved right hand carved the open air as he worked on the virtual display visible in his goggles. Manolo had tried the BattleSpace VR rig as part of his command training, and the damn thing had left him seasick. So much for technology.

The holographic display flickered and two new, red icons appeared. Surface ships. The lieutenant spoke in a calm voice. "Admiral, two new sonar contacts reported from *Key West,* correlated with AWACS data. Classified as Luyang-class guided-missile destroyers. The ships are on a parallel track with the strike group."

Finally, Manolo thought. *Time for some payback.* "Very well. Order the *Zumwalt* to engage both contacts with long-range missiles."

He watched as the order went out. The *Zumwalt's* status flashed and a spool of data trailed across the wall screen.

"Missiles inbound!" The BattleSpace table blinked red and a cluster of fast-moving red tracks speared across the holographic space. "Admiral, we have twelve inbound missiles. Probable Chinese C-805s."

Manolo grimaced. In their current damaged state, even one or two of those missiles might finish off the *Ford.*

"Very well," Manolo said. "Transfer the telemetry data to the strike force. All ships engage."

BattleSpace went blank. "We've lost the data link with the strike force, sir," the BattleSpace operator called out, a note of panic in his voice.

The admiral wheeled around. "On any available circuit, transmit in the clear: Incoming missiles, all ships engage."

He rushed out to Vulture's Row just in time to see the *Zumwalt's* vertical launch batteries release a slew of surface-to-air missiles. On the horizon, forward of the *Ford*'s beam, the USS *Mustin*—an Arleigh Burke–class guided-missile destroyer—followed suit with a fiery launch. The air filled with dozens of points of light. There was an explosion as one of the friendly SAMs destroyed an incoming Chinese antiship cruise missile. Then another, and another, and another. He lost count. Six destroyed, seven?

"Missiles inbound. Brace for impact." The 1MC public-address system rang through the ship.

Manolo walked back inside Flag Watch. The Battle-Space table was still blank. The lieutenant still had the VR goggles on, and his right hand pawed at the open space in front of him as he tried to reboot the system.

His petty officer shadow with the sound-powered telephone headset was back. The whites of his eyes flashed at Manolo in the dimness of the space. Manolo put his hand on the young man's arm and gave him a squeeze.

A small explosion sounded outside. *Chaff,* Manolo thought. The air around the carrier would be full of metal confetti in a last attempt to draw away the Chinese missiles. The wind was favorable; it might fool the missiles. At least some of them.

The SeaRAM defenses punched out airframe missiles with a steady beat. The *bzzzt* of the CIWS started, sounding like a buzzer in the next room. An explosion rocked the ship. *Chalk another kill up to the CIWS,* Manolo thought.

He gripped a steel stanchion and said to the petty officer, "Hang on, son. This is gonna hurt."

The heavy steel deck of the mighty ship trembled under his feet, and then a searing light consumed the world of Admiral Han Manolo.

CHAPTER 49

Don scanned past the message header info to the heart of the flash message from the USS *Zumwalt:*

USS FORD ATTACKED BY CHINESE DDGS. SHIP IS ON FIRE AND AFLOAT, BUT DAMAGED BEYOND REPAIR AND SINKING. XO ORDERED ABANDON SHIP. STRIKE GROUP FLAG SHIFTED TO USS ZUMWALT. CDR FORD STRIKE GROUP KIA.

Don cursed under his breath and passed the message to Lieutenant Jackson. An American aircraft carrier sunk? Unthinkable—except it had just happened.

"Six thousand, including the air wing," Jackson whispered.

"What?"

"That's the crew of the *Ford.* More than six thousand people—including my brother," Jackson said.

"I'm sorry." It sounded lame. It *was* lame.

"These comms outages," Jackson said. "I'll bet they had a lot to do with it."

"Look, Lieutenant—"

"Don't, sir. Don't say it." She flung out her arm, encompassing the packed ops center in a violent sweep.

"The modern navy, all this technology, the Trident program? Without good comms, it's just a bunch of junk. They're sitting ducks out there unless we do our part." Her eyes flashed at him.

Don wasn't sure whether to hug her or tell her to take five and pull herself together. He did neither. "So, let's do that. Assume you're right. Assume we've been hacked. How? Why? Who's doing it? Unless we can find those answers, we'll never get anywhere." He pointed at the workstations. "This is *your* front line. Get to work, Lieutenant."

Don watched her go. His speech wasn't going to go down in the history books as great motivation, but it got the job done. For now.

They'd divided the available staff into different groups, some looking at system architecture flaws, some looking at peer-to-peer protocol, and still others looking at source code for any suspicious malware traces. The three midshipmen had been put into the last group.

Looking for "suspicious code" within a program as complex as Trident was like a cop staring at a random highway at rush hour hoping his murder suspect would drive by. But, as usual, the mids had cooked up some shortcuts to speed up the process.

Goodwin was watching lines of code scroll down four screens at once, his body still, his eyes unblinking, staring at a fixed point. Don knew the kid was somehow processing all four screens, but he was damned if he knew how he did it. Every so often he would stop, highlight a section, and transfer a chunk of code to Everett's screen for deeper analysis. Ramirez was busy writing small routines to feed Goodwin's workflow.

Don came up behind them. "Can I interrupt?"

All three stopped what they were doing and spun in their chairs.

"What've you got so far?" he asked.

Everett spoke up. "There's a whole lot of trash in the code. Lines of extra commands that don't seem to be part of the system, but we have no idea what they do."

"Michael's able to find the same code—in different places—across multiple platforms," Ramirez said, "but we're just finding bits and pieces, not a whole working program."

"What if we had a baseline?" Goodwin said.

Don looked at him. "Explain."

The midshipman stood up. "When you read us into Trident, you told us it was a viral supercomputing network. Each node carries an independent copy of the source code, right?"

"Go on."

"What if the malware we're looking for isn't in the system architecture; what if it's in each node?" He carved the air with his hands as he spoke.

"Maybe it's a worm," Ramirez said.

Goodwin grimaced. "Sort of. It infects like a worm, but it doesn't hijack a single program, it takes over the whole node. The node becomes a slave to some larger program . . ." His voice trailed off.

Don considered the young man. "Say you're right. How do we prove that theory?"

"If Goodwin's right," Everett said, "then all we're finding are bits and pieces of random code. We need to figure out a way to get the whole program."

Don paused. "We need to infect a new node. On purpose."

It turned out they needed to infect four new nodes before they had enough data to make a conclusion. Each time, the infection added thousands of lines of new code fragments, sprinkled throughout the existing programs—the same code fragments, but in a different order each time.

"It's a jigsaw puzzle," Everett said.

"So there has to be another program that assembles the picture," Ramirez added.

"And then what?" Don asked. "What does the assembled program do?"

The midshipmen looked at each other.

"Figure it out," Don said. "Call Jackson if you need help."

Don strode out of the main ops center to the adjacent SCIF, using the retina scanner to gain entrance. Two of his best operators were manning workstations. They looked up as he entered.

"Well," Don said, "how happy is the panda?"

They'd all been relieved to find their back door into the Chinese network still available. For the last few hours, his team had been combing through the Chinese system in preparation for a cyberoffensive that would destroy their command and control network. But before they launched an attack, they needed to find out what was going on inside the Chinese military and why their battle tactics were so different than anticipated.

It just didn't make sense.

A young woman, a fluent Mandarin speaker and an expert on Chinese cybertactics, stripped earbuds from her ears and shook her head. "It's the damnedest thing, sir. I mean, the Chinese are definitely ordering these attacks—we found clear evidence—but their military is freaking out that these are phantom orders."

"But the orders are real?"

Both operators nodded. "Absolutely. Every single one came from Beijing through proper channels."

"And your working theory is?"

"Somebody's trying to cover this up?" She frowned.

"I've studied the Chinese military for years and this makes no sense. Unless someone has hijacked their entire network, these orders to attack the US are the real deal."

"Is that possible?" Don asked.

"Hijack their entire network without the Chinese knowing they'd been hacked? No way, not possible."

Don stared at her.

"Sir? Are you okay?"

"Keep at it. I'll be back in a few minutes with some reinforcements. I have an idea."

Don rapped lightly on the office door of his boss, Air Force Brigadier General Tom Price, known as the J2 in the parlance of the military intelligence world.

"Sir, I have an unusual request," he began.

Price sat back in his chair and pulled off his reading glasses. A wiry man with a fringe of gray hair, he looked more like an accountant than a one-star general. Don also knew the man was whip-smart and possessed a temper that could flare at inconvenient times.

Price pointed his chin at the open chair across from his desk. "Out with it, Riley."

There was no use beating around the bush, so Don dove in. "I want to read the midshipmen into Happy Panda."

Price held his gaze without emotion. "You're right, that is unusual. Explain."

"They've managed to find a bucket of code that's resident on each node of the Trident system."

"So I've heard, but we don't know what it's for. It's just trash."

"But what if it's not? What if there's another program, an assembly program that uses this code to build another—a much larger and more dangerous—program? What if it just hasn't been activated yet?"

"To what end?"

Don shrugged. "We don't know yet. This is just a theory, but we have been able to verify that it shows up on multiple nodes in Trident."

Price fiddled with his glasses. "I'm not tracking, Riley. What does this have to do with Panda?"

"I think the same program is on the Chinese system—and it's been turned on."

"I think I see where you are going with this. You think that by seeing what it did to the Chinese we can make sure the same thing doesn't happen to us."

"Exactly."

Don was afraid if Price twisted his glasses any more, he'd break the frames. The ticking of the wall clock behind Don sounded like a hammer blow in the silence.

"And you're convinced one of these midshipmen can figure this out? They need access to Panda?"

"No, sir, I'm sure all three of the midshipmen—together—can give us a shot at figuring this thing out before it hits us." He paused. "If my theory is right, sir."

General Price threw his glasses onto his desk. He stared at Don for what seemed like a full minute.

"Do it."

CHAPTER 50

US Cyber Command, Fort Meade, Maryland

Don led the midshipmen into a conference room and pointed to a row of chairs across the table from him. All three slumped to a sitting position wearing the thousand-yard stare of people who had spent far too long looking at a computer monitor.

He passed each of them a sheet of paper. "Remember when I asked you to sign a special NDA so you could look at Trident?"

They nodded. Ramirez scanned the sheet and grinned. "Happy Panda—sounds like a Chinese restaurant." Everett looked at her and Ramirez stopped smiling. "This is about China, sir?"

Don pointed at the paper. "Read carefully and sign, then we can talk."

When the pages were signed and returned, Don began. "The working theory you've laid out for me—and I've sold up the chain of command—is that we've been hacked. Someone installed a virus that has salted our operational code with what looks like trash, the kind of stuff left over from any programming effort. When the time is right, someone activates an assembler routine that uses all these pieces to make a master program. We don't know who's behind it, or why, or what this master program does. Do I have it right so far?"

His trio of midshipmen watched him with rapt gazes. Everett nodded for all of them.

"Well, I buy your theory, lock, stock, and barrel. Now I'll add to it. I think the Chinese got hacked also, and whoever it is has successfully run the assembly routine on their system."

The midshipmen exchanged glances. Everett spoke. "But we're in a shooting war with China. What are we going to do? Call them up and ask them?"

Don shook his head. "We're going to have a look inside their system and see if we can figure out what's going on."

"We can do that?" Ramirez asked.

"Happy Panda is an access point. We discovered this flaw in their security and rather than exploit it immediately, we set it aside for a rainy day, for a time when we might need access to their network."

"A time like right now," Goodwin said.

"Exactly."

"And you're going to let us poke around inside the Chinese military network?" Everett asked. Her eyes shone with excitement, boosting Don's own mood.

He stood. "Follow me."

With Don, his two civilian operators, and the three midshipmen, the SCIF was at capacity. The operators, Kang and Able, gave up their seats to Ramirez and Goodwin but hovered over their shoulders. Don ignored the glares he received from his operators.

"Ignore the data files," said Kang to Goodwin. "Unless you speak Mandarin, you won't be able to make heads or tails of them."

"Let's take a few of the more complicated lines of code from the seed program and see if we can find them in the Chinese network," Goodwin said.

Ramirez cracked her knuckles. "What'd you have in mind?"

Goodwin gave her four sequences that he recalled from the Trident code, which Ramirez cobbled together into a search sequence that yielded several hundred possible matches. She routed the results to Goodwin's screen and they painstakingly opened and reviewed each file.

An hour ticked by before Goodwin spoke. "I think I might have something." They crowded around his screen. He pursed his lips. "This is way more extensive than we thought. It looks like a monitoring system—at least this part does. It's got hooks everywhere." He highlighted a section of code. "This section allows someone to override a comms channel. Whoever's behind this could send their own commands without the real operators even knowing it. But there's this other section. I have no idea what's going on here. It looks like some sort of pattern-recognition function." He looked up at Don. "We need to download this program so we can analyze it."

"How is it controlled?" one of the operators asked.

Ramirez dropped her cursor on a section. "The hackers have total control of the comms systems, so the inputs can come from literally any external channel—satellite, internal, even a mobile phone if it got close enough. This is genius-level stuff. The required inputs are minimal, the assembled program on the infected network does all the work.

"But it gets even worse," Ramirez continued. "The Chinese probably don't even know the master program is there. It's designed like a supervisory system, a shell program. It overlays their network. They're probably going crazy trying to figure out what's happening."

"But how did it get there in the first place?" Able said. "The Chinese are sharp operators and the original code had to be gigabytes of data. An upload of that size would have triggered all kinds of alarms."

Don closed his eyes as the full realization of the problem hit him. "They hid it in plain sight," he said. "Someone uploaded the file, broke it apart, and disguised it as junk code, leftover trash from programmers. When they were ready, they assembled the shell program and took over the Chinese command and control network."

"But we found the same code on Trident," Everett said.

"Exactly," Don said. "It's just a matter of time. Can we download this?" Don pointed at the screen.

Kang frowned. "If we try to download something of that size, I'll set off alarms on their end. The only way to do it safely is to save the program into small packets and ship them out at random intervals. Hopefully, we can fly under the radar that way."

"How long?"

Kang shrugged. "For a supervisory program of this size? Maybe ten or twelve hours."

"Do it," Don said. "I want the midshipmen to stay here. Figure out what the rest of the program does and how we can stop it."

US Navy brig
Yokosuka Naval Base, Japan

Brendan took another sip of the truly awful coffee. He could feel the jet lag headache building at the base of his skull.

"That's him, sir." NCIS agent Mincer nodded at the monitor. The man in the interrogation room looked a few years younger than Brendan, and a two-day growth of stubble covered his weak chin. He'd had to roll up the cuffs on the too-big orange prison coveralls.

"He hasn't said anything?" Brendan asked.

Mincer grimaced. "Just sits there with a fucking grin like the cat that ate the canary. I sure hope you've got something that'll rock his world, because we got nothing on this guy that'll stick."

Brendan looked over at Jenkins, the only technical person he'd felt comfortable sparing from the Trident watch floor. "You ready?" he said.

Jenkins nodded, but he kept jiggling his leg.

Brendan tucked a folder under his arm. "Let's do this."

The lights inside the interrogation room turned Merville's sallow skin a sickly shade of pale yellow.

"I'd like a cup of coffee," Merville said. Brendan ignored him and drew out a chair. Jenkins sat to his right.

Brendan let the silence lengthen. Finally, he said, "I understand you have refused to cooperate with NCIS, Weston."

"I prefer to be addressed by my rank, sir."

The only sound in the room was the patter of Jenkins's foot on the cement floor. Brendan met Merville's defiant gaze. "Do you know who I am, Weston?"

Merville shrugged.

"My name is Captain Brendan McHugh. I run the Trident network." A shadow flickered across Merville's features. "Do you have any idea what you've done?"

"I haven't done anything. If NCIS had anything, they would've already hit me with it. I'm telling you what I told them: This is all a big mistake."

Jenkins's foot tapped on.

"How did they get to you, Weston? Was it money? Ideology?"

Merville's lip curled and he sat back in his chair. "I don't know what you're talking about, Captain."

Brendan opened the folder and slid their only picture of Rafiq Roshed across the table. "Was it him?"

Merville went pale. "Who is that?" he said.

"That is an international terrorist, Weston. He's working for the North Koreans now. Remember the hack of the US power grid last year? That was his work. Do you remember how many people died in that attack? That's nothing compared to what you've done."

Merville stared at the picture, his lips working as he tried to say something. Brendan nudged Jenkins. "Go get Lieutenant Commander Merville a cup of coffee, Jenkins."

Brendan heard the door close behind his colleague. He kept his eyes locked on Merville. In the space of a few seconds, the man seemed to have shrunk into himself.

"Commander, you took an oath. To some people, that doesn't mean much, but to guys like you and me, it's everything." He paused. "How did he get to you?"

Merville squinted at the picture.

"There was an accident. In Australia," he said. "He said he was a cop, said he could help me." His eyes filled with tears. "I knew he wasn't a cop."

Jenkins opened the door and froze. Brendan beckoned for the coffee and set it in front of Merville.

"Drink this," Brendan said. "And start from the beginning."

CHAPTER 51

"Raise missiles to launch position," Lieutenant Han Bingwen ordered.

The checklist trembled in his hand. Outside, he heard the hoists on the trailers strain to lift the massive Dong-Feng 21D missiles into their vertical launch attitude. He peeked out the window of the command trailer. Slowly, the pointed shapes, like statues across the landscape, came to attention, sharp against the dawn sky.

"Missiles in launch position, sir."

"Verify targeting data."

In training, their instructors called the Dong-Feng 21D the "carrier killer," the People's Liberation Army's answer to the overwhelming might of the US Navy's aircraft carriers. They would be on the front lines, the trainees were told. The Second Artillery Corps was the tip of the spear in the defense of the People's Republic of China.

These orders were crazy, but one did not question launch orders from Beijing. Not a single trainee in Lieutenant Han's missile battery ever expected to fire a shot. He loved America. Every single member of his extended family worked in a Guangdong factory that made mobile phones for an American company. And now he was about to fire on American ships.

"Targeting data verified and locked in, sir."

Lieutenant Han's throat constricted, his mouth went dry. His eyes swung to the plot on the wall. Two US Navy carriers operating east of Taiwan were the target.

He took the key from around his neck and inserted it into the fire-control system. He turned it to the right. The screen indicator went from a yellow STANDBY to a green FIRE.

"Missile is ready to fire," the technician announced.

Lieutenant Han took a step back and drew a deep breath. "Fire," he said.

The technician flipped open the plastic cover on his panel, revealing a square red button. The button pulsed like a heartbeat. As the lieutenant watched, the technician depressed the button.

Outside, the world exploded into roaring fire as six missiles launched into the night sky. The command trailer shook, and the technician strained to shout over the noise.

The missiles lifted away, leaving ringing ears and the smell of singed grass and burned rocket fuel. A small tree had caught on fire. A team of enlisted men attacked the blaze with fire extinguishers.

"All missiles away, sir." The fire-control tech was shouting.

"Very well." Lieutenant Han's eyes slid to the plot showing the missile's track relative to the target. He could imagine the American ships going to general quarters, their destroyers deploying their antiballistic missile defenses.

He'd seen that simulation a hundred times. How many other batteries had fired on the Americans? There might be dozens of Chinese missiles on their way to the American carriers right now.

The US ships would chip away at the number of incoming Dong-Feng ballistic missiles, but they wouldn't get them all.

CHAPTER 52

USS Gerald R. Ford *(CVN-78)*
50 miles south of Taiwan

Captain Diane Henderson boarded the SH-60 Seahawk helicopter only seconds before it lifted off the deck of the *Ford*. Normally, the helo carried a crew of four with room for six passengers. Today, they had a crew of two and ten passengers.

All the passengers were pilots—the only commodity the wounded *Ford* could contribute to the fight against the Chinese navy. After taking a direct hit in the hangar bay and multiple strikes on the flight deck, the only fighter aircraft the *Ford* could muster was the lone CAP in the air at the time of the attack. Apart from the helos, not a single aircraft had launched off the *Ford* since the second attack.

Nearly seventy aircraft dead, dying, or otherwise out of the fight for good.

And that wasn't even the worst of it. She twisted in her seat for a last look at what was left of her home at sea. Despite the best efforts of the XO—Captain Gutterman, the CO of the *Ford,* had been killed in the attack—the mighty carrier was sinking. Fast.

Helos from all over the fleet were landing and taking

off from the bomb-damaged deck like honeybees, ferrying wounded off and damage-control crews on to the ship.

Taking the pilots to the *Reagan* was her idea. Admiral Manolo, her boss, had died in the attack along with half of the personnel in Flag Watch. The crew of the *Ford* were professionals, she decided. They knew how to deal with an emergency without her. She wasn't a ship driver, she was a pilot with no planes to fly, so she did the next best thing—took her pilots to a place where they could get back in the fight.

She signaled the crew chief for a set of headphones and slid them on.

"We're about three-zero minutes out from the *Reagan*, ma'am," he said. "They're headed this way at speed, so maybe a little sooner."

She nodded and cast a final glance back at the *Ford*. Her heart ached at the sight. The massive ship was dead in the water, showing a discernible list now. Yellow life rafts clung to her side, and a pair of frigates were taking on hundreds of refugees.

At least it was light and the weather was decent. Thank God for small favors.

"Ma'am?" The crew chief's voice snapped her back to the moment. "The pilot wanted me to tell you that Seventh Fleet just authorized an alpha strike."

She nodded her thanks. Alpha strike! An all-out air assault on every PLA Navy combatant within range. Now *that* was a response—and about damn time, too.

The *Ford* was nothing but a smudge of dirty smoke on the horizon now. She put her old ship behind her. Surely there was something she and her pilots could do to support the *Reagan* and the *Roosevelt* as they took the fight to the enemy.

One of her pilots tapped her on the shoulder and

motioned out the window. The USS *Ronald Reagan* was just coming into sight. As she watched, an F/A-18 shot off the catapult and made a steep climb away from the ship. Less than a minute later, another aircraft launched, this one an F-35. The *Roosevelt* was running a parallel track, five miles distant, and was pumping aircraft into the skies on a similar tempo. Henderson craned her neck upward, shielding her eyes against the sun.

The sky above them was thick with US Navy warplanes. She fought back a rush of pride mixed with rage. God, she wished she could be in a cockpit right now.

Payback's a bitch, China.

The SH-60 pilot wasted no time. He swung them wide around the carrier and landed on the flight deck just aft of the island. Henderson was first off and relieved to see a petty officer waiting for her. "Captain Ransom sent me to get you, ma'am," she shouted over the roar of the helo's rotors as it took off again for another trip to the *Ford*.

The relatively quiet interior of the island was a welcome relief to her ears. The petty officer moved swiftly through the passageways, calling ahead to "make a hole" if she saw any impediments to their progress up to Flag Watch. When she arrived, Captain Bill "Handsome" Ransom, the air wing commander on the *Reagan,* was frowning at the BattleSpace table.

"Diane," he said, extending a hand. "It's good to see you. How's the *Ford*?"

She ignored the question, looking past him to BattleSpace. "What've you got, Bill? I'm here to help."

He took the hint and waved at the holographic display. "That's what an alpha strike force of one hundred thirty-two planes looks like. For the *Reagan* and the *Teddy,* if it has wings and a gas tank, we launched it."

He pointed to the scattering of some forty PLA Navy ships that ranged along China's coast. "Those mother-fuckers are about to feel the wrath."

Captain Diane Henderson felt her lips peel away from her teeth in a feral smile.

"Sir," the lieutenant running the BattleSpace table called, "Alpha Whiskey is releasing strike packages now."

Alpha Whiskey was the air warfare commander, embarked on the USS *Zumwalt*. The state-of-the-art guided-missile destroyer had the most advanced radar and computer processing capacity in the entire fleet, making it the obvious choice to quarterback the combined air assault.

Henderson stood next to Ransom as the 3-D display crisscrossed with vectors showing which aircraft teams were assigned to which targets. The vectors blinked until the flight leaders accepted the assignments.

"All strike assignments accepted, sir." The entire table flashed green twice. "Alpha Whiskey has released the alpha strike."

"Very well," Ransom muttered.

The open channel circuit crackled in the background. "Ramrod, Disco One, over." Ramrod was the call sign for Alpha Whiskey.

Henderson's head snapped up. A flight leader's call direct to Alpha Whiskey indicated a problem. "Turn that up, please," she called.

Louder now. "Disco One, this is Ramrod, go ahead."

"Ramrod, we're flight level two-five-zero. We're see-ing dozens of contrails from mainland China rising fast to high altitude. Possible missile strike. Break." He paused. "Are you picking up anything on radar?"

As if on cue, the door to SUPPLOT burst open and a harried-looking lieutenant commander rushed in. "Admiral, satellites are showing a massive salvo of Dong-Feng antiship ballistic missiles, headed our way."

The admiral appeared on the other side of BattleSpace. A tall man, bald, with hooded eyes. "How many?"

"Between thirty and forty, sir."

The incoming missiles began to appear on BattleSpace as red streaks across the holographic display. Every second more appeared. Henderson's breath hitched. The Dong-Fengs were nicknamed "carrier killers" for a reason.

"Nukes?"

"Unknown, sir." The intel officer hesitated. "It's possible."

"Time to first impact—seven minutes, sir," said the BattleSpace operator.

"Run a clock on those missiles. Let's keep track of how much time we have left to do some damage," said the admiral as he snatched the red phone from its cradle, the one that connected him to the combined warfare elements in the battle force. "All ships, this is Bulldog. We have inbound Dong-Feng ballistic missiles. All ships engage in evasive maneuvers. Let's make their targeting as tough as possible. Break." He lifted his finger off the transmit button for a second. Flag Watch held its collective breath. "Alpha Whiskey, over."

"Bulldog, this is Alpha Whiskey."

"Dave, this is up to you now. Make 'em bleed."

"Will do, sir. Good luck. Alpha Whiskey, out."

The carrier heeled to starboard as the ship's captain began evasive maneuvers.

"Admiral, the first strike teams are engaging targets," said the BattleSpace operator. Two of the Chinese destroyers that were less than thirty miles out blinked red and disappeared. "Two targets destroyed, sir."

"Very well," the admiral said, but his eyes were on the countdown clock that had sprung up to show the time to impact on the inbound Dong-Fengs. It read 5:32.

There was nothing she could do here. Henderson stepped out onto Vulture's Row, her eyes cast skyward for telltale contrails.

The destroyers had oriented themselves in a picket line along the threat vector. The ships began ripple-firing their batteries of SM-6 surface-to-air missiles until it seemed the sky was massed with crisscrossing contrails. Smoke hugged the waves and small explosions poofed far above them as the defensive missile screen found its targets. She counted three . . . four . . . seven. Kinetic kills. Essentially, the SM-6 was a supersonic bullet hitting the incoming supersonic missile, destroying both. Another six explosions peppered the blue morning sky in rapid succession.

She squinted. Unverified intel claimed the Dong-Feng 21D warhead could separate into multiples, called MaRVs, maneuverable reentry vehicles, with independent targeting. She was about to verify intel—the hard way.

Captain Ransom joined her on the catwalk of Vulture's Row.

"There!" Henderson spotted an incoming contrail burst into four separate trails. Out of the corner of her eye, she saw the closest carrier escort release a flurry of Block III missiles, designed for short-range protection of the carrier. The Block III missiles moved at Mach 6, and one of them found a mark immediately. Then another.

But the sky was full of missiles now as the attacking

warheads split into quarters and entered their terminal descent.

Shiny chaff clouds sprouted from the *Reagan* and her escorts, a final effort to fool the incoming missiles.

Captain Henderson hurried to the door just as the IMC blared out, "Missiles inbound, brace for impact."

CHAPTER 53

US Cyber Command, Fort Meade, Maryland

Don wanted to pace, but the tight space of the SCIF did not allow it. Goodwin and Ramirez hunched over the workstations, with Everett seated on a spare chair she had wedged between them. The three of them spoke in low voices as they concentrated on the screens.

"How much have we downloaded?" Don asked.

Ramirez checked her monitor. "Twenty percent, sir."

"Any idea what the third section of the master program is for?"

Ramirez shot a glance over her shoulder. "No, sir."

"Not even ideas?"

"Sir?" Everett's voice held a note of irritation. "Maybe you can let them work the problem. We'll call you if we find anything."

"Sorry." Don pushed toward the door. "I'll be on the watch floor."

He was surprised to find General Price waiting for him. The J2's normally calm features were pinched with worry. "You were right, Riley. We checked the Japanese command and control network and found the same trash code. They've been infected as well."

Don absorbed the new information. "But so far whoever is behind this has only activated the Chinese network. What does that tell us?"

Price grimaced. "That's what I want to know. If it's not the Chinese behind this, then who? Russia? Would they be that stupid? Putin likes instability, but he likes instability he can control—and what do they have to gain from a shooting war in Asia?"

"Takes the pressure off them in Europe," Don said.

"Putin's an egomaniac, but he's not a fool. He knows when countries start blowing up each other's shit, it doesn't usually stop at a border."

"North Koreans?" Don ventured.

"Latest intel I've seen says they don't have the juice for this," Price said.

Don flashed on Rafiq Roshed. "Are you sure about that, sir?"

"You know something." Price didn't make it a question.

"Maybe. . . . The most important thing right now is to figure out what this program does."

"Good point. Where are we on that?"

"Not far enough. We've isolated the program on the Chinese network and we're downloading it in packets to avoid getting noticed. So far, we've got twenty percent in house. Meanwhile, we've got the mids studying it to see if we can figure out what it does."

Price shook his head. "Midshipmen. I never thought I'd see the day where technology moved so fast we had to bring in baby officers just to keep up."

Don resisted the desire to roll his eyes. "These three are special, sir." He tried to change the subject. "Have we given any thought to telling the Chinese they've been hacked?"

"Well, you can ask the president yourself when you brief him in an hour," Price replied.

Don paled. "Sir, we don't know enough to give him good advice yet. I need more time."

"Time's up, Riley. While we're screwing around in the virtual world, real missiles are flying around in the real world. People are getting killed. If you really believe the Chinese are being used, then you need to tell the commander in chief."

An alert sounded on the watch floor indicating another communications interruption. As Don watched, the front wall screen went blank. Operators looked up from their workstations in alarm. A few stood. "Anybody else offline?" someone called.

Price looked at Don. "Get that program downloaded, Riley. I don't care if the Chinese find us. Do it!"

Don rushed to the SCIF, tapping his foot as he paused to scan his retina. He burst into the secure area. "Download the entire program from the Chinese network. Do it now."

Kang stared at him. "Mr. Riley, we're only at twenty-two percent. If we try to download it all the Chinese will—"

"Do it! That's an order."

Ramirez's hands flew across the keyboard. She punched a final button. "Downloading now."

Goodwin watched from the other screen. "Twenty-seven percent, twenty-nine . . ."

"They'll be onto us any second now," Kang said.

"Thirty-eight."

"They found us," Ramirez said. Several seconds later, her screen went blank. "Download's terminated."

"How much did we get?" Don asked.

"Forty percent," Goodwin said.

Don nodded. "Okay, we've got a partial download and what you were able to observe online. Get to work. We know this thing is in Trident. It's just a matter of time before whoever's behind this turns it on. I want to know what it does and how to kill it—before it's too late."

"I think we figured it out, sir." Goodwin's voice was cool.

Everyone in the room stared at the midshipman.

"Go on, Goodwin," Don said.

The young man shot a glance at Everett, who nodded. "I think the third part is a machine learning module," Goodwin said finally.

"You mean like artificial intelligence?" Kang said.

"No, ma'am. The term 'AI' implies sentience. This is a program, not a being."

"It's teaching itself how to play war?" Johnson said.

Ramirez jumped in. "Not exactly, sir—at least not yet. Someone is feeding it examples, molding its behavior. After enough inputs, it will start to act independently. To think on its own."

"And now this thing is in our system?" Kang said, looking at Don. "It's in Trident?"

Don bit his lip, then nodded once. "Who's teaching it?" he said.

The midshipmen looked at one another.

"Not good enough," Don said. "We're looking at a situation where the greatest navy in the history of the world is in the hands of a rogue computer program. Figure it out. Now."

CHAPTER 54

White House Situation Room, Washington, DC

The president looked down the long table at Admiral Trafton, General Price, and the heavyset young man next to him. The room around him was packed to capacity. In addition to the normal national security, cabinet, and military representatives, he'd invited the House and Senate leadership from both parties. Lord knew he was going to need all the political cover he could muster for this one.

He consulted the page in front of him. "Mr. Riley, I see your boss has generously offered you up as a subject matter expert on this cyber problem. Please explain to the room how it is that the Chinese have attacked us but are not responsible."

Riley tugged at his collar. The president felt for the man. The room was hotter than usual, and the laser stares of the nation's most powerful people didn't make it any more comfortable.

"The Chinese were hacked, sir. In simple terms, someone uploaded a computer virus that managed to seed their entire network with what looked like stray bits of code. When the hacker turned on an assembly tool, it built a new program inside the Chinese network and took it over."

"Define 'took it over,'" said the secretary of defense.

"The program has hijacked their existing command and control structure. Whoever's behind this can intervene in their communications at will."

"You mean to tell us this virus can send out an order to attack an American ship and the Chinese brass doesn't even know it?" the secretary said.

Don nodded.

"So why can't the Chinese just turn it off?" the CIA director asked.

"Initially, they probably didn't know it was there, sir," Don said. "The master program exists outside of any monitoring systems on their network."

"But they know it now," said the CIA director.

"Probably. I'm sure they figured out they'd been compromised when their field commanders started firing on American ships without legitimate orders from the top brass in Beijing."

"So why haven't they dealt with it themselves?"

Don drew in a deep breath. "The only sure way to get rid of this is to take their entire network offline and reload everything from scratch. They would be without communications for twelve hours, maybe longer. Right now, everything works ninety-nine percent of the time—except when the program intervenes and sends a rogue order. That might only be one message in ten thousand. They might be playing the odds that they can limp along until they figure out a way to debug their system." Don hesitated. "What the Chinese probably don't know is that they're on the clock."

"Meaning?" the president asked.

"The program has three parts, sir. There's the monitoring, the intervention, and a third part that we're only just now figuring out. It appears to be a machine learning component. Someone is teaching this master program how to use the Chinese military to conduct war."

"You mean like an AI?" asked the secretary of defense.

"More basic than that, but the same idea. At some point, this program will run on its own with no outside intervention required. At that point, it might be too late to shut it down."

"And you know this how?" asked the Senate majority leader.

Don looked at Price, who nodded. "We hacked the Chinese, sir. We saw the program in action. It's a preview of what's going to happen to us."

The Senate minority leader jumped in. "But we've got a backup communications system, right?" Don recognized that he was a member of the Armed Services Committee who had approved the funding for Trident and later for Piggyback.

Price shook his head. "No, sir, I'm sorry. When we made the decision to link the Trident intelligence system to the military command and control network, we compromised both. Trident is infected. It's only a matter of time before they take over our network."

The chairman of the Joint Chiefs weighed in. "That means we're going to need to . . ."

"Shut down the entire military command and control network and the intelligence-gathering network. Both of them. At the same time," Don said. It wasn't hard to interpret the expression on the chairman's face. The Chinese and American militaries would be completely vulnerable. What would the Russians do with that kind of power?

The president cleared his throat. "There's one piece

of this puzzle you haven't discussed, Mr. Riley. Who's responsible?"

The chairman muttered something about the fucking Russians under his breath.

Don shifted in his chair. "The Russians are at the top of the list. They have the skills to pull this off, but they lack the motivation. What do they have to gain by training a program to coopt a country's entire military and then setting it loose? Pardon, sir, but there's only one way that scenario ends: total destruction. This program will eventually make it into the Chinese Second Artillery Corps nuclear strike forces. There's no way this conflict stays limited to us and the Chinese. It's even possible the Russians were hacked and nobody knows it yet."

The president leveled his gaze at Riley. "I assume you have a theory, Mr. Riley?"

Don shot a confirming glance at Price and said, "Rafiq Roshed." A stir went through the room. Everyone knew the name. "We know he's in North Korea. If he had enough time and money he could pull this off. And the motivation fits: chaos. He wants to see the world burn."

"Do you have any evidence to back that up, Mr. Riley?"

"Not yet, sir."

"Then find some." The president's eyes swept around the table. "Defense, what are we going to do in the meantime?"

"Sir, I've met with the Joint Chiefs. We recommend we withdraw all naval assets from the western Pacific and reset our force structure."

"What about the Japanese?" the president said. "Or the South Koreans, for that matter? They can't withdraw, and they can't stand down with Kim Jong-un breathing down their necks."

The secretary of defense shook his head. "We don't have a choice, sir. If the Chinese attack we have to respond in kind. Whether their military leaders are in charge or not, we must defend ourselves. The only way we avoid more bloodshed is by not being in the line of potential fire."

"Wait! You want to run away?" said the Speaker of the House. "After having one US Navy aircraft carrier sunk and two others gravely damaged, you want to cut and run?"

The president trained his gaze on the Speaker, who glared back. The Speaker was a wiry man, on the shorter side, with a weak chin and pale blue eyes. *This* was his biggest problem. While the president tried to save lives—hell, maybe even save the world—he had this self-righteous asshole lobbing sound bites at him.

"I'm glad you brought that up, Mr. Speaker. I invited you here so that you could get the whole story. That kind of talk doesn't help anyone. We need to be together on this. American lives have been lost, American blood spilled, but if we don't work together, this gets much, much worse."

The Speaker pursed his lips and exchanged glances with his Senate counterpart. "You can count on us."

The president thanked him, but he didn't believe him for a minute. "Mr. Chairman," he said.

"Sir?"

"I want to see a campaign plan to hit the Chinese mainland, defeat the PLA on their own soil. If Mr. Riley's theory doesn't pan out, we're going to end this thing before it spins out of control."

CHAPTER 55

Pyongyang, North Korea

In the years Pak Myung-rok had worked directly for the Supreme Leader, he had seen dozens of people experience the wrath of Kim Jong-un. Powerful men, with decades of experience. Especially generals. Kim loved to destroy high-ranking military men, especially ones with ideas about modernizing his armed forces in ways inconsistent with the Supreme Leader's vision. Some went to face a firing squad, some to reeducation camps, and some were just never seen again.

Pak's theory was that Kim associated him with a life separate from North Korea. Western luxuries, beautiful women, the thrilling intrigue of thumbing his nose at the Western world, all the while living apart from the façade of their collectively shitty existence in North Korea. Pak had convinced himself that the Supreme Leader actually liked him. He might even go so far as to say that the Supreme Leader wanted to be Pak. In short, Pak Myung-rok had lived a life immune to the ire of the most powerful man in the DPRK.

That was about to change.

Pak felt his knees quiver and wondered if they would

bear his weight. He turned the door handle and entered the boardroom. The polished wood table was turned lengthwise in the room, facing the door. Kim sat in the center of the long table in a high-back wood and leather chair. His advisers ranged on either side of him: generals, intelligence officers, his personal astrologer, and some faces that Pak had not seen before.

None of them looked like they'd slept, but the Supreme Leader looked particularly worn. His heavy jowls sagged even more than normal, and his brush cut was rumpled where he'd run his hands through his hair.

Pak scanned the crowd, seeking out a covert signal of support. He found none.

I'm a dead man. He bowed so deeply his lower back cracked. *I should have run.*

He flashed back to his last meeting with Rafiq. The signs of the man's mental disintegration were there if he had just taken the time to see them. The mood swings, the disinterest in money, the warning for Pak to leave . . .

"Rise," Kim said.

Pak straightened, averting his eyes.

"What have you done?" Kim's voice was flat, without emotion.

Pak was used to the Supreme Leader's tantrums when he was displeased. The childish outbursts, throwing things, red-faced screaming—Pak had even seen Kim's father beat a man almost to death with a golf club—then a swift sentence. Pak was prepared for all possible moods and actions of the most powerful man in his life—except for this one.

He's afraid, Pak thought. *He's afraid for his own life. And I can work with that.*

"Excellency, it seems Jung Chul has taken advantage of your generosity—"

"This is the work of your pet foreigner?" said General Zhu, seated at the Supreme Leader's right hand. "He's started a war between the Chinese and the Americans. If we are blamed for this—"

"I can make sure that does not happen," Pak said quickly.

"You know where he is then?" Kim asked.

Pak nodded. "Yang-do Island, near Hwadae. There's an abandoned bunker there."

"Excellency," said Zhu, "I will personally lead an assault on the island and destroy this traitor."

"I wouldn't advise that, General," Pak shot back. He had the full attention of the room now. Time to close the deal. "Do you believe that a man clever enough to hack the Chinese, the Japanese, and the American military networks will not have contingency plans in place to ensure his survival? He has his own soldiers; he will resist." He stopped. Kim was staring at him, his face reddening by the second.

"He hacked the Americans?" Kim said, his voice rising in pitch. "Who gave him permission to hack the Americans?"

Pak blanched. "I don't know that he did, Excellency. But how else could you explain the Chinese being able to sink an American aircraft carrier?" He knew the Supreme Leader secretly lusted after the US Navy's carriers. He kept a scale model of the USS *Ronald Reagan* in his private chambers.

The Supreme Leader's face regained some composure, but Pak felt the general's eyes on him. The room was listening to him now, but he was far from safe.

"Excellency," Pak continued. "Jung Chul trusts me. I can get close to him, get him to stop this madness." He shot a glare at the general. "If necessary, I will deal with him myself. Permanently."

Kim's color had returned to normal. He nodded. The general, sensing he'd lost the momentum of his argument, tried again.

"Excellency, I advise against this course of action," he said in a brash voice. "We don't need weak half measures now. You must show real strength in this crisis."

It took all Pak's willpower not to smile. By implying that Kim was weak and then telling him what must be done, the general had committed the ultimate act of stupidity. Whatever support he'd had from the other members of the Supreme Leader's advisers evaporated like rain in the summer sun.

Kim smacked his hand down on the table. In the silence that followed, he stabbed a pudgy index finger at Pak. "You will go to Hwadae immediately and stop this madness. All traces of our involvement must be erased. Is that clear, Pak?"

Pak allowed himself a ghostly smirk at the glowering general. Then he bowed to the Supreme Leader. "As you command, Excellency. It shall be done." He backed out of the room. When the boardroom door closed behind him, Pak began walking. His knees were still weak, but he dared not pause even for a second. His bravura performance in front of the Supreme Leader had bought him a window of opportunity, but it would not last. He would never be able to stop Rafiq—and he had no intention of trying.

Dawn was breaking when he stepped outside the Supreme Leader's residence. The damp smell of freshly turned earth in the great man's personal gardens hung in the air. *The smell of new life,* Pak thought. *How appropriate.*

He rapped on the roof of his car to wake his driver but opened the door himself and collapsed into the backseat.

"Home, quickly," he said to the driver. The departing car left a divot in the raked gravel drive.

Pak turned on his mobile phone and dialed his pilot. "We're going to Yang-do Island. Have the plane ready in an hour."

He paused at his front door, listening. He was taking a risk by coming home, but he needed to play out his part. Any deviation in his expected behavior would be all the general needed to raise suspicion. He entered his home and snapped on the light.

Silence.

Pak filled a small overnight bag and dressed with care. He eyed the rows of beautiful suits, bespoke shirts, and expensive shoes in his walk-in closet. He would miss them. Finally, after he had walked through the entire house looking for any sign of an intruder, he went back to the foyer. A huge ceramic planter with live bamboo stood in the entryway. He braced himself and pushed against the planter. It barely budged. He put his back into the effort, rocking the tall planter back and forth until he managed to push it over.

Dirt spilled across the tile floor. Pak grabbed the bamboo shoots and heaved until he had dragged the roots and dirt onto the floor. On his hands and knees, he reached into the planter, digging through the sandy soil until he felt a plastic brick. He pulled it out onto a towel he had brought from the bathroom and rubbed away the dirt. Then he slit open the double-sealed package. Two fake passports and fifty thousand dollars in various currencies went into the false bottom of his briefcase. The small handgun fit into his jacket pocket.

At the airport, he waited for his driver to open his door. The wind blowing across the tarmac was warm, another promise of spring—for those who would live long enough to see it. His pilot waited by the plane steps. "We're ready to leave immediately, sir."

Pak nodded vigorously. "Excellent! We're on a mission for the Supreme Leader himself." He bounded up the steps.

The pilot retracted the steps behind him and took his place in the cockpit. Pak sipped a bottle of water and watched his car drive away. The early-morning tarmac was quiet except for the muted roar of the twin engines as they taxied to the runway. The engine's pitch ramped up, and the plane began to roll forward, gathering speed. There was a moment of weightlessness as the craft left the ground; then the steep climb pushed Pak back in his seat.

The city of Pyongyang was stirring beneath him. He saw the lights still blazing in the residence of the Supreme Leader and wondered if General Zhu was still there trying to convince his boss that Pak was screwing them all.

When the city was behind them and the sun was up, Pak rose and went to the cockpit. He drew out the small handgun and placed the muzzle on the back of the pilot's neck.

"Fly to Tokyo," he said.

The plane made a wide turn toward the rising sun.

CHAPTER 56

Narita Airport, Tokyo, Japan

Pak laid his cheek flat against the cool laminate of the table in the interrogation room. They'd taken his watch and there was no clock in the room, but hours must have passed. He was hungry, he was tired, but most of all, he was afraid. The information he possessed was perishable, and these idiots were wasting his best bargaining chip.

When his plane landed at Narita Airport, the Japanese authorities had been surprisingly gentle. In his country, the authorities would have seized someone landing uninvited at a North Korean airport and thrown him in jail—maybe even shot him first.

Here, a contingent of airport security arrived at his plane, their white helmets gleaming in the weak spring sunshine. It was even warmer in Japan, and a freshening breeze made it hard to talk unless they were close. Pak had raised his hands and said in English, "I am a diplomat from the Democratic People's Republic of Korea. I am seeking asylum."

The man in charge of the detail stared at him,

responding with a burst of Japanese. Pak shook his head and tried French. No response. "Speak English?" he said, pointing to the airport terminal. "Find someone."

After another twenty minutes, a car arrived bearing a young man with glasses who spoke excellent English. His eyes widened when he told the security detail about Pak's desire to seek asylum.

"I need to speak to the American embassy," Pak said. "It is urgent." What he really needed was their CIA station chief, but good luck getting that message across.

They didn't even bother to handcuff him when they transported him into the bowels of the massive terminal. He waited another two hours while the customs officials argued with a rotating cast of bureaucrats about how to handle Pak's entry paperwork.

The door to the room opened. "Mr. Pak?" Pak stood, still bleary-eyed, and nodded. The man was of medium height, with powerful shoulders and short dark hair. His mixed parentage appeared to be Japanese and some darker-skinned ancestry. "I'm Michael Willis from the US embassy."

Pak extended his hand. The man's grip was powerful. "I need to speak to your CIA station chief."

"I'm afraid that's not possible, sir."

Pak sighed. "We're wasting time, Mr. Willis. Even as we speak, your military command and control networks have been infected with a very potent computer virus—the same one that has infected the Chinese systems. I can give you valuable information about this situation, but my information is time-sensitive."

Willis watched him without blinking. "Why don't you tell me your information and I'll make sure it gets to the right person."

"I insist on speaking—"

"Assume that you are speaking with him."

"What assurances do I have that I will receive asylum?"

"I'll make that recommendation when I hear what you have to say, Mr. Pak."

Pak felt his stomach clench. He was holding a weak hand, but if Rafiq's cyberweapon destroyed the Americans his hand would be even weaker. . . .

He sat down and indicated for Willis to take a seat. At least he could exert some modicum of control on the situation.

"You know the name Rafiq Roshed?" he asked.

Willis did not flinch. "I'm listening."

"He's behind this."

"And he is in North Korea now? You know where he is?"

Pak nodded. "Asylum first."

Willis folded his arms. "Convince me this is real."

So Pak talked. If he could bolster his story about Rafiq, then the secret of his location would be even more valuable.

"We were contacted by the Russian Bratva to stir up regional tensions with China—"

Willis leaned forward. "So the Russians are behind this?"

Pak held up his palm. "No, the Russian Brotherhood contracted with Kim Jong-un to hack the Chinese. They wanted to sell more weapons, but they stipulated no actual fighting."

"That seems very unlike the Russians, Mr. Pak. How do you know about all this?"

"I was the one who made the deal."

Willis stood abruptly. "Wait here."

It was forty minutes before he returned with a man

in tow. His face showed two days of stubble and his eyes were red-rimmed. He wore his business suit like a uniform.

The man disregarded Pak's outstretched hand and sat down. "If you lead us to Roshed, you'll get asylum. Start talking, Mr. Pak."

"I need to see the details in writing, Mr. . . ."

The man ignored the fishing for his name. "Don't try my patience, Mr. Pak. The conditions of your asylum will be in direct proportion to the amount of damage you help us avoid. You came to us, remember?" He paused. "If you prefer, we can put you on your plane back to North Korea. It seems your pilot is anxious to return home, and I'm sure the Supreme Leader is looking for you."

Pak swallowed hard. "Roshed is out of control. He developed a computer virus that learns—I mean, he's teaching it. He infected the Chinese, the Japanese, and the American military networks."

"We know that much," the man said. "Where is he?"

Pak hung his head. "Yang-do Island, near Hwadae, on the east coast."

The man called for a map of North Korea, and Willis appeared in the doorway almost immediately. He unrolled a detailed map on the table.

"Show me," he said.

Pak's finger traced the coastline until he found the tiny island. "Here. This used to be a missile launch facility. There's a bunker there, and barracks."

"What about his utilities? Power? Communications?" Willis asked.

"He has generators and he's severed the telecom lines with the mainland. He's completely self-sufficient."

"You've been there?" Willis said.

Pak nodded. The two Americans exchanged glances.

"I want you to tell me everything you can remember about the island," the man said. "Don't leave out a single detail. No matter how small. Most important, I want to know where to find Roshed."

CHAPTER 57

The cold coffee tasted sour in Don's mouth, adding another level of complexity to the roiling in his gut. He pushed the cup out of view of the video camera. He hadn't slept in . . . he was too tired to even do the math. These status calls with the heads of all the agencies plus the White House every few hours weren't helping either.

He looked across the table at General Price. He didn't seem to be faring any better than Don.

The director of the CIA went offscreen for a second, then reappeared. "Excuse me, everyone, but I've got a useful update. A North Korean defector showed up in Narita claiming knowledge of Rafiq Roshed and the computer virus."

"Does he have a location?" Price asked.

Don had just spent the last few minutes briefing the conference that his team had tracked the command signal for the virus to the commercial satellite network. The globe was surrounded by a ring of interconnected telecom satellites in geosynchronous orbit. These were workhorse satellites, carrying everything from emails to telephone calls to HBO. There was no way they could

shut down that network and not cause a worldwide up-
roar. From there the trail ran cold. Roshed could be
transmitting from anywhere on the planet.

The CIA director said, "The station chief in Tokyo
is uploading the whole interview, but I'm patching
Brendan McHugh through now to give us an update."

Brendan's face filled the screen. Don's friend looked
like he hadn't slept in several days, but he managed a
weary smile.

"Captain McHugh, you're live," said the operator.

He nodded. "Thank you. Earlier today, a North Korean diplomat arrived unannounced at Narita Airport
and claimed asylum." A picture of a dour-faced Korean
man flashed on the screen. "This is Pak Myung-rok, a
close confidant of Kim Jong-un. He showed up demanding to speak with the CIA station chief in Tokyo. I was
already in Yokosuka investigating the hack on the Trident network, so I caught a chopper to Narita. Mr. Pak
claimed to have direct knowledge of the communications hack and Rafiq Roshed's whereabouts."

"And?" the chairman of the Joint Chiefs said. "Is he
still in North Korea?"

"Yes, sir." The screen showed a map with a tiny
island circled in red. "He's holed up in what used to be
a missile test site off the east coast of North Korea. The
agent who handled the interview is writing up the notes
and will transmit them as soon as we have them in a
form you can use."

Don sagged with relief. He looked across the table at
Price. The general nodded in satisfaction.

"Finally," the chairman said. "We'll blast this fucker
into the Stone Age. Good work, Captain."

Price caught Don's eye and pointed to the row of seats
behind Don and out of view of the camera. He'd forgotten that he'd invited the three midshipmen to the

briefing in case he needed any technical details addressed. Everett was waving at him and miming, *No!*

He slipped out of view of the camera. "What is it?"

"Sir, if you destroy the originating site, we may not be able to shut the computer program down. It's still learning. We don't know what it will do if it's not educated."

"You mean it could be worse?" Don said.

"It could be much worse," Goodwin replied. "It's code, but it's like a living thing. It needs to be shut down at the source or . . ."

"How bad could this get?"

The three looked at each other blankly and shrugged. Don's mind immediately went to North Korean nukes. A man like Roshed would have a fail-safe plan in case he was taken out—and by "fail-safe," Roshed would mean "world-ending."

Don rolled back into the screen, where there was a vigorous debate between State and Defense about how bombing a sovereign nation would impact global politics.

"Excuse me, Mr. Secretary, we have another problem. My technical team here believes the safest way to deal with the computer virus is to shut it down at the source."

The line went silent for a full ten seconds.

"How certain are they, Mr. Riley?" the chairman asked.

Don looked behind him. "Sir, I'm going to ask them to explain it. There's no sense in me being a middleman on this issue." He widened the camera view and had the midshipmen roll their chairs into view.

The chairman made a choking noise. "Are those Naval Academy midshipmen? Riley, what the hell is going on over—"

"Sir," General Price broke in. "Give them a chance. I was skeptical at first, but without them I'm afraid we'd be sitting here with our thumbs in our posteriors. I stand behind their work."

Don threw Price a look of thanks.

"Proceed," the chairman said in a curt voice.

Everett swallowed, sitting ramrod-straight in her chair. "My name is Midshipman First Class Everett, this is Ramirez and Goodwin. Our analysis on the virus shows that it has a learning component. Someone, presumably this Roshed person, is teaching the program to do what he wants."

"The AI part. We know about that," said the chairman.

"It's not an AI, sir," Goodwin said. "There's no sentience here. It has to be taught, like . . ." He scowled, and then his face cleared. "Think of it like training a puppy. Are you training a hunting dog or a show dog or a fighting dog? If you stop the training midway and release the dog into the wild, what happens? Will it be tame or go feral? It depends on the environment. The program might have defenses that we don't know about."

Everyone on the call seemed to be processing the concept of a feral computer virus.

"Assume we bomb the island and kill the puppy's master, Midshipman," the chairman said. "What's the best-case scenario?"

Ramirez jumped in. "It could go dormant. A tame dog, if you will. In that case, we'd still have to take the entire Trident network offline to make sure we got the virus cleaned from our system. Same for the Chinese and the Japanese networks."

"The Russians are going to love that," someone said.

"What's the worst case?" the chairman asked.

The three midshipmen looked at each other. "Can't say, sir," Everett replied.

"Could this virus access nuclear weapons?"

"It's possible."

Another period of stony silence.

"And you think if we have someone at the source, they can shut this thing down safely? Make the virus destroy itself?"

"Yes, sir," Goodwin said. "If someone wrote it, someone else can take it apart."

"Anyone against a raid on this island to shut down this virus at the source?" the chairman asked.

There were no dissenters.

"I'm calling the president as soon as we're done to get JSOC activated. Be back in two hours for a full brief." The chairman paused. "Captain McHugh, I'm directing you to act as my direct liaison on that raid."

"Absolutely, sir," Brendan said.

"Mr. Riley?" The chairman's tone was stern.

"Sir?"

"Tell your midshipmen to pack their bags. You're all going to Korea."

CHAPTER 58

Yang-do Island, North Korea

The wolves were coming. Rafiq could feel it in his bones. But *who* were they?

He briefly considered the North Koreans. Maybe Pak had talked, but that seemed unlikely. To admit to the Supreme Leader the extent of Rafiq's cyberwarfare plans would have implicated Pak himself. But if Pak had grown a conscience—even more unlikely—they might be fighting North Korean special forces. They would be able to find detailed plans of the island, which would put his men at a disadvantage.

The North Koreans would come from the mainland, probably by boat.

Rafiq directed one of his technicians to man the ancient radar system and keep a close watch for any ships leaving the mainland toward the island.

Even as he gave the order, he knew it was no more than a precaution. Rafiq knew Pak Myung-rok, and if his old friend had not already taken Rafiq's advice and fled the country, he would at the very first sign of trouble.

Pak had been feathering his nest at the expense of the Supreme Leader just for a rainy day like this one. He was most likely already somewhere in Southeast Asia, sipping mai tais from the deck of an expensive villa overlooking the ocean.

What about the Chinese? Surely they knew their forces were being manipulated, but had they been able to track the signal all the way back to Rafiq's tiny island?

So-won was confident in her algorithm that piggybacked their command signals onto the global telecom network. By using commercial satellites, she ensured they would not be shut down quickly, and she was equally confident she could hide their tiny commands in the sea of commercial digital traffic.

Rafiq watched So-won working. Her head was bowed as if she might butt the monitor. She was a woman with a mission, and her work to this point had been all but flawless. He had no reason to distrust the quality of her work or her analysis.

Still, one young woman against an army of Chinese cyberwarriors . . . was it fair to expect anyone to win that matchup? The Chinese would be coming, he decided. It was only a matter of time.

He wandered over to the radar station, peering over the young man's shoulder. "What is that?" he said, pointing at a fast-moving air contact on the edge of the radar's range.

"Commercial airliner, sir. It came out of Yangyang Airport in South Korea and has maintained course and speed."

Rafiq grunted, watching the blip as it went out of range. He should have upgraded the radar capability in the facility when he had the chance. This system was years out of date.

He walked back to So-won and put a hand on her shoulder. "How's it going with the Americans?" he asked.

She shook her head. "I never imagined their network was this large. We still don't have the ability to take over their system without slowing everything else down to a crawl—it might even crash our system. There's just too many nodes." She hung her head. "I'm sorry, Chul."

He cupped her cheek. Her jawline felt fragile in his grip. "You've done excellent work, So-won. I am pleased. For now, it's enough to goad them into counterattacking the PLA. Focus on the Chinese. Get access to their strategic weapons. That's the prize now."

She thanked him with her smile and went back to work. Rafiq resumed pacing between his workstation and the radar.

The Americans might not know the extent of the hack, but they knew enough to pull their forces back from the reach of the Chinese. They would figure out the rest eventually.

There was still no sign of any ships departing the mainland—

A sudden thought stopped Rafiq's nervous pacing.

The Russians.

What if Pak had spilled his guts to the men who'd hired him?

Rafiq and his operation were shielded from discovery by the Americans and the Chinese, but the Russians could draw a straight line from Pak to him—and the Bratva would be eager to cover up its involvement in the mess. And that's what Rafiq and Pak would be to the Brotherhood: a mess of unnecessary complications that would expose their organization to the kind of international notoriety that no one wanted.

Rafiq's skin crawled as he imagined Spetsnaz soldiers creeping out of the icy waters of the Pacific to attack his bunker.

That was it, the source of his unease. The Russians were coming.

He called the officer on duty in the barracks. "Wake your men. Tell them to be ready for an attack."

Six miles above Yang-do Island, North Korea

It was amazing how long it took to fall from thirty-one thousand feet. Almost two full minutes.

Lieutenant Commander John Winkler—Winky, to his teammates—found an odd sort of peace in a HALO jump. In the blackness of a night like this one, diving out of the red-lit cargo hold of the C-17 Globemaster was like jumping into a cave . . . and falling for a really, really long time. The sound of the rushing wind consumed his senses.

Sidney, the sixty-pound Belgian Malinois working dog strapped to his chest, didn't find the experience as peaceful as his partner. He wormed his head into Winky's armpit. The man patted the vest that covered the dog's flank and pressed his lips to the animal's ear. "Hang in there, buddy. We'll be on the ground soon."

Using the heads-up display embedded in his visor, Winky checked his alignment in the formation of the twelve SEALs jumping with him. He angled his arms to move his body a few meters farther to the left.

The altimeter on his display spooled away numbers. 10,000 . . . 9,000 . . .

The topographical map of the target island showed on his screen, along with their projected trajectory. They were landing on the western end of the landmass, on a grassy plain a hundred meters from the bunker. The barracks were on the other end of the island, nearly a kilometer away. Their mission was to get inside the bunker and secure it before the AC-130 gunship arrived on scene to rain holy hell on the barracks.

4,000 . . . 3,000 . . .

He eye-scanned the display to energize comms. "Night vision, on." His own display bloomed ghostly green.

2,000 . . . 1,000 . . .

Winkler wrapped his arms around Sidney, taking care to cradle the dog's neck.

At 750 feet, his chute deployed, snapping his body vertical as if a giant hand had plucked him by the shoulders. A stiff breeze blew across their landing zone. He grabbed the steering toggles and adjusted their course toward the open field.

Winkler patted Sidney twice, their signal that he was about to release the dog's tether. He felt the animal tense against his chest. He jerked on the quick release, and Sidney dropped between his legs.

Winkler flared his chute to reduce their speed. Ten feet below, Sidney touched the ground first and raced ahead. Then the SEAL's feet touched ground. He ran out the landing, releasing his chute and scanning his surroundings, M4 carbine with IR laser designator at the ready. The sparse tree line was clear. The dog crouched in the grass next to him. He raised the camera and antenna on the dog's tactical assault vest.

"All clear, boy?"

Sidney chuffed an affirmative.

Winkler gathered the billows of black nylon parachute and S-rolled the material so it didn't blow away.

He checked his HUD and switched to open comms. "Five minutes till the AC-130 lights this place up. Let's move."

The landed SEALs broke into two teams, one for each entrance. Winkler, with Sidney on point, fast-walked his men across the open field to the small rise that shielded them from the bunker entrance. A pair of guards flanked a steel door set into a low concrete wall.

"Pogo and Wolfman, take them."

Two men melted away from the rear of his team, reappearing a few seconds later in his peripheral vision. They crept forward, the silenced muzzles of their rifles parsing the thin underbrush.

A series of muffled pops, like rim shots on a drum, and the two guards sank to the ground.

"Get those charges on the door. Move!"

Two more SEALs rushed past him. They knelt at the steel door, pressing shaped charges into the hinges and locks, then backed away to cover.

"Charges set."

Winkler checked the clock on his display. "Stand by." The plan was to blow both doors at the same time. "Blow it."

"Fire in the hole!" came the response.

The resulting blast crashed through the nighttime silence like a car wreck. In the dust, pulverized concrete, and smoke, the shattered door wobbled and fell open.

Winkler and Sidney were already running at the bright square of light.

Now the real work began.

CHAPTER 59

Sea of Japan, 30 miles east of Yang-do Island

Midshipman First Class Janet Everett tugged her shoulder straps even tighter as the MH-47 Chinook helicopter hit an air pocket. Her headphones crackled, and a voice said, "Nervous flier, Everett?"

She looked around the red-lit cabin to find Captain McHugh grinning at her. He held up three fingers and mimed at her to switch her headset channel.

"You okay?" he said, when they were on a private channel.

She nodded. "I've only been on a helo twice before and it wasn't anything like this." She sat between Goodwin and Ramirez, opposite McHugh and Riley, toward the front of the open cargo bay. A few seats separated them from a squad of SEALs. They were serious men, armed to the teeth and looking none too happy to be escorting three baby officers into a firefight.

"Mr. Riley said you used to be a SEAL, sir," she said.

McHugh let his gaze wander toward the rear of the helo. "Long time ago. I was injured by a North Korean sailor. My own fault. Kid with a knife got me when I let my guard down. Maybe this mission is payback, in a way." He smiled again.

"Do you miss it?"

Brendan shook his head. "No—well, sort of. Yeah, I guess I do. It's complicated." He gestured at her fellow mids. "You guys really figured out this computer virus all on your own? That's some good work, Everett."

She was glad the darkness hid her blushing. "It wasn't on our own, sir. We had lots of help, and Mr. Riley, too. He believed in us." She looked at Goodwin and Ramirez, both sitting with their eyes closed. "Besides, they're the smart ones. I just sorta translate what they're doing and fill in the gaps when I can."

"Don't sell yourself short, Everett. You're their leader."

"I guess so, sir." She felt herself blushing again.

McHugh switched subjects on her. "You know how to use that sidearm?" His eyes dropped to the holstered nine-millimeter at her waist. Neither Ramirez nor Goodwin was armed.

"Yes, sir. My dad was an Army Ranger. I think deep down he wanted a boy, but we made it work. I made the academy pistol team my plebe year and we went to nationals."

The older man's eyes met hers. "Okay, that's good to know, but shooting a target and shooting a man are different. These guys"—he jerked his head toward the exit ramp—"are here to handle the rough stuff. You just make sure your team gets the real job done. As their leader, that's your mission. Got it?"

Everett nodded.

The helo heeled over as they took a turn at high speed. Everett, looking out the small window, felt like she could reach out and touch the tops of the waves below them.

The pilot's voice broke into their conversation. "The advance team has started the assault. Landing in one-five minutes." She felt a shift in the atmosphere of the cabin, a tightening of the tension.

McHugh switched back to the shared channel. "Hey, Everett, did you know Riley was my plebe at the academy?"

Riley, looking miserable strapped into his jump seat, gave her a wan smile and nodded. The helo went into a steep dive.

"Yup," McHugh continued with a laugh, "my wife, Liz, and I met young Don when he was no older than Goodwin there. He was a terrible plebe, but he turned out okay, don'tcha think?"

Goodwin and Ramirez smiled.

"I guess he just had a good leader in his life, sir," Everett said.

Yang-do Island

Rafiq felt his ears pop from a change in air pressure . . . or an explosion. The emergency alarm screeched out a warning.

The wolves had arrived.

He raced to the security monitors in time to see a line of helmeted men in dark camouflage stream past. One by one, the camera feeds winked out as the intruders moved deeper into the bunker.

He fixed the image in his mind, especially the weapons. They were carrying M4 carbines. Definitely not Chinese. Americans?

Rafiq whirled on the two guards at the door. "Go!" he shouted. "They must not get into this room!"

He walked through the watch floor, pointing at the men and women sitting behind their workstations.

"You, stand . . . and you." When he had finished, only three operators and So-won were sitting.

Rafiq strode to the front of the room, planting himself underneath the large portrait of the Supreme Leader. "The Americans are here! On the sacred soil of your homeland! You are all cyberwarriors, but now you must become *real* warriors." He scanned the room. They were smiling, nodding; some even had tears in their eyes. "Your nation is under attack! I need your sacrifice." He pointed at the picture above him. "He demands your sacrifice."

One of the young men in the front row raised his arms over his head and screamed, his head thrown back, teeth bared in a war cry. He rushed to the small arms locker, seized a rifle, and ran out of the room. The rest of them stood frozen in place.

"Go!" Rafiq yelled at them. There was a mad rush for the locker and a few more shouts; then the room fell silent.

Rafiq followed them to the exit, closing the heavy steel door and dogging it shut. They were sealed off from the rest of the bunker.

He walked to his desk and took his Glock 19 from the drawer. He chambered a round and calmly shot the three remaining coders in the head. Their eyes were still wide with shock as their corpses collapsed to the floor.

So-won screamed from behind him. "What are you doing? They were our best coders! We need them."

"Exactly. They knew the most about what we've built. I don't want that knowledge falling into the wrong hands. The Americans call it tying up loose ends."

"You bastard. They trusted you. *I* trusted you."

Rafiq smiled. "No, So-won, you're different. I gave you the chance to build a beautiful cyberweapon and you loved every minute of it." He stepped close and gripped her chin in his hand. Her skin was warm, the bones of her jaw like twigs in his grip. Her pulse beat rapidly against his fingers.

She would not meet his gaze, so he pulled her face close to his. "Admit it," he said.

Her dark eyes met his—and he knew he had her.

"What do you need me to do?" she said.

"The Chinese," he said. "Give the command to use nuclear weapons."

Her eyes flared but stayed locked with his. "I need to gain access to their nuclear codes. That will take time."

He released her. "Then get started."

CHAPTER 60

Sea of Japan, 5 miles off Yang-do Island

Everett listened as information streamed across the JSOC raid force channel. They all sounded so calm—not bored, just emotionless and precise.

"Spectres commencing fire."

Captain McHugh pointed out the window behind her, and she twisted in her seat. The bulk of the island was dark. Suddenly, a string of explosions began on the ground. She switched her comm channel to the private circuit they'd been on before.

"AC-130 gunships," he said.

"But I don't see any firing going on," she replied.

"Drop your night-vision device."

She lowered the night vision goggles mounted to the front of her helmet and was surprised to see brilliant beams of light shoot from the air to the ground. They lasted a second, then winked out.

"High-energy lasers. UV spectrum. Invisible to the naked eye, but oh so deadly to anything on the ground." He paused as a massive explosion bloomed into the night. "That would be an ammo dump."

"Touchdown in two minutes," came the pilot's voice.

The MH-47 banked hard and started a steep descent. Everett could see another MH-47 out the window mirroring their movements.

A pinpoint of light shot up from the ground toward them. A second later, the flanking helo's engine exploded.

"This is Eagle Two, I'm hit, I'm hit. Emergency landing." The helo dropped from sight.

"Spectre One, this is Eagle One. We are taking fire. Request assistance." The pilot of their helo rattled off a string of coordinates.

"Roger that, Eagle One. Commencing fire." Everett detected a flicker of movement far above them, and the ground next to their landing zone erupted in fire and pulverized earth. Another secondary explosion blossomed out of the darkness.

"Cease fire, Spectre One. Cease fire."

Ramirez and Goodwin were both looking out the window now. She saw Ramirez mouth, *Holy shit.*

"Hundred-and-five-millimeter shells, pinpoint accuracy," Brendan said, switching back to the group channel. "Those guys could shoot a golf ball off a tee from a mile away. Hang on, Midshipmen, we're coming in hot."

The exit ramp dropped as the helo touched down. The SEALs at the rear of the craft ran out of the cabin with weapons up. Brendan shepherded the mids down the ramp, where their escort had formed a wedge. At the bottom, he halted and crunched the midshipmen and Riley together, then leaned in to shout in their faces.

"Listen up. This is not a movie. You can get shot. Stay behind me, keep your heads down, and you'll be fine. Got it?"

They nodded. Brendan keyed his throat mic. "Let's move out."

Yang-do Island

"How much longer?" Rafiq peered over So-won's shoulder at the screen. The Chinese Second Artillery Corps nuclear forces had an additional level of security, an unfortunate twist in his plans, but So-won was confident she could crack it—if she had enough time.

She frowned at the screen. "Thirty minutes? Maybe an hour? It's not an exact science." Her tone was sharp, and her gaze kept drifting back to the corpses of her fellow coders.

He moved back to the security station. Most of the screens were blank now, but the assault forces had missed a few of the less obvious cameras. They were being attacked by Americans, probably Special Forces. How had they found him so quickly?

Pak. That rat bastard must have defected and sold his soul to the United States.

He returned to So-won's side. "Put the program on automatic. It's time to go."

"Does that mean you're going to kill me now?" Her eyes were dark slits.

He hesitated. That was the plan, of course. No loose ends, no dead weight, nothing to slow him down. He had a boat waiting in a hidden cove along the rocky coast. A small craft that would pass a cursory inspection as a Japanese fishing vessel. With her clearly North Korean features and accented English, she was a liability he couldn't afford.

Rafiq surprised himself by replying, "No, you're coming with me." He checked the security cameras. The commandos were on this level now, and they had at least one dog with them. He heard the distant rattle of gunfire as his former technical team tried to hold them off. The wolves were outside, but it would take time to break through the steel door of the control room.

So-won heard the gunfire, too. Her dark eyes found his. "Chul, we're trapped."

"How much longer?" he barked back at her.

Tears streaked down her pocked cheeks. "I don't know. The decryption program is running, but it takes time."

Rafiq studied her workstation, wishing for a status bar or some indication of when it would be done. He chewed his lip in frustration. If he stayed, he might hold them off for a few more precious minutes.

Or he could run.

He grabbed So-won by the hand, pulling her toward the back of the room. She resisted, crying, and Rafiq realized she thought he was about to kill her.

"Stop it, So-won. I'm taking you with me. You'll be safe."

He paused at the bookcase at the back of the room and slipped his hand into the second shelf, pressing the release at the back of the cabinet. The bookcase moved away from the wall, revealing a door with a worn sign that said MISSILE BAYS.

"There's always another way." He pulled her into the passageway and dragged the door shut behind them.

CHAPTER 61

As the helo plunged into a steep dive, Dre Ramirez's body strained against the three-point harness that kept her strapped into her seat. She felt more than saw the squad of SEALs tense. As a group, they dropped the unwieldy night-vision goggles from the front of their helmets down across their eyes, the four lenses making them look like something out of a science-fiction movie.

When Ramirez followed suit, the effect on her vision was stunning. During their hasty briefing session, the petty officer who outfitted Dre and her friends had called them GPNV goggles, short for ground panoramic night vision. Although they looked like two sets of binoculars mashed together, she immediately saw the benefit. Not only could she see the ghostly green of night-vision goggles she'd worn before, but these had an infrared heat display and expanded her field of view to somewhere slightly forward of her ears.

"Whoa," Dre heard Everett say. "I can almost see behind me. These are cool."

The helo touched down and Captain McHugh was on his feet, herding them down the ramp.

The second MH-47, its damaged engine still smoking, had managed to land in one piece. SEALs, their faces highlighted in her vision by the IR detector, streamed out of the belly of the damaged craft and automatically broke into squads. They disappeared into the green shadows of the surrounding terrain.

Their group moved swiftly up an incline, the SEALs forming a protective cordon around them. They ran across a grassy field; then she felt gravel crunch under her boots. A wall of concrete rose out of the landscape and a square of light appeared in her night-vision goggles. Two dead North Korean soldiers were sprawled to either side of the entrance, and a steel door crusted with rust lay on the ground, blown off its hinges. In the heat register of the IR detector, the dead men's faces registered as cooler than the live soldiers around her.

Apart from her grandfather's at his funeral a few years ago, they were the first dead bodies she'd ever seen.

Two of the armed men around her raised the night-vision goggles off their faces, snapping them into a locked position above their helmets. Ramirez did the same, following the squad into the wide concrete hallway.

They encountered another pair of dead North Koreans at the first turn in the hallway. The walls were raked with deep gouges from stray bullets, and there was a blast pattern on the wall from some kind of explosion. Her boots stuck to the floor as they walked through the fresh blood, and the sharp scent of expended rounds penetrated her sinuses.

Deep inside the bunker, she heard more gunfire, then a pause, and return fire.

Their escort advanced at a steady pace. No rushing, just a constant movement forward. They passed another half-dozen dead men, then a wounded SEAL with a tourniquet applied to his leg. The medic in their squad peeled off to treat the injured man.

The lead man held up a closed fist and everyone stopped. She could hear Goodwin's heavy breathing next to her. Ramirez gripped his elbow, and he nodded in reply, still staring straight ahead.

"Captain McHugh?" the lead man called out. "The strike team is at the ops center. They're placing charges now. We'll hold till the space is secured."

"Give us a warning," Brendan said. He turned to the mids and Don. "When you hear 'fire in the hole,' you cover your ears and open your mouth. Got it?"

Ramirez nodded, as did Goodwin and Everett. In the harsh fluorescent light, Goodwin's dark skin had an ashen undertone.

A few seconds later: "Fire in the hole!"

She clamped her hands over her ears and threw her jaw wide open. Under her feet she felt a heavy bump, and her ears popped. The lights flickered. Dust filtered down from the overhead.

The lead man stood. "Let's go." He set a new, faster pace through the dim tunnels. They went down two flights of steps into what looked more like an office space. Instead of raw concrete, industrial linoleum covered the floor. Heavy dust in the air caught in her throat.

There were more dead bodies here, but whereas the dead men in the upper levels had worn full battle dress, these corpses were in dress uniforms and looked like office workers. She saw at least four women among the dead, and the air was heavy with the scent of blood and vomit and shit. She stole a glance at her friends. Goodwin was gagging at the stench, and Everett stared straight at the back of the man in front of her.

"It's all right, Michael," Ramirez whispered. She gripped his biceps, and he nodded back.

A SEAL met them next to an open doorway. A heavy steel door, charred and twisted from an explosion but still hanging on its hinges, was jammed back against the wall. To Ramirez's surprise, a dog sat by his side. The animal wore a bulletproof vest over his rib cage, and his attentive gaze flitted from his partner to Captain McHugh.

"What've we got, Winky?" McHugh asked.

"This is definitely their ops center, sir. Three dead inside, execution-style. Computer geeks, not soldiers. No sign of Roshed." His eyes passed over Riley, Ramirez, and the other two mids. "The room's cleared for your team."

McHugh cursed. "Roshed's here somewhere. Tear this place apart if you have to but find him. I'll stay here with the tech team. You can take these guys with you." He jerked his thumb at their escort.

"Aye, aye, sir. Sidney, with me." The dog leaped up at the sound of his name.

Apart from the obvious language differences on signs, to Ramirez's eye, the North Korean control room looked remarkably like the watch floor at Cyber Command back home. The computer workstations were arranged arena-style facing large wall screens. The screens showed the East China Sea and the landmasses of China's east coast, with Taiwan to the south and Japan and the Korean peninsula to the north. The digital map was covered with color-coded symbols that she took to be ships and other military assets.

Ramirez paused when she saw the three dead bodies on the floor. Two women and a young man; they'd each been shot once in the forehead.

"That's what you get when you work for Rafiq Roshed," McHugh said in an acid tone.

"Oh my God," Riley said, pointing at the wall screen. "That's the entire Chinese and Japanese militaries up there. Ships, planes, even bombers sitting on the runway and their weapons loadout."

McHugh moved to what looked like the watch supervisor's station. "Don, you need to see this."

Ramirez, Riley, and the other mids crowded around the screen.

"It's a decryption program," Riley said. "It looks like it's trying to access a separate Chinese system." He tapped the space bar on the keyboard. "We're locked out." He pulled out the chair and sat down. "You three mids, find a terminal and let's figure out how to shut this thing down."

Minutes ticked by. Ramirez sorted through the screens, sampling code she could gain access to, looking for a way into the system. She rolled her chair close to Goodwin and said loud enough for Everett, who was sitting on the other side of Goodwin, to hear, "What do you think, Michael?"

He shook his head like he was trying to shake off a bee. "I don't know. This is the first time I'm seeing the full program. It's . . . a little overwhelming."

Everett put a hand on his shoulder. "You need to focus. They're counting on us."

"I see it," Goodwin said. He was staring at the screen.

"They're trying to break into the Chinese nuclear launch system. That's the final step."

Ramirez crowded closer. Although the room was cool, Goodwin was sweating.

"Can you shut it off?" she whispered.

Goodwin shook his head. "It'll just keep going until it gets what it wants. The only way is if the Chinese shut down their entire network. Everything, at the same time." He looked up at Riley and his friends. "And I mean, like, now."

"There has to be another way, Michael," Ramirez said, acutely aware that her voice had a begging quality. "Think."

"If there is, I don't see it," he said. "They've trained the puppy. This is the last lesson."

Everett sat back in her chair. "What if we give it something else to do? Distract it."

"I don't follow," Goodwin said.

Ramirez fell back in her own chair, thunderstruck at the simplicity of the idea. "Janet's right. We can't stop the puppy, but we can distract it. Teach the dog a new trick. Move its attention away from the nukes."

"Like what?" Goodwin asked.

Everett threw up her hands. "I don't know. Inventory all the toilet paper in the entire Chinese army or calculate the number of bullets in the Japanese arsenal."

"Too easy," Ramirez said, hunching over her keyboard, her strength renewed. It was all so clear now—she knew what she had to do. "It's a distributed system. The program will just pass along the command and wait for an answer. It won't actually tax the resources here on the island. We need a *huge* task, something that will suck up all the computing power in this place . . ." Her gaze rose to the wall screen festooned with symbols representing the Chinese and Japanese military units. She looked at Everett, who said, "Like activating the US Trident network."

Everett dragged Riley away from one of the workstations to where the mids were sitting. "We want the program to go live on Trident," she said.

Riley stared at them. "Are you out of your minds? You want to activate a computer virus inside the US military's most secret network?"

Everett grabbed his arm. "Listen. The program already has control of the Chinese command and control network. It's going for their nukes and it will get there eventually. We need to distract it, slow it down, suck up resources to buy us some time."

"But what if you turn it on and you can't turn it off?"

Everett looked at Goodwin and Ramirez. "We'll figure it out. I promise."

Ramirez felt the first twinge of doubt. She was the one who would have to figure it out. *They* had to figure it out. Together.

"I need to call this in," Don said. "Get permission." His face was twisted in a grimace, and he rubbed his chin in rapid strokes.

Ramirez stood. "Mr. Riley—Don, they'll never give you permission, or if they do it'll be too late. We need to do this, and we need to do it now."

Riley threw a questioning look at Brendan, who said, "Your call, Don. I'll back it."

Riley swallowed hard. He nodded.

"Do it."

The command to activate the virus inside the US Trident network was already queued on her screen. Ramirez dropped back into her chair and hit the return key. "Done," she said.

Seconds ticked by; the only sound was the hiss of the air ducts. Goodwin pursed his lips at his screen.

"It's working. The program is reallocating computer resources to the new problem."

On the wall screen, a US ship popped up as an active symbol. Then another, and another.

Riley gnawed at a fingernail. "Good, now put a bullet in this thing once and for all."

CHAPTER 62

Yang-do Island, North Korea

The underground missile bays of the bunker reminded Rafiq of catacombs. Entire rooms carved out of living rock and filled with abandoned junk, including a complete mobile launcher that had been stripped for parts and left to rust away in the dampness of the tunnels.

He cursed Pak under his breath. There was no other explanation for the speed and accuracy with which the Americans had penetrated the bunker. But Pak had never been in the abandoned missile bays. He and So-won would be safe from the attackers in here—at least for now.

The Americans had dogs with them. A strange tickle rose from deep inside his chest. A part of his brain tried to analyze it, to categorize the new sensation. He grappled with the answer—fear. He was afraid.

When he lost his beloved Nadine and his family was taken away from him, he swore that the world would pay his price. All this time, all these years, Rafiq had convinced himself there was no personal sacrifice too high; even death was fine with him.

Now, with death panting at his heels, he wasn't so sure.

"Chul, stop!" So-won said, her voice echoing in the chamber. Her thin figure was nearly lost in the shadows.

"What?" They were running out of time to get off the island.

She pointed to a network terminal atop a dirty desk. "I want to see if the program has completed the task."

Rafiq peered down the corridor. These tunnels went on forever and the island might be crawling with American commandos by now. Then he looked into So-won's eyes and saw her resolve. The kind of strength he should be showing. "Okay, but quickly."

She turned on the terminal. The ancient machine beeped and whirred to life. Rafiq tried to still his foot from tapping the floor. Finally, So-won got to the command prompt screen. "I set up a remote-access program in case we needed to look at the program from offsite."

Rafiq frowned. She'd never mentioned that to him before. He wondered what else she hadn't told him.

"Oh, no," she said, gripping the sides of the dusty monitor. "No, no, no!"

Rafiq squinted at the screen, but it was all a jumble to him in his heightened state of awareness. "What happened?"

"They're trying to activate the program on the American network."

"That's a good thing, right? That will take over the US military command and control systems."

"No, they're doing it to slow down the system, refocus the computing power away from the Chinese network. They'll use the extra time to shut the program down."

Rafiq tried to absorb what she was saying.

"We have to go back," she said, standing.

Rafiq's mouth went dry.

Yang-do Island

Everett's gaze flicked between Goodwin and Ramirez. She felt like a third wheel. The pair were completely absorbed in their work, talking in shorthand she found difficult to follow. Goodwin seemed to be onto a possible solution, but Ramirez wasn't convinced. She kept one eye on the wall screen as the system added US assets at what felt like an increasing rate.

Riley was hunched over another workstation, with Captain McHugh standing behind him. Their attention shifted from the computer monitor to the wall screen, where at least a dozen US Navy assets were showing, each ready to be taken over with the touch of a button. They talked back and forth in low tones.

She was the only one with nothing to do.

This room felt odd, and it wasn't just the scent of the dead North Korean bodies lined up in a neat row in one of the aisles. It felt like she was being watched.

She allowed her gaze to rove across the space. The SEAL team had turned all the overhead lights on when they'd searched the room, and they were still on, the harsh fluorescents casting everything in a stark cold glare. That's what she could do: dim the lights so it was easier to see the screens.

As she stood, a flicker of movement along the back wall caught her eye. Her brain registered it as a shadow, but in this light-drenched space there were no shadows. She turned back.

The bookcase on the far wall was moving, easing open. She thought she saw a gun—

"Get down!" she screamed. She threw her arms across Ramirez and Goodwin, dragging them to the floor. Out of the corner of her eye, she was Captain McHugh draw his weapon. Gunshots blasted into the enclosed space with a deafening boom. Her ears rang.

Her two friends' eyes were white with fear. She slapped the floor and pointed to the door. "Stay down and get out," she said.

Everett clawed the Glock out of her hip holster and wriggled forward to peek around the corner of the workstation.

Don was kneeling, his hand pressed against Captain McHugh's chest. The unconscious officer still held his sidearm. Riley's face was rigid with fear.

Everett gripped her weapon. "You get him out of here. I'll hold them off." She belly-crawled past him before he could say anything.

She could hear someone moving in the back of the room, and another sound—the clatter of a keyboard. A thought chilled her. The program now had control of the US forces. If someone accessed the system now, they could attack anything.

Everett got on her hands and knees to move faster. The typing sounds grew louder. She zeroed in on them as coming from a workstation near the back of the room. She could hear heavy breathing and the rapid patter of keys just on the other side of the barrier.

She drew her weapon, gathered her legs underneath her, and stood, bringing the handgun to bear on the typist.

Everett blinked. The girl behind the keyboard had a narrow, acne-pocked face and shoulder-length stringy black hair. She looked up at Everett in mutual surprise.

"Take your hands off the keyboard." The girl raised her hands, her thin fingers splayed out like twigs.

"Stand up."

The girl stood. "Chul," she said.

"What?"

The reply came in English—excellent English, in fact. "His name is Chul." Her eyes slid past Everett just as the midshipman heard the scuff of a shoe from behind her. Everett spun, firing her weapon once, twice, three times.

The first shot took Everett high on her left arm and slammed her back against the workstation. Her breath burst from her like an explosion. A second shot hammered her center mass, a punch in the gut that robbed her of any breath she might have had left. Everett's legs lost all strength, and she slid to the ground.

A booted foot clamped over her wrist, pinning the handgun to the floor. The man looking down at her had dark features and hard eyes, half closed in a fierce squint. His lips twisted in a cruel smile.

"You're Roshed," she gasped. Her voice sounded breathy, distant, like she was hearing the words from someone else.

He nodded. The deep black hole of the gun muzzle swung toward her, and Janet Everett wanted to scream, but her lungs were empty. The linoleum felt slick beneath her cheek. She was numb, so still and cold, as the warmth of life fled her body.

The image of the man and the gun darkened in her vision. Her hearing, still dulled from her own shots, registered shots in rapid-fire succession.

But they sounded very far away.

CHAPTER 63

Yang-do Island, North Korea

Lieutenant Winkler was clearing rooms on the lower level with Sidney when his headset burst with a frantic call. "We're under attack! Help!"

"Who is this?" he said.

"Riley," the voice screamed back. "I'm in the control room. Brendan's down—"

The sound of a single gunshot rang over his headset.

Winkler and his canine partner got to the control room in under a minute. Riley was just outside the control room door, his hand clamped high on McHugh's chest. A trail of blood streaked the floor where he'd dragged the captain's body out of the room.

"The midshipmen," Winkler barked, "where are they?"

"Inside," Riley's round face was white as paper and his words came out in a rush. "Ramirez took my weapon and went back in. I heard shots . . . I don't know about Everett. She was still in there . . . she went after them. There was a lot of shooting."

Winkler cursed. The room had been cleared, but he

should have left men with them anyway. He entered the ops center with his carbine up. "Midshipmen? Sound off. Where are you?"

"Over here, sir."

Winkler made his way through the aisles of computer workstations until he got to the back of the room. Goodwin had both hands pressing down on Everett's upper arm. The young woman's eyes were closed, but she was still breathing. Leaked blood formed a dark red halo around her upper body.

Ramirez clutched a handgun with both hands, standing over her friends, her gaze slowly circling the room.

"They came out of nowhere, sir. I fired back . . . and they just disappeared." Her hands shook; her face was pale. "Is—is Janet dead?"

Winkler felt for Everett's pulse and was rewarded with a strong beat. He squeezed Goodwin's hands, nodding for him to keep up the pressure. "She'll make it as long we get her out of here soon." He called for a medic, then raced back to Riley.

Winkler knelt next to McHugh. The bullet had entered near his neck where the body armor was lightest, shattering his collarbone. He felt for a pulse. Weak, but there. He slipped his hand behind McHugh's neck, searching for an exit wound, and cursed when he realized the bullet had deflected down into the man's chest. Sidney nosed the man's body, whining.

"Keep the pressure on." Winkler said. "The corpsman will be here soon." He stood. "On me, Sid."

Back in the room, next to the still unconscious Everett, Sidney sniffed at a spray of blood on the floor that held the imprint of a man's boot. He whined.

The corpsman hustled in, displacing Goodwin. Winkler pulled Sidney back so he could inspect the boot print. A man's shoe, judging by size. It had to be Roshed. "She winged him." He looked around. "But where did he come from?"

The mids exchanged glances. "We don't know," Goodwin said, watching the corpsman work on Everett. "Janet saw something and knocked us down. Then the shooting started. It all happened so fast."

Winkler turned to his canine partner. He slapped the floor twice. "Sidney, hunt!" The dog's nose swept across the linoleum. He ranged through the aisle, Winkler following. They stopped at a computer workstation. "Someone was using this computer," he called to the midshipmen.

Ramirez turned, her face alight. "They're logged in?"

Winkler shrugged. "Looks like it."

She brushed past Winkler, her expression hopeful. "Michael, this station is logged in as system admin. We're in!" Her fingers flew across the keyboard. "I'm giving you admin privileges. Your password is . . . Janet." She typed the last few keystrokes, then sat back.

Winkler followed Sidney as the animal continued along the wall, finally stopping at a floor-to-ceiling bookcase. The dog whined and pawed at the wall. "Must be a door here," Winkler said. He knelt, searching for the handle.

"Midshipmen!" Riley's voice was sharp, borderline angry. The two mids stood. "We've got a job to do. What's our status?"

"We've got admin access, sir. We can figure out a way to turn this thing off."

Riley avoided looking at Everett. "Good. Get to work."

Winkler found the catch hidden on the second shelf. The bookcase swung away from the wall to reveal a concrete tunnel. He shone a light into the darkness, then pressed his throat mic. "This is Winky. I need a squad down here in the control room to clear out a rabbit hole."

"Sir?"

Winkler turned back to the mids. Goodwin pointed at the wall screen. "They launched a cruise missile. Salvo Tomahawks."

"Who did?"

"We did. The USS *John McCain*." His finger trembled, and Winkler could see the rust red of Everett's blood on his fingernails.

"What's the target?"

Goodwin stared at him. "Us."

Winkler felt a chill run up his spine. They had at least twenty men topside, plus helos. "You mean here? This island?"

Goodwin nodded. "ETA fifteen minutes. Give or take."

"Can you turn it off? Retarget it?"

The young man shook his head. "They locked out the retargeting function. I can try, but we're running out of time." Goodwin looked at the screen. "If the system gets those Chinese nukes . . ."

Winkler spoke into his mic. "All units, all units, this is team leader. Be advised we have inbound Tomahawks for this location. ETA one-five mikes. Clear the surface and get the helos airborne ASAP."

Acknowledgments flowed in fast. Winkler watched the two mids work. He owed one to Riley and his team for the warning. He'd seen firsthand the damage a conventional Tomahawk could do.

Sidney pawed at his leg, whining toward the open door. "Not now, boy."

The dog persisted, and Winkler looked around. "Where's Riley?"

The two mids looked up. "Don't know," said Ramirez, and they went back to work.

Sidney whined at the open door.

"Oh no he didn't," Winkler said.

Yang-do Island

Don Riley ran until he thought his heart would gallop out of his chest. He grabbed the rough wall, dragging in deep lungfuls of air. He hauled at the sweaty neckline of the heavy bulletproof vest.

Brendan shot, maybe dead. He swiped his left hand across his face and realized he was crying. His Glock was still clenched in his right fist.

Pull it together, Riley.

Every rational thought in his head told him to turn around and let the SEALs handle this. They were the pros. It was their job to take this asshole down.

No. Rafiq Roshed had left a track of devastation in Don Riley's life that must be accounted for. This was personal.

A disused launcher minus the missile loomed in his night-vision goggles, the sharp outline softened by a thick layer of dust. A soft glow shone from the space beyond the rotting hulk. He flattened himself against the vehicle and peeked around the edge. An ancient computer terminal, so old it had only a basic green CRT display, was running.

Roshed had come this way.

He searched in the dust for footprints and found them leading into another tunnel carved out of living rock. And there were two sets of prints: a man-sized boot, and then a smaller, narrower footprint. A woman? The prints were tangled, as if he was dragging the woman. A prisoner?

He dropped to his knee to get a closer look. The larger boot on the right side made a trailing scuff in the dirt. He touched a dark blot on the rock floor. Wet, sticky. *Blood*. He wasn't dragging her, she was helping him.

Rafiq Roshed was injured.

He gripped his Glock and moved until his shoulder brushed the rough surface of the rock wall. With steady steps, he advanced down the corridor, weapon at the ready, every sense screaming for a sign of his prey.

No running, no tears, no drama.

It was time for payback.

Yang-do Island

Michael forced the image of a wounded Everett out of his head.

He focused on the monitor, trying to get his mind to see beyond the strings of information on the screen. The structure of the program, the way each piece fit together, was . . . elegant. He would like to have met the person who built this program. They would have a lot in common, he suspected.

"Michael, we need to hurry," Dre said.

He ignored her. This could not be rushed. The answer was here—somewhere. His solution needed to be as elegant as the thing he sought to destroy. He needed to put the pin back in the grenade.

The genius of the virus was that none of it resided here in the bunker—it was all resident on the networks it had infected. Somehow this Roshed person had managed to upload the building blocks of his code onto the servers of his targets like a child who had hidden Lego pieces all over his house.

From those hidden pieces, he had built his own shadow command and control network. The resulting program was massive, and it was about to become alive. A feral network controlling some of the most powerful weapons on earth.

All of those pieces would need an assembly program . . .

"That's it!"

Ramirez looked at him like he'd lost his mind. She'd rigged up a counter on her screen. The inbound cruise missile would destroy the satellite uplink, cutting off their only chance of shutting the program down remotely. If it received no direction from them, the virus—including the version they'd activated on the US Trident network—would revert to its training. Roshed had taught the Chinese system to execute attacks, but they hadn't taught the US system anything. Their forces would be sitting ducks in the Chinese line of fire.

He read all this in Ramirez's eyes—and she was afraid.

The counter read 3:02.

"The assembly routine," Goodwin said. "They built this program from bits and pieces of code. There had to be assembly instructions, and if there's instructions to assemble it, then—"

"We can tell it to disassemble itself," she finished for him. Ramirez turned to the monitor. "There has to be a command sequence here. . . ." She blasted through screen after screen of information.

"Our forces tried to shoot down the cruise missile," Winkler said from behind them. "No joy."

The counter read 2:14.

"There's too much here, Michael, help me." She threw him a screen of data. He allowed it to spool, increasing the feed rate until the lines almost blurred in his vision. He could hear Winkler's heavy breathing behind him, Ramirez's staccato gasps at his side.

There! His brain registered commands used to search for and link together some of the junk code he'd been searching for back at Cyber Command. He stopped the data feed and scrolled backwards. What he found were more of the linking commands. "I think I found it," he whispered.

1:47

Ramirez pushed him out of the way. She highlighted the chunk of code and threw it onto a new screen. She muttered to herself; it sounded like chanting. Goodwin couldn't make out the words.

0:45

Her fingers paused over the keyboard, twitching.

"Send it," Goodwin said.

Ramirez punched the return key. A confirmation box flashed on the screen.

"It's gone."

0:15

The dog whined and looked up at his partner. "It's okay, Sid," Winkler said.

The big man put his arms around Goodwin and Ramirez. Gently, he forced them to the floor, using his body to shield them and his animal partner. Sidney's panting was warm against the back of Goodwin's neck. He heard Ramirez muttering to herself again. This time he could make out the words.

"Our Father, who art in Heaven . . ."

Then a giant force smashed him flat against the floor.

Yang-do Island

Rafiq leaned even more on So-won, her thin frame nearly buckling under his weight.

His leg was on fire. The bullet from the girl's weapon

had passed through his calf, touching his shinbone. Probably not broken, but he could not put weight on it.

Still, they'd disrupted the Americans' progress. There was no way they would be able to stop the program before it cracked the Chinese nuclear codes. And the hidden door let them make a clean escape.

So-won stumbled, forcing Rafiq to stand on his injured leg.

"Ahh!" he cried. He felt a flash of self-anger. He was old, feeble. The Rafiq of his earlier days would have laughed this injury off as a scratch.

And worse than that, he was afraid. He admitted it to himself now. His fear shadowed him in the dark, whispering in his ear.

"Look!" So-won said, pointing forward. A shimmer of gray in the darkness, the outlet of the tunnel. From there, all they needed to do was make it down the slope to the dock and they were free.

He increased their pace. So-won's nape fit snugly in his armpit, like a human crutch. She was sweating and panting, but they were working as a unit.

"You've done well," he said.

"We need to hurry, Chul—"

"I could not have done this without you." He could smell the ocean now, taste the fresh salty air blowing in the entrance. They were free.

Her arm tightened on his waist. "You don't understand. When we were in the control room I launched a—"

Rafiq heard a noise behind them and spun them both around. It sounded like the scrape of a boot on rock. Too late, he realized their bodies were outlined in the light of the cave entrance. He dropped to the ground and pulled his handgun, firing wildly into the darkness of the tunnel behind them.

So-won stood alone. Flashes sparked deep in the tunnel, and he saw one, two, three dark spots bloom on her jumpsuit. She toppled over.

Rafiq waited, his breath coming in sharp gasps. He pointed his weapon back into the dark. By his reckoning, he had one round left. His ears strained to hear something, anything to let him know his attacker's whereabouts.

He held his breath, but all he could hear was the sound of the surf a few hundred feet below him. The soothing noise made him want to close his eyes.

His weapon still pointed behind him, he shifted his weight, wincing at the noise.

No response.

He slid half a foot toward the entrance. He tensed. Was that a moan? Or the sound of the wind?

Rafiq was running out of time. The Americans would bring reinforcements. They would find the tunnel and come after him. He needed to move now.

Rafiq slid over and used the wall to pull himself to his feet. The smell of So-won's blood mixed with the scent of the ocean. Not unpleasant to his senses.

He took a tentative step outside. In the starlight, he could make out the narrow trail down to the hidden dock. He took another step. The pain was not so bad now.

Rafiq Roshed banished fear from his heart. A moment of softness, nothing more. Fear was for the weak. He was strong, and he won. Always.

Another step.

A noise like a sustained crack of thunder sounded high above him. He looked up to see a bolt of flame dropping straight down from the heavens.

The world erupted in fire. He felt the kiss of heat on his cheek, and his breath was sucked out of his lungs.

The fear he had so recently banished screamed back into his brain.

The shock wave from the Tomahawk cruise missile threw Rafiq Roshed's broken body far out to sea.

CHAPTER 64

Undisclosed location in the Russian Far East

The hood came off Borodin Gerasimov's head with a snap. His brain ached, and his mouth was gummy with thirst. How long had he been drugged? Hours? Days?

He squinted into the softly lit surroundings. He'd lost his glasses in the struggle, making everything appear as shapes and blurs in his diminished eyesight.

But the smells. Moisture, chlorine, scented oils . . . his heart seized with fear.

Aminev's bathhouse.

He drew in a deep breath of the humid air and calmed his brain. If Alexi Aminev wanted him dead, he'd already be dead. The fact that he was here meant Alexi wanted something else. Money, Gerasimov decided. This was a shakedown.

One of the blurs in front of him moved, drew closer, and sharpened into Alexi Aminev's bearded face. "Did you have a good trip, Borodin? Were my boys too rough on you?" His voice was so low it was almost drowned out by the white noise of the hot tub jets in the water behind him.

He tried a smile. "No, Alexi. No problem, they had a

job to do. They just got carried away." Gerasimov tried to rise but found he was cuffed to one of the teak deck chairs that littered the bathhouse.

Don't lose your head. Be cool.

"Alexi . . ." He paused. How to play this? Casual or penitent? "I—I was just about . . ."

Alexi's face loomed into sharp detail. His breath smelled of sour vodka and rotten meat, and there was a chunk of something caught in his front teeth. His pupils were dark pinpoints in the muddy brown of his eyes.

Gerasimov dismissed the tingle of fear that tried to worm its way into his thoughts. Alexi Aminev was a businessman. Gerasimov was a businessman. They would reach an agreement and go their separate ways. He'd made enough in profits from the China deal that he could afford to share. Hell, he'd made enough from the China deal that he could afford to retire.

This was a negotiation. Treat it that way.

"What? You were just about to *what,* Borodin?" Aminev was so close that his whiskers scraped across Gerasimov's cheek. And they were alone. Gerasimov noticed that for the first time. Where were all the women? And his ever-present entourage of tattooed confidants?

He drew his head back as far as he could. "Call you, of course. The China deal was ten times what we expected. I think success like this calls for some celebration."

Aminev's hairy face moved even closer, snuffling his neck. "I agree," he said, his words almost lost in the hollow of Gerasimov's collarbone. The other man's beard scratched his skin as it traveled up his neck. Gerasimov's flesh shrank in disgust.

The snuffling reached his jawline. Hot, fetid breath tickled his ear canal, offering a sick thrill of pleasure.

He opened his mouth to speak but closed it again when Alexi planted a wet kiss on his temple. Then the other man bit down on his ear.

Gerasimov screamed, his voice echoing in the open space.

Aminev's face loomed in his field of view again, his lips twisted into a leer, mouth dripping blood. A piece of flesh—*his flesh*—poked from between Aminev's teeth. The other man started chewing. Then he made an exaggerated swallow and a dumb show of opening his mouth to demonstrate that Gerasimov's ear was all gone.

"You were saying, Borodin?"

A warm flow ran down Gerasimov's neck, pooled in the hollow of his collarbone, and dripped down his chest. His breath came in quick, ragged gasps, and his vision started to close in.

A chilled glass pressed against his lips. Vodka flooded across his tongue, cutting through the gumminess of his mouth. Aminev's meaty paw slid behind his neck, tilting his head back. "Let's not pass out yet, Borodin. We're just getting started."

He choked on the vodka, but the bite of the cool alcohol cleared his head. His mind slipped into frantic calculations. "You've seen the news," he said. "There's no way they can trace it back to us."

Aminev stood. "Hold that thought." He padded away into the blurry land beyond Gerasimov's vision. There was the sound of snorting. *Good Christ, the man is taking more drugs.*

When Aminev came back, he was shirtless. His broad chest was completely covered in fur. His heavy pectorals swung like hairy breasts, and his belly bulged over the belt. He bowed closer. "You were saying, Borodin?"

Gerasimov couldn't tear his eyes away from the drop

of blood in the man's beard. A pink tongue snaked out and worried at the blood. Gerasimov felt the sourness rise in the back of his throat as he grappled with the truth.

He wasn't getting out of here alive.

"Take the money!" he screamed. "All of it. It's yours. You can still get away."

Aminev's eyes glittered. His hand slid behind Gerasimov's neck again. Powerful, but strangely comforting. He pressed his forehead against Gerasimov's. "You don't get away from the Brotherhood, Boris. You know that." He giggled. "They're coming for me. It's just a matter of time."

He reached behind his back and drew out a Grach handgun. Gerasimov's eyes followed the weapon as the other man laid it on the stone floor. He grinned up at Gerasimov. "You thought this was for you? Too easy, Borodin. This is for me. But before I go I have one thing to take care of."

He stood and stretched, the powerful muscles of his upper body rippling. "You, Borodin, you fucked me." One set of hairy knuckles pawed at his belt buckle. Gerasimov heard the sound of a zipper.

"Get ready, Borodin, because now I'm going to fuck you."

Gerasimov tore at his restraints. The heavy chair rocked on the stone floor.

Aminev stepped out of his trousers, and Gerasimov caught a flash of red silk underwear. The other man hooked a thumb in the waistband and dragged them down his thighs.

Gerasimov screamed and pushed back against the chair with all his might. The front legs rose off the floor; the chair teetered for an instant, then fell backwards.

Hot water and shiny bubbles surrounded him in the

hot tub. The chair sank slowly until it clunked against the cement bottom of the pool.

He opened his eyes in the frothy hot water. Alexi Aminev, fully unclothed, stood on the rim of the pool.

Gerasimov blew all the air out of his lungs and opened his mouth wide.

CHAPTER 65

North of Fortaleza, Brazil

Pak Myung-rok lowered his body into the lounge chair and listened to the surf crashing far below the stone veranda. A full moon was rising on the horizon, turning the glassy water molten silver.

He sucked on the end of his cigar and realized it had gone out again. Sparking the lighter on the teak table next to his chair, he lifted the flame and puffed until the end of the Cuban glowed. He followed the smoky taste with a sip of cognac.

Pak exhaled and closed his eyes. Bliss.

If he had planned it this way, it could not have gone better. The Americans were so appreciative of his timely information that they'd been happy to chip in to his private retirement fund. There was already more than enough in his Caymans account, but one could never have too much cash on hand.

He could have taken them up on their offer of relocation, but some information was better kept on a need-to-know basis.

Cash the check and disappear. It had all worked out

so well. A just reward for his honorable service to the Democratic People's Republic of Korea.

Another puff and a sip. The night air was perfect, like velvet on his skin. Pak dozed.

He was awoken by the sound of the doorbell. He rolled his shoulders and stretched his back. The evening's entertainment had arrived. He paused to drink off his cognac before he strode inside.

The video camera next to the steel-reinforced front door showed two women in skintight minidresses. One blond, one dark-haired, both stunning. Pak licked his lips. Apparently, the agency was getting a better handle on his tastes.

"Yes, ladies?" he said through the intercom in his accented Portuguese. It was a frightfully difficult language to learn, but he was determined to fit in.

The dark-haired woman unleashed a torrent of unintelligible Portuguese, then cupped her breasts at the camera.

Ah, the international language of lust.

Pak unbolted the door and threw it open. He spread his arms. *"Bem vinda, senhoras."*

The brunette stepped forward, her lips set in a sultry pout. She raised a tiny spray bottle.

"Boa noite."

Pak's mouth was dry, and his head throbbed with each heartbeat. He blinked, but there was something across his eyes. As far as he could tell, he was still wearing the silk pajamas from last night. The pants were damp where he'd soiled himself.

And his hands were tied behind his back. Panic set in.

He writhed on the cold ground, a chill wind cutting

through the thin material of his pajamas. His panicked pulse thundered in his ears.

Strong hands gripped him by the elbows and jerked him to his feet in one jarring motion. His back touched a solid wall. Cold. Concrete.

The blindfold was ripped away. Pak blinked in the weak sunlight. His knees almost gave out when his eyes met the icy stare of the Supreme Leader.

"Excellency," he gasped. "Thank goodness you brought me home. I was abducted by the Americans on my way to . . ."

Kim Jong-un turned slowly and walked away, his hands clasped behind his back.

"Excellency!" Pak called. "I have money! It's all for you. I was saving it for you."

The broad back of the Supreme Leader did not even miss a step.

That's when Pak saw the field gun. A massive weapon; the bore was so large he could have fit his fist inside of it. Pointed at him.

Fresh wetness ran down his leg.

"Excellency, please!"

The Supreme Leader reached the viewing stand built at a safe distance behind the field gun. He mounted the steps and accepted a pair of earphones from General Zhu.

The general screamed out an order, and the men standing at attention next to the gun sprang into action. Pak heard the sharp crack of the breech being opened and the slip of metal on metal as a round was loaded. The crew fitted their own hearing protection, then snapped back to attention.

Except for one soldier, who held a lanyard in his hand and faced the viewing stand.

The Supreme Leader raised his hand; the general screamed an order.

Pak stared at the pudgy palm, lit by the morning sun, and tried to will it to stay in the air.

The hand fell.

CHAPTER 66

United States Naval Academy, Annapolis, Maryland

A stiff breeze, unseasonably raw and cold for April, blew in from the Chesapeake Bay and straight into Janet Everett's eyes. She stood at attention, or as best she could with the arm sling beneath the service dress blue jacket making an unsightly bulge in her uniform. Medically, she was not required to wear her uniform, but she felt like it was the right thing to do. She'd gotten her roommates to pin the front of the double-breasted uniform coat closed. The empty left sleeve hung slack at her side, moving with the breeze.

Her shoulder throbbed where Roshed's bullet had pierced the inside of her arm, nicking the humerus bone and severing the brachial artery. Had it not been for Michael Goodwin's first-aid skills and the SEAL medic she would have bled to death on the floor of that dingy control room deep inside a North Korean island.

The Academy psychiatrist told Janet she'd suffered a trauma and to go easy on herself. She wrote her a prescription for sleeping pills.

She didn't take them, not even once. Instead of having nightmares, Janet found she liked the nighttime. The quiet helped her think, helped her make sense of everything that had happened.

Don Riley, standing next to her between a pair of aluminum crutches, wavered, and she put her good hand on his arm. The man looked like he'd come out on the losing end of a prizefight, with bruises still shadowing the side of his face. Dre and Michael had told her how Don Riley had pursued Roshed into the tunnels of Yang-do Island without telling anyone. After the explosion, the SEAL team dog had found Riley, unconscious, half buried in the rubble of a collapsed tunnel, and shot through the thigh.

But alive. Janet was glad for that.

"You okay, sir?" she murmured.

Riley nodded, his gaze stealing for the hundredth time to the front of the funeral assembly, where Captain McHugh's widow sat with her two children on either side of her. Liz Soroush's face was still and beautiful, and her dark eyes were dry. Her children, a girl with dark hair and skin coloring like her mother, and a boy, younger, with a blond crew cut, each held one of their mother's hands tightly, as if they were tethering her to the earth.

Captain McHugh visited Janet's thoughts again, as he often did. This time, she remembered him in the back of the Chinook helo before they landed on Yang-do Island. His easy grace under pressure, the way he spoke to her in calming tones when her own mind was about to spin out of control. He'd known exactly what to say to her in that moment. His experience talking, she figured at the time.

It was more than just his manner, though. Certainly, he was wary about the action to come, they all were, but as she remembered it now, there had been another layer to his mood.

Captain McHugh had been happy in that moment. Fulfilled.

The honor guard of six midshipmen, including Ramirez and Goodwin, lifted the American flag from Captain McHugh's casket and moved away in lockstep to perform the elaborate folding ceremony. The chief of naval operations presented the folded flag to Liz Soroush and bent low to say a few words that Janet couldn't hear.

The widow murmured a reply. Janet's heart ached as she saw the children watch their mother, eyes wide, looking for cues on how to act. She wondered if the reality of their loss had settled yet. Captain McHugh's widow left the flag in her lap and reached for her children's hands again, searching for her tether.

The sharp crack of the rifle squad delivering a twenty-one-gun salute snapped Janet back to reality. From somewhere behind them, the mournful sound of "Taps" floated in the air. The wind whistled through the crowd, making the lone bugler's lament fade and swell.

The domed lid of the mahogany-and-brass casket reflected the low clouds, their patterns shifting subtly on its surface. The priest nodded. The casket began to recede into the earth.

"Ashes to ashes, dust to dust," the priest intoned, and next to her Riley's body convulsed in a suppressed sob. He hung his head. Tears rained down. Janet put her good arm across his shoulders and held him as best she could.

In that moment, as she saw Riley's grief and the strength of McHugh's widow, the pieces clicked for Janet Everett. All those sleepless nights staring at the ceiling while her roommates snored gently. Every session with the psychiatrist where it felt like she talked endlessly about every emotion she had felt in every moment of every day since the raid. Every time she saw how Ramirez and Goodwin watched her.

All that time she was searching for an answer, the answer had been staring her in the face.

Captain McHugh's life had meant something. His death had been the price to make the world a better, safer place. He was a hero, not because he'd died, but because of how he had lived.

But now, he was gone, and a new generation needed to step in to continue the fight. She would honor Captain McHugh's life with her own service.

For the first time since the raid, Janet Everett wept.

Liz Soroush rose to her feet, her figure in a long dark coat bold against the blustery clouds hanging over the Chesapeake. She had a child on each hand as they stepped to a small mound of dirt next to the open grave. They each took a handful of dirt and threw it onto the coffin. The hollow sound was like hail on a window.

Then it was over. Janet huddled with Riley as the strangers who had assembled around the hole in the ground slowly dispersed. She watched a parade of brass offer their condolences to Liz, then hurry to their waiting cars for the trip back to Washington and the inertia of their own lives.

Ramirez and Goodwin joined Janet and Riley.

Finally, the widow said goodbye to the last well-wisher, sent her children off with a pair of grandparents, and turned toward the three midshipmen and Riley. She came straight at Riley and threw her arms around him so forcefully she might have knocked him down had Janet not been there to steady him. The subtle jasmine scent of her perfume flowed around them as she buried her face in Don Riley's shoulder.

"I'm so sorry, Lizzie," he said. "I—"

"Don't you dare, Don." She pushed back and gripped him by the lapels of his jacket. "Don't you dare. Brendan was there because he wanted—no, he needed—to be there." Her dark eyes were bright with emotion. "That's how he lived, and that's why I loved him."

She released Riley and patted his lapels flat before she turned to the midshipmen. "And how are you three holding up?"

Janet said nothing, so Ramirez put her arm around Goodwin. "We're keeping it together, ma'am—"

"Don't you 'ma'am' me, Midshipman. I'm Liz to you, and anything this guy taught you"—she hooked a thumb at Riley—"he learned as my plebe. Brendan and I had a long history of doing great things together. Don was just one of many."

Riley blinked hard but made a solid attempt to smile.

Liz turned in to the freshening breeze, her eyes glassy now. She took Janet's good arm and hugged the younger woman to her. Together, their gazes roved over the stately buildings of the Naval Academy grounds.

"He always loved it up here," she said in a whisper. Janet nodded, not daring to break the spell. "I'm so glad you're all safe. He wouldn't have been able to live with himself if something had happened to any of you."

Janet didn't know what to say. She was so choked up, it would have just come out as a wail anyway.

Liz drew in a deep breath and blew it out between trembling lips. She patted Janet's arm. "My Brendan's watch is done. It's up to you now, Midshipmen."

"We're ready, ma'am," Janet said.

Something in her tone must have caught Liz's attention, because she locked eyes with Janet. The widow's gaze was sad, still full of unspent grief, and yet somehow still fierce. The eyes of a fighter.

"Yes." Liz nodded slowly. "I believe you are."

She squeezed Janet's arm one last time, shook hands with Ramirez and Goodwin, and hugged Riley again. Then she walked away through the headstones.

ACKNOWLEDGMENTS

If it takes a village to raise a child, it takes at least that many people to nurture a book from a vague idea to a finished product sitting on the shelf of your local bookstore. And since this book has two authors, the number of people we need to thank totals something approaching a small town.

We'll do our best.

Although we're both graduates of the United States Naval Academy and former US Navy officers, we only met in 2013 at an alumni breakfast event in Minneapolis. We struck up a friendship, and a few months later, we were asked to speak to the local Minnesota chapter of the USNA Parent's Association about careers post-graduation from Annapolis. At the time, David had recently left his corporate job to write science fiction full-time and J. R. was retired from a twenty-one-year career as a naval intelligence officer. After hearing our dueling biographies, one of the parents raised his hand and suggested we write a book together.

Our first thank-you goes out to the Naval Academy parent who unknowingly launched two writing careers.

For our first two novels, *Weapons of Mass Deception* and *Jihadi Apprentice,* released in 2015 and 2016, we didn't even bother looking for an agent. Instead, we crowdfunded and independently published them to build a readership. Our first forays into publishing yielded modest results. We sold a few thousand copies and garnered dozens of kind reviews that compared our storytelling to "early Clancy," which is the highest possible praise, in our opinion.

Our second thank-you is for all those early supporters. They are too numerous to list here, but if you can find a print edition of our early novels, we thanked them all by name.

Along our path in independent publishing, we worked with some true professionals to produce the best possible work product in all forms: digital, hardcover, paperback, and audio. Thanks to Sarah Kolb-Williams, our editor; Steven Novak for his fabulous covers; John Hamilton, fellow writer and our photographer; audiobook narrators Aimee Kuzenski and Clay Lomakayu, and our team of technical experts and beta/advance readers: Jennifer Schumacher, Chris Pourteau, Pete and Cami Bruns, Maria Lenartowicz, Doug Baden (West Point '88), Dr. James Densley, Charly Salonius-Pasternak, Jackie Olson, Ed Wallin, Shena Crowe, Shemi Hart, Will Swardstrom, Caleb Lang, Bob Mayer (West Point '81), and Steve Konkoly (USNA '93).

There are a few local champions who really assisted us in our early marketing efforts. These include fellow USNA grads Chip Sharratt ('74), Alex Plechash ('75), and Chris Bentley ('79), as well as Mike Farley (West Point '88). Also, a big thanks to WCCO radio hosts Roshini Rajkumar and Al Malmberg.

Before we even finished writing the novel that eventually became *Rules of Engagement*, we decided to see if we could interest a major publishing house in our little story. Once again, our connection to the US Naval Academy paid off as fellow author Rick Campbell introduced us to his agent, John Talbot of the Talbot Fortune Agency.

John had a plan for us from the moment we signed with him, and he worked tirelessly to get our manuscript in front of the right editors. To our good fortune, Keith Kahla, editor at St. Martin's Press, saw a diamond in the rough and gave us this chance.

We want to especially thank John and Keith for all the support they've given us as we worked through the final draft of *Rules of Engagement*.

And that brings us to family, the center of our village of thanks. For David, that includes parents Dick and Regina Bruns, sister Jenny and brother Pete, daughter Cate, and son Alex, who suffered through shooting and producing videos for two Kickstarter campaigns. J. R. would like to thank his mother Pam, brother Doug, and sister-in-law Jackie.

Finally, our wives gave us lots of room to pursue this writing dream and we are grateful beyond words to have their support. All the hours spent in story meetings, research, writing, editing, and everything else—it's finally paid off.

Thank you, Christine and Melissa.

If you've read this far, the role that the US Navy has played in our lives is obvious. We are privileged to have attended the finest service academy in the world and have served our country in the finest navy on the planet. It is no exaggeration to say that without the Naval Academy, this book would not exist.

Read on for an excerpt from *The Pandora Deception*, the next explosive novel from David Bruns and J. R. Olson, available soon in hardcover from St. Martin's Press!

Mocimba da Praia, Mozambique

It was well past midnight before the young prostitute made her way down the alley toward Rachel Jaeger. Rachel stood in the dark, hearing the distant pounding of the surf and the occasional roar of a plane taking off from the nearby airport.

The night was dark and humid and overlaid with a heavy, sweet smell from the battered dumpster a few meters away. A small furry creature scurried across the young prostitute's path, but the girl didn't flinch. Rachel crossed her arms and waited.

The woman stopped a few paces from Rachel. Like most of the prostitutes in the area, she was from Tanzania, working in Mozambique to send money home. She was half a head shorter than Rachel with a long, lean frame and a generous bosom. She was dressed in neon yellow hot pants and matching halter top that left little to the buyer's imagination. Her hair was braided and when she turned to look behind her, Rachel saw the scar on her right cheek. She also noticed the young woman's fierce expression.

Rachel relaxed a tiny bit. Whatever this woman's

motivations for being here, she was unafraid of the consequences.

"Neema?" she asked.

The woman's smile of acknowledgement made a slash of white in the dimness of the alley.

"I have the information you seek." She spoke in broken Portuguese, the native language of Mozambique. She pointed back toward the light at the end of the alley. Rachel took a step to the right so she could see the neon sign: Estrella's Bar and Restaurant. "He's in there now, drinking, and alone. He likes this place. I sent all the other girls away for the rest of the night." She smiled again. "He's all yours."

Rachel nodded, feeling a thrill of excitement race up her spine. Neema was involved in the two oldest professions on earth: prostitution and spying. The Mata Hari network in this region of Africa had originally been put in place by al-Shabab, a radical Islamist group, as a way to spy on corrupt police officers.

Rachel, a Mossad agent, had been looking forward to this particular job for a very long time.

"Tell me about him," Rachel said. "Anything you know, even the smallest detail. His favorite drink, his preferences in bed. Anything."

Neema grimaced. "You can't miss Abdul. He takes the"—she mimicked a hypodermic being inserted into a bicep—"I don't know what you call them. Muscle drugs."

"Steroids?" Rachel asked.

The young woman shrugged and mimed big puffy muscles on her arms. "He has big strong muscles, but a very little prick." She held her thumb and forefinger a few centimeters apart.

Rachel shared her laughter. "What else?"

Neema made the local crude hand sign for anal sex.

"He is a pig. He hits the girls, too." She touched the scar on her cheek and her face twisted into a mask of fierce fury. "I'm glad you're going to kill him."

Rachel froze. Was that just an expression or did she understand what Rachel was here to do?

"Why do you say that?" she said as casually as she dared, wishing they had a better common language.

The young woman grinned again. "I know who you are." She pointed at Rachel's black lace bustier, flaming red miniskirt, and four-inch high heels. "You are no prostitute. You not from here."

Rachel allowed herself to take a beat. That admission alone was enough to kill the operation. If Neema knew, then there had to be others, possibly including her mark. She was alone in a strange city with no backup.

On the other hand, she had tracked this asshole for months, carefully figuring out the best way to get close to him. Leaving now would mean starting over, letting a known murderer walk free for another day.

Abdul Wenje and his al-Sunna gang were nothing but common thugs hiding behind a thin veil of Islamic rhetoric to extort money from local business. The murder of ten Israeli tourists on the Quirimbas Islands had more to do with real estate than religion.

Rachel was assigned to end him—but quietly. The last thing Mossad wanted was international headlines about revenge killings, no matter how justified.

As a lone operator, she had leeway to interpret the local conditions. Rachel decided to trust Neema. "Who else knows?"

The young woman shrugged. "The girls, we talk, we see things. But we do not say things."

Rachel's mind raced. The threads of intel that she had gathered to pull this op together were not reproducible. If Abdul slipped away tonight, it might be years before her agency had another chance at him. Years before those ten innocent tourists were avenged.

"Can I count on you to stay quiet?"

Neema's braids silhouetted in the light of the bar, swayed as she nodded. "Like I said, he is a pig. You are doing us a favor."

Rachel reached into her tiny clutch purse for some money. Neema shook her head again. "This I do for free."

Rachel forced the money into her hand. "Take it," she said. "Divide it among the other girls, but stay quiet."

Neema stuffed the bills into her bra. "Wait," she said. "I fix." She hooked a finger into Rachel's bustier and tore the lace apart so the flesh of her breast squeezed out the side. Then, gripping the hem of her miniskirt, ripped it open all the way to her hip. She stepped back to survey her modifications to Rachel's disguise. "Now you look like one of us."

Rachel watched Neema hurry out of the alley. If she was ever in a fight in a dark alley, she would want that one beside her.

The interior of Estrella's Bar was as tacky and run-down as it looked from the outside. The place seemed to be in the midst of an identity crisis. With the Mozambique airport less than a mile away, it had the feel of a bar for weary business travelers. But it was also near the beach and tried to play on that theme with a spray of neon palm trees on the wall. Lastly, Estrella's bordered a seedy neighborhood and gave off a dive bar vibe.

Rachel paused in the doorway, peering through the thick clouds of cigarette smoke darkening the interior. Besides the neon palm trees, lighted signs for European beers and Tipo Tinto, the local rum, penetrated the gloom.

She headed to the bar in a slow saunter, allowing her hips to roll suggestively underneath her now-ventilated miniskirt. She parked herself in the center of the bar between two men, a heavyset European who was sweating despite the air conditioning and a large black man in a business suit.

She caught the bartender's eye. "Rum and coke," she said as she extracted a pack of cigarettes from her clutch and put one between her painted lips. The bartender gave her a light and she sipped her drink.

She felt the two men on either side of her sizing her up, trying to decide if they wanted to make an offer. She smiled at the heavyset white man first.

"Good evening," she said in Portuguese.

"Beautiful night," the man responded in English. She shifted into his language.

"You are from Europe?" she said.

The man's jowly face creased into a smile. "Scotland," he said, as if his accent didn't make that fact abundantly clear to her. "Here bidding on a construction project at the airport. You speak very good English."

Rachel nodded and let her eyes slide past him to a man sitting along the far wall. The man wore a short-sleeved, collared shirt, but he had rolled up the sleeves to his armpits to expose his biceps. He was tall, easily six feet, with neck muscles sprouting from the collar of his shirt.

His eyes met hers for an instant and she took a pull of her cigarette before she looked away. He lifted a shot glass of brown liquid and drank it in one go. A rum drinker, then.

Rachel turned back to the bar, flirting with the large black man on her right. He was a chemical engineer from South Africa in town to work on a water treatment project. He seemed in a hurry and made her an offer quickly. Rachel refused him and he left quickly.

She slid into his seat, leaving an open space between her and the Scot, who continued to chatter away. Another patron took the seat next to her and made an offer. She pretended to consider it, then countered with what she knew was a very high price.

The new john laughed in her face and called her a whore in a loud voice as he left. Rachel flipped him off as he walked away, then ordered another drink.

It took nearly an hour for her mark to come off the back wall. He inserted himself into the space between her and the voluble Scot who tried to lean forward to continue his conversation with Rachel.

Abdul Wenje glared at him. "Move on."

The Scot paid his tab and left.

Rachel sighed and ran a finger down Abdul's bulging bicep. "Impressive," she said. "How often do you work out?"

"Every day," he said. He twisted his arm so the triceps popped. "Sometimes twice a day."

Rachel slid closer so the flesh of her exposed breast brushed against his bicep. "I like a man who takes his work seriously. Buy me a drink?"

His eyes narrowed. "I saw you refuse two offers tonight."

Rachel took his newly poured shot of rum and drank it in one gulp. The liquid burned all the way to her stomach. "Tonight is my night off. I'm looking for something more than just money." She leaned over and let her tongue trail along his bicep. "I was planning to walk the beach later . . . maybe you'll join me."

Abdul snorted and tossed back another shot of rum,

but Rachel noted the way his pupils dilated and his posture stiffened.

She had him hooked. Now to reel him in.

"Another rum for me," she said to the bartender. "He's buying."

Abdul looked at her sharply but said nothing. He gave a wolfish smile. "Why not?"

Rachel drank one more shot, then feigned drunkenness and spilled the next one. She laughed loudly at the mess, all the while sidling closer to Abdul. She rubbed her hand up his thigh. "I think I want to go to the beach now," she whispered, nipping his ear with her teeth. Rachel stood, pretending to sway.

Abdul was in the mood now. He dropped some bills on the bar and seized her hand, causing Rachel to nearly trip in her ridiculous heels.

The street outside was deserted and quiet. Besides the tap of her own shoes, the only sound was the surf a few blocks away. The night air was humid and still, settling on Rachel's bare shoulders like a thin damp blanket.

Abdul held her hand firmly and walked at a fast clip. They moved between pools of light from the few functioning streetlights. Rachel, still feigning drunkenness, clung to his meaty arm with her free hand.

At the corner, she leaned left, toward the beach, but Abdul pulled her to the right, deeper into the city.

Rachel balked. "I want to go to the beach," she cooed. "It's romantic."

Abdul crushed her hand, then reached across to grip her free arm. He pulled her close enough for Rachel to smell the sourness of his breath. "Is there a problem?"

Her heart beat quickly, but she let her head droop and her words slur together as she replied. "The beach . . ."

Abdul released her arm. He slid his hand into the

ripped side of her miniskirt and dug his fingers deep into the cleft of her buttocks. Rachel kept her face impassive as her stomach recoiled at the violation. Instead, she nuzzled his chest and moaned.

He withdrew his hand and reversed his direction, now drawing Rachel toward the beach.

Rachel's instincts flared an alert. He was toying with her. Something was wrong.

"You're hurting me," Rachel said, trying to extract her hand from his grip. With her free hand, she fumbled with her clutch, trying to get at the tiny syringe inside. One quick stab of the needle and the bastard's heart would stop for good.

Abdul ignored her. Midway along the block, between streetlights, he paused at the opening to a dark alley and gave a low whistle. There was a dragging sound, then a man stepped out of the shadows. He threw something at Abdul's feet that made a wet, slapping sound as it hit the pavement.

Rachel looked down, focusing on a yellow glow in the bundle. With horror, she realized she was looking at Neema's neon yellow halter top, which meant the ropy mass above that was . . .

She sensed more than saw Abdul's fist swinging toward her. Rachel ducked and jammed the spike of her high heels into his instep, causing him to release her. With the second man, she wasn't so lucky. He tackled her, driving her body into the brick wall.

Rachel felt all the air leave her lungs and saw stars as her head cracked into the wall. She dropped both elbows onto his back as hard as she could, then launched a knee up into his face. His grip weakened, and she hammered her knee up in another strike. He slid to the ground.

Frantically, she ripped open the clutch purse, her

fingers seeking the two-inch syringe hidden inside a tampon.

But Abdul was back in action. The big man loomed before her, his shadowed face a mask of fury. He gripped her throat with both hands and pressed her back against the wall. The clutch purse slipped from her hands as she tried to free herself.

She felt the skin on her back scrape away as he pressed her flat against the wall and slid her upwards. Rachel kicked at his chest, but it seemed to make no difference. She tried to claw at his eyes, but the big man had a longer reach and all she did was scrape at the flesh of his upper arms.

She gasped for breath, feeling her vision starting to tunnel. She tried to kick at his chest with her heels, but she had no leverage . . . Heels. High heels.

Rachel twisted her leg up and clawed at the clasp on her shoes. She felt the blood vessels in her eye start to rupture. The clasp came free and she tore off the shoe.

Her strength was draining away. With all her remaining might, Rachel drove the tip of the four-inch heel into Abdul's eye.

He screamed as he let her drop to the ground. The damp, foul air of Mozambique was the sweetest breath she had ever drawn. Rachel stripped off the other heel and clawed herself upright. A weeping Abdul staggered down the street. She stalked after him, feeling stronger with each step, the shoe still in her hand.

Abdul stopped, turning to face her, his fists up. "Who are you?" he yelled at her.

Rachel moved with a speed and fluidity born from years of training. She rushed him, seeing him telegraph his punch and ducking under it. She used the spiked heel to dig into his ribs, then stepped away.

Abdul lowered his hand to clutch the injury and she

struck again. This time delivering a round house kick that dropped the big man to his knees. He jabbed out a fist. She let it slip past her, then kicked him in the teeth. He fell backwards and she leaped onto his chest.

"Who are you?" he said again. His right eye was a deep hole of welling blood, his left glassy with tears.

Rachel positioned the point of the heel under his chin.

"My name is Death," she said in Hebrew. She used her fist to jam the heel up into Abdul Wenje's skull.

Rachel rolled off the corpse, lying flat on her back in the dirty street. With a grunt, she got to her feet and went back to the alley.

Neema was dead, beaten to death. Abdul's accomplice was unconscious. She felt along the ground for her lost clutch purse. The syringe hidden in the tampon was still there, as was the infrared flashlight. She needed that to signal her extraction team waiting for her offshore.

Rachel drove the tip of the needle into the unconscious man's neck and waited for his heart to stop.

Then Rachel got to her feet and walked toward the sound of the surf.

Nadia Hirsi-Simpson sighed as she considered the queue of incoming intercepts on her computer screen. She imagined computers all over the world hoovering up streams of data from computers, mobile phones, and every other digital device. The data were sifted by algorithms, and suspicious bits were sent to analysts like her for further investigation.

Without meaning to, her eyes slid to the clock in the lower right-hand corner of her monitor. Only one hour to go until the weekend. She had reservations with her husband at the new Indian restaurant on Dupont Circle, then maybe a movie . . . anything but listening in on the conversations of other people from the other side of the planet.

It was heartbreaking to watch the news here in the US and realize that the average American couldn't even find the country of Yemen on a map, much less give a fig about the fact that Iran and Saudi Arabia were fighting a proxy war on the backs of the Yemeni people.

She sighed as she highlighted an audio file on her

secure terminal. Nadia adjusted her headset and clicked the little arrow to play the recording.

The file was a poor quality audio recording of a woman's voice, strained across distance and partially unintelligible in places. It sounded like she was weeping.

"Hamdi!" the voice sobbed. There was a long pause. "Hamdi, can you hear me?"

"Yes, Zahra. I can hear you." The man was shouting. "Go ahead. The connection is very bad."

"They're all dead! Everyone in the village is dead." The digital signal faded and Nadia lost Hamdi's response.

". . . Mira is dead. The children are dead. Everyone in Yousap." The woman was ranting, repeating herself. The man tried to stop her, but she just kept going, babbling about dead people and blood and bodies melting. It made no sense.

Nadia paused the recording and listened to it again. After tracing the call to the cell tower near the town of Haydan and studying fine-scale maps of the area, she finally found a place called Yousap. It was a flyspeck on the map, not even dignified with a population estimate.

One eye on the clock, Nadia studied the latest intel. These places were far from the front lines of the fighting. Nothing added up.

Nadia flagged her supervisor. Mark Gallarita was a heavyset NSA analyst lifer with a perpetual frown and dark hair that flopped into his eyes whenever he moved his head. The Yemen desk was not where Mark wanted to be in his career and he made that point perfectly clear every day. "What is it, Nadia?"

She colored slightly. Mark's demeanor was brusque, but she told herself he was just a guy trying to do his best on an assignment he hated.

"I got a fragment of a cell phone call," Nadia said. "It sounds like a bunch of civilians are dead."

Mark leaned over her terminal where she had the maps pulled up.

"The caller made a reference to this village." Nadia pointed to a tiny dot fifteen kilometers past Haydan. "It looks like it's only accessible by footpath, not even a place to drive a car up there. Subsistence farmers, goat herders. Maybe fifty people at the most."

Mark stared at the screen.

"She was panicked." Nadia realized she was talking faster, trying to convince her supervisor she was right. She tried to calm her voice and slow down. "Said everyone was dead. She mentioned the bodies looked like they were melting."

That piqued Mark's interest. "Melted? Chemical weapons, maybe? But why in the middle of nowhere?"

Nadia tried to backpedal. "Well, I think she said melted. It's a terrible connection and the dialect was tough for me." There were dozens of Arabic dialects in the country of Yemen alone, especially when you went into the deep countryside. Her parents had insisted she learn Arabic when she was growing up, but her parents had both been raised in Sanaa, the capital city of Yemen, and were born to wealth. She could understand the gist of any conversation well enough, but the subtleties might be lost in translation. On reflection, Nadia was increasingly concerned that maybe she was misinterpreting some of the words from the intercepted phone call.

Mark straightened up. "Okay, here's what we're going to do. Send this intel on to the theater commander as unverified. Then get on the horn with Creech and see if we can get a Reaper to make a surveillance pass for us. Maybe they can pick something up from the air."

Nadia nodded, looking at the clock. If she hurried, she might just have enough time to do this before she got off shift. Overtime on Friday night was not in her plans.

She routed a secure call to Creech Air Force Base in Nevada into her headset and spoke to the duty officer. "This is Nadia from the NSA Yemen desk. Requesting a flyby on these coordinates." She read out the location of the tiny village in the mountains of Yemen.

A tired voice repeated the coordinates back. "Standby, ma'am."

Nadia listened to the muzak in her headphones until the duty officer came back on the line. "We have an MQ-9 UAV in the area, ma'am," he said, using the official designation of the Air Force Reaper drone. "I'm patching you through to the operator now."

Her phone clicked and a new voice came on the line. "NSA, this is your pilot, Charlie," the voice drawled. "To whom do I have the pleasure of speaking to this fine day?"

"Hello, Charlie, this is Nadia from the Yemen desk in DC."

"Well, welcome aboard, Nadia. Please place your tray tables in an upright and locked position and fasten your seat belt. You will be seeing a live feed from my drone in three . . . two . . . one . . . mark."

Nadia's screen popped to life, showing an image of the mountainous Yemen countryside at night using a low-light camera.

"Looks like it's about one in the morning in lovely Yemen, Nadia. Our low light cameras are pretty good, so I'll do a visual pass first, okay?"

"Acknowledged." She raised her hand to beckon Mark to her desk and handed him a spare set of headphones to listen in on.

The mountain hamlet of Yousap came into view on her screen. To call it a village was an insult to villages. It consisted of ten structures bisected by a footpath barely large enough to accommodate a donkey cart. A few crude corrals surrounded the buildings and some gardens.

"I believe that is our target, Nadia. Looks like a lovely rustic—make that *very* rustic—hideaway. What are we looking for?"

Nadia quickly filled him in on the basic situation.

"Roger that. The fastest way to tell if we have any warm bodies is to use infrared. Stand by."

The screen updated to show a ghostly screen of heat register. Nadia could make out at least a dozen person-shaped images with very little heat signature. Inside one of the houses, she made out a warm body—probably the woman who made the phone call.

Charlie's voice was subdued when he spoke again. "Based on what I am seeing here, Nadia, I would say we have a whole lot of dead people in this little burg."

Nadia leaned closer to the screen. "Concur, Charlie. I'd like to see if we can ascertain a cause of death. The eyewitness described the dead looked like they had melted."

"Roger that. Let me see how much detail I can get for you. Stand by."

Nadia and Mark watched as the remote pilot increased magnification. Charlie's voice sharpened. "Nadia, we have a high-speed incoming bogey on an intercept vector."

"I don't understand, Charlie. What is—"

An aircraft entered the field of view. Charlie froze the image and Nadia was able to make out the desert camouflage painted on the top of the fuselage and the blue seal of the Royal Saudi Air Force.

"Jesus," Mark said, "that's an F-15E."

"Nadia," Charlie said, "we have been ordered by in-theater commander to vacate. Breaking off now."

"Charlie, wait!" Nadia said. "Give us a visual of the target for as long as you can."

There was no reply from the pilot, but the image stayed on her screen.

The F-15 released a weapon from under its wing. It streaked down toward the tiny hamlet of Yousap. Seconds later, the mountaintop erupted in a ball of flame.

"Laser-guided bomb," Mark whispered. "Two thousand pounder. Enough to vaporize a city block. What the fuck is going on over there?"

"Nadia, this is Charlie. It's been a pleasure, but I'm outta here."

Nadia's screen went dead.

"That woman was alive," Nadia said. "We saw her heat signature. She was the one who made the call."

Mark blew out a long breath and pushed his glasses up his nose. "We don't know that for sure, Nadia." He stripped off his headphones and handed them to her. "We don't know what happened. This is a war zone over there, for all we know that heat signature might have been the next Osama bin Laden."

Nadia stared at him until Mark looked away.

"All right, I'll tell you what. There's a new group over at CIA called Emerging Threats. My new standing orders are if it smells funny and doesn't fit in our mission, we're supposed to send it over to the ET Group."

"The ET Group, really?" Nadia looked askance at her supervisor.

"Hey, if it is chemical warfare, this certainly falls outside our normal mission."

Nadia looked at the clock on her screen. Quarter past five.

"Fine. Emerging Threats it is."